# Praise for *The Outcast*

"Petersheim's emotional story leaves readers intrigued by the purity of Rachel's strong will, resilience, and loyalty."

*PUBLISHERS WEEKLY*

"Petersheim makes an outstanding debut with . . . well-drawn characters and good, old-fashioned storytelling."

*LIBRARY JOURNAL*, STARRED REVIEW

"Petersheim sets a retelling of a classic piece of literature against the backdrop of bonnets and buggies . . . [revealing] the power of confession and God's willingness to forgive and restore."

*CBA RETAILERS+RESOURCES*

"A must-read that will draw you into a secretive world of sin and senselessness and leave you with the hope of one set free."

***JULIE CANTRELL***

*New York Times* bestselling author of *Into the Free*

"I have to say, I've never been a fan of the Amish fiction genre. I'm still not. But Jolina Petersheim's *The Outcast* was the only Amish fiction book I've ever read from cover to cover. There are some really powerful passages in there. I especially related to Judah and his wanderings."

***IRA WAGLER***

*New York Times* bestselling author of *Growing Up Amish*

"Surprising and satisfying, this epic first novel of love and betrayal, forgiveness and redemption will resonate with people from every corner of life."

***RIVER JORDAN***

Bestselling author of *Praying for Strangers: An Adventure of the Human Spirit*

"*The Outcast* is an insightful look at the complexities of living in community while living out one's faith."

***KAREN SPEARS ZACHARIAS***

Author of *Will Jesus Buy Me a Doublewide? 'cause I need more room for my plasma TV*

"[This] riveting portrait of life behind this curious and ofttimes mysterious world captivated me from the first word and left me breathless for more. Do yourself a favor and place *The Outcast* at the top of your reading list."

***LISA PATTON***

Bestselling author of *Whistlin' Dixie in a Nor'easter*

"From the first word until the last, *The Outcast* captivates and charms, reminding us that forgiveness and love are two of life's greatest gifts. A brilliant must-read debut novel."

***RENEA WINCHESTER***

Author of *In the Garden with Billy: Lessons about Life, Love & Tomatoes*

# *the* OUTCAST

JOLINA PETERSHEIM

*Tyndale House Publishers, Inc.*
*Carol Stream, Illinois*

Visit Jolina Petersheim online at www.jolinapetersheim.com.

*TYNDALE* and Tyndale's quill logo are registered trademarks of Tyndale House Publishers, Inc.

*The Outcast*



Designed by Dean H. Renninger

Edited by Kathryn S. Olson

Published in association with Ambassador Literary Agency, Nashville, TN.



ISBN 978-1-61129-030-1

Printed in the United States of America

*To my kindred spirit, Misty, the bravest person I know.*

*I love you to life, friend.*

# ACKNOWLEDGMENTS

From the beautiful teacher who helped a struggling seven-year-old read *Lassie Come-Home*, to the compassionate professor who read my first manuscript and kindly told me it was not yet time, all my life I have been surrounded by a village of supporters who have helped raise this child, my novel.

Firstly, I want to thank my parents, who provided me with a childhood devoid of TV and teeming with books and silver minnows in shallow creeks and acres of deep woods to explore. You both have calloused hands so that I can now callous these fingertips pressing a keyboard. Thank you for your sacrifice and for never doubting my ability to write, even when I doubted it myself. I love you both from the bottom of my heart, and I pray I will be as great a supporter of my daughter's dreams.

I would like to thank the patient instructors who have gone above and beyond the call of duty to streamline this superfluous writer: Carey Boggs, Brent Coley, Regina Blazer, Gina Herring, Tom and Kathy Fish, Marianne Worthington. All writing accolades are yours; all compound modifiers are mine.

A humble thank-you to my friends who have supported me through reading, listening, editing, endorsing, and hooking my feet back into the stirrups whenever I got bucked off: Susie and Carl Roberts, Chris Peters, Joanne Petersheim, Chris Painter, Paige Crutcher, Kat Wood, Katie Rulketter, Jessi Buck, Candace Smith, Crystal Hillis, Hannah Alaniz, Kaitlin Alms Belcher, Rebekah Mason, Niki Cecil, Brenda McClain, Melissa Crytzer-Fry, Kimberly Brock, Julia Monroe Martin, Cynthia Robertson, Erika Robuck, Erika Marks, Renea Winchester, Shellie Rushing Tomlinson, Karen Spears Zacharias, Julie Cantrell.

To my dear mother-in-law: Thank you for your example of unconditional love and for telling me that this story needed to be told. Thank you, also, for watching Baby Girl and bringing over that pan of lasagna while I was on deadline.

Thank you, Nancy Jensen, for turning your creative writing classes into something akin to therapy. I don't know what I would have done that difficult semester without your cups of Bigelow tea and grace-filled words.

Wes Yoder: Thank you for agreeing to represent this story that unveils a hidden side of our Plain heritage. I know it was a risk for a seasoned agent to take on an untried writer, and I am honored to be working with you.

Thank you, Misty Brianne Adams, for letting me read my journal entries to you from the time I was in sixth grade until college, and for taking long walks with me while I untangled plot snarls. Thank you, also, for just being you—a compassionate, loving woman who faces life with a quiet peace concealing the strength of William Wallace, to which Vanderbilt doctors will attest. You have his sword, after all.

River Jordan: Thank you, *thank you* for taking this trembling fledgling under your wings and inviting me to lunches and other events where you introduced me to a community of loving writers and friends. I would not be here if it weren't for you; I am so glad I clogged that night.

To the Tyndale fiction team composed of Karen Watson, Kathy Olson, Stephanie Broene, Shaina Turner, Babette Rea, and Dean Renninger: You all work with an efficiency that turns this convoluted publishing process into a joy. I cannot think of anyplace I would rather be.

To my firstborn child, my daughter: It was no coincidence that your birth took place during the birth of my novel. You are my magnum opus, my life's work, and I pray that I will continue to put your precious life before my art. But that through my art, you will also find the courage to follow your dreams. I will love you always.

To my beloved husband and the father of my child: You are my bulwark and my sails. Thank you for supporting my dreams day in and day out and for saying the laptop's glow didn't bother you when you were trying to sleep at night. Life with you has been an incredible adventure, and I cannot wait to see what others are in store. I love you so very much.

To my Savior: Thank you for planting in my heart the seed for story. I pray that I will have the discernment to root out the ones you don't want told and nourish the ones you do. May I draw closer to you during their telling, and may my readers draw closer to you in their reading. Keep my knees bent, my heart open, and my gaze fixed solely on you.

To the unsung prophet of the London Underground: I believe our meeting was not happenstance, but divinely appointed, as your word that I would abandon my current manuscript and write one that was God-inspired has come to pass. Strange how I had to travel overseas just to hear one still small voice amid the clamor of so many others. Thank you for letting him speak through you.

# 1

## Rachel

My face burns with the heat of a hundred stares. No one is looking down at Amos King's handmade casket because they are all too busy looking at me. Even Tobias cannot hide his disgust when he reaches out a hand, and then realizes he has not extended it to his angelic wife, who was too weak to come, but to her fallen twin. Drawing the proffered hand back, Tobias buffs the knuckles against his jacket as if to clean them and slips his hand beneath the Bible. All the while his black eyes remain fixed on me until Eli emits a whimper that awakens the new bishop to consciousness. Clearing his throat, Tobias resumes reading from the German Bible: "'Yea, though I walk through the valley of the shadow of death . . .'"

I cannot help but listen to such a well-chosen verse, despite the person reading it. I feel I am walking through the valley of death even as this new life, my child, yawns against my ribs. Slipping a hand beneath Eli's diapered bottom, I jiggle him so that his ribbon mouth slackens into a smile. I then glance across the earthen hole and up into Judah King's staring, honey-colored eyes. His are softer than his elder brother Tobias's: there is no judgment in them, only the slightest veiling of confusion not thick enough to hide the pain of his unrequited love, a love I have been denying since childhood.

Dropping my gaze, I recall how my braided pigtails would fly out behind me as I sprinted barefoot down the grassy hill toward ten-year-old Judah. I remember how he would scream, *"Springa! Springa!"* and instead of being caught by Leah or Eugene or whoever was doing the chasing, I would run right toward the safety of base and the safety of him. Afterward, the two of us would slink away from our unfinished chores and go sit in the milking barn with our sweat-soaked backs against the coolness of the storage tanks. Judah would pass milk to me from a jelly jar and I would take a sip, read a page of the Hardy Boys or the Boxcar Children, and then pass his contraband book and jelly jar back.

Because of those afternoons, Judah taught me how to speak, write, and read English far better and far earlier than our Old Order Mennonite teachers ever could have. As our playmates were busy speaking Pennsylvania Dutch, Judah and I had our own secret language, and sheathed in its safety, he would often confide how desperately he wanted to leave this world for the larger one beyond it. A world he had explored only through the books he would purchase at Root's Market when his father wasn't looking and read until the pages were sticky with the sweat of a thousand secret turnings.

Summer was slipping into fall by the time my *mamm*, Helen, discovered our hiding spot. Judah and I had just returned from making mud pies along the banks of the Kings' cow pond when she stepped out of the fierce sun into the barn's shaded doorway and found us sitting, once again, beside the milking tanks with the fifth book in the Boxcar Children series draped over our laps. Each of us was so covered in grime that the jelly jar from which we drank our milk was marred with a lipstick kiss of mud. But we were pristine up to the elbows, because Judah feared we would damage his book's precious pages if we did not redd up before reading them.

That afternoon, all my *mamm* had to do was stand in the doorway of the barn with one hand on her hip and wag the nubby index finger of her other hand (nubby since it had gotten caught in the corn grinder when she was a child), and I leaped to my feet with my face aflame.

For hours and hours afterward, my stomach churned. I thought that when *Dawdy* got home from the New

Holland horse sales he would take me out to the barn and whip me. But he didn't.

To this day, I'm not even sure *Mamm* told him she'd caught Judah and me sitting very close together as we read from our *Englischer* books. I think she kept our meeting spot a secret because she did not want to root out the basis of our newly sprouted friendship, which she hoped would one day turn into fully grown love. Since my *mamm* was as private as a woman in such a small community could be, I never knew these were her thoughts until nine years later when I wrote to tell her I was with child.

She arrived, haggard and alone, two days after receiving my letter. When she disembarked from the van that had brought her on the twelve-hour journey from Pennsylvania to Tennessee, she walked with me into Leah and Tobias's white farmhouse, up the stairs into my bedroom, and asked in hurried Pennsylvania Dutch, "Is Judah the *vadder*?"

Shocked, I just looked at her a moment, then shook my head.

She took me by the shoulders and squeezed them until they ached. "If not him, who?"

"I cannot say."

"What do you mean, you cannot say? Rachel, I am your *mudder*. You can trust me, *jah*?"

"Some things go beyond trust," I whispered.

My *mamm*'s blue eyes narrowed as they bored into mine. I wanted to look away, but I couldn't. Although I was nineteen, I felt like I was a child all over again, like she still held the power to know when I had done something wrong and who I had done it with.

At last, she released me and dabbed her tears with the index nub of her left hand. "You're going to have a long row to hoe," she whispered.

"I know."

"You'll have to do it alone. Your *dawdy* won't let you come back . . . not like this."

"I know that, too."

"Did you tell Leah?"

Again, I shook my head.

My *mamm* pressed her hand against the melon of my stomach as if checking its ripeness. "She'll find out soon enough." She sighed. "What are you? Three months, four?"

"Three months." I couldn't meet her eyes.

"Hide it for two more. 'Til Leah and the baby are stronger. In the meantime, you'll have to find a place of your own. Tobias won't let you stay here."

"But where will I go? Who will take me in?" Even in my despondent state, I hated the panic that had crept into my voice.

My *mamm* must have hated it as well. Her nostrils flared as she snapped, "You should've thought of this before, Rachel! You have sinned in haste. Now you must repent at leisure!"

This exchange between my *mamm* and me took place eight months ago, but I still haven't found a place to stay. Although the Mennonites do not practice the shunning enforced by the Amish *Ordnung*, anyone who has joined the Old Order Mennonite church as I had and then falls outside its moral guidelines without repentance is still treated with the abhorrence of a leper. Therefore, once the swelling in my belly was obvious to all, the Copper Creek Community, who'd welcomed me with such open arms when I moved down to care for my bedridden sister, began to retreat until I knew my child and I would be facing our uncertain future alone. Tobias, more easily swayed by the community than he lets on, surely would have cast me and my bastard child out onto the street if it weren't for his wife. Night after night I would overhear my sister in their bedroom next to mine, begging Tobias, like Esther beseeching the king, to forgive my sins and allow me to remain sheltered beneath their roof—at least until after my baby was born.

"Tobias, please," Leah would entreat in her soft, high-pitched voice, "if you don't want to do it for Rachel, then do it for *me*!"

Twisting in the quilts, I would burrow my head beneath the pillow and imagine my sister's face as she begged her husband: it would be as white as the cotton sheet on which I lay, her cheeks and temples hollowed at first by chronic morning sickness, then later—after Jonathan's excruciating birth—by the emergency C-section that forced her back into the prison bed from which she'd just been released.

Although I knew everything external about my twin, for in that way she and I were one and the same, lying there as Tobias and Leah argued, I could not understand the internal differences between us. She was selfless to her core—a trait I once took merciless advantage of. She would always take the drumstick of the chicken and give me the breast; she would always sleep on the outside of the bed despite feeling more secure against the wall; she would always let me wear her new dresses until a majority of the straight pins tacking them together had gone missing and they had frayed at the seams.

Then, the ultimate test: at eighteen Leah married Tobias King. Not out of love, as I would have required of a potential marriage, but out of duty. His wife had passed away five months after the birth of their daughter Sarah, and Tobias needed a *mudder* to care for the newborn along with her three siblings. Years ago, my family's home had neighbored the Kings'. I suppose when Tobias realized he needed a wife to replace the one he'd lost, he recalled my docile, sweet-spoken twin and wrote, asking if she would be willing to marry a man twelve years her senior and move away to a place that might as well have been a foreign land.

I often wonder if Leah said yes to widower Tobias King because her selfless nature would not allow her to say no. Whenever she imagined saying no and instead waiting for a union with someone she might actually love, she would probably envision those four motherless children down in Tennessee with the Kings' dark complexion and angular build, and her tender heart would swell with compassion and the determination to marry a complete stranger.

I think, at least in the back of her mind, Leah also knew that an opportunity to escape our yellow house on Hilltop Road might not present itself again. I had never wanted for admirers, so I did not fear this fate, but then I had never trembled at the sight of a man other than my father, either. As far back as I can recall, Leah surely did, and I remember how I had to peel her hands from my forearms as the wedding day's festivities drew to a close, and *Mamm* and I finished preparing her for her and Tobias's final unifying ceremony.

"*Ach*, Rachel," she stammered, dark-blue eyes flooded with tears. "I—I can't."

"You goose," I replied, "*sure* you can! No one's died from their wedding night so far, and if all these children are a sign, I'd say most even like it!"

It was a joy to watch my sister's wan cheeks burn with embarrassment, and that night I suppose they burned with something entirely new. Two months later she wrote to say that she was with child—Tobias King's child—but there were some complications, and would I mind terribly much to move down until the baby's birth?

Now Tobias finishes reading from the Psalms, closes the heavy Bible, and bows his head. The community follows suit. For five whole minutes not a word is spoken, but each of us is supposed to remain in a state of silent prayer. I want to pray, but I find even the combined vocabulary of the English and Pennsylvania Dutch languages insufficient for the turbulent emotions I feel. Instead, I just close my eyes and listen to the wind brushing its fingertips through the autumnal tresses of the trees, to the trilling melody of snow geese migrating south, to the horses stomping in the churchyard, eager to be freed from their cumbersome buggies and returned to the comfort of the stall.

Although Tobias gives us no sign, the community becomes aware that the prayer time is over, and everyone lifts his or her head. The men then harness ropes around Amos's casket, slide out the boards that were bracing it over the hole, and begin to lower him into his grave.

I cannot account for the tears that form in my eyes as that pine box begins its jerky descent into darkness. I did not know Amos well enough to mourn him, but I did know that he was a good man, a righteous man, who had extended his hand of mercy to me without asking questions. Now that his son has taken over as bishop of Copper Creek, I fear that hand will be retracted, and perhaps the tears are more for myself and my child than they are for the man who has just left this life behind.

## AMOS

I never thought I would enjoy the day of my own funeral, yet that's exactly what I find myself doing. Outside my and my wife's *haus*, which has been scoured from top to bottom by my sisters, I watch my grandsons discard their sorrow like a worn-out garment and begin to rollick with the enthusiasm of pups. Before you can count to *zehn*, the knees of their best pants are stained brown with dirt, and their straw hats with the black bands have gone sailing off into the yard, causing the fine hair not constrained in the bowl cuts to poke into their eyes.

If the mothers, aunts, and sisters of these boys could see them all now, they would surely wag their fingers along with their tongues. But they can't. They are too busy slicing *schunke* and mashing *grummbeere*, beating egg whites into stiff meringue peaks and pouring pickled chowchow into crystal relish bowls. My wife brushes a tendril beneath her black bonnet and stoops to slide an apple strudel into the *kochoffe*. If given another chance, I would pull that black bonnet and prayer *kapp* back and burnish every silvered tendril of hers with a kiss. I imagine how Verna would scold while swatting me out of the kitchen, but all the while her dark eyes would shine as she reveled in the fact that she was loved by a man no longer afraid to show it.

I imagine, too, how I would go up to my three daughters—Irene, Mary, and Ruth—who are right now filling the chocolate whoopee pies with peanut butter cream, and I would hug them. Oh, how I would *hug* them! All these years as husband and father, I allowed my stiff German upbringing to inhibit the demonstrativeness of my love, for I thought the congregation might perceive physical touch to be improper. Now that my mortal eyes have been replaced with something far more heavenly,

I can see how my girls yearned for my touch until they became women who expected it no longer.

The banter of my wife, sisters, and daughters as they prepare the evening *esse* reassures my heart that theirs will mend, despite eyes still being swelled from tears and chests heaving with the flood of those they have not shed. The only one who worries me is Rachel Stoltzfus. Though she is of no immediate relation, I wish I could do something to ease the pain etched across her features because I feel responsible for it.

You see, when the heat of a Tennessee summer no longer allowed Rachel to conceal her illegitimate pregnancy beneath a shawl, she was placed amid those few who remain in the church while living outside its doctrinal parameters. The community, as they'd been taught by the generations before them, withdrew from Rachel so she could see the error of her carnal ways, ask for forgiveness, and rejoin the flock. I had always counted myself blessed that I was not bishop over a congregation that enforced the shunning. But watching everything unfold from this higher plane, I have to wonder if the shunning might be easier on the person it is placed upon. Without it, Rachel does not know her place, and the community does not know where to place her. They cannot be cruel—for what is Christlike in that?—but neither can they have her around the young women and men who haven't joined the church and could still be lured into leaving Plain life for the glamour of the *Englischer* world.

## Rachel

Eli and I take a seat at the far end of the five tables. Although I have no appetite, I know that I must eat or my body will not produce enough milk to supply my ravenous son. I give him a knuckle of my left hand to suck, and his scrunched face relaxes until he realizes that nothing is coming out. Stiffening his body in its cocoon of blankets, his face darkens and his mouth splits open in a silent, frustrated wail. Then he gets his breath, and oh, what a breath it is! The entire house seems to reverberate with the intensity of his screams, and I am again amazed at how much noise can come from one so young.

Placing him against my shoulder, I sing the lullaby my *mamm* sang to Leah and me: *"Schlaf, kindlein, schlaf! Der vater hüt' die schaf; die mutter schüttelt 's bäumelein, da fällt herab ein träumelein. Schlaf, kindlein, schlaf!"* I stroke his downy hair and pat his bottom, but this does nothing to help. I am working my legs over the bench so I can go into the next room and not disturb anyone's meal, when a hand brushes my shoulder.

Turning, I look up into the smiling face of Judah King.

"Let me take him," he says. "You eat." I glance down the long row of tables flanked by my sister's family and friends, who are all watching us with a knowing gleam in their eyes.

"No," I whisper. "They'll talk."

Judah shrugs. "What does that matter? They'll talk anyway."

With great reluctance, I pass Eli up to him. My eyes well with the image of my child tucked against a man's work-hardened chest. I know that feeling of masculine security is not one Eli will often experience.

Judah sits on the bench across from me. I won't give everyone the satisfaction of glancing down the table again, but inside my heart skitters against my ribs.

"What're you doing?" I whisper, staring at my plate. "Your name will be mud if you sit with me."

Judah tears off a piece of my *brot* and pops it into his mouth. Swallowing, he says, "What do I care about names?"

"You will once you lose it."

"Do *you* care?"

I nod but keep my eyes where they are. The pineapple gravy pooled on the *schunke* and *gemaeschde grummbeere* has started to congeal. "Yes, I care," I say. "But not for me. For *him*." I look up long enough to nod at Eli.

"Then why don't the two of you leave?"

"And go where?" I snap.

"I don't know, back to Lancaster?"

"I can't bring more shame upon my parents by raising a fatherless child under their roof. Besides, my *dawdy* won't let me come back."

Judah winces at this. Then he says, "Why don't we just leave?"

"What do you mean?"

"You and I, we could leave the church."

Hope causes my eyes to rise up to meet Judah's, and I see there is not a hint of jesting in them.

"But why? Why would you suggest that?"

He looks down at Eli, whose fingers are curled around his face like a starflower. "Because nobody should live in a place where they're not welcomed."

"Oh, Eli'll be welcomed. The community won't punish him for my sins."

"That's not what I'm talking about. I'm saying that *you* shouldn't live in a place where you're not welcomed."

"We must stop talking like this," I say. "I'm not just going to run away with you. I—I can't."

Judah King extends a hand toward me, and then looks down the length of the table to where his brother sits, watching us with disapproval in his eyes. Retracting his hand just as Tobias had done at the funeral, Judah's jaw begins to throb. "I'm not talking about running away; I'm talking about getting married."

"So you can make an honest woman of me?"

"No, Rachel. So I can make you my wife."

I point to the bright bundle nestled against Judah's chest. "And are you ready to be Eli's father, even though you don't know who the real father is?"

"Wouldn't you tell me if we were married?"

"Never. That's a secret I'll take to my grave."

"Never?" Judah leans back on the bench and searches my eyes. "You'll never tell?"

"No."

He nods. "Well, I can respect that decision, but I want you to know that it doesn't change mine. I'm leaving Copper Creek in a month. I hope you'll have your answer by then."

"I can't promise I will."

"I know. I never asked you to promise anything."

He comes around to my side of the table and passes back my son. In just a few minutes, my arms have grown unaccustomed to Eli's warm weight. As I watch Judah King stride out of his family home with his shoulders squared, I let myself imagine how it would be to share the burden of raising this child together.

Even with a man I can never let myself love.

# 2

## AMOS

"*Ju*-dah!" Tobias's voice zigzags across the floor like a lightning bolt. As my youngest closes the front door and shrugs off his jacket and hat, there is something stronger than frustration yet weaker than anger simmering in his eyes. Perhaps because of this, he does not enter the den where the call emanated from, but walks over to the kitchen to kiss my wife's cheek. Her round face blossoms with love, and she reaches into the jar behind the *kochoffe* and passes Judah two molasses cookies.

"You want *millich*?" she asks as if our youngest is two instead of twenty.

Judah shakes his head and grins until his eyes sparkle and dimples appear. Passing the cookies back to his mother, he sighs and strides into the den. "Yeah?" Judah says before he's even seen his brother. "What do you want?"

Tobias's lips tighten. Folding his hands on my old desk, he says, "I just wanted to see how you are. You left the meal early today."

"It being *Dawdy*'s funeral and all, I thought people would understand that I wasn't hungry."

"Yes, that's understandable. What *isn't* is why you were speaking with Rachel Stoltzfus."

Judah slouches against the doorframe. "I'd say what isn't understandable is why nobody *will* speak with Rachel Stoltzfus."

"She's borne a child out of wedlock. Do I really need to give you any more explanation than that?"

"Actually," Judah says, "you do. It's obvious Rachel did not conceive that child alone. Why aren't measures being taken to find out who the father is?"

"Because it may be difficult. How are we to know she's only been with one man?"

The angles of my young son's face sharpen; the hands that have been dangling at his sides clench into fists. "Because I know Rachel."

Tilting his dark head, Tobias rests one finger against his skull and smiles. "Do you, Judah? The two of you were just children when we moved. A lot can happen in ten years. A person can really change."

Looking straight at his brother, Judah says, "Tell me about it."

Tobias's smile disappears. He refolds his hands. "Why are you being so defensive of her? Is there something between you and Rachel that I should know about?"

"No," Judah replies, staring at the hook rug beneath the desk. "There's never been anything but friendship between us."

"That's a relief."

Judah's head pops up. "Why? Did you really think I could be Eli's father?"

"Over the past few months, the thought's crossed my mind. I'd have to be blind not to see how crazy you are about her."

"Then I guess you're about to think I'm even crazier. Today I asked Rachel to be my wife, and she said she'd give me her decision soon."

"Oh, Judah," Tobias moans. "You didn't."

Striding up to my desk, Judah places his hands on the oiled wood. "Yes. I did. Somebody's got to do right by that woman, and it's going to be me."

"This isn't some charity act here; we're talking about marriage!"

Judah forcefully presses his palms on top of the desk until the veins crisscrossing his hands protrude. "I know *exactly* what we're talking about!"

"No, you don't! You're twenty years old, and you still live at home with your *mudder*!"

"Yeah, well, you're thirty-two, and you're just following in your dead *vadder*'s footsteps!"

It hurts so much to eavesdrop on this conversation between my sons that I wish I could turn away. Then Tobias clenches his jaw and says, "I forbid it. Now that *Dawdy*'s gone, I'm the bishop, and I refuse to bless your union with Rachel."

"You wouldn't be the one to marry us, anyway! If she says yes, we're leaving the church. There's no way I would keep subjecting Rachel and Eli to this community's cruel treatment!"

Tobias looks out the window. The sky is so black and starless, I know he cannot see anything. Still, his gaze does not waver as he says, "We're both tired; we're both grieving. I fear that if this conversation continues, we will both say things we will later regret."

Judah nods. "You're right; this conversation *does* need to stop. But you should know that I meant everything I've said tonight, and I would say it all over again if we continued this conversation in the morning."

With this, Judah pivots on his booted feet and marches toward the door. Before he opens it, Tobias calls out to him. Judah pauses but does not turn around as his brother says, "She won't marry you, you know."

My youngest asks once his breath returns, "And how do you know that?"

"Because Rachel won't leave her twin behind, especially considering Leah's condition, and if she won't leave her twin, you will have to remain in the church to be near her. And if you remain in the church, I won't marry you." Tobias pauses and stares at his brother's back. "It's as simple as that."

Straightening his spine, Judah says, "We'll see," then flings open the door and stalks out of the house.

He spends the rest of the night in the barn grieving for many things. Although the haze of my own emotions will not allow me to see his thoughts, I know the majority of his tears are not shed over me.

## Rachel

After I return from the Kings', I check in on Leah and find that she is sleeping as soundly as when I left. Her eight-month-old, Jonathan, is curled in the crook of her arm. A sparkling chain of drool drips from his mouth and connects to Leah's nightgown like an umbilical cord. Laying Eli, who drifted off during the short buggy ride home, on the bed, I carry Jonathan over to the cedar chest to change his diaper and clothes.

Jonathan's eyes peek open as I wipe his bottom with a soapy cloth. Although he's known since birth that I am not Leah, once I button his pants and pick him up, his mouth nuzzles at my breast. Instinctively, my milk lets down. I carry Jonathan over to the rocking chair and unfasten the top layer of my cape dress. Latching onto me, he roots and kneads like a greedy kitten. I am about to switch sides when he stops suckling and looks up. The almond-colored liquid dribbles from the corner of his smiling mouth. I run a hand over his thin brown hair.

"You're a sweet *bobbel*," I croon. "Yes, a very sweet *bobbel*."

Leah rasps from the bed, "Rachel? That you?"

"Yes, Sister. It's me."

Leah struggles to sit up. Even that small effort expends her energy. I watch the blue tributary throb at the hollow of my sister's temple; her once-berry-red lips pinch with pain. Being as private as our *mamm*, if not more so, Leah does not often reveal her physical ailments. But I am also the one who changes her sheets and does her laundry, and I know the bleeding has not stopped since Jonathan was born.

"How was the funeral?"

I blink and look over. Leah's eyes mirror her worry. But her selflessness would never permit Leah to worry about herself. No, she is worried about me.

"Just great," I say. "Everyone's so kind here in Copper Creek."

Leah flinches. I am flooded with guilt, yet still infuriated that she has made herself sick worrying over the fate of her newly fallen sister, when she needs to focus on regaining her strength.

Contrite, I add, "No, really. It was a nice service. Tobias did a good job."

A smile smooths the furrows plowed across her forehead. "I'm glad," she whispers. "I wish I could have gone. To be there for him, you know."

*And when has Bishop Tobias ever been there for you?* But I know this question would only fill Leah with more pain than her answer would be worth.

So I say instead, "I'm sure Tobias missed you, but I'm also sure he understands your need for rest."

My sister's gaze falls to her child in my arms. Tears fill her eyes.

I ask, *"Vas es letz?"*

"I'm not fit to be his *mudder*. Not—" swallowing, Leah plucks at her lank hair and thin cotton gown—"not like this. The other *kinner* are old enough to get by, especially with Miriam almost grown, but what about Jonathan?"

Just like when we were children, I dart over to try and calm Leah's fears. I stroke her hair and hold her birdbone hand in mine, but it is as if she doesn't even know I am here.

"You're tired, Leah. That is all. If we could just rebuild your strength, you'd soon be back to your normal self."

"My normal self?" She laughs. "Even at my best, I was never like you. You gave birth less than three months ago, and already you're back taking care of me."

"What if I wrote *Mamm* and asked her to send some herbs?"

Leah holds out a hand. "Tobias doesn't like putting faith in such things."

I bite my tongue to prevent a scathing reply, but Leah can still read my expression.

"What is it, Rachel?" she asks. "What about my husband bothers you so?"

Instead of looking at my twin, I glance down the length of bed where my own son slumbers with his chubby arms far flung and mouth gaping wide. How amazing it must feel to be protected. It seems like years since I haven't felt vulnerable, but I know it must be only months.

"I don't know, Leah. I guess, at first, I resented Tobias because he took you away from me. Now . . . now it seems he holds this strange power over you, and you can't say or do anything without asking his permission, just like *Dawdy* always lorded over *Mamm* and us."

Sitting up, my sister reaches for Jonathan. I pass him to her without disturbing his rest, and she drapes him across her lap like a blanket. "Tobias is my husband," she says. "The head of our home. The Bible calls me to submit to him, to get his permission before I do things."

"Like take an herb? Like going to see a doctor when you so obviously need to? *That* kind of submission you will never see from me!"

"Are you saying that I am in the wrong? That I should defy my husband?"

"No. I am saying that *he* is in the wrong by not getting you the help you need!"

Either from the severity in our voices or the bony thighs he is resting upon, Jonathan awakens and begins to cry.

Leah mistakes his *brutzing* for hunger and brings him to her breast, which he will not take since he is already full from mine.

Her face twisted with anguish, Leah looks up. "See?" she says. "My own body can't bring him nourishment!"

"You don't know that."

"Yes, I do. I think *you* should nurse Jonathan. Just until he's stronger or I am stronger. The way I am now, he is not getting the nourishment he needs. Look at the differences in our sons, Rachel."

My eyes do as they've been told. I note that though there is a five-and-a-half-month gap between Eli and Jonathan, their bodies are almost the same size. Jonathan has a balding scalp that is spotted with flakes of dandruff; Eli's hair is corn-tassel blond that already shows hints of curl.

"Will you do that for me, Rachel?" my twin asks, clenching my hand between hers. "Will you take care of my son as if he is your own?"

Removing myself from her grip, I say, "I can't. You know I can't. Tobias wouldn't want Jonathan being nursed by me."

Leah leans in until her stale breath fluffs the few hairs that have slipped from my *kapp*. "Tobias *will* let you nurse Jonathan," she says. "At least 'til I can get back on my feet. You must trust me on this."

I look into my twin's face, at the passion that dabs color into her thin cheeks and stirs the blue cauldrons of her eyes. "All right," I say, only to appease her. "If Tobias agrees to it, I'll be a nursemaid to Jonathan, but you will always be his mother."

Satisfied, Leah leans back against the pillows and closes her eyes. "Oh, I'm not worried about that. Somehow children always know who their real parents are."

## AMOS

Two hours after everyone in the *haus* has gone to bed and an hour after Rachel began her vigil, Tobias returns, unhitches his buggy in the barn, and leads the horse to its stall. It takes over thirty minutes for him to fill the horse trough with sweet grain, replenish the water supply, and brush down the black mare with the starburst blaze and four white socks (a wedding gift from his *vadder*-in-law, the horse trader). But even after all this, the heat of the words he and Judah exchanged causes Tobias's body to hum with an energy only forgiveness or death—as I have so recently experienced—can diminish. He returns the currycomb and shoe pick to the tack room and, after checking that Reuben has milked the three Holsteins and one Guernsey and given them corn silage, makes his way out of the barn.

A sigh passes his lips. He looks up at the plain ten-room farmhouse with ten plain unshuttered windows and finds the one in his and Leah's bedroom as black as the sky stretching beyond it—signaling that she has not had the strength to wait up for him, as she has not had the strength to wait up for him time and time again.

Tobias plods up the porch steps on weary feet and unlaces his boots. Holding them in one hand, he opens the door and enters the foyer. The moment the door closes behind him, my son's nostrils are pricked by smoke. He turns to see an oil lamp whose untrimmed wick casts strange shadows across the kitchen cabinets. He walks toward the intermingling of shadow and light with his boots still clenched in his hands.

"What are you doing up?" he asks.

By the sharpness of his voice, Rachel knows that he has not mistaken her for Leah again. She does not turn or even blink as she says, "Waiting for you."

"Why?"

"Because we need to talk."

Only on that last word does Rachel look over her shoulder to meet her *bruder*-in-law's gaze, which is so heavy with dread, he looks like he could fall asleep standing. "I haven't changed my mind, Rachel," he says. "And I won't. You have two weeks to get off my land."

Taking a sip from the mug of meadow tea that has grown cold in her hands, Rachel shrugs. "I know. That's not what I wanted to talk to you about. What I want to talk to you about is Leah."

"What about her?"

"She needs to see a *doktor*. *Should* have seen a *doktor*

weeks ago. She's so weak right now, she can barely take care of Jonathan. She even asked me to—"

"No," Tobias interrupts as he drops his boots to the floor. "I lost one wife to an *Englischer doktor*; I won't lose another."

"That was different. Your wife got an infection after a botched hysterectomy. They might not even have to do a hysterectomy on Leah. They just need to find out how to make the bleeding stop. She can't keep living like this, or she's certainly going to die."

Tobias walks around the table and leans against the doorframe with his thumbs locked behind his suspenders. "How can you say that? You don't know anything—"

"I know what my mother taught me."

"*Jah*, nothing but witchcraft."

In the lamplight, Rachel's eyes glitter as her mind forms words she won't allow herself to speak. Once her temper has abated, she says, "At your request, I haven't done anything to help my sister heal. All I now ask is that you allow me to make her an appointment with a reputable English doctor."

Taking his thumbs from behind his suspenders, Tobias folds his arms. "Leah may be your sister, but she is my *wife*. My answer is no. Will *always* be no. Leah's body will heal itself in due time. She doesn't need some *doktor* taking out an organ God has placed there for good purpose."

"That is your choice," Rachel says. "A bad one, but

wholly yours. The only thing I ask is that you don't make my sister with child, for her body won't be able to withstand another pregnancy."

Tobias's jaw pulses. "What happens in my marriage bed is entirely between my wife and me!"

Scraping back the kitchen chair, Rachel stands to face him. "It would be entirely between the two of you if what you were doing weren't risking my sister's life!"

"Tobias?" At the sound of Leah's weak voice, Rachel and Tobias step back from each other and look toward the staircase where Rachel's twin stands, her hands clutching the sturdy railing as her questioning eyes flit between the two people she loves most in the world. When neither of them will reveal anything, she asks, "What's wrong? Did something happen to the children?"

"No, Leah," Tobias says, offering her a reassuring smile. "Rachel and I were just discussing the funeral."

Leah looks down at the step beneath her bare feet. "I'm sorry I couldn't make it. I thought I could, but—" Her lips clamp shut, blocking her words.

Tobias runs forward as Leah crumples onto the staircase. Crying his wife's name, Tobias kneels on the step and takes Leah in his arms. Her head lolls back, her waist-length hair brushing dust from the steps.

Crouching over her sister, Rachel places her right index and middle fingers against the side of Leah's neck. "We need to call 911," she says. When Tobias does not respond, Rachel digs her fingernails into the muscles of his shoulder.

"If you do not run out to the barn and call 911, you will lose your wife. Do you understand?"

Tobias nods as Rachel comes to take his place and supports Leah's head, which feels as heavy as a stone. "Get me a *hunlomma* before you go," Rachel calls.

Tobias turns from the front door and looks at her in confusion. Rachel motions to her sister's nightgown where patches of blood have started seeping through. Tobias's eyes widen. He darts toward the kitchen table and jerks down the clothesline that hangs high above it during colder months.

Tossing the threadbare *hunlomma* at Rachel, Tobias gives his wife one last fret-filled look before running out the front door and slamming it behind him.

I watch him sprint in his stocking feet the whole way to the barn.

# 3

## Rachel

At lunchtime, when Tobias returns, I press my sister's forehead with a kiss, leave the hospital room without acknowledging her husband, and enter the maze of corridors. One by one, the nurses lower their clipboards and stare as I walk past, still in the black cape dress and white *kapp* I was wearing at Amos's funeral. I am not accustomed to such scrutiny. In Lancaster County, there is such a large concentration of Mennonites, Brethren, and Amish, tourists are the only ones to ever give us a second look. I nod and smile at one nurse. Her penciled eyebrows disappear into her bangs, but then she nods and smiles in return. Long ago, I decided I was not going to bow my head and shuffle along like the rest of our community when faced with rude stares. No, I'd stare right back and remind them that I was a human being just living my life, not an oddity to be captured on film.

Exiting the double doors, I sit on a concrete bench and watch for Gerald's conversion van that is never hard to spot since he spray-painted it black due to his black-bumper Mennonite restrictions. Ten minutes pass . . . fifteen . . . but still our driver does not come. My adrenaline wears off and exhaustion slips over my shoulders like a cloak. I am becoming more and more frustrated by the stares of passing strangers when a huge truck lurches to a stop in front of the hospital's double doors, a tinted window lowers, and a heavyset woman bawls, "You're the girl I come to pick up, right?"

I stare at the woman just as unabashedly as those who have been staring at me. All I can see of her is the bottom of her chest to the top of her head, but that is more than enough. She is so well endowed, her bosom strains against the snap buttons of her Western shirt. Her wiry gray hair looks like it has been shorn with a dull razor blade. One of those Indian dream catchers I once saw at Root's Market in Manheim swings from the truck's rearview mirror, and country music blares from the sound system.

"Welp, girl," she calls, "you gonna get in here or not? I can't be waiting round all day."

Getting up from the bench, I walk toward the truck. "Where's Gerald Martin?"

The woman shifts a wad of snuff to her other cheek. "Dunno. All I know's I got a call to pick up some Amish girl from the hospital."

"I'm Mennonite," I correct. "You're sure you're here for me?"

"Honey, I doubt there're too many Amish *or* Mennonites running round this place. I'm sure it's you. Now get in. I ain't gonna bite."

Sighing, I walk around to the passenger's side and open the door. The truck is so high off the ground, I don't know how to get in it without exposing myself.

Seeing my predicament, the woman points to my cape dress and says, "Just tuck that skirt between your knees and jump. Nobody's paying you no mind."

I glance around the parking lot to see if this is the case. It isn't. Three paramedics, two nurses, and one janitor on his smoke break are watching this exchange. I cannot say that I blame them; if there ever was an oddity to capture on film, this is it. Coiling the seat belt around my hand, I use it to lever my body inside. Before I have even closed the door, the woman starts driving out of the parking lot.

"Kinda like Indiana Jones getting up here, ain't it?" she says. I look at her blankly, and she waves her hand. "Never mind."

Once we're back on the highway, she asks, "Where should I take ya?"

"Copper Creek Community," I reply. "Up on the mountain."

"No need to direct me," she says. "I know right where you live."

"You do?"

"'Course I do. That's where I get my sorghums and jams."

Staring out the window, I watch the colorful trees zip past, but we are driving at such a frightful speed, the blurred kaleidoscope of them makes me sick. I instead focus on the four-lane highway unwinding in front of us. "Do you buy a lot?" I ask.

"What?" the woman asks.

"Sorghum and jams."

"Yeah, but not for me. I sell 'em in my store."

"What kind of store is that?"

"An Amish one." Pausing to spit in a small green bottle, she says, "Ida Mae's Amish Country Store."

"Are you Ida Mae?"

"The one and the only."

"Were you Amish?"

"Not exactly, but I got kin that was." She nods and points out the window. "Somewhere up in Ohio."

I pause to imagine how Bishop Tobias would react if he entered an Amish store and saw a tobacco-chewing, men's-shirt-wearing, big-bosomed, big-mouthed Ida Mae behind the counter. The thought makes me smile.

"You get a lot of customers?" I ask.

"Boatloads." She lazily moves her hand over the steering

wheel. "They come up from Nashville, and most of them don't care that I'm not even Amish—just that my stuff is. The Amish and Mennonites I buy from, they don't care about me not being Plain, neither. They just care that I can sell their stuff for a higher price than what they'd get in their little podunk communities."

"You work on commission?" I ask.

Ida Mae nods, looks over at me with calculators in her eyes. "Why? You got something you wanna sell?"

I open my mouth to answer, then close it fast. If Tobias knew I was using my skills on the public, he would find a way to banish me from the community and my sister for sure. But if he never found out . . . "I don't have anything to sell, but I do have a service."

Ida Mae raises one eyebrow. "What kinda service is that?"

"Reflexology." She gives me as blank a look as I did when she mentioned Indiana Jones. "Do you know what reflexology is?" I ask.

"Ain't that Chinese stuff? Where you stick people with pins and things?"

I shake my head. "No, I just know the pressure points in people's feet and hands and massage them until the tension goes away. It's simple science, really."

Ida Mae snorts. "Sounds it."

For a few miles we're silent as each of our business wheels are busy turning, and then she says, "How would you get to my store? I reckon you can't drive if I was called here to drive ya."

"No, I can't. But I could come to your store two days a week if you could pick me up. I'd give you 30 percent of my earnings."

Ida Mae stops to consider my offer. "Gas money would have to be pulled from that too, ya know."

"If I was driving, I'd be spending money on gas anyway."

My new driver shoots me an admiring grin. "You sure got a business head on your shoulders for being such a scrawny runt."

I try to take this as a compliment. As Ida Mae turns on the blinker and barrels her truck up Copper Creek Mountain, she suddenly slaps the steering wheel and laughs until I can see the silver filling her cavities. "Whew," she says. "An Amish massage therapist. That's really gonna bring my customers in."

"I'm Mennonite, you know."

"Not when you're working in my Amish store you ain't."

I just nod, wondering what in the world I have gotten myself into.

## AMOS

When the truck drops Rachel off at Tobias and Leah's, she walks up the porch steps, takes a deep breath, and goes inside. My older daughters are both in the kitchen. Irene is washing up the lunch dishes; Ruth drops *rivvels* into boiling *hinkel* broth for a side dish to go with supper. Although it is early afternoon, the lack of electricity plunges the kitchen into darkness, making it hard for Rachel to read my daughters' expressions. As their *vadder*, though, I can read them each like a book, and I am ashamed to see the disdain lurking beneath their *mudder*'s precious features. I don't know where my children have picked up such self-importance. They did not learn it from Verna or me. My children act like they've never done anything wrong (despite my belt and their behinds knowing far better), and it is their personal mission to ensure that the community knows this and is therefore writhing over their own past mistakes.

Well, all except for our youngest. Even when Judah was a child, I could never place him in the same category as his siblings. He was always sensitive toward God's creatures no matter how insubstantial those creatures might be. So sensitive, in fact, that he was often ridiculed by his schoolmates, who would flatten anthills with a solid stomp or place toads under buggy wheels and force Judah to watch as those wheels slowly turned. There aren't enough stars arcing over this celestial sky to number all the times my son would come running to me with tears snaking down his dusty cheeks. Cradled in his hands would be a rabbit, bird, kitten, or puppy whose body had been caught in a piece of farm machinery or in a larger creature's jaws.

Time and time again, Judah would try reviving the

animal with milk through an eyedropper or worms or tiny rodents or insects, but their end was always the same: he would find the animal's small chest shuddering for breath, and then it would shudder no more. My son's own chest would start shuddering as his mournful tears started to fall, but Judah would still pick up the hapless creature and wrap it in whatever spare quilting material Verna had saved for this very occasion. After swaddling the animal, Judah would carry it to the strawflower field beside our house. There he would dig a hole with a little spade before placing the animal in its six-inch grave.

Now, watching Rachel's wide-eyed stare around that gloomy kitchen, I wonder if Judah wants to marry her because he loves her, or if he wants to marry her because she is another one of God's hapless creatures he hopes he can save.

Stepping toward the sink, Rachel takes a dish from Irene, dries, and returns it to the cupboard without making a sound.

Ruth dispels the uncomfortable silence by asking her, "How's Leah?"

"The doctors say if she keeps improving, she'll be home by the end of the week."

Irene and Ruth exchange glances, and Irene—the more domineering of the two—says, "Where you going to stay in the meantime?"

Being careful to keep her eyes fixed on the plate she is drying, Rachel replies, "I haven't given it much thought."

"Well. You should." I wince at Irene's tone of voice, which is as formidable as the set of her jaw. "It's not proper for you and Tobias to stay here alone."

Rachel wipes and wipes the dish, although there is no moisture on it. "We'd hardly be alone," she says, pointing over to the living room, where Sarah and Matthew are on the floor playing with a marble chaser. "Not with all the children around."

Ruth says, "Things are different now that Tobias is bishop. With that position comes a certain responsibility. An . . . an image to maintain."

Returning the dish to the cupboard, Rachel bangs the door closed and clenches the countertop. "Is it Tobias's image or your own that you're both so concerned about?"

My daughters look at each other and raise their eyebrows. Ruth opens her mouth to speak, but Irene shakes her head.

Raising her gaze from the countertop, Rachel looks them each in the eye. It would be impossible not to see the fire banked in hers even if the kitchen were as black as pitch. "That's what I thought," she says, then marches up the steps and closes her bedroom door.

The gentle knock two hours later awakens Rachel with a gasp. Sitting up, she looks out the window to the sun that has started sliding behind the mountains, leaving a buttery streak across the pines. Swinging her legs off the bed, Rachel smooths the quilt to hide that she's been sleeping on it and pulls open the door.

My wife, Verna, is standing on the other side. The skin around her eyes is smudged with gray; sorrow has carved lines in between her eyebrows and along the sides of her mouth. Her plump frame seems to droop with the yoke of grief hanging from her shoulders. But despite this obvious exhaustion, Verna smiles at Rachel and passes her the sleeping child.

"Has he been good?" Rachel whispers.

My wife nods and smiles again. "He's a precious little *bobbel.* Barely woke up all day except to nurse."

As Eli nestles against his mother's familiar bosom, Rachel says, "Tell Mary thank you for me."

"I will." My wife bites the inside of her lip and looks down, a sign that she has something to say but does not know how to say it. When Rachel has started to fluster from the uncomfortable silence, Verna asks, "Would you like to stay with us until your *schweschder* is out of the hospital?"

Rachel does not reply, so my wife continues, "Miriam can care for Tobias and Leah's little ones, and my *dechder* can check in on them from time to time. Make sure they have plenty to eat and such."

Rachel cannot seem to muster the same snap and fire she displayed with Irene and Ruth. Perhaps it is due to my wife's sweet demeanor, or perhaps Rachel's just tired of fighting a battle she knows she will lose. "All right," she says. "Just let me pack a few things."

"If you forget something, Miriam can bring it up."

"You mean, you don't want me to come back here at all?"

Pausing, my wife says, "Irene, Ruth, and I thought this would be the easier way. Just until we can figure something better out."

Rachel nods and pulls her baby against her chest. "I'll be ready in fifteen minutes."

My wife nods and turns to head down the steps before Rachel has even closed the door.

## Rachel

Threading my cape dress with straight pins and rolling my hair into its standard middle part and bun, I don my prayer *kapp* and secure it with bobby pins. I dab a *hunlomma* in the bowl of water on the Kings' dresser and wipe Eli's face. He moans a little but does not wake up enough to cry. I change his cloth diaper and sit in the rocking chair to nurse him, which brings immense relief since he only ate once the night before.

Tucking Eli against my shoulder, I pull open the bedroom door to find Verna's kitchen table already laden with breakfast. In the center is a plate heaped with *grummbeere*, eggs, and slabs of honeyed *schunke*. Yesterday's sourdough *brot* has been cut, toasted, and lathered with *budder* and rhubarb preserves. Hearing a noise in the cold cellar below the kitchen, I walk over and call down the stairs in Pennsylvania Dutch, "Can I help with anything?"

To my shock, Judah is the one who begins clomping up the steps. "No," he replies in English, "we're almost ready."

"You made all this?" I ask. I've never seen my *dawdy* enter the kitchen unless he knows there is something in there for him to eat.

Judah smiles. "Yes, I can make breakfast. I can't bake any desserts except shoofly pie, but I've got *fleesch* and *grummbeere* down pat." He mounts the final step and stands there, towering over me. I look at him in the darkness wafting up from the cellar floor, and although his shirt and suspenders are splattered with lard and there is a pungent bowl of *koppche* cheese in his arms, I have never seen him look so masculine. As his golden head leans closer to mine and his lips part, I almost wish that I could say yes to marriage with Judah King as easily as my sister had said yes to his brother, Tobias. I wish that I could go back and make my choices again. But different choices would mean this accidental child would not be in my arms, and I would not trade him for ten lifetimes of marital ease.

Turning my head, I break the spell that had cast itself over both of us. I am thankful for the darkness, as my cheeks are ablaze with the embarrassment of wanting. Judah walks around me without a word and enters the kitchen. I hear him whistle as he makes final preparations for the meal. This unusual sound causes Eli to stir and his blue eyes to open. Extending a fist, he waves it back and forth as if in time to the tune, then his eyes drift shut even as a smile remains on his face.

Despite all the uncertainty that I am facing, as I stand in the darkness waiting for the heat in my cheeks to subside, I am surprised to find that there is also a smile on mine.

## AMOS

It is almost two o'clock before Tobias sees the huge truck pull up in the hospital's circular parking lot and deposit Rachel and Eli in front of the double doors. Glancing over at his wife to reassure himself that she is sleeping, Tobias strides down the corridor, cuts a right, and punches the button for the elevator. When the doors slide open, he steps inside and barks, "One!"

The *Englischer* nurse gives the Mennonite man with the fearsome disposition a puzzled once-over and presses the button for the first floor. With his muscular arms crossed and bearded jaw throbbing, Tobias descends the two floors and steps up to the door before it has even opened with a mechanical ding. He marches through the lobby, almost colliding with Rachel and Eli as she hurries around the corner.

"Excuse me," she says, before glancing up and seeing

that it is him. As if a magic veil draws itself over her face, her apologetic smile is replaced with a scowl.

Rachel moves to sidestep Tobias, but he grabs the arm not holding Eli and drags her down the hall. "You need to leave," he says. "Tonight."

"I already *have* left. Your sisters and mother made sure of that."

"No. I don't mean you need to leave our house. I mean you need to leave Copper Creek."

Rachel looks up with confusion and the first glimmer of fear. Her voice betrays none of this as she says, "Bishop or not, you have no power to excommunicate me."

"No, I don't. But I *will* do whatever it takes to protect Leah, and if you love her as much as you claim, you will try to protect her as well."

"Leah? What does she have to do with this?"

"Everything. She's upstairs in that hospital bed because she's worried herself to death over you, and I'm *sick* of it." After a pause, he says, "If you haven't left the community by this evening, I swear I'll tell Leah the truth."

"But that would kill her faster than worrying over me ever would!"

"Exactly. Is that a chance you're willing to take?"

Rachel hangs her head. "No, it's not. You know it's not." Looking up at him, she holds Eli against her chest and narrows her eyes. "You've really thought this through, haven't you?"

Tobias growls, "I thought somebody should."

# 4

## Rachel

Pulling the hospital's pay phone closer to my mouth, I whisper into the receiver as if the baby in my arms can understand my words. "I need to be picked up. Something's happened."

"To your sister?" Ida Mae asks.

"No, to me."

"You sick?"

"I'm fine. I just need you to come."

"It'll probably take half an hour 'fore I can get back. You and Eli be all right 'til then?"

I nod before realizing that Ida Mae can't see me. I have

only talked on the phone a handful of times and haven't grown accustomed to the sightless communication. "Yes. We'll be waiting at the entrance."

Returning the phone to its hook, I gather the leftover coins that clink into the slot and slip them into the front pocket of my black purse. I take two steps toward the bench before my legs grow too weak to support me. Panic pierces through the haze of my thoughts like the pale November sunbeams slice through the clouds above my head: Where will I go? What will I do? More than that, with my eighth-grade education, how am I ever supposed to provide for my son? Sure, thanks to Judah King I can read, write, and speak English better than my Mennonite peers, yet these days every decent-paying job involves computers, which I have seen only from a distance. And although my accounting skills probably rate lower than those of an *Englischer* eight-year-old, I still know I cannot afford to keep a roof over Eli's and my head and food in our bellies on what I'd make doing reflexology alone.

As my stomach heaves, I stumble over to the concrete bench so I don't fall to the ground. Eli pays no attention to my erratic movements despite the way they cause his head to wobble against my chest. Sitting down, I lay my child on my lap and fold my trembling body over his. *Will you ever know your cousin Jonathan?* I wonder, breathing in Eli's calming smell of baby powder and newborn skin. *Will you ever know your aunt?*

These questions might never have answers, but unless

I want Tobias revealing my past, that is something I am going to have to live with. Taking a deep breath, I sit up and wipe my eyes. Eli looks at me with an expression too serious for his age. "Oh, little one," I whisper, "what has this world got in store for you?"

A cloud scuttles across the sun, blotting out the light that had been shining down on Eli's face, casting him into premature darkness. I pick him up and kiss his forehead as if sealing it with life.

"Nothing's taking you away from me," I whisper into his ear before pulling him close. "Nothing. You have nothing to fear. *Mammi* will see to that."

Eli is concerned about neither my fear nor my promise, but I keep holding him until the foreseeing shadow has passed, and we are bathed in sunlight once again. I cannot fathom how I will keep my promise to this child, but I know to the maternal core of my being that I will find a way.

Fifteen minutes later, when Ida Mae's truck swoops into the parking lot and pulls up at the hospital's entrance, I rise from the bench with Eli in my arms and look up at the third floor. The shades have been pulled across every window except one. I stare up at that window and see Tobias King staring down. As I walk toward Ida Mae's truck, Tobias's face wears an expression of triumph so pronounced that my blood is on fire. Opening the door, I strap Eli into Ida Mae's car seat, which swallows his tiny frame.

"What're you doing?" Ida Mae asks as I step back down.

I say, "Just hold on."

Reaching up with both hands, I rip bobby pins from my *kapp*, and they begin dropping at my feet with the sound of metallic rain. Yanking out the last two pins, I jerk the *kapp* off my head and clamber up into the truck. Ida Mae gives me a confused look, but still shifts into drive and guns the truck's engine without a word. As we pull out of the parking lot, I turn and look up at that hospital window to ensure that Tobias is still watching me. I then release that white prayer *kapp* out into the wind. At first it glides through the sky like a dove, but by the time we've pulled onto the highway, I watch the filmy netting plummet to the earth, where it will be trampled into the ground until the purity it represents is completely unrecognizable.

The ticking of the truck blinker snaps me out of my numbness as Ida Mae prepares to turn up Copper Creek Mountain. Pointing out the window, I say in my mother tongue, "We're not allowed up there."

My driver pulls onto the side of the road and switches off the radio. "What happened?" she asks in rusty Pennsylvania Dutch. "Why'd you remove your *kapp*?"

Astonished, I turn and look at Ida Mae, who must have more of a Plain background than she lets on. Shifting to English, I say, "Eli and I've been kicked out of the community by Tobias King."

Ida Mae's calloused hands clench the steering wheel until her knuckles turn white. "That man!" she spits. "He wouldn't know kindness if it bit him in the butt!"

Despite my distress, I cannot help but smile at Ida Mae's audacity in saying what I have been thinking for the past two years. "You know Tobias?" I ask.

"Know him?" she crows. "I'd say I know him. He was my farrier for years 'til the day I come early and saw him grab my mare by her nostrils and smack her across the muzzle to stop her from leaning on him. I wouldn't let Tobias touch my horses after that. Only worked with Judah."

"Judah's very different from his brother."

Ida Mae sniffs. "'Bout as different as Cain and Abel. I can't believe they even share the same blood."

I would usually smile at such a unique turn of phrase, but as I look out the window, I find instead that I want to cry.

Ida Mae touches my knee. "Where should I take ya?"

"I don't know," I whisper.

"Welp, I've already given you a job, ain't I?"

"Yes, but—"

Ida Mae holds up her hand. "Now, no buts. A deal's a deal." She cranks the engine and pulls the truck out onto the highway, back in the direction of the hospital.

"Where're we going?" I ask.

"Blackbrier. You're coming home with me."

When I look over in alarm, she punches the brake without checking her mirrors. "Or you want me to just drop you off right here, and you can find your way up Copper Creek Mountain by yourself?"

"No, no," I say, not wanting to lose my job or a free place to sleep. "Going home with you will be fine. At least—at least for tonight. Eli can get fussy, though. You sure you're okay with that?"

Ida Mae nods and turns up the radio. "Say so. Can't hear nothing since I snore like a freight train anyway."

## AMOS

As the fever ravaging Leah's body increases, she no longer remembers that her twin has been removed from her and Tobias's home. Leah no longer remembers that Tobias has convinced her that this is a good thing since Rachel will now be out of sin's—and Judah King's—way. All Leah's crazed mind understands is that her twin is not beside her sickbed. The fever seems to spike in direct proportion to the urgency of Leah's cries.

Tobias attempts to silence his wife by spooning more ice into her parched mouth. Leah swats the spoon away so that the chips spray across the tile floor and turn into puddles the size of melted snowflakes. Dropping the plastic spoon into the Styrofoam cup, Tobias leans his head back against the hospital chair and stares out at the bruised sky. In this moment of desperation, he considers finding Rachel and asking her to forgive his impulsive demand. He even considers asking her to return to his home and to his ailing wife's side. But the truth is, Tobias was not being impulsive when he asked Rachel to leave Copper Creek. Ever since Rachel's sin began to show, Tobias knew she would have to leave, but he also knew he would have to bide his time until his wife could not interfere with her twin's removal from the sanctuary of their godly home.

Around seven, when the night nurses have taken Leah's vitals and the orderlies have cleared her untouched food away, her fevered question changes. Instead of asking for her sister with every toss and turn, she simply says, *"Mudder."*

My firstborn sighs upon hearing this, takes his wife's hand, and presses her hot fingers to his cool lips. He knows what he has to do.

Forty-five minutes later, Gerald Martin pulls up in front of the hospital's double doors in his once-silver van, now spray-painted black. Tobias climbs into the passenger's seat.

"Where to?" Gerald asks.

"Home. Please just take me home."

Gerald nods and shifts into drive. A taciturn man under normal circumstances, Gerald senses that these are not your normal circumstances. He is quiet the whole journey up Copper Creek Mountain.

Before Tobias disembarks outside his white farmhouse, my son reaches into the right pocket of his black pants and draws out a money clip. He lays a fifty-dollar bill on the console despite Gerald's protests. "You lost some money because of my request," he says. "I hope this'll make up for it."

Nodding his compliance, Gerald smiles at his charitable passenger and pulls away.

Tobias watches the lane until the van's red taillights are extinguished by the darkness. He turns and plods up the porch steps, more fatigued than when he spent his days lifting up the feet belonging to two-thousand-pound mares. When he enters the silent dwelling, Tobias breathes a sigh of relief.

But not for long.

At his brother's arrival, Judah stands. His features are awash with frustration as he asks, "Where is she?"

Shrugging off his jacket, Tobias hangs it on the back of the kitchen chair but keeps his hat on to further obscure his eyes. "I don't know what you're talking about."

Judah steps closer to his brother. "Yes, you do!" he hisses through his teeth. "Don't you lie!"

Wiping Judah's spittle from his face, Tobias says, "Would you please keep your voice down? You're going to wake the entire *haus*."

"Let's go outside, then."

Like a dog that feels secure on his own marked ground, Tobias moves closer to his brother and peers down with eyes that dare Judah to strike out the way his anger desires. "Rachel left the community," Tobias says. "She came and told me at the hospital."

"And who forced her to go?"

"No one. She just thought it was the best choice."

"Best choice?" Judah's face twists with a sneer. "Two days ago, you told me that Rachel would never leave her twin. Now you're saying she thought that was the best choice? Bishops aren't supposed to lie, Tobias, and this is the third lie you've told in the past five minutes." Smiling without a trace of humor, Judah shakes his head. "Then again, I guess it's fitting: you should be allowed to tell as many lies as you want, considering your life itself is one."

## Rachel

Ida Mae hops down out of the cab. I look over while freeing Eli from his car seat and stifle a gasp. This is the first time I've seen her outside the truck, and I never noticed that she was short. Her legs, squashed into Wranglers so tight they must be cutting off her circulation, are the same as a chicken's: plump at the top but narrowing down to ankles that are as bony as mine. She wears mud-caked boots that lace up, and as she stalks off toward her Amish store, I see there's a perfect worn circle on the backside of her jeans from where she keeps her tobacco tin.

After spreading a blanket on the truck seat and changing Eli's diaper, I tug a knitted hat down over his ears and carry him across the gravel driveway toward the store.

Ida Mae comes out the green door of a tiny outbuilding attached to the main one and clomps down the three steps, waving a brass key in her hand.

"If you ever need in the store and I ain't around, make sure you remember that I keep the key in the bathroom. I hang it on a little hook behind the curtain." I nod, and she says, "Welp, c'mon. Don't just stand there gawking at me, girl. Let's go round to the front."

I follow Ida Mae to the entrance of the square white building with a striped awning and green shutters with star cutouts. After using the porch steps to scrape mud from her boots, Ida Mae opens the glass storm door, wedges her key into the lock, and knocks open the door with a hip like a battering ram. A high-pitched bell tinkles above it.

She takes a step inside, then looks back over her shoulder. "Am I gonna hafta give you permission to breathe?"

I shake my head and enter the store right as Ida Mae flicks on the lights. It's a small building—no bigger than most of the storage sheds Ida Mae has for sale outside—but every inch of space is organized in an attractive manner I would not have thought my new employer capable of. In the center of the store is a wooden shelving unit lined with a green gingham pattern. When Ida Mae sees me looking at it, she says, "That's for the baked goods. I bring 'em in twice a week from Hostetler's."

"The bakery at Copper Creek?"

She nods. "I ain't much of a baker myself. Don't like such time-consuming things."

An antique wrought-iron bed is in the far right corner of the room. It is heaped with quilts with hand-stitched nursery themes and tiny postage-stamp designs or the classic wedding-ring pattern that Amish and Mennonites like to give as housewarming gifts. I know Ida Mae must have gotten these quilts on commission from various communities because I could never imagine her hunched over "such time-consuming things" for hours and hours on end.

The shelves on the opposite wall are filled with jars of jewel-colored jams, honey with chunks of floating comb trapped inside like flies in amber, and sorghum as thick as tar. Hanging from wooden pegs are children's Amish outfits, each complete with a boy's suspenders or a little girl's mini *kapp*. On a low table is a tiered arrangement of handcrafted soaps made from oatmeal, coconut oil, or cocoa powder. Each small square is tied up with brown burlap string and a cardboard tag reading, *Ida Mae's Amish Country Store*.

"I tried that cocoa soap out once," Ida Mae says. "But it tasted so good, I 'bout drowned in my bubble bath."

I don't know which causes me to laugh more: the thought of this loud-mouthed, quick-tempered woman in a gray army jacket and muddy boots taking a bubble bath, or the thought of her being such a glutton for chocolate that she would taste her own bathwater.

Regardless, the laughter takes hold of me and will not let go. Ida Mae is startled at first, for this is the most noise I've made yet; then she tosses her head back and laughs too.

When we have both regained our breath, Ida Mae elbows me lightly. "You didn't know your boss was a comedian, didja?" I shake my head and she says, "Welp, Rachel-girl, get yourself prepared. There are plenty of sides to me nobody but my cats has seen."

Ida Mae shows me the tiny back room where she keeps her containers for transporting baked goods; it will now serve as my "reflexology station." She locks up the store and leads me to her house. Four soaring trees with knotty trunks and sweeping limbs overshadow the whitewashed dwelling with a steeply pitched roof, their leaves bathing the green tin in a tangy wash of orange and red. The small yard is enclosed by a white picket fence, and a long-haired calico with striking green eyes slinks along the fence top, mewing and arching its back in an attempt to get rubbed or attract a mate.

"Get down, you!" Ida Mae yells, swatting at the feline. But it's obvious that Ida Mae's bark is worse than her bite as she cradles the cat and runs rough fingers through its sleek coat. "This here's Bathsheba," Ida Mae says. "The last of Jezebel's babies."

My eyes widen at the choice of names. Depositing Bathsheba on the ground like she's made from glass, Ida Mae straightens, claps her hands, and calls, *"Lay-dee!"* A shaggy creature gets up from where it was slumbering in the flower beds and waddles toward us. I've never seen an animal so obese. Stopping in front of us, it collapses on its haunches and lifts a paw up to touch Ida Mae's thigh.

"What *is* that?" I whisper, my voice muted by the hand over my nose.

Ida Mae hunkers over and runs two hands down the animal's thick neck. "This here's Lady, a golden retriever."

Recoiling from the dog that's decided to place her dirty paw on my dress, I say, "I've never seen a golden retriever so . . ."

"Fat?" Ida Mae suggests.

I nod. Ida Mae scratches the dog behind her ears. She drops to the ground and rolls onto her back. Ida Mae rubs her boot on the dog's extended stomach, and Lady thumps her tail as drool oozes from either side of her mouth.

"Does she have a thyroid problem?" I ask, wondering if my mother has an herb we could use to fix the poor animal.

Ida Mae shakes her head. "No, ma'am. This dog here's got a little carbo-hydrate problem. I've been feeding her my leftover baked goods since I opened. I think they're starting to catch up with her." Smacking her own backside, Ida Mae adds, "But then, I shouldn't talk."

Ida Mae steps over the obese animal—who's still stretched on her back, hoping for another rub—and walks down the cracked sidewalk toward the house.

"How many cats do you have?" I glance at the line of beds under the porch and a tin nine-by-thirteen pan heaped with kibble. Having been raised on a farm, my family's always thought of cats as one step above mice, and that's only because they kill them.

"Oh, I'd say 'bout fifteen or twenty, but a few of them are feral as mountain lions." Ida Mae reaches out and touches Eli's head, which I don't like, since she has just been rubbing on Lady—a dog who does not live up to her name. "But don't you worry, Rachel-girl, they don't come in my house. I got a little shed for them out back."

Ida Mae opens the door to her house and ushers me inside. The same as in the store, I am surprised by the organization and attractiveness of the modest dwelling. There's a fireplace flanked by bookshelves. A quilt is draped over a threadbare couch, but neither are covered in the cat hair I had steeled myself to expect. The coffee table has the same crocheted doily beneath a glass bowl filled with dark molasses candy that my parents have on theirs. Really, the only difference between this house and my parents' is the small TV and VCR combo stowed in a painted cupboard and the gas fireplace rather than wood.

Touching my elbow, Ida Mae says, "I'll show you to you and Eli's room." She leads me through a narrow doorway and points to a blue room that has a lasso and a pair of rusty horseshoes hanging from nails embedded in the far left wall. A child's red cowboy hat dangles from a chin strap looped over the top of the bunk bed; the blue and red comforter is splashed with a Western theme. The LEGO magazines on the low chest in the right corner of the room are yellowed and the pages are curled. The window ledge is dotted with flies and speckled with dust. Looking closer, I see that *everything* is coated in dust, which seems strange compared to the cleanliness of the rest of the house.

Holding Eli tighter, for I can feel the shadow's coolness passing over us again, I ask, "Ida Mae? Was this room your little boy's?"

My employer looks at me with a mixture of annoyance and dismay. "No, it wasn't," she snaps, and then turns to leave. Before she does, she puts one hand on the doorframe and glances over her shoulder at the child in my arms. She opens her mouth, closes it, opens it again. "The bathroom's in my bedroom if ya need it," she says without meeting my eyes. "It's the size of a closet, but it works."

"That's fine. I'm not used to anything fancy."

"No," Ida Mae says, "I don't suppose you are."

By four in the morning, after I have counted the whistles of a dozen trains blaring past Ida Mae's house, I am resigned to the fact that sleep will not come. Lacing my arms, I pillow them behind my head and stare up at the ceiling, which is strewn with a constellation of glow-in-the-dark stars. "Who are you?" I whisper to the sleeping Ida Mae, whose snoring is as loud as she had claimed. "How'd you leave the church?"

I know this is a question I will have to answer for myself soon enough. I cannot go back to Copper Creek, perhaps not even to gather my things. If I go back, I might not have the strength to leave. And if I don't leave, I fear that Tobias will do as he threatens: tell my sister everything I have tried to shield her from for months. I know there is a possibility that Leah knows everything already, but I cannot take the risk that she does. I would rather live an hour from her and keep her tender heart safe than live under her roof and watch how my sins ravage the person I would do anything in this world to protect.

A train rumbles down the tracks again, causing dishes to rattle in the kitchen cupboards. The instant its whistle pierces the quiet night, I remember the Boxcar Children series Judah and I devoured that first summer he taught me how to read. I remember how those orphaned children made a new beginning for themselves out of an old boxcar they found in the woods. Although their lives were not what they once were, they were happy in their own right. Would Judah and I be happy if I said yes to his proposal of marriage and we fled the community's ties? Would we be like those children, hacking a future for ourselves out of a worldly wilderness? Mennonite couples often marry soon after joining the church at age seventeen, but for a year afterward, they travel from community to community: visiting with friends and family, eating meals that are prepared for them, sleeping in beds whose sheets they do not change or own. How would Judah and I ever build a life outside the cloistered boundaries of the church? Judah might have a better education than most Old Order Mennonites, but what is that compared to the English?

Flipping onto my stomach, I mash the pillow over my head and groan into the mattress as my tangled thoughts continue to unwind. And if I did say yes to Judah's proposal, what would he expect in the marriage bed? With my womb still swollen from Eli's birth and my breasts so heavy with milk they hurt to touch, my body is not one that can bring pleasure to a man; besides, I don't want it to bring pleasure to a man ever again. I am a mother now; that is all. I might have failed in every other area—disappointing my parents, worrying my sister to the point of death, burdening Judah King with a whiplash of gossip—but I will not fail my son, no matter what it takes. And for now that means finding a way to support our family so we can have a chance to survive.

# 5

## AMOS

The morning after my sons' confrontation, Judah awakens as the birds start twittering in the trees and slips into the spare room. He stuffs the black valise with the few garments that were folded on the rocking chair beside the bed. He grabs the crocheted blanket in the cradle and rolls it up, slipping it beneath his arm. It does not take Judah long to gather and pack the rest of the items, but he knows he must hurry before those in the house begin to stir.

Once everything is arranged, he exits the spare room just as quietly as he had entered and grabs the small bag he'd packed last night and placed outside his own room this morning. He tiptoes down the stairs, being careful to avoid the third-to-last one, which squeaks in the center, and places the letter explaining his actions beneath the pot of rhubarb preserves on the kitchen table, where he is sure his mother will find it.

Judah has to swallow as he glances around his childhood home for what he hopes, and fears, is the final time. With the perspective of leaving, the old is changed back to new. Even Verna's crocheted doilies draping the worn arms of the couch and the potted violets on the windowsills hold a special place in my son's sentimental heart. The wooden floor is scarred and warped from years of abrading rocking horses and chairs and afternoons of grandchildren tromping through snow, then coming inside to thaw in front of the woodstove with a cup of Verna's cocoa held between mittened hands. But in Judah's biased eyes it is as unmarred as the face of an ancient lover. The miniature barn, plastic fence, and animals that have been worn smooth and featureless by our children and then our grandchildren evoke in Judah memories that he never knew he had of the two of us playing farmer together.

If Tobias had not tightened his reins on the community as soon as they were taken out of my cold hands, vowing to squeeze out anyone who had the slightest rebellious twinge, Judah might have been comfortable to remain in Copper Creek all his life. He would've found a beautiful, soft-spoken girl at a hymn sing, and after a few months of open-buggy courting, he would have brought his bride into our home and raised their family in it just as his mother and I had done. But Tobias's tyrannical actions no longer allow this to be Judah's choice. Now all my younger son hopes for is a life with Rachel and her little boy, whose father she will never name.

The thought of their future together, even as he's in the midst of abandoning his past, brings a smile to my son's handsome face. Gripping the bags held in each of his hands a little tighter, a slight bounce enters his step as he opens the front door and makes his way down the long gravel lane. Judah passes the path that branches off to Tobias and Leah's home, and then takes the main road he used to walk on his way to the smithy. The place where he worked alongside his elder brother until my death forced Tobias to sit in the schoolhouse with two other deacons and withdraw one hardback *Ausbund* from a stack of three. When he cracked the black spine scrawled with dulled gold, a slip of paper fluttered from between the deckled pages like a moth. That simple luck of the draw promoted Tobias from blacksmith to bishop, a mantle he had never intended to wear.

Now, despite the fog pouring down the mountain ridges and pooling in the fields, Kauffman's General Store, Risser's Sorghum Mill, Hostetler's Bakery, Mast's Cannery, and Schlabach's Leatherworks all come into Judah's view. Out toward the end of the lane—where Copper Creek would become just another dead end if not for the signs used to lure *Englischer* tourists—a white, one-room schoolhouse is adorned with only the cast-iron bell the teacher uses to call the children back from lunch at their homes.

After taking advantage of the outhouse located behind the school, Judah settles in to wait for his driver to appear. It is impossible for an Old Order Mennonite to run away without transportation that goes faster than ten miles an hour. But when Judah learned of Rachel's banishment from Copper Creek, he hid in the barn and whispered through the phone receiver that the driver should pick him up at five o'clock Tuesday morning in front of the school. Judah knew there was a chance the truck's engine would be overheard, and the families preparing to open up the surrounding stores would put two and two together. But Judah also knew he would be long gone before his brother would receive the news and attempt to chase him down.

Sitting on the schoolhouse steps with the bags between his feet, Judah finds that the only person he feels guilty leaving behind is his mother, who is so burdened with grief over my death, she can barely open her eyes. For years after our first four children were born, my wife begged the Lord for another child. But nothing ever happened. Then one morning she awoke and realized she hadn't gotten her monthly in the past three of them. At first, she credited it to the onset of menopause, but after she went downstairs and the sight and smell of Mary's poached egg started making her sick, and the slight cramping in her stomach wouldn't go away, she decided to visit the midwife, who confirmed my wife's growing suspicions.

Six months later, when the improbable became possible, Verna and I could not help but love our surprising blessing all the more. Tobias, at twelve, was far too old to resent Judah, but the lack of attention he paid his brother communicated the feelings his mouth would not. To our consternation, our daughters followed their eldest brother's lead. My wife and I tried to make up for our children's slight by coddling Judah. We didn't give him as many chores as the others; Verna would always keep the bread box stocked with his favorite baked goods and her ragbag heaped with bright scraps that would have been beautiful woven into a quilt but wrapped Judah's woodland creatures instead. Rather than softening his siblings' apathy toward him, our attention only seemed to carve it into stone. To counterbalance this, we were soon treating Judah more like a grandchild than a son. I think this is why Tobias assumed the role of the father, one which he tries to enforce to this day, and the very reason, more than any other, Judah is bound and determined to leave Copper Creek.

Ida Mae's radio is turned as low as a hum, and she lets the truck engine purr as Judah slings the two small bags inside the cab, then climbs in behind them.

"You runnin' away?" Ida Mae asks.

Strapping the seat belt across his chest, Judah shakes his head. "No, I'm running toward something."

"It wouldn't be no girl, now, would it?"

Judah looks over with frustration in his eyes. "Why do you say that?"

Pulling out of the schoolyard onto Copper Creek Road, Ida Mae hides her smile by looking out the driver's-side window.

Judah, too tired to fall into her trap, shrugs. "I guess it doesn't matter how you found out since you're taking me to her anyway."

"Oh, am I? And how do you know where this girl even is?" Ida Mae points out the windshield where the community's peaked roofs are pricking through the fog. "She ain't living here no more, is she?"

My son says, "No. I don't know where she is, but somehow I've got to find her."

"It won't take you too long, I bet."

"How do you know?"

Ida Mae doesn't answer, just pulls down out of the mountain onto the highway. Taking a left back toward her store, she turns the radio to a country station. "Dunno," she says and smiles. "Love's got a way of taking us where we belong."

Placing her hands on either side of the sink, Rachel takes a deep breath and then pulls a freckled banana loose from the bundle sitting on top of the microwave. She peels it and takes a bite. For the first time since Amos's funeral, her stomach feels hollow from want of food, and a piece of fruit is the only thing in this *ferhoodled haus* she knows how to give it. Rachel isn't expecting Ida Mae to return until the store opens three hours from now, so she does not clean up the kitchen but just leaves it and pads into the blue bedroom with the glow-in-the-dark stars that have vanished with the dawn.

"How'd you get in here?" Rachel asks in Pennsylvania Dutch, shooing the feline off Eli's bed. Jezebel bats at her with retracted claws before leaping down onto the floor and exiting the room with the miffed air of royalty.

At that moment, Ida Mae opens the front door to her house, and Jezebel is a multicolored streak who darts between her master's legs into the fresh air outside. Ida Mae takes one whiff of the singed sugary smell pervading the room and does not blame Jezebel her hasty escape.

"What's burning?" Judah asks, coming in behind her.

Ida Mae calls out, "Rachel?"

Not having heard the front door open or the unmistakable timbre of Judah's voice, Rachel has no qualms about stepping from the bedroom into the living room. Her dark-blonde hair, released from its standard *kapp* and bun, trails down to the waist of her nightgown. My son just stands there with his mouth agape and eyes wide, thinking that hair and the person attached to it are the most glorious sight he has ever seen.

Clearing her throat, Ida Mae sidesteps the young couple and walks through the living room into the kitchen. She has to smile at the pan of charbroiled cinnamon rolls and pot of jet-black coffee sitting on the countertop. She'd made just as appetizing a meal the first night she moved into an apartment on the shady side of a Tennessee town where no one knew her name or her story. Tuning one ear to the low murmurs in the living room and another to the child who is starting to whimper from his bed, Ida Mae grabs a Brillo pad and begins scouring the countertops and the burners on the stove. She dumps the pot of coffee and pan of cinnamon rolls out the back door, but even Lady turns her nose up at the pastries that look nothing like the leftovers from her master's store.

Ten minutes later, the kitchen looks like it had never collided with an Old Order Mennonite woman's first attempt at technology. As if on cue, Eli's whimpers increase to outraged wails. Ida Mae wrings out the Brillo pad and sets it on top of the sink, then scurries into the blue room and lifts the infant from his makeshift bed. Startled by the unfamiliar, peach-shaped face, Eli opens his mouth to scream, but Ida Mae widens her pitted brown eyes and opens her mouth in an O that mirrors his own.

Eli's pale brows wrinkle as he stares at this unusual woman who holds him against her cushy bosom like she will never let him go. If Ida Mae had her choice, she wouldn't. And for the first time since the arrival of the young girl and her illegitimate child, Ida Mae Speck's hoping Rachel will *not* leave with that young man who bit his nails the whole drive from Copper Creek to Blackbrier, but will stay with her in the little tin-roofed cottage between an Amish store and the train tracks, which houses the remnants of lives that were never truly lived.

## Rachel

Once Ida Mae tactfully leaves, I grab the blanket off the armchair and drape it around my shoulders. Bowing my arms behind me, I begin to fold my hair into a braid, but Judah touches my arm and says, "Don't. I like it down."

I want to tell Judah King that he has no right to determine the way I do my hair or clothes; that from an overbearing father to the man who fathered my child, men have been superimposing their desires upon mine until I couldn't even tell that they were not one and the same. Even if Judah's heart is good, that does not mean his intentions are what they should be.

He must sense these thoughts from the firmness of my mouth trying to keep them all in, for he tilts his head and asks, "Did I say something wrong?"

"No. I'm just tired from yesterday."

Judah nods, looks over at the unblinking gray eye of the TV, and then to my brown bag, which he had placed by the door. "You never have to go back there," he says. "I packed up everything I saw. But if something's missing, we can buy it for you. I've saved up some money from smithing over the years. Not a lot, but it'll hold us over. At least until I can get a job."

Trying not to appear as disquieted as I feel, I move to the front door and gesture for Judah to follow. I sit on a wicker rocking chair on the porch; Judah's lips crook into a grin as he takes the seat beside me. I don't know what he is expecting, but I have a feeling he is going to be disappointed. Pulling the blanket tighter around my shoulders, I tuck my feet on the rung of the rocking chair and use my body to set it into motion. A light rain begins to fall, the contact on the tin roof making it sound like a deluge. An orange tomcat darts from under the porch and curls into a woolly ball at my feet. I scoot my chair back so it won't land on his tail. To Judah's credit, he says nothing, but just lets me rock in silence.

"I appreciate . . ." I pause and try to think of a less formal beginning. "It was very kind of you to get my things for me."

Judah just nods and stares out at the yard whose dirt is turning to mud beneath the steady trickle of rain. Knowing then that nothing will penetrate his dreamy mind but the truth, I say, "It was kind of you to pack up my things, but there should be no mention of 'we'; there should be no mention of 'us' until I'm sure that's a pronoun I want to use."

Judah says, "But even as children, I've always thought of you as just an extension of me."

Risking a glance at him, I see the profile of the young

boy who taught me how to read and write English for hours without the smallest complaint. Judah does not deserve the harsh vocalization of my thoughts, but neither can he keep holding out such foolish hope for something that can never be.

"Until I know the mistakes I've made no longer have the power to hurt those I love," I say, "I have no choice but to be a single mother to Eli."

Judah stops rocking his chair and reaches over to stop mine. "That's where you're wrong," he says, his cheeks flushed. "I don't know what mistakes you've made or who you've made them with, but I know marrying me wouldn't be one of them."

Dropping the blanket from my shoulders, I snap, "No, that's where *you're* wrong. You think I'm still that innocent little girl who was your childhood friend. Well, I'm not. You don't even know who I am. *I* don't even know who I am. Until I've gotten that figured out, you and I can never be 'us.'"

Judah looks over, and I can see the reality of my refusal sinking in. As if walking in a trance, he rises and comes over to stand before me. "When you've figured out who you are, you let me know. Until then . . ." Stooping, he places his blacksmith's hands on either side of my chair and slants his body parallel to mine. I flinch at his closeness, at the lure of his proximity. Ignoring my withdrawal, he places a light kiss on the center of my part created by years of braided pigtails and scalping buns. "Good-bye, Rachel," Judah whispers.

He then straightens and walks off the porch into the pouring rain.

His leaving is not quite the dramatic exit his words deserve. Judah first must grab a bag from Ida Mae's truck before he can walk up to the four-lane highway running past the store.

I sit on the white wicker chair when I want to sprint after him, when I want to ask how he is going to leave or how he thinks he can. Judah has no vehicle, and he wouldn't know how to drive one if he did. By his own admission, he does not have much money to pay a driver.

None of this deters him. I watch how the rain plasters his homemade shirt to his lean body and drips off the back of his black felt hat. Judah lifts his thumb like the hitchhikers we sometimes see on the roads and begins walking up the highway.

Only when I know he is out of sight do I stand and walk barefoot into the sodden yard, trying to catch one more glimpse of him. It is too late. Judah is already gone, despite not knowing where he is going or how he will get there.

For all our differences, it seems Judah King and I are living lives that are one and the same.

I have no idea how much time has passed when Ida Mae appears with a mug of black coffee and a bowl of something that looks like porridge.

"Grits," she explains, thrusting the bowl at me. "The staple food for everybody beneath the Mason-Dixon Line."

The warm bowl feels good in my hands, but the thought of eating anything right now is appalling. Ida Mae collapses into the chair that Judah had occupied and starts rocking with the rolling of her tiny booted foot. Taking a sip of coffee, she keeps staring straight ahead as she says, "Welp, Rachel-girl, didja send him packing?"

I nod.

"I think you done right. Judah's a sweet boy, but you can't be raising two kids when you're just a kid yourself."

Feeling defensive, I say, "He's hardly had a chance to prove himself to anyone."

Ida Mae pats Lady's head. The dog has wobbled over to rest a dirty paw on her master's knee. "I reckon he's left the church?" she asks.

"Yes," I reply, realizing the enormity of his departure. "I believe he has."

"That's for the best too. Judah can never find himself, tied to his momma's apron strings."

"Or under his brother's thumb."

Ida Mae glances over at the vehemence in my voice. "Gerald drives Tobias here sometimes," she says. "Along with some other menfolk from Copper Creek. They fix the storage barns and bring me quilts from their women that I can sell. In the summer, they bring their produce. You gonna be all right working round all that?"

Taking a bite of grits, I swallow the buttery granules and say, "That'll be fine. I'll just stay in the store."

"And have you thought 'bout where you and that young'un are gonna live?"

"Actually, I was wondering if . . ."

"Yeah?" Ida Mae stares out into the yard with a bored look.

"Well, if Eli and I could maybe stay here? For a while, at least? I can cook and clean for you, and I could grocery-shop if a store's within walking distance."

My stomach sinks as Ida Mae shakes her head. "You telling me you're gonna make those sorry cinnamon rolls every morning and coffee that could replace the oil in a car?"

"I'll have to learn how to use an electric stove, but I'm a fast learner."

Ida Mae gives me a skeptical look. "From that twister in my kitchen, I'd say you clean 'bout as good as you cook."

"I'm actually a very tidy person. This morning was just a little . . . different."

"I'll say." She sniffs, setting the empty mug on the porch and shooing the orange tomcat away. "Nothing's been the same since I picked you and that kid up from the hospital."

I stand to go inside, carrying my bowl of grits. Before I open the storm door, I turn back to Ida Mae. "I don't think anything's been the same for me, either."

She smiles even though tears shine in her eyes. "Nah, honey, and it's never gonna be. You can bet your bottom dollar on that."

On my way to the kitchen, I glance around at the blue room and see the yellowed LEGO magazines and nailed horseshoes that have turned crumbly with rust. I no longer think I can ask Ida Mae if we can redecorate this room, for as we were talking, I saw in her eyes the same strange sorrow I know must be reflected in mine.

## AMOS

Had Samuel and Helen Stoltzfus known that their young driver left the Amish church only three months before so he could become the next Dale Earnhardt, they surely would have asked for a refund rather than paying him that extra hundred dollars to make it from Pennsylvania to Tennessee in eleven hours instead of the standard twelve. But Helen takes pride in sticking to her word, especially since her husband doesn't, so, standing outside the hospital with a large suitcase leaning against her skirted legs, Helen hands over the crisp Ben Franklin without giving the young driver the scolding his terrible driving deserves.

Samuel and Helen ride the elevator up to the third floor, where their daughter lies in a hospital bed recuperating from severe blood loss and dehydration. As the elevator doors slide open, ushering them down the corridor's maze, Helen reaches for Samuel's hand in a demonstration of affection considered odd to them both. Still, their fingers remain intertwined as they hurry toward Leah's room and Helen knocks on the door.

Tobias opens it at once, his rumpled face relaying the feelings of anxiety and relief his eccentric in-laws somehow always bring.

Helen's lips are poised to ask, "How is she?" but she can see for herself the pallid tone of her daughter's features, the skeletal hands overlaid with parchment skin and an embroidery of thin blue veins. Clucking her tongue, Helen strides to the end of the bed and takes Leah's feet in her hands. She presses her thumbs into the swollen arches, and Leah, still asleep, emits a soft moan.

Moving away from Samuel, whose one-track mind is causing him to discuss his latest set of matching ponies rather than his daughter's health, Tobias looks at his mother-in-law and barks, "What're you doing?"

Nothing about Helen acknowledges Tobias but her lips. "I'm seeing which of her organs are inflamed."

Tobias's thick eyebrows form a V over his eyes and his jaws clench. Striding over, he jerks the thin blue blanket over Leah's feet. "I did *not* invite you down here to do witchcraft on my wife!"

It is easy to see where Rachel inherited her temper as Helen Stoltzfus looks up at the man towering over her and snaps, "I guess you invited me down here to watch her die, then." She points to the machines clustered around the bed and the IV filtering fluids into her daughter's arm. "These

*Englischer* contraptions are only masking the problem; they're not getting to the source."

"And you think your powwow *doktor*ing can?"

Helen shakes her head. "It's not powwow *doktor*ing, Tobias. It's holistic medicine."

"Still sounds like witchcraft to me."

"That's because you don't understand it."

Looking at Leah lying there in a shifting purgatory of wakefulness and sleep, Tobias says, "That's not the only thing I don't understand."

Samuel drags a hand over his white beard. "I'm hungry." He yawns.

Not attempting to hide his annoyance, Tobias asks, "I take it you want to go down to the cafeteria?"

Samuel nods and gets up from the hospital chair. "You want anything, *Fraa*?"

Helen shakes her head. Only when she hears the sound of the door clicking shut does she feel like she can breathe again. Getting up and walking over to the suitcase, Helen kneels down, unzips it, and throws back the flap. She digs into the netted compartment where she packed her black tights. In the left heel of one pair she feels the small glass bottle. Glancing over her shoulder, trying to listen for the sound of the nurses' rubber shoes squeaking across the tile, Helen rolls the bottle out of the tights, unscrews the cap, and gets to her feet.

If Leah were in her right state of mind, she would never drink this elixir of healing herbs. Helen knows this; that is why she must work fast. Leaning over the hospital bed, Helen whispers, "Open your mouth, *Dochder*."

Leah, always complaisant about everything except what Tobias has trained her to avoid, lowers her bottom lip and even smiles at the sound of her mother's purposefully soothing voice.

"That's right, my *meedel*," Helen says, tipping the bottle's contents into her mouth and then rubbing Leah's throat, forcing her to swallow.

Leah's eyes open. She grimaces at the bitter taste ballooning inside her mouth, and her bleary gaze comes to rest on the woman who is putting the cap back on the vial.

*"Mammi?"* she rasps. "That you?"

"Yes, *meedel*." Tears deepen the timbre of Helen's voice. "I'm here."

"What did you give me? What's in the bottle?"

"Just a blend of healing herbs. . . . Norman Troyer made it for you."

"You know Tobias doesn't like Norman."

"It doesn't matter who Tobias likes or who he doesn't. What matters is getting you well."

Leah looks down and plucks at her IV. "Why do you and Rachel despise my husband?"

Sighing, Helen sits on the edge of the bed and takes her daughter's feet in her lap. "I guess the reason I get so angry with Tobias is because . . . well, because I feel responsible for your union. That letter—"

Leah holds up the hand trailing the IV and shakes her

head. "Please don't bring up that letter again. What's done is done. I've said my vows, and I will live by them until I die."

Staring down at the bed to hide her fear, Helen rubs and rubs her daughter's feet as if she can cure Leah's ailments by her determination alone.

# 6

## Rachel

Today is my first day working at Ida Mae's Amish Country Store. Her only stipulations are that Eli and I dress as Amish as possible and that I speak to him in Pennsylvania Dutch whenever *Englischer* customers enter the store. I told her that dressing Amish is difficult, since all my Mennonite cape dresses are printed with tiny flower patterns, whereas Amish dresses are cut from plain cloth. Ida Mae just waved her hand and said, "Honey, nobody round here's gonna know the difference."

I just nodded and smiled, but I'm not as gullible as Ida Mae must think. I know she's hired me more for decorative purposes than for reflexology, though I am not about to complain. McDonald's wouldn't see my Plain heritage as a benefit, nor would they allow me to flip burgers with one hand and juggle my son with the other. Plus, $8.50 an hour just to sit around and mutter nonsense at Eli, whom Ida Mae placed in some Amish doll clothes and matching straw hat so he'd look "more authentic," is not that bad. I have no need for pride, and if I raise Eli up the way I intend, neither will my son. As far as I have seen, pride's never gotten the people of Copper Creek very far.

Ida Mae calls out, "Somebody's comin'!" and reaches to turn up the CD player lilting instrumental hymns. Smoothing the green gingham apron over her bust, she sits up higher on the stool and runs fingers through her mop. Although Ida Mae has left the "Amish" garb up to me, whenever she's in the store, she trades her tight Wranglers for an ankle-length skirt whose stretchy material suctions to her backside. Her muddied boots she trades for clogs, and her gray army jacket for a jewel-toned sweater over a red turtleneck.

"You ain't the only one who can play dress-up," she snapped when she caught me giving her outfit a double take over breakfast. "Tourists don't wanna come in my store and see an ol' biddy behind the counter. They wanna see their *grossmammi*, so that's what I give 'em. I fawn over their young'uns. I hand 'em peppermint sticks and slivers of fudge in wax paper. I let 'em set in little tables and color in the Amish books I get from

Lehman's. I'm telling ya, it makes the parents come back. Not just for my baked goods and pickled beet eggs, neither, but 'cause coming to Ida Mae's Amish Country Store is an *ex-peri-ence*."

Looking at my new employer now, smiling from ear to ear and calling out to the customer, "Velcome! Let me know if ve can help vith anything!" I have to agree.

The bleach-blonde woman wearing dark sunglasses on a sunless day, on the other hand, does not see the appeal. "Are these baked goods fresh?" she asks, poking the bread with one manicured nail.

"Fresh this morning," Ida Mae says, even though I know she tugged them out of the freezer last night.

Pushing her sunglasses on top of her head, the woman squints at the ingredients on the baked goods label. "Shortening!" she exclaims. "But I thought *Om*-mish people cook organically!"

"Look at it like this," Ida Mae says with a stiff smile. "Everything's organic one way or another, even shortening."

"I see," the woman says, then flounces toward the door in her designer heels and lets it slam behind her.

Ida Mae looks out the window as the woman whips around the store in her champagne SUV. "I'm telling ya, Rachel-girl," she sighs, "this organic kick's really gonna do us in."

"Then why don't you tell Hostetler's to bake organically? Couldn't they just charge a little extra to cover the ingredients?"

Ida Mae rolls her eyes. "I've tried telling them that, but they've been using the same recipes since the days of Menno Simons. They ain't 'bout to change their ways now."

"Why don't we do the baking? We'd just need a few really good mixers and ovens. I've been baking since I was a little girl. I know how it's done."

"I'll think about it," she says. "But I know one thing you *ain't* gonna bake."

"What's that?"

Ida Mae slaps my back as a Frito-Lay truck pulls into the parking lot. "Cinnamon rolls!"

When the broad-shouldered trucker in the tan Carhartt jacket and steel-toe boots enters the store, the bell above the door is the only thing heralding his arrival. I find this strange, since Ida Mae practically fell off her stool trying to make the last customer feel "velcome."

"How are you, Miz Speck?" the man asks, unmoved by her stony silence.

She takes out a ledger from beneath the table. Flipping it open, she begins entering debits with a red ballpoint and credits with a black one.

"Did that honey ever come in?"

Ida Mae points to the shelf without looking up.

"Is it local? I can only do local honey or it won't help my allergies."

Scribbling out an entry in the ledger, Ida Mae snaps, "Read the label."

The man lumbers over and takes out a pair of glasses from his jacket pocket. Putting them on, he picks up the honey jar and scans the bottom. "Sure enough," he says. "Bottled in Blackbrier, Tennessee."

"So, you ready to check out?" Ida Mae asks like we're about to close rather than just having opened.

The man shakes his head, his eyes crinkling up behind his glasses. "You sure are in a good mood," he says. "I bet it's that pretty sweater you're wearing. Puts some color in your cheeks."

"My cheeks and their color are none of your business."

I would be cowering beneath the baked goods shelf if Ida Mae said these things to me and in such a threatening tone, but this man just says, "Oh, but I wish they were my business."

Ida Mae slaps the ledger closed and glares up at him. "If you don't come over here and pay for that honey right this minute," she says from between clenched teeth, "I'm gonna get my new girl here to throw you right outta the store."

Alarmed, I look at the man, but he just glances at me and smiles. "Why, that baby she's holding's bigger than her. She couldn't throw out a brute like me."

"You might be surprised," Ida Mae says. "She was corn fed."

Ambling up to the counter with his right hand tucked in the pocket of his jeans and the other holding the honey, the man sets the jar on the countertop and I glimpse a wedding band.

"Can I writcha a check?" he asks.

Ida Mae nods. "Long as it ain't rubber."

Reaching in the basket beside the cash register, the man grabs a peach fried pie and sets it next to the honey. "I'll take that, too," he says.

Ida Mae says, "No, you won't. Those things will give ya a heart attack."

The man shrugs. "Already had two."

"Like I don't know it . . . you out picking ginseng seven miles from home."

"And *you* keeping me in bed for a day rather than taking me to the hospital. Shoulda known you were trying to get rid of me then."

My eyes dart between Ida Mae and this man as I try to understand the dynamics of their relationship. Maybe he's her brother? But that doesn't make sense because the look in the man's eyes isn't the least bit brotherly. No wonder Ida Mae is being so rude to him. She's trying to deflect the attentions of a married man.

He finishes signing his name with Ida Mae's black ballpoint and plinks the pen into the empty coffee mug next to the register. Turning the check over, Ida Mae stamps it with the store's name and address and slips it into the bottom drawer of the cash register.

"You want your receipt?" she asks, tearing it off and holding it up.

The man shakes his head. "I never doubted you were honest."

Ida Mae flips open the ledger again like she can't wait for him to leave. Not until he *has* left (with his paper sack of honey minus the peach fried pie) does Ida Mae hit N/S on the cash register.

Pulling out his check, she inspects it under the fluorescent lighting as if it's a counterfeit. "Ugh, that man. I can never read his writing. You mind?" she asks.

I nod and take the check. His cursive letters and numbers are equally difficult to read, but after a moment of compare and contrast, they become clear. "Two hundred and fifty dollars seems pretty expensive for honey," I say. "Even if it *is* local."

"That scoundrel keeps doing this," Ida Mae says. "Paying for a little something, then giving me a whole bunch of extra money."

I glance down at the check again, reading the name in the top left corner: Russell Speck, 317 Red Herring Road, Blackbrier, Tennessee 37842.

Speck, Speck. Somewhere I've heard that last name before; then I realize and look over at Ida Mae in confusion. "Russell Speck? Is he your brother?"

Snatching the check from my fingers, she rips it in two, and then in four. "No," she says. "My husband. My *second* husband. And my first *ex*-husband. The other one, we didn't divorce. He died."

"How?" I ask.

She drops the check pieces into the trash can beneath the counter and wipes her hand off on her apron as if it is dirty. "That Russell Speck," she says, "my second husband, my first ex-husband?"

I nod.

"Welp, he killed him. He killed my first husband."

The words are out before I can think of how accusing they will sound: "Then why did you marry him?"

Ida Mae uncaps her red and black ballpoints and resumes entering debits and credits in the ledger. "It's a long story," she says. "And honestly, Rachel-girl, I'm in no mood to tell it."

## AMOS

The hospital releases Leah the day after her mother arrived in Tennessee. If Tobias suspects that something has been used to accelerate his wife's recovery, he keeps it to himself, for he is just happy to have her home. Leah is not so grateful. In the hospital, it had been easy to distance herself from the fact that her sister was truly gone. Tobias had even planned it that way. He had waited until his wife's mind was softened by medication to whisper into her ear that Rachel had not only left their home, but Copper Creek as well.

Now, unmitigated by sleep aids, the reality of Leah's

twin's departure comes rushing in, and with it, a pain of separation so pronounced it is as if Rachel and Leah were Siamese twins severed without their consent.

*Why'd she leave without saying good-bye?* Leah wonders, walking through Rachel's room and seeing remnants of hers still there—a baby bootie, a box of nursing pads, a sheaf of bobby pins. Comforting herself with the fact that perhaps Rachel *had* come to the hospital to say good-bye but Leah had been too addled to respond, she turns to exit the room and jumps when she sees her mother standing in the doorway.

"Did you know Judah's left too?" Helen asks.

"No. When?"

"Two mornings ago. He hired a driver and no one knows where he's gone."

"You think he's with Rachel?"

Helen folds her arms. "It's possible, but I don't think she'd do that."

"Why not?"

"It makes sense. It's what the community expects of her. And of him. Rachel often refuses to do things when they're expected of her."

Leah picks up the baby bootie Rachel left behind. Slipping two fingers into the delicate yellow and white sock, she sighs. "*Jah*, she does." After a moment, she adds, "How do you think we can find her?"

"The drivers." Helen says this without hesitation, letting Leah know that she has thought this through already. "We just need to find out who drove Rachel that day, maybe even who drove Judah, too."

"Gerald Martin?"

Helen shakes her head. "No, I already asked. It wasn't him. He said he'd been asked not to help Rachel."

"What?" Leah drops the baby bootie to the dresser and whirls around, incensed. "Who would do that to a young mother?"

Seconds pass. Helen stares at her daughter with blue eyes conveying a message Leah cannot decode. "Your husband," she finally says. "Your husband paid Gerald Martin not to drive Rachel around."

When Tobias climbs into bed beside his wife, eager to make up for the conjugal separation her hospital stay had required, he finds Leah's body as rigid as a board and her waterfall of hair—a reservoir formulated for his pleasure alone—still twisted into its bun. My son does not understand this, but lately there have been a lot of things about Leah and her family that he has not understood. Trying to remain patient, he puts an arm around Leah's frail shoulders and attempts to turn her body toward his. She remains planted on her side.

Tobias gives up and flips onto his back. "What's wrong?" he says, failing to keep the irritation from his voice. "Are you in pain?"

Leah shakes her head but does not say a word. Tobias sighs and glares up at the ceiling, thinking she is just being emotional again. But if he could see how her eyes glitter in the moonlight flickering through the window, he would know the emotion she is feeling is not sorrow, but the first stirrings of anger. Not anger toward her husband, exactly, but anger toward the irreparable situation in which she has placed herself. For the first time Leah allows herself to imagine what her life would be like if she had never responded to my son's urgent request for a wife to mother his children, if she had stayed in that yellow house on Hilltop Road where her and her sister's lives revolved completely around each other.

There is no question that Rachel would have married one of the boys vying for her attention and left Leah alone, in the same way that Leah, shockingly enough for everyone in the Muddy Pond Community, had left her. But at least Leah could have gone and stayed with Rachel and her new husband, who would've never forced his sister-in-law out into the street. At least Leah's and Rachel's days could have been lived together, even if at night Rachel went off to her marriage bed. Now, Rachel is gone—taking her child and irrepressible spirit with her. Even if Helen somehow makes contact with Rachel through her driver, Leah knows that Tobias won't allow her to visit Rachel again. He might not even allow them to *speak* ever again. This, more than anything, is the reason Leah remains on her side, facing the window rather than her husband. A year and a half ago, if she could have known that by choosing Tobias she would be choosing to abandon her twin, she would have never done it. She would've rather lived out her days in spinsterhood than marry a man who would sever the bond between two people so intertwined it was hard not to see them as one, for with Rachel's departure, Leah understands that it is easier to leave than to be left behind.

This realization crashes over Leah like a wave. With it comes an undertow of tears. At first they trickle down her face without effort or sound, but as their intensity increases, Leah's body begins to convulse with sobs, and she loses both her rigid back and her resolve.

Tobias, sensing her will's breakdown, reaches over and turns his wife to face him. Her small body is as malleable as a child's, and Leah curls up against his warm chest not because she wants her husband's comfort, but because she cannot stand to be alone on such a cold and lonely night. Unaware of any of these emotions—because he will not ask and does not want the answer—Tobias kisses the brine of his wife's tear-streaked face, and then her mouth. With every gesture of affection, the decibel of Leah's wails increases until Tobias stops and grips her by the shoulders.

"Stop it! Just stop, Leah!" he barks, his lips curled back as he shakes her. "She's gone! Rachel's gone! You *must* get used to this!"

Leah nods and turns to bury her head in the pillow.

Hitting the headboard behind him with the flat of his

hand, Tobias rolls onto his side and looks toward their bedroom door. Leah flips onto her side and faces the wall.

Hours pass with Leah biting her sobs into the feather pillow, but Tobias has hardened his heart against her unrelenting emotions and forces himself not to hear.

## Rachel

Ida Mae has not been her talkative, bossy self since Russell Speck was here a couple of days ago, and the more I ponder our conversation, the less I understand it. Although Ida Mae's personality is a rare one, I still cannot imagine that she would marry the man who killed her spouse. I know from one glimpse into her murky brown eyes that Ida Mae must've loved deeply for them to reflect such loss. But is that loss over the husband who was killed or over the second marriage that ended just as devastatingly as the first?

I've been asking myself these questions for the past two days, but they have gotten me nowhere. I have to admit, though, it's been a relief to have something to occupy my mind besides my own life's uncertainty. Perhaps this is why *Englischers* spend so much time tapping on their cell phones or reading glossy tabloids. They want to watch someone else's drama unfold; they want to watch someone else's life crash and burn, as it takes away the heat of their own.

I have just switched off the oven where I'm baking potatoes wrapped in layers of foil (Ida Mae set the temperature beforehand), when she comes in the kitchen and hands me her cell phone.

I am so startled, I ask, *"Was ist das?"*

Ida Mae answers, "Your *mudder*."

I feel the color drain from my face. My hands shake as I take the cell phone and look at the black numbers on the gray screen.

Leaning over, Ida Mae taps the bottom of the phone. "It's ready," she says. "Just talk."

"Is it Leah?" I ask into the receiver, the words barely audible even to me.

My *mamm* hollers, as if her voice must carry across the miles. "No, it's not Leah! She's out of the hospital and everything!"

I move backward until my spine rests against the oven. I had thought she was calling to tell me of my sister's passing. I was almost certain of it; I could feel Leah's death reverberating throughout my body as if my mind had already received the news. The only time my *mamm* has ever used the barn phone is for emergencies or to cancel an appointment with a reflexology customer, so why is she calling from it now?

"Then who is it?" I ask and swallow. "Is it *Dawdy*?" Although my father is physically fine, his mental capacity has diminished since the afternoon he was kicked by a horse and his brain bled, causing his thoughts to now revolve around the only subject that has ever brought him joy: horse auctions.

"No, it's not *Dawdy*!" *Mamm* shouts. "We're worried about *you*. You just ran off without telling Leah good-bye."

"It wasn't like I had a choice," I say, my tone annoyed. "Tobias forced me to go."

There is a muffled sound. My *mamm*'s voice is lower as she says, "I thought as much. He seemed pretty upset when we saw him at the hospital."

"What do you mean? . . . You saw him? Are you here in Tennessee?"

I can tell my *mamm* nods, because there is a long pause before she says, "Yes. *Dawdy* and I got down here *Mittwoch* afternoon. Tobias called and told us to come. He even hired a driver."

"How generous of him."

My mother clucks her tongue, whether in agreement or chastisement I cannot tell. After a moment, she says, "Are you and Eli safe there with that *Englischer weibsmensch*?"

"Ida Mae's not English or Plain. But yes, we're safe. She's been very kind to us."

"Can *Dawdy* and I come see you tomorrow? I'd try bringing Leah, too, but I don't think Tobias would allow it."

"Don't even ask him," I warn. "You'll only make it harder for her." After giving *Mamm* the address, I explain, "If you have any trouble finding it, just tell Gerald it's the Amish store in Blackbrier."

"I'm not hiring Gerald to drive us," *Mamm* says. "He's got no backbone."

"Who else, then?"

"Your *Englischer* friend, you think she'd come get us?"

"Yes. She'll come. But—" I glance around the kitchen and the blue room to make sure Ida Mae's out of earshot—"well, *Mamm*, she *is* a little different."

"And our *familye*'s not?" she says.

I have to smile as I hang up. She's got a point there.

At first Ida Mae isn't too keen on picking my parents up and bringing them back to her store. I have a hard time understanding why, but then I notice how she keeps staring at Eli asleep in his handcrafted cradle next to our stools and how she won't meet my eyes when she passes the free-range eggs, warm *brot*, and smoked cheeses for me to bag up. To test my theory, I wait until the customers leave and say, "I'm not going back with my parents to Pennsylvania, you know."

Ida Mae just snorts, hops off her stool, and goes over to straighten the jars of jam. I have all but forgotten what I said when Ida Mae replies, "You say that now, but when your *mammi*'s here, loving on her *grosskind*, you'll be saying something different."

"That's not true," I insist, remaining focused on the storage barn and swing set flyers I am restocking so she won't see my frustration. "I won't be going back because I'm not *allowed* to go back."

For the first time since I asked Ida Mae if she could drive my parents, she glances over her shoulder and looks me right in the eyes. "Who?" she asks.

"Who what?"

"Who won't let you go back?"

"My father."

Ida Mae just stands there, rough hands on aproned hips, waiting for the further explanation I am reluctant to give.

Trying to dispel all seriousness, I shrug. "I guess he thinks it would hurt his horse-trading business with the Amish and Mennonites. That they wouldn't want to purchase something that had contact with such a scandalous family."

"Hogwash!" Ida Mae fumes, leaning down for the small Mountain Dew bottle she keeps tucked in the front pocket of her apron. After spitting into the bottle—a brown dribble down green glass—she screws the cap back on, wipes her chin with her hand, and says, "It burns me up how those Amish and Mennonites sin just like the rest of the world, but they act like they're all high and mighty."

"Please," I entreat, taking a step closer to her. "Don't bring anything like that up with my father. He—he doesn't do so well with confrontation."

Ida Mae climbs onto her stool again, her miniature feet (the only thing miniature about her) tucked in the silver rungs because they don't reach the floor. Leaning over to start the CD player again, she says, "I ain't making no promises, Rachel-girl. If I see your *dawdy* talking ugly to you, I might just have to give him a piece of my mind."

Watching heat climb up the ladder of Ida Mae's neck to her full cheeks, I can only imagine what a generous piece that will be.

# 7

## AMOS

Strange as it is, ever since Ida Mae picked Samuel and Helen up from Tobias's *haus* in Copper Creek and brought them back to her store, she has become selectively deaf. She will leap to her feet at Eli's smallest whimper or Rachel's lightest sigh, but she will sit with her stone face turned to the brick wall as Helen pays her some banal compliment about the store that Ida Mae knows she does not mean.

But Samuel's really the cross that Ida Mae has to bear. With his bushy black eyebrows contrasted with a shocking amount of white hair, he looks just like her father, Jacob Miller, did when she left her community soon after the accident. The physical resemblance is not their only similarity; Samuel's attitude is the same as Jacob Miller's was too. He has no time for any ideas or comments except his own—which, in Samuel's case, are all about the matching ponies he's bought and sold at the New Holland horse auction over the past forty-some years.

"Did ya know you can drug a horse in the show ring to make it look broke?" he asks the four people, counting Eli, in the room.

Having been informed of this fact many times before, Helen and Rachel nod, but Ida Mae just stares at Samuel and then says, "Is that what you do? You sell a horse to people that could kill 'em?"

Samuel's brows act like an awning over his squinty blue eyes. Even with the damage to his brain, he can recognize a challenge when he hears one. "You calling me a *schwindler*!" he rails in his thick Pennsylvania Dutch accent, sliding thumbs between his suspenders and shirt.

Ida Mae says, "If the horseshoe fits," and slaps the ledger closed.

You'd have to be blind in addition to selectively deaf to miss the tension escalating between Samuel Stoltzfus and Ida Mae Speck. Passing Eli to her mother, Rachel stands and walks over to them. "Why don't we have some *middaagesse*?" she asks. "I've got some fudge pie for dessert."

Samuel shrugs but not before glowering at Ida Mae. "I guess we'll *esse*," he says, not willing to relinquish, even for the sake of an argument, the only thing that brings him pleasure besides his matching ponies.

Ida Mae says, "Y'all go on back and help yourselves. I'm gonna watch the store."

Settling Eli on her hip, Rachel herds her mother and father out through the back of the store and mouths over her shoulder, "Sorry."

Ida Mae nods and, once the door shuts, sighs. It's only been two hours since Samuel and Helen's arrival. It is going to be a long day.

Once the remainders of *kiehfleesch* and *gemaeschde grummbeere* have been wiped clean from the plates by Samuel Stoltzfus's buttery piece of sourdough *brot* (courtesy of Ida Mae's Amish Country Store), Helen leans forward on the table and looks at her daughter with eyes that reveal her impending words: "Why'd Tobias force you to leave?"

Rachel knew this conversation was going to happen, but the dread of it still knocks the breath from her. "I don't know for sure, *Mamm*," she says, "but I think a lot of it had to do with that child over there." She nods at Eli, who is being rocked in the swing that Ida Mae says she picked up at a yard sale even though the tags said it came from Walmart.

"Don't be smart with your *mudder*," Helen says, whipping the strands of her *kapp* behind her neck. "Just answer the question."

Tired of the lies and even more tired of telling them, Rachel says, "I think he blamed me for Leah being sick."

Helen Stoltzfus's thin lips snap shut. She sits up straighter in the kitchen chair. In the waning afternoon sunlight coming through the curtained windows, Helen peers over at her husband to see if he is starting to patch together the disparate parts of their daughter's life. But the dull look in his eyes tells her he isn't; of course he isn't. Even before that stallion got tired of the man picking at his hooves and dented in Samuel's skull with a casual swoop of his hind leg, Samuel never cared to pay attention to conversations concerning relationships and love. All he knows is what he needs to: his daughter has given birth to a fatherless son, and she is now living in the home of an *Englischer* woman who has a voice as gruff as a man's.

Mopping his beard with a napkin, he looks over his shoulder as if the fudge pie will appear. "Where's dessert?" he asks.

Rachel gets to her feet and escapes to Ida Mae's galley-size kitchen, where she dissects the pie and slips the pieces onto plates, her knuckles whitening as she clutches the server. From this, I know that she is not yet ready to face the truth of her unresolved feelings for her father and the role they have played in bringing her to this point. But in the strange state in which I find myself, I seem to understand far more than I should.

## Rachel

It is suppertime when Ida Mae returns from dropping my parents off at Copper Creek. The table is already set and the leftovers laid out. I know she must see the modest meal that I have prepared, but she doesn't acknowledge it. Instead, she just hangs her jacket on the coat tree, staggers back to her bedroom, and closes the door.

After the day's frustrations, I have no appetite myself, but I want to keep up my end of the room-and-board bargain by making sure Ida Mae's house remains clean and her stomach well fed. Snapping the swing straps around Eli's waist, I turn the dial to thirty minutes and walk down the hallway to Ida Mae's room. I knock on the door, but she doesn't respond.

"Ida Mae?" I ask. "You in there?" She *has* to be in there unless she escaped through her bedroom window, which would be some feat considering her girth, but I don't know what else to say. After a minute or two has passed, I knock again. "You okay? You need something?"

Frightened by her silence, I try the door handle and find it unlocked. I push the door open slowly, trying to give Ida Mae enough time to call out if she's getting changed or taking a bath, but she says nothing. I half expect to see her buxom body sprawled across the floor with her chest barely moving. Instead, she's just sitting on the bed with a book made from magazine cutouts in her lap.

On rainy afternoons or days when it was too cold to

play outside, Leah and I would sometimes cut out pictures from *Dawdy*'s old *Farm Journal* magazines and paste them together in a book, which we would then laminate with contact paper, stitching around the edges with *Mamm*'s colorful yarn. I never knew any Plain children shared our pastime, but I know this is the kind of creation Ida Mae is looking at. What I don't understand is why this crude assemblage is causing her lips to quaver and tears to trickle from her eyes. She doesn't look up at my entrance, just continues flipping through the pages with an odd reverence.

"Do you feel okay?" I ask. "Want some water?"

Ida Mae's head pops up, the surprise on her face letting me know she hasn't heard me enter her room or one word I have said before now. Wiping her eyes with her sleeve, she closes the book and nods. "I'm fine," she says. "Just got a touch of hay fever."

"In November?" I ask.

Ida Mae's eyes snap with their old fire, and the familiar look brings me relief. "Yeah, in November," she says. "You think you can't get the crud now, too?" Sliding off the bed, she pushes the book under a pillow and straightens the quilt. "Today was hard, wasn't it?" Ida Mae asks, her back to me.

"It wasn't easy."

"And don't you think it's ever gonna *get* easy. I've been living away from my family longer than you've been alive, and I still get this ache to see them that won't go away. Then I see somebody who reminds me of them, and all this anger comes flooding back that I didn't even know was there."

"Yes, that's how it is," I whisper, recalling how my parents didn't even glance down at their *grosskind* in my arms—the first they'd ever seen of him—but were focused on my lack of a prayer *kapp*. A sign, my father said, of my being brainwashed by this *Englischer* woman into leaving the Mennonite church.

"What you hafta remember," Ida Mae continues, "is that your mom and dad ain't gonna change their ways, 'cause they don't even know they need changing. The only reason you're starting to see everything clear is 'cause you're removed from it. When you're living smack-dab in those little podunk communities, it's like you think you're the only people in the world. Not until you've left can you realize that your little community don't even make up a *corner* of that world."

Keeping my eyes fixed on the quilt pattern on the bed, I ask, "What was your community like?"

Ida Mae is silent for so long, I look up. "Whoever said I was from a community?" she says, her murky brown eyes peering right down through my innocent-sounding question to the purpose beneath.

"You just did. You said you can't see that something needs changed in the community until you've been removed from it. I assumed you were talking about yours."

"You know what they say about assuming things, don't you?"

I shake my head and Ida Mae sighs. "Well, it ain't good. I'll say that."

Running a hand through her hair, making it stick up worse than it already did, she asks, "Now, what's this you got for supper? I'm smelling something awful good."

"Just leftovers," I mumble, knowing this is Ida Mae's end to a conversation I had only found the courage to begin.

At three in the morning, a train rattles past, its shrill whistle blows, and Eli awakens and begins to cry. Only this is not his normal cry, but a high-pitched gasp that sounds more animal than human. Clambering down the bunk bed ladder so fast a splinter spears my palm, I lean over Eli's bed, which is hemmed in with blankets and pillows, and put a hand to his chest. Eli's blue eyes are open wide and his face pinched as his tiny rib cage fights to draw in oxygen.

Whisking Eli's sweaty body up from the bed so fast he startles and cries even louder, I sprint across the carpet and fling open the door to Ida Mae's bedroom. It is as black as a cellar, so I flip on the lights and run back toward her tiny bathroom. Twisting on the faucets above the claw-foot tub, I blast hot water as fast as it will go and reach over with my foot to kick the bathroom door shut. I sit on the closed toilet seat with my infant gasping on my lap. It seems like his lips are turning blue even as his face is tomato-red.

Five seconds pass before the bathroom door smacks open and an irate Ida Mae is standing there with her wild hair askew and flannel nightgown twisted up around her knees. "What in the world!" she cries. "You got a mind to wake the dead as well as the living?" Then her groggy eyes seem to clear because she runs over to the basket where she keeps her towels and hands one to me. "Put this over your head," she instructs. "And lean over that steam. If we can just get him to cough up that phlegm, he'll be fine."

"But what if he *can't*?" I am surprised to hear my words are as high-pitched as Eli's wheezing.

"He will, Rachel-girl." Ida Mae puts a hand to my cheek, which I didn't know until now was wet with tears. "He's gotta."

The whole night passes this way: Ida Mae cycling out wet towels that she drapes over my head so the bathtub's hot steam will rise up and be trapped, helping free my son's clogged lungs. When his coughing becomes violent, I jerk back the towel and stare down at Eli as he struggles to breathe.

Ida Mae asks, "Should we take him to the emergency room?"

I look up at her standing over my shoulder and see genuine fear in her eyes. "I don't have insurance."

"That don't matter," Ida Mae says. "Not when he's bad as this."

My *mamm* nursed Leah and me through numerous bouts of childhood illness without once having to take us to the *doktor*, but I don't know the herbal remedies she used and would not have the supplies on hand even if I did.

I can feel my resolve weakening. I am about to have Ida Mae drive us to the closest hospital when Eli's body stiffens, his breathing stops, and then his mouth projects a clump of mucus so small, it seems impossible it could have been enough to block his passageways.

But it was, for as soon as it passes, his rasping coughs return to wheezes and he's breathing again.

I then start crying so hard that Eli does too. I press him against my shoulder and rub and rub his back, which feels so bony and vulnerable after he had to put up such a fight.

Ida Mae leans down to massage my shoulders with tough old hands, and if the situation weren't so serious, I would smile at the image the three of us must make. "You did real good, Rachel-girl. Your baby boy's gonna be just fine. Now y'all both just need some sleep."

"Thanks," I murmur in between sobs.

She pats my back. "Think nothing of it. Any woman with a momma heart woulda done the same."

# 8

## « AMOS »

Leah takes a seat at the long pine *disch* that had been a wedding gift from Tobias's first wife's parents and writes by the light of that oil lamp whose wick still needs trimmed. Last week, she wrote about the steady goings-on in their lives: what quilt patterns the women were making for the Fairview auction in the spring (wedding ring, spinning star, log cabin, compass, and postage stamp); how business in Copper Creek had picked up since Hostetler's Bakery put an ad in the *Bargain Hunter*; that Matthew had lost his first tooth to his older brother, Reuben, who looped a piece of string around it and tied the string to the door, which he then slammed with glee. Soon, though, Leah found that this piffle was not enough. The standard opening, "Greetings sent to you on the wings of love," does not suffice for what is truly going on inside her heart, which has nothing to do with quilts, jams, or business dealings in Copper Creek. My daughter-in-law wants to reveal how she contemplated, just for an hour, leaving my son so she could rejoin her sister. She wishes she could tell Rachel that her husband forced her to choose, and although she knew it was wrong in the eyes of both God and man, she had to choose her twin. Their bond is impenetrable by distance or even death, and she cannot imagine a life apart from her. But over a month has passed, and she's only now found the courage to commit this treasonous thought to paper.

Long after the pages blur in the flickering light, Leah sets down the pen and folds up the letter. She slips it into one of the business envelopes left over from Tobias's days as the Copper Creek blacksmith and seals it with a quick swipe of her tongue. Leah dare not write Rachel's address on the front in case one of the children or her husband stumbles upon the letter. Instead, she writes *Geld* and hopes the envelope's label will discourage any interest from her children and husband.

Tonight, one week since her clandestine letter-writing began, Leah decides that she cannot risk having these letters scattered about until her and Rachel's paths somehow cross. So she bundles them up with baling twine, spools a shawl around her shoulders, and carries them—barefoot in the December cold—out beneath a navy sky thickened with stars. At first, Leah has no idea where to put the letters. She contemplates the barn, but fears that mice will get to the pages before she can devise a way to get them to Rachel. Then she remembers the birdhouse. It is for the purple martins—a white, multitiered structure that Tobias built far more intricately than their own dwelling. The only problem with the construction was that the children had wanted to peer down inside the birdhouse to see if any eggs were about to hatch. Accommodating only when it comes to his dead wife's offspring, Tobias agreed. Instead of suspending the birdhouse on a standard twenty-foot pole, he kept it close to the ground, and he put a hinge on the roof so it could flip up to reveal the purple martin hatchlings. But in the past twelve seasons, not one purple martin has occupied the dwelling because it is so vulnerable to predators—children and cats alike. The beautiful birdhouse has just hunkered down beneath the sycamore, wilting in the elements.

Leah remembers all of this and, smiling, flits down the porch steps and across the yard. Lifting up the roof to the purple martin house like a benevolent giant, she places the bundled letters inside. She takes a step back and peers at the birdhouse from every angle, making sure the letters cannot be seen through the numerous outside holes. Reassured that they cannot, she scampers back to the farmhouse and into her marriage bed as quickly as she had left it, eager for Ida Mae Speck's next visit to

Copper Creek, when Leah can retrieve the letters explaining her plans to her sister.

Ida Mae's next visit to Copper Creek happens sooner than Leah could have anticipated. With Christmas just around the corner, Ida Mae has numerous orders for "Amish" wares: dollhouses and miniature furniture to fill them; quilted tea cozies, hot pads, and pillowcases; crocheted baby sweaters and bonnets in every spectrum of the pastel rainbow. *Englischer* tourists are even willing to pay twice as much for candles that supposedly last longer when made by Amish hands. To Rachel's chagrin, Ida Mae forces her to ride along to Copper Creek by saying that she needs help loading the truck with these orders. But Rachel knows better. Living with Ida Mae for a month and a half has allowed Rachel to see through her employer's many well-intentioned guises, and this is the worst of them all.

Ida Mae does not want Rachel running from her problems as she herself did twenty years ago, so she gives Rachel an ultimatum: face them head-on or lose her job. Of course, Ida Mae might have been kidding when she threatened this, but Rachel does not want to take the chance. As soon as Rachel transformed the little back room of the store into her reflexology office, word spread throughout Blackbrier about the soft-spoken Amish girl (Ida Mae was right: *Englischers* don't know the difference between

Mennonites and Amish) who massages people's feet for twenty-five dollars an hour. Rachel's meager income tripled within the month. She is not about to let such a financial opportunity slip through her grasp, even with Ida Mae receiving 30 percent of her earnings, for Rachel knows another one might not present itself.

Job security is the only reason she is now riding along with Ida Mae, and it's easy to see that Rachel is not enjoying the trip. During the past weeks, Rachel has forced herself to forget everything about Copper Creek: the events leading up to her banishment; the loss of her sister who lives only an hour away; how revolted Tobias's face was when—on the day of my funeral—he reached out a welcoming hand, and then realized who he had extended it to; every scene between herself and Judah. Rachel tries to remember why she sent him away, knowing if he were here, she would be embracing a future with him rather than sifting through the past to find out where she went so wrong.

As the diesel truck swerves off the highway and begins switchbacking up the craggy mountainside, every memory comes rushing back, and with them, a pain of regret that causes tears to nip at Rachel's eyes. The emotional change within the cab is like snow tumbling through a sunroof in the middle of July. But Ida Mae says nothing, just turns down the radio and covers Eli's legs with a blanket when he kicks it from his car seat onto the floor.

"We're stopping by Hostetler's first," Ida Mae says once the community's buildings come into view.

Rachel nods but doesn't say anything, as she fears she will be sick. It makes no sense how she could have lived in Copper Creek for so long, and had Tobias not forced her to leave that fall day they had their confrontation in the hospital, she would *still* be living in the very place where she had conceived a lifetime of guilt and one innocent child. If everything weren't so complex, Rachel could almost envision walking up to the new Bishop King and thanking him for blackmailing her into leaving Copper Creek. This would never happen, of course, but the image still helps Rachel breathe easier as Ida Mae pulls the truck up outside the bakery and shifts into park.

"You staying?" Ida Mae asks, turning off the ignition.

Rachel shakes her head and somehow manages a smile. "No, I'll go inside. It'll be nice to see everyone again."

Nodding, Ida Mae says, "That's my girl," and reaches over to pat Rachel's knee. Ida Mae then hops out of the cab, slides two long containers from the covered truck bed, and swaggers up to the bakery door.

Cinching the blanket extra tight around her son so the cold air won't induce another coughing spell like the ones he's been battling on and off for weeks, Rachel steps out of the cab and cradles him against her bosom, staring at the line of quaint Copper Creek stores. It is amazing what comfort such a tiny child can bring. Rachel understands that without this child, her soul would have been shattered by the betrayal she'd so callously dealt, even as her life beneath her sister's roof appeared the same as it had before. She is glad her facade wasn't allowed to continue; she is glad her sin was truly found out. Without it having bloomed inside her for the entire community to see, she would be hiding it to this very day—deep within the Pandora's box of her chest—the same as Eli's father is doing.

## Rachel

I hoped the Hostetlers would treat me with the casual respect of a customer, but they stare right through Eli and me as if we are transparent. Ida Mae is too busy stacking pound and hummingbird cakes into plastic containers to notice their slight, and I am thankful. The two things I have learned about my employer over the past month and a half are that she is protective of those she loves and that she has no qualms about speaking her mind.

"There's seventy here," Ida Mae says, snapping the lids shut and wiping her brow. "I ordered eighty. Didn't you get my fax?"

Lemuel nods, but his wife, Elvina, comes bustling around the counter and peers in at Ida Mae's containers, which are already condensing with steam from the hot baked goods. I can see Elvina's miserly mouth working as she counts everything again.

"What?" Ida Mae puts hands on her hips. "You think I'm gonna lie?"

I face the row of angel food cakes—plain, strawberry, lemon, and chocolate chip—to keep my smile from giving my amusement away. I had lived in Copper Creek for only a few weeks when I understood that no one dares cross Elvina Hostetler, not even her husband, who's watching this interaction with an apologetic expression on his ancient face.

From the corner of my eye, I watch Elvina fold her arms. Their fleshiness strains against the material of her sleeves. "I just counted up seventy-three," she says, one eyebrow raised.

"So?" Ida Mae retorts. "That still ain't eighty."

"Perhaps the others are in the back," Lemuel says.

Elvina rolls her eyes. "Those are for the tea shoppe, Lemuel."

"We could make some more before Claudette comes this afternoon."

"We'll do no such thing." Wheeling back toward Ida Mae, Elvina says, "This is what happens when you don't send us the fax the night before."

"No," Ida Mae says, "this is what happens when you run your business like a circus show."

Elvina Hostetler's nostrils flare; her mouth tightens into a hard little knot. "If you want your seven other pound cakes, *you* can wait. Not the tea shoppe."

"If you want to keep my business, you'd better learn how to treat your customers."

With this, Ida Mae jerks up the two plastic containers

bowing beneath the weight of fifty pound cakes and twenty-three hummingbird and starts heading toward the door. "Wait!" I call. "Let me put Eli in the truck, and I'll help you!"

But Ida Mae is so infuriated that her burden seems to weigh nothing. Holding the awkward tubs at chest height, she stalks down the cement handicap ramp, across the gravel, and tosses the containers in the back of the truck before I can even get out of the store.

Over the roar of the truck engine, Ida Mae yells, "You coming?"

I scramble into the passenger's side. Eli isn't even strapped in when Ida Mae shifts into reverse and guns it out of the bakery. "That woman makes me so mad, I could spit!" she fumes.

"Have you two always been at each other like this?"

"Me and Elvina?" Ida Mae asks.

I nod.

"Yeah. She's jealous."

"Of you? Why?"

Pinning her eyes on me, Ida Mae says, "Believe it or not, Rachel-girl, back when I was skinny as a whip like you, I had my share of admirers." She pulls into Mast's Cannery and shuts off the truck. "I guess Elvina thinks that since I'm a divorced woman, I'm after anything in suspenders . . . including her husband."

"Lemuel?" I ask.

Ida Mae pockets the keys. "I know," she answers, shuddering. "What makes her think I'd want a piece of that?"

My heartbeat reverberating in my ears, I take Eli from his car seat and carry him up the tree-lined pathway to Verna King's house. I have no idea why six horses and buggies are waiting in front of the barn, so I am grateful when Ida Mae opens the storm door and steps inside first. Her unique appearance and personality are a diversion until I gather my bearings and glance around. At least ten Plain women are circled in front of the *kochoffe*, the position of their bodies mimicking the unfinished compass quilt draping their laps. One hundred unadorned fingers move deftly over the vibrant fabric they are hemming in with thread as ten mouths, equally unadorned, zigzag so fast over the Pennsylvania Dutch language, it is difficult even for me—a native speaker—to understand.

Then the casual banter is broken apart by one high-pitched gasp, and I know that I have been spotted. Turning toward the source of the exclamation, I see my sister, whom I yearn to run to and throw my arms around, yet at the sight of all these Copper Creek women, my feet have forgotten how to move. I remain paralyzed by the door as Leah comes across the kitchen with her arms outstretched. I am amazed by the straightness of her spine and the blossoms in her cheeks. I feel a pang, wondering if the reason my sister is now thriving is because I am no longer here.

"Rachel!" Leah embraces Eli between our bodies. He awakens and tilts his head up to first peer at me and then at my sister. Frightened by our identical appearance, he burrows his head in the cleft of my bosom and begins to cry.

She laughs at this, and then clasps my shoulders. "How *are* you?"

My head swims as I stare into Leah's warm blue eyes. From her elated expression, you would never guess that I have been removed from Copper Creek, that this child in my arms is proof of my dalliance with sin. No, Leah embraces me like the father in Scripture embraced his prodigal son: without one word of complaint or censure, as if nothing I had done in my past were ever wrong. I wish I was so forgiving of the events that have transpired. But I am not. I am as filled with hatred toward myself as I am filled with hatred toward her husband, Bishop Tobias King, who has forced me away from this one person, other than my son, whom I love more than life. I know Tobias's reasons for doing so, and I do not question them, but I *do* question what he must have told Leah for her to act in such a nonchalant manner. I have not returned to Copper Creek after a trip to another Mennonite community; I have not been gone for a few days or a few weeks, but for a month and a half. How can my sister smile at me like this? How can her eyes reflect only joy despite mine being filled with sorrow? Is she glad that I am gone from her life, that her life can now continue on its standard course in a way it never has before?

"Rachel?" At the sound of her voice, I refocus on my

sister's face, which is erased of its winsome smile. "Rachel, do you need to sit down?"

When I cannot answer, Leah guides me into a kitchen chair, sits in the one next to it, and takes my hand in hers. I look over at my twin, who is exuding such strength and confidence, and I realize that the two of us have switched places—the comforter being comforted—that with my banishment from Copper Creek, the tables have finally turned.

An hour later, Ida Mae settles commission accounts and opens new ones for Christmas wares. Verna King uses this diverting activity to speak with me about her younger son, Judah.

"Have you heard from him?" she asks. The intensity in her eyes contradicts the relaxation of her smile. "Have you heard from Judah?"

All chatter ceases. Clutching needles and dark spools of thread, the women turn toward me with tilted ears, dogs hungry for the meat of my reply.

"No," I say. "Have you?"

Verna shakes her head. "Ach, no. Judah left a letter saying he was going to leave; that is all."

"Maybe he went to stay with his *freindschaft* in Lancaster?"

"I've contacted the Kings and the Fishers. They've heard nothing."

The older woman traces the quilt pattern in her lap, but I can see from her trembling mouth and fingers that Verna King is about to cry.

Leah stands and passes her sleeping child to me. "Who wants some *fastnachts*?" she asks, dispelling the tension with the prospect of sweets.

As my sister takes requests and goes into her mother-in-law's kitchen to fill them, Ida Mae comes over carrying three large garbage bags stuffed with quilts and a spiral notebook full of commission information balanced on top. "You ready?" she asks. I nod and give Jonathan to his *grossmammi*.

Verna leans forward and whispers, "I hope I didn't make you uncomfortable just then."

"It's fine," I say. "I'm sure you're not the only one who thought Judah was with me."

To my surprise, Verna reaches out and clasps my wrist. "If you hear from him," she says, "please . . . let me know."

I tell her I will. But I don't tell her that after the way Judah and I parted, I have a feeling she has a far better chance of hearing from him than I.

"You're leaving?" My sister's panicked voice echoes across the lawn. "But I haven't gotten to . . . to give you the letter!"

"Mail it to me or something, Leah," I call, without

turning around. "I've got to go. I don't belong here. Not anymore."

"That can change."

I wait until Ida Mae has climbed inside the truck cab before shifting Eli to my hip and looking back. "I saw how the women in there looked at me. How Elvina and Lemuel at the bakery wouldn't. I don't think changing this situation is possible."

Leah says, "Maybe it'd be easier if I just told you."

"Told me what?"

"What was in my letter." Smiling, she links her arm with mine. "I want to move *Mammi* and *Dawdy* into the *dawdi haus* on our land, and then you and Eli could live here . . . with them."

"That place hasn't been lived in since *Grossdawdy* Fisher died. Anyway, I could *not* live with *Dawdy*. I don't have the patience for him that you do."

"It'd take work, I know that," she says, leading me down the sidewalk. "But just think: if you lived here with them, you and I could be *nochberen*."

"That would be the only benefit," I drawl. At Leah's horrified face, for she has a different relationship with our *dawdy* and cannot begin to imagine mine, I change the subject. "You really think *Mamm* and *Dawdy* would just give up the *bauerei*?"

My sister stops walking. The tree branches overhanging the path cast a lattice of shadows across her face. "They're losing it anyway, Rachel," she says. "*Dawdy*'s not making the sales he used to, and *Mammi's* arthritis is getting so bad, she has to turn new reflexology patients away."

"How come they didn't tell me when they were down?"

Leah shrugs. "Maybe they didn't want you to worry? Maybe they were ashamed? A developer's made them a good offer, and they're going to accept. *Dawdy's* horses and tools will be auctioned off at New Holland next week."

My mind reels with the weight of this news. For years after the Lancaster County area had exploded with expansion and our neighbors had cashed in on their properties and moved farther south, my parents continued turning down offer after offer. How bad must their finances be if they're now allowing our yellow house on Hilltop Road and the land surrounding it to be transformed into another cookie-cutter subdivision?

"You and Tobias are going up for the auction, I guess?"

Leah nods.

The impromptu timing of everything is the only reason I find the courage to say, "You think he'd let me ride along?"

"I—I don't know." Leah looks at the cracks fissuring the sidewalk. "But I promise I'll ask."

"I know you will." I reach out and give my sister a hug. With our bodies pressed so close and Eli on my hip, I can feel how our stomachs—both changed since the birth of our sons—touch each other like two halves of one whole.

"It was awful good to see you," Leah says, her voice catching. "I've missed you terribly."

"I've missed you too," I whisper into her hair, and then

turn and head down the sidewalk before she can see the remorse in my eyes.

## AMOS

Before Tobias falls asleep and Leah sneaks downstairs to begin her cathartic letter-writing, Leah asks if Rachel can join their journey to Pennsylvania.

"No. Absolutely not," her husband answers, the question not having fully left Leah's mouth. "There's no way."

"How is there no way? Gerald's van's not even full."

"It will be full when it comes to the likes of Rachel."

"The likes of Rachel?" Leah bolts upright in bed. "She's still my flesh and blood, Tobias, and I would appreciate if you spoke about her with a little more respect."

"I would speak about your sister with a little more respect if she had earned it."

Swallowing the words that threaten to career off her tongue, Leah stares down at her husband's back, and for the first time in her twenty years, understands her sister's temper. "I know you do not agree that my sister should accompany us on our trip," she says. "But there have been many things you have done that I have not agreed with, and still I have complied."

"That is how it is supposed to be. You are my wife."

"And *you* are my husband, who has made decisions that have devastated me. I think the least you owe me is this!"

My son's breathing grows shallow.

"Tobias?" Leah asks. "Did you hear me?"

Nodding, my son clears his throat so his voice will not crack when he replies, "Yes. I heard you."

"Then Rachel can go with us?"

*"Jah."* Tobias punches the pillow beneath his head. "She can go."

Leah has a sudden impulse to reach out and embrace her husband, but they haven't really touched since she returned from the hospital, and any caress would probably seem like manipulation to him now. So Leah simply turns toward her husband rather than the window and stays in bed for the first time since her nightly letter-writing began.

Tobias does not fall asleep until the sun begins to rise over the pines, for the sentence his wife had uttered about her sister's banishment from Copper Creek held another meaning entirely for him.

Ida Mae says, "You sure 'bout this?"

Looping the car seat, heavy with Eli's weight, over her arm, Rachel watches Tobias stow suitcases and pillows in the back of Gerald's van. "No," she says. "I'm not."

"Welp, if you get into trouble, just give me a holler. I'll come up there and fetch ya."

"The whole way to Pennsylvania?"

Ida Mae nods. "I could get one of the gals over at the high school to run my store, so don't you think twice about calling me."

"I'm sure it'll be fine," Rachel says, blinking doubt from her eyes. "It's only for a few days."

Once Rachel closes the truck door, Ida Mae starts driving down Copper Creek Road, but she watches Rachel and Eli in her rearview mirror until they become nothing but blond specks decorating the horizon. It takes the whole drive back to Blackbrier for fear to stop clutching at Ida Mae's throat and her fingers to loosen their death grip on the steering wheel. And in her dreams that night, the memories that have haunted Ida Mae for twenty years come to life again.

Not until they have crossed into Virginia does Tobias acknowledge that Rachel is along for the ride. Even then it is only because he happens to glance up in Gerald's rearview mirror and catch her sitting on the bench seat, nursing Eli.

"Have you no modesty?" Tobias barks, averting his gaze.

Rachel's cheeks burn from irritation more than embarrassment. "Obviously I do or I wouldn't be wearing *this*." She uses the hand not supporting Eli's head to tug at the afghan.

Rachel is incensed by his rebuke and rightly so; Leah has nursed Jonathan three times over the past seven hours, and Tobias hasn't said one word to her. Rachel tried to sate Eli's *brutzing* for as long as possible, but when she realized that Gerald Martin wasn't going to stop at another gas station until his full tank emptied into the red, she covered herself up to the neck with the afghan she'd packed, took Eli from his car seat, and let him suckle.

Tobias huffs, "You could've at least gone to the back of the van."

"And what if Gerald got pulled over, and I couldn't get Eli back into his car seat in time? He could lose his license."

"I've never gotten pulled over," Gerald says. The first sentence he's spoken since the trip began.

Minutes pass before Leah says, "If you're not going to allow us to get out to stretch our legs and use the restroom, we have no choice but to nurse our children while we drive."

Astonished, Rachel stares at her sister. Tobias is so shocked by his wife's forthright tone that he turns in the seat, as if looking for proof that she and Rachel haven't switched places. He then remembers that Rachel is still nursing and, cheekbones striped with red, faces the front again. Gerald Martin says nothing, just keeps his hands positioned at the ten and the two and pushes his white sneaker down on the gas pedal until his black van is cruising just under the speed limit—the fastest he has ever gone.

Once Eli and Jonathan are lulled to sleep by the rhythmic bumps of the van moving over the patched Pennsylvania roads, Rachel and Leah climb into the backseat and get Lebanon bologna and Swiss cheese sandwiches from the cooler. They pass four up to the men and then grab two for themselves and unwrap the wax paper.

After taking a bite, Leah wipes mayonnaise from her mouth and whispers, "You okay?"

"My back's a little stiff." Rachel yawns. "But I'm sure it'll loosen up once we get out."

"I don't mean how you are feeling." Leah looks toward the front of the van and then lowers her voice. "I was wondering if you're okay after what my husband said."

Rachel balls up the wax paper and sets it in her lap. "I'm getting pretty used to him by now."

Leah sighs. "I still wish he wouldn't treat you the way he does."

Rachel chews a bite of sandwich rather than responding.

"I'm hoping you and I can get some alone time up here," Leah continues. "I'm sure Tobias will be helping *Dawdy*. That should make things easier."

"That would be nice," Rachel agrees.

"Wouldn't it be wonderful?" Leah smiles. "The two of us? Just like old times."

Rachel sets the sandwich in her lap. She feels carsick, which she has never struggled with before. How can she tell Leah that no matter how hard they try, no matter how much alone time they have while sifting through the memories in that yellow house on Hilltop Road, they can never go back to the innocence of old times again? Leah would not understand Rachel even if she said this. All their lives, she was the one who believed in the good of people and the good in the world. If Leah only knew how the people she loved most in the world had betrayed her, her naive life would be stripped of its innocent perspective.

Leaning over, Leah begins to massage the muscles of Rachel's neck. "Are you worried about *Mamm* and *Dawdy*?"

Rachel turns toward the van window and nods, even though the situation involving Helen and Samuel is the last worry on her mind. Only when Leah has drifted off with her head on her sister's lap does Rachel stare at her young, trusting face and allow the tears she has been holding back to flow down. Observing movement at the front of the van, she glances up to see Tobias watching Jonathan and Eli asleep in their matching car seats. He then looks up at her. For the first time since her pregnancy became apparent, in his gaze Rachel sees not anger, but sorrow. As if she is not the only one who has failed someone she so desperately loves.

## Rachel

We arrive at my parents' house on Hilltop Road at two in the morning Pennsylvania time. It has taken over thirteen hours for us to make the usual twelve-hour journey, and that is without the rest stops one is required to make with a group our size. The only reason I can give for Gerald Martin's driving at the speed he does is that he is still becoming accustomed to his "liberal" black-bumper Mennonite ways after being in the Amish church for so long. Going fifty miles an hour, even on the interstate with a speed limit of sixty-five, must feel like flying to him.

Pushing open the side door into the mudroom, I find that *Mamm* and *Dawdy* have not waited up. But downstairs clean sheets and blankets are stretched across the couch, and a rickety cot is set up in the reflexology office. Leah and Tobias will take the upstairs room my sister and I used to share, with its wood-paneled walls, iron bedstead, and flowered *debbich* my *mamm*, not the best of housekeepers, has probably allowed to become sheathed in dust as thick as the quilt backing itself.

I smile as Leah comes in carrying Jonathan. She tries to smile too, but the expression does not reach her eyes. I do not have to ask what she is feeling; I am feeling it as well. It is hard coming back to my childhood home for the first time since I left it, knowing this visit will also be my last. As children, we sat at this table—in these chairs with the fuchsia rosettes painted on the back by masculine Amish hands—making homemade play dough with flour, water, salt, and a splash of the food coloring not often used. Together, Leah and I would tug a stool over to the *kochoffe* and peer down into the pot churning with whichever *supp* my *mamm* was making. Sometimes in the winters, when the horse sales had slowed because of the buyers at New Holland not having funds left over from their summer crops, *Mamm* would start adding water to the *supp*. All we had for supper one night was tomato *supp*—so diluted it looked more pink than red—and runny rice pudding.

But my sister and I were almost into our teens before we realized just how poor our family was. Our dresses and shoes were often hand-me-downs from wealthier *freindschaft*, and at Christmas, our toys were ones *Mamm* had found at charity shops throughout the year. Because my *dawdy* often purchased horses and tack he could not pay for, our family was on the brink of bankruptcy numerous times. Still, my *mamm* never let us out the door with our hair strubbly or shoes unshined. Leah and I might return from the Mennonite school within walking distance of our *haus* and, regardless of the weather, be sent out to pick dandelions, walnuts, strawberries, or meadow tea to sell to local restaurants, but *Mamm* was adamant that we did not have to look as close to poverty as we were.

Leah says, "I'm going to bed."

I bid her good night and carry Eli's car seat into my *mamm*'s reflexology office. Stretching my son out on the pallet already prepared on the floor, I tuck the afghan under his chin and lean in to kiss his cheek. It is then I hear the wheezing of his breath despite all the precautions I have taken to keep him from catching another cold. I climb onto the narrow cot and bunch the quilts around my shivering frame. Perhaps it is the panic coursing through my veins like caffeine serum, juxtaposed with the calming scent of echinacea, oregano, and olive-leaf extract wafting from the green and blue bottles lining the dusty walnut shelf, but my weary mind soon drifts to the holistic *doktor*, Norman Troyer.

For years, my family's purse remained weighted only

with my *dawdy*'s debts until the afternoon my *mamm* visited a little hovel next to the sprawling Masonic Lodge in Elizabethtown. Cluster headaches had plagued her for as long as my sister and I had been alive, but the only reason she wanted to address the ailment now was because of its thwarting her ability to work. We were not with *Mamm* that summer day she met Norman Troyer. Still, I can imagine her skepticism as he picked up a cheap flashlight from his desk and used it to peer at the navy rimming the irises of her cornflower-blue eyes. After five minutes of perusal not involving a single touch, Norman pinpointed the source of my *mamm*'s cluster headaches: a pinched nerve on the side of her neck, which she'd probably strained giving birth to twin daughters thirteen years before.

To this day, I do not know what made that renowned holistic *doktor* take my mother on as his apprentice, teaching her everything he knew, then—when the Muddy Pond Community objected to the prospect of a woman iridologist—giving her textbooks on reflexology that she could market as a foot massage instead. Maybe it was the hunger Norman Troyer read in her eyes—physical hunger, yes, for she encouraged Leah and me to take seconds before she had even had firsts—but there was another hunger present, an insatiable hunger, a thirst, for knowledge beyond what the mundane tasks of an Old Order Mennonite woman required, and alternative medicine soon became her never-ending smorgasbord.

# 9

## AMOS

The New Holland sale, where Samuel Stoltzfus's horses and tack will be auctioned off to the highest bidder, takes place the morning after Tobias and the twins arrive. Because of the auction, both Samuel and Helen are out working in the barn when everyone else wakes up. Eli and Jonathan will not stop *brutzing* during breakfast, where the adults eat banana nut muffins and fruit that Helen has prepared. Nobody mentions it, but after having spent the previous day on the road, they are as tired and irritable as the children. Thankfully, Gerald Martin has agreed to shuttle everyone around rather than spend the three days with his extended family in Lititz, so Tobias and the twins will not have to leave the *haus* for another hour.

But Rachel finds no rest, since Eli's breathing is becoming more labored. After his bath in the *becken* where Helen gave her twin infants theirs, Rachel rubs Eli's body down with grapeseed oil to try to soothe him. She turns him over to massage his back and sees the buttonlike protrusions of his spine. Tracing her hand over them, she runs fingers along his hairline and the small column of his neck. That is when Rachel feels it: a knot tucked in the hollow of his clavicle, no bigger than a pea.

A shard of worry wedges itself between Rachel's shoulder blades as she recalls the severe cold her son just cannot seem to shake. The only reason Rachel has not taken Eli to see the *doktor* is that none of his coughing fits have been as bad as that night she and Ida Mae spent in the bathroom. Well, that, and the fact that Rachel believes, just like her *mamm*, that *Englischer doktors* will only pump children full of antibiotics—killing the good bacteria along with the bad, hampering their bodies' ability to fight back before they have learned to fight at all.

By the time everyone, including Helen and Samuel, loads up in Gerald's van and heads toward the auction, Rachel has tried to put her fears regarding her son's health to rest. But as Eli holds on to one of her fingers with all of his, her worries awaken anew; even his grip seems to have weakened since the night before.

*"Mamm?"* Helen turns toward her. "Is Norman Troyer still around?"

"Of course," she says. "Why?"

"I thought I'd get him to look at Eli while we're up."

Seated in the passenger seat as he was on the journey from Tennessee to Pennsylvania, Tobias says, without shifting his gaze from the windshield, "Isn't he that powwow *doktor* over near the Masonic Lodge?"

Helen says, "No, Tobias, Norman just looks at the whole body when finding a cure."

Her son-in-law says nothing, nor does Rachel.

It is a quiet drive until they reach New Holland.

The New Holland auction is a flea market that sells animals rather than antiques. Outside the enormous tin barn housing the sale, vendors layered in wool and checkered flannel sit behind tables, hawking cut-rate goods. Just outside the huge double doors that have been slid shut to block the cold, a young Amish boy with Judah's fair coloring stamps his feet and blows into chapped hands while a snow globe of flurries swirls around him. In front of the boy, a folding table is crowded with Christmas poinsettias featured in pink, yellow, and red, along with a heavy metal box. The poster board taped to the front of the table, which conveys the price of the *blummen* for sale, is misspelled and written in a child's hand. Just observing for five minutes, as my loved ones unload from Gerald Martin's van, the boy has six pictures taken of him and two cups of hot cocoa placed on the table beside his money box.

Only one *Englischer* buys his *blummen*.

Shifting my attention, I watch Leah and Rachel enter the barn, carrying a bundled child each. The main arena has been mucked and covered with sawdust. Thick corral gates and a holding pen, where the horses wait their turn to be led out by the trader and pranced around the ring, bracket off this area from the bleachers flanking each side. Although the auction has just begun, Amish and Mennonite men—each wearing different-width *hut* brims according to their bishops' varying stipulations—are already clustered around these gates, their mud-crusted boots hooked over the bottom rung. A few of the men have pipes or cigars clamped between their teeth, giving the air a smoky, festive scent contrasted by the manure swathing the grounds.

Hemming in the outskirts of this arena is a section stacked with cages of live chickens, turkeys, peacocks, guinea pigs, guinea hens, bunnies, and bleating sheep accompanied by collie pups supposedly trained to guard them. Beyond even this, in cramped wooden stalls lit by a row of low-watt bulbs, is the place that broke Judah's heart when he came here as a child, the place where horses not fit for auction are kept. They are the ones with bad feet from years of hauling buggies and clomping over paved roads, swaybacks from being ridden too early, or joints weakened by age. I often glossed over the truth by telling young Judah that these horses would find good homes when the fact is most, if not all, would end up at local dog food companies.

But the Amish and Old Order Mennonite farmers (and the *Englischer* tourists who are hoping to spot the Amish and Old Order Mennonite farmers) do not often go to this area. Instead, they remain gathered either on the corral gates or up in the stands eating hot dogs piled with sauerkraut and mustard, sloppy joes that more than live up to their name, chicken *welschkann supp* from deep Styrofoam cups. Sloshing this assortment down with birch beer or root beer, they then unwrap the cellophane around whoopee pies that have crumbled from passing through so many hands.

Their bellies thus filled with this typical auction menu, they sit back in the stands and wait for the horses. Sometimes in the arena you can spot the poor creatures that have been drugged. Their heads will hang, lips droop, legs splay wide in a subservient gesture out of place in an area considered the show ring. Back before the price of land increased so much that our community had to leave Lancaster for the South, I used to have Amish and Mennonite friends who were horse traders at New Holland. But they knew the tricks of the trade that did not involve drugging the animals or risking the life and limb of the *Englischers* gullible enough to purchase the strangely docile horses. No, these friends of mine used vegetable oil to buff their horses' coats until they gleamed. They rubbed their hooves down with this same oil and washed and brushed the manes and tails so many times that the wiry hair hung like a skein of silk.

If an animal could be trusted not to spook, my friends would get their young daughters or sons to slide off the rumps of the horses or run a hand over the animals' twitching bellies or flanks—proving to the awestruck crowd just how safe these auction horses were. With every stunt like this, the price of the horses would increase. The quicksilver mouth of the auctioneer would become parched as it struggled to keep up with the climbing bids. And once that card-flashing frenzy began, there was no stopping it. I remember sitting up in the stands (the left side, I think), watching Samuel Stoltzfus play that crowd into his hands as effortlessly as a circus master under the big top. Even then, years before we became *nochberen*, I did not think he was your typical Old Order Mennonite man. He strutted too much, leading those flashy sets of matching ponies and the jet-black stallions with the white socks and brilliant starburst blazes. His clothes, though cut from the same cloth as mine and patterned after the same style, somehow accentuated his broad shoulders that tapered down to a lean waist in a way that seemed far more worldly than Plain. He didn't have a beard then, as he was not yet married, and I remember how his pink lips would peel back and his white teeth flash as he took that crowd into his hands and had them begging for more than an auction, had them begging for a show.

An introvert who did not understand the personality

type opposite mine, I knew, as I watched Samuel lather that crowd up into a horse-buying frenzy, that he and I would never really become friends. I thought of him as a *schwindler*, someone who would do anything, say anything, just to make a sale. I watched how he manipulated the female portion of that audience, both Plain and *Englischer* alike. How he would whip his wavy black hair to the side and smile, his blue eyes flitting up into the stands to see if they were watching, which they somehow always were. I remember how he would touch his crop to the hindquarters of those mares to prove his control. How, in response, they would prance their oiled hooves through that sawdusted earth, tossing their glistening manes and whinnying as if they were enjoying the show as much as their master was.

Once these horses had all sold for astronomical prices, auction after auction I would watch the *Englischer* women march down out of the stands in their tight-fitting jeans and ruffled shirts and introduce themselves to Samuel. He would then take on another role and leave the one of the ringmaster behind. From high up in those stands, I saw how those women ate up this new role as much as Samuel's old: the blushing, stammering Mennonite boy who needed to be shown the ways of their carnal *Englischer* world. By the end of this awkward exchange, the women would be scribbling down numbers on crinkled hot dog paper or napkins and passing them to him. Samuel would take that paper into his hands and smile. But after they'd left, he would throw their numbers to the sawdusted ground now sprinkled with manure and bottle-green flies. He did not care about the prize of the women so much as his conquest of them. Plus, there was no way Samuel could call; he didn't have a phone.

Looking back on the days I sat up in those New Holland stands observing and judging Samuel, I understand that I was jealous of him. My being a blushing and stammering Mennonite boy was no convenient role I knew the *Englischer* women would love. I was so shy, I couldn't even open my mouth at our community hymn sings if Verna Fisher was there, and I knew it was going to take a miracle to open my mouth when asking that dark-haired woman with the soft brown eyes if she wanted to court. Yet at the ripening age of eighteen, Samuel Stoltzfus made everything I struggled with seem so easy. And up until the point we became *nochberen*, and I understood his swaggering self-confidence masked insecurities far greater than my own, I envied him for it.

The auctioneer's strident voice causes time to zip forward again, covering half a century in seconds. I look down—not from the stands as I had before, but from a height far greater—and see that Samuel's slot in the New Holland horse sale has begun. There is not an ounce of malice in my heart (for who can be malicious where I am?) when I say these forty years have not been kind to the blue-eyed ringmaster with his penchant for matching ponies. Samuel still has a head full of hair, which I could not boast of fifteen years back, but his broad shoulders have collapsed in on themselves like two halves of an accordion, his lean waist expanded with years of hearty Lancaster County fare, his swaggering stride reduced to a hobbled-over shuffle.

As Samuel walks into the arena leading one set of matching bay ponies and one set of dun, his face reddens and his once clear-blue eyes water. He draws his right hand up to his chest, the nostalgia in his gaze replaced with confusion and pain, and I watch his body topple forward onto the freshly strewn dust. The two sets of matching ponies go nowhere. They just lean down with their silken manes draping him and snuffle and huff at his pants and shirt. The horse dealer's collapse takes place in the smallest fragment of time, and then the quiet reverence that had permeated the auction returns to its previous noise. A few of the men who'd been holding the next set of Samuel's horses run across the arena and turn Samuel onto his back. They pound on his chest and blow hard into his mouth, but it is obvious they do not know what they are doing.

A woman's voice cuts through the din. "Somebody call the doctor!"

Samuel's family has just reached the corral entrance when its gate opens. Rachel's eyes fill as she watches the man with a black hat and a long white beard force his body to move faster across that arena's floor than it has moved in a quarter of his lifetime.

When the silver braces supporting his arms assist the man enough that his legs are able to reach Samuel, he collapses onto atrophied knees and takes a small white bottle from his pants pocket. He twists it open and pours one of the capsules into his hand. Tucking the capsule under Samuel's tongue, he reaches for the water bottle one of the corral keepers has brought. He squirts some liquid into Samuel's mouth and massages his throat.

The Stoltzfuses and Kings have just made it to Samuel's side when Tobias eyes the white bottle with suspicion. "What did you give him?" he asks.

Norman Troyer looks up and smiles without a trace of annoyance. "Nitroglycerin," he says. "Samuel's not the only one with heart trouble."

## *Rachel*

Tobias and I were arguing near the concession stands when my *dawdy* collapsed in the arena. I had walked over to get a cup of cocoa when Tobias tapped my shoulder and said, "We need to talk." The last thing I wanted on little sleep and less patience was to have a conversation with a man whose very presence made my blood run cold.

"Sure," I said, faking a smile. "Let me get my drink." After stirring the cocoa powder into the hot water with a plastic stick, I threw the stick in the barrel trash can and said without looking at him, "All right. What is it?"

"I don't want Eli going to that witch *doktor*."

"And I don't think what I do with my son is any of your business."

Tobias's jaw throbbed. "He's still *familye*."

"Really? I didn't know it was common practice to force family out into the streets."

Looking back at the arena and then down at me, he hissed, "You know very well you were not out in the streets!"

"That's because Ida Mae was kind enough to take us in."

"Judah would've taken you in if you had let him."

"If I had let him?" I could feel my entire body flush with anger. "You ruined *any* chance Judah and I had!"

"Keep your voice down!"

"I am *not* the one who wanted to talk in the first place. I will not be told to keep my voice down!"

It was at this point we noticed the strange silence blanketing the arena, which was only magnified by the volume of our words.

"What's happened?" I tried forcing my way through the throng of people, but they all seemed taller than I. "Tobias, what do you see?"

He turned around, his face ashen. "Your *vadder*," he said. "There's been an accident."

My mind bloomed with the image of my *dawdy* in the barn after the stallion had kicked him: how blood, dark as oil, had drained from his ears and puddled on the concrete floor. Standing there, viewing such a horrific sight, I had thought for sure that *Dawdy* was dead or that he was in the midst of dying. His accident took place years before Eli was conceived, but even then I regretted the things he and I had never talked about, the things I wished I'd never said. If I'd heeded that call to mend the chasm silence had created, could a few words have made a difference? Or would my *dawdy* have dismissed my emotions as easily as he had dismissed me?

"Is he okay?" I cried. "Talk to me, Tobias. Tell me what you see!"

"He's not moving." Tobias turned and wrapped his hand around my arm. "C'mon, we must reach him before your *mudder*."

I jerked free of his grasp. "Don't you touch me!"

Leah's husband dragged a hand over his beard. "Fine," he muttered before marching through the crowd.

The doctors claim Norman Troyer's quick use of nitroglycerin was what opened my *dawdy*'s blocked arteries and saved his life. Even though his heart attack was minor enough that he could eat the *supp* and pie my mother brought along in the ambulance, hospital policy requires him to remain under their observation for the rest of the night. Leah and I offer to stay, but everyone can see that we are as exhausted as our children. So the night watch will be shared between Tobias, Norman Troyer, and *Mamm*, who is just as tired as we are, but she won't hear of leaving *Dawdy* on his first night after the heart attack.

"I don't want to stay in this *ferhoodled* hospital!" my *dawdy* rages, picking at the regulatory gown. "Anyone with two eyes in their skulls can see I'm good as new!"

"Now, Samuel," our *mamm* chides in the same voice she used when Leah and I were children, "you know the *doktors* are just taking precautions."

Seeing that Tobias is distracted by my *dawdy*, I touch Norman's elbow and ask if I could speak with him outside. The day's physical toil must have worn him out, yet Norman staggers onto his distorted feet.

"You worried about your *vadder*, Rachel?" he asks as we enter the hall, his light eyes kind.

I shake my head and jiggle Eli on my hip. "No, Mr. Troyer, I'm worried about my son."

"Your son?" Norman uses the braces to move closer and peers down into Eli's eyes. Six hours ago, when my *dawdy*'s heart attack occurred, Eli was in dire need of a nap. Now he is tired beyond all reason. This perusal from a stranger causes his bottom lip to quiver before his mouth opens up in a rattling cry.

"Hear that?" I ask Norman, although there is no doubt he can.

"May I?"

I pass Eli to Norman, who places my son's small chest flush against his own.

"What do you think's wrong?"

Norman Troyer lifts up the hand not supporting Eli and looks down, listening rather than responding to me. Next, he holds my son out with hands tucked beneath his armpits and tries to peer into Eli's eyes. But Eli only screams louder, chokes, and pedals his hanging legs as if trying to climb higher to breathe.

Finally, Norman passes Eli to me and shakes his head. "I don't know what's wrong. Your son's crying too hard to look into his eyes, but from the way he's breathing, I can tell he's not getting enough oxygen into his lungs." Norman looks into my eyes as if trying to read the navy rimming the cornflower blue just like, seven years ago, he tried to read my *mamm*'s. "Perhaps, Rachel, you should take Eli to see the *doktor*?"

"But aren't *you* a doctor?"

Norman spreads long fingers across the blue shirt spanning his chest. "In a way, yes. I look into people's eyes. I prescribe herbs that can soften the effects of rheumatism, take the edge off menstrual cramps and migraines. Your son, though . . ." Norman runs a finger down Eli's tearstained cheek. "Your son, I fear, needs more knowledge than I have to give."

The past seven years, my faith in Norman Troyer's knowledge has convinced me that holistic medicine is the remedy for every ailment under the sun. Now, looking at the self-doubt lurking in his eyes, I find my faith beginning to wane. "What do you mean?" I ask. "What do you think's wrong?"

Norman stares at the wall adorned with a print of a seaside landscape shaded in a color spectrum only known to man. "Has Eli been fighting colds, coughing up mucus, or having difficulties breathing at night? Has he recently lost weight or had fevers, night sweats?" I stop nodding as his words rumble in my ears. "Have you noticed that any of his lymph nodes are swollen?"

My vision floods. Norman's face transforms into someone I cannot recognize. "What are you saying? That my son's really sick?"

Norman shakes his head. "No, Rachel. I'm not saying anything like that. I just don't think it'd hurt to have your son checked out by a *doktor* when you get home."

Leaning against the wall with Eli in my arms, I realize that everything bad seems to take place inside hospital facilities such as this one. "But why, Mr. Troyer, have you given up faith in holistic medicine and placed it in *here*?" I gesture to a harried orderly wheeling down the corridor with a cart of evening meals covered in white domes like spaceships.

Norman Troyer smiles. "I haven't." Taking out the nitroglycerin bottle he keeps in his pants pocket, he rattles the contents and says, "Sometimes, I just think you do not have to choose one over the other. I think, when treating an illness, you can apply a mixture of both."

Gerald Martin drives Leah and me home from the hospital around ten o'clock. He then grabs his small duffel from beside the couch and leaves to stay at his family's home in

Lititz because Tobias thought it improper for Gerald to remain behind with us. Watching through the storm door as the van lights cut across the driveway, I roll my eyes and sigh at the hypocrisy of Tobias's request.

Leah sets a kettle on the stove for tea. "What is it?" she asks.

"Nothing." Rummaging through the cupboards for something to eat, for I haven't touched a morsel since lunch, I find an old Good's potato chip tin filled with oatmeal cookies. I take a bite of one, and the cookie crumbles into a hundred pieces despite the *budder* meant to keep it together. "*Mamm*'s still using the same recipe," I say. "Even after all these years."

Leah doesn't turn, smile, or nod. Stepping closer, I can see by the light of the kerosene lamp hanging overhead that her small shoulders are shaking.

"Leah," I ask, touching her back, "what is it?"

My sister stabs a finger toward the storm door. "Like *you* should expect an answer from me! You who tells me nothing!"

"What are you talking about? What didn't I tell you?"

Pivoting to face me, Leah sets her jaw. In all our conjoined lives, I have never seen her like this. "Why did you sigh when Gerald Martin pulled away just now, and why did Tobias pay him not to drive you? Is he . . ." My sister wipes the tears from her face and takes a breath. "Is Gerald Martin Eli's father?"

I can't help it. As the image of Gerald Martin—pudgy,

self-conscious Gerald Martin with his immaculate sneakers and ragged bowl-cut hair—filters into my mind along with the idea of his being Eli's father, I begin to laugh. Then the reality of Leah's question and the answer only two people in this world know comes flooding back. With it, all humor is gone.

"No, Leah," I say, "Gerald Martin is not Eli's father. I think your husband paid Gerald not to drive me around and asked him not to stay here tonight because . . . well, because Tobias feels it is his duty not to protect us from men like Gerald, but to protect men like Gerald from me."

Fresh tears replace the ones my sister's just dried. "But you made one mistake. *One.* Why can't the people of Copper Creek—why can't my own husband—forgive you?"

I feel like I am standing on uneven ground. The sensation is so intense, I drag out a kitchen chair and lower myself into it. "I don't know," I say. "Maybe because—"

The teakettle screams. Leah snatches a hot pad and whisks the kettle off the burner before the sound can awaken our children, who were so exhausted in the hospital they cried themselves to sleep. I am relieved by the distraction, by the noise. I am hoping I will now not have to finish my sentence, when Leah takes off the hot pad and sits in the chair opposite mine.

"Because what?" my sister prods, reaching across the table to clasp my hand.

Silence hisses like steam from the teakettle, as the explanations long prepared in my mind refuse to come out my lips. They would only be more lies added to those the Copper Creek Community spread in their quest for truth. The lies that have turned my heart from the church as well as from God, as I perceived their judgment and his to be one and the same.

"Maybe because, Leah, I refused to repent to the church."

The kerosene light inside the wire netting flares, illuminating our joined hands, whose only difference is the small scar snaking across Leah's where she sliced it during canning years ago. I look up and smile, remembering how we used to sit like this when we were children praying a wordless blessing over the meal. But I do not see any fond remembrances in my sister's eyes, only sadness. I hate knowing I have put that sadness there, and I hate knowing how much deeper that sadness would travel if she knew the truth.

This is when I realize I cannot unburden myself while sitting at the comfort of our parents' kitchen table in their yellow house on Hilltop Road. For a moment—fortified by our *dawdy*'s brush with death and its reminder of the fragility of life—I imagined that I could unburden myself of my secrets and all would be well.

But even without speaking the truth, looking into Leah's sorrowful gaze, I realize that I have already hurt the one person my silence was meant to protect.

# 10

## AMOS

Fortified with a cup of stout black tea purchased in the hospital cafeteria, Norman Troyer comes to take over the graveyard shift and finds that Helen is still occupying the chair beside Samuel Stoltzfus's bed. "Why don't you go home and sleep?" he asks.

Helen looks over her shoulder with reddened eyes. "Gerald's in Lititz," she says. "I'd have no way to get there."

"I could call a cab. They run twenty-four hours."

"That won't be necessary." Helen stands and stretches the muscles of her lower back. "If I need to sleep, I can just use the pullout bed."

Norman shuffles closer to Helen. "Trust me," he whispers,

"those pullout beds are terrible. If you can ever get to sleep, the plastic covering them will wake you at every turn."

Helen looks down at Norman's legs. "Did you sleep in one after your accident?"

*"Jah."*

"Why didn't they give you a real bed?"

"They did. But after I got out, I would come here to stay with my nephew."

Helen muffles her yawn with a cupped hand. "Your nephew?"

"Both my nephews were with me that day." He pauses, takes a sip of tea. "As was their father—my brother, Henry."

She wipes sleep from her eyes, now fully awake. "Were they all right?"

"No," Norman Troyer says. "My nephew was on life support for a while, but in the end, I was the only one in that buggy who survived."

Helen says, "I'm sorry," knowing those words are an inept covering for such a loss.

"It's fine." Norman reaches out and lightly touches Helen's arm. "It really was a long time ago."

## *Rachel*

The cot bows beneath the weight of someone crawling into my bed. I cry out, and a hand claps over my mouth.

"You want to wake the *kinner*?" Leah whispers. "I can't sleep in that big bed by myself. Move over."

I groan but draw back the covers, ushering my sister inside. "You've never slept by yourself."

"You're right." Leah turns onto her side and straightens out her legs so that she and I can both fit on the narrow cot. "And just between you and me, you're a better sleep partner. You don't smell like sweat." She laughs. "And you *don't* snore."

"Why are you so awake?" I grumble, pulling the pillow up around my ears. "It's almost dawn."

"I thought that tea was decaffeinated."

"Let me guess. It wasn't." I place my spine against the wall and straighten my legs as Leah has done.

"Rachel?" Leah says.

*"Jah?"*

"Don't you *want* to get married?"

I squint at her in the moonlight slanting through the office window. Our unbound hair strewn across the shared pillow and cotton nightgowns buttoned up to our necks remind me of us as children. The thought of the innocence I have desecrated brings me to tears; I close my eyes again before she can see.

"What makes you bring that up now?"

Leah shrugs, the small movement making the bed quake. "I guess just talking about moving from your bed to Tobias's."

"And are you glad you did?"

"You can't answer my question with a question."

"You've woken me up in the middle of the night, Leah. I say I can do whatever I want."

"Fine." Turning onto her back, Leah folds her arms behind her head and stares up at the ceiling. "*Jah*, I'm glad I married him. I wouldn't have Jonathan otherwise."

"You could've just had an illegitimate child like me and skipped crawling into bed every night with a sweaty husband."

Leah elbows me. "That's not funny."

"I never said it was." I elbow her back. "Seriously, though. Why'd you marry him?"

It is a long time before Leah whispers, "Because I knew nobody else would ask."

"That's ridiculous!"

"No, it's not. *Mammi* told me Tobias might be my only chance."

I can feel anger bubbling up from somewhere deep within my chest. "Yeah, well," I snap, "*Mamm*'s not always right."

"And she's not always wrong." Leah then adds, her voice softened, "Tobias needed a wife and I wanted to get out of Muddy Pond, so I knew I needed a husband."

"Why didn't you just get a job? You could've worked as a seamstress or a baker in town. You could've taught school."

"Rachel, come on. You've always said that *I'm* too naive, and now you're the one looking at life through a rose-colored lens. How would I ever support myself on what a seamstress or baker makes? The only school I could ever teach on an eighth-grade education would be a Mennonite one, and in another community I would still have to rely on someone else to take me in . . . to feed me, to clothe me. No, agreeing to marry Tobias was the only way."

"You could've told me your plans. We could've figured something out."

"I didn't want to figure something out! I wanted to make my own way—"

"But to marry a man you did not love—you *do* not love!" I cry. "That is no way to begin a life!"

The cot threatens to collapse as Leah flips to face me. "I *do* love Tobias," she says. "Maybe not like I imagined as a little girl, but I never really expected to have that kind of love, that kind of marriage. All my life it seemed like everything was lined up for you, and I had to scrape by on what remained. I guess I never expected my marriage, my love for my husband, to be any different. I dreamed it would be different, yes. But I never expected it. I never expected to have a marriage or a love like the one I knew you would have."

"Look around you," I command, pointing to the floor where Eli sleeps. "I *have* no marriage. I have no home. I don't even have the benefit of a good reputation. You have all this and still you think that I—*I* am the one whose life is lined up for her? The one who gives *you* the leftovers?"

"You don't think our parents chose their favorites from

our birth? That I was our *mudder*'s Jacob and you, our *vadder*'s Esau?"

"No. I *don't*. You had *Dawdy*'s attention in a way I never did. You were his precious, delicate Leah while I was less like his *dochder* and more like his field hand."

"I tried . . ." Leah chokes down a sob. "I tried to help him, but he'd always send me away. Tell me to go back to the *haus* and do something with *Mamm*."

"That's because he wanted to protect you."

"Protect me?" Leah resentfully asks. "From what?"

I realize then that *Dawdy*'s pushing Leah away perpetuated in her the same rejection that I always felt. Are these complicated childhood scars the reason I wanted to be more than just the daughter who could never be the son, or the daughter who could never be her sister, but rather everything one man had ever wanted, even if only for one night?

"I don't know, Leah," I say, sorrow burning my eyes. "I think . . . I think *Dawdy* wanted to shield you from the realities of life found in that barn. Horses sometimes hanged themselves after their bridles got tangled up in the cherry trees in the pasture. Our Brown Swiss, Bossy—you remember Bossy, the one *Dawdy* said he sold at New Holland?" Leah nods. "Well, she *wasn't* sold. She really sliced open her stomach on the barbed-wire fence and was put down, then eaten for supper that night. And that was just the beginning. We had colts that were stillborn. Colts that were born premature and had to be bottle-fed for weeks, only to die after I had grown attached enough to name them. Glimpses of life and death were everywhere in that barn. *Dawdy* didn't let me work beside him because he loved me more; *Dawdy* had me work beside him because he didn't care if, even as a young child, I could handle that level of labor and stress or not."

"I never knew." Leah tries to muffle her cries with the pillow. "I never knew any of this."

I run my fingers through the tangled tresses of my sister's hair. "How could you have known? I never told you, and you never told me that you felt I was *Dawdy*'s favorite."

"I didn't want to . . . to ruin your relationship with him," Leah says. "I thought you would've given up your time in the barn; you would've tried to get me to take your place. And that—that scared me more than anything. I didn't know him at all. He was a stranger to me." She pauses and wipes tears with her sleeve. "He is a stranger still."

"If it makes you feel any better, I'm about as comfortable around him as you are."

"But why? Why was it like that, and why is it like that now?"

I stop scratching my sister's back and ponder the question I have asked myself so many times. "I think it's because we never talked to *Dawdy*, and *Dawdy* never listened. He never asked how our day was or what we did. He never told us about his day or what *he* did. It seems simple, I know, but all that time we were out in the barn, he never made an effort to establish any kind of relationship with me. He only saw me as an extra set of hands, as a strong back, not as his *dochder*."

"Is that why you did what you did?"

My spine stiffens. "What do you mean?"

"Did you sleep with Eli's father because you were looking for the father you never had?"

Closing my eyes, I see myself as that naive, pigtailed girl who hauled water and mucked stalls, polished tack and picked hooves for the payment of glimpsing her reflection in her father's smiling eyes. Ten years later, that girl became a woman whose pigtails were *kapped*. Deep beneath the layers, though, I remained that scarred little child, scrambling for her father's approval. And though I knew it was wrong, I relished the fact that even when my sister and I were in the same room, in her husband's dark eyes I saw only me.

"I don't know," I say, hedging truth. "I could ask you the same question: Did you marry Tobias because you thought in him you could find the father *you* never had? The one who would pay attention to you; the one who would draw you out, let you talk and he would listen?"

Leah's stifled sobs are the only reply. I feel guilty for once again answering her question with a question of my own, but I can't answer hers. *Dawdy* might have been an emotionally absent father, yet I have free will, and I am the one who fell. He did not push me.

I turn onto my side and face the wall to hide the hot tears streaming down my cheeks in accord with Leah's sobs. I act like I am asleep, but in light of my culpability, sleep will not come.

## AMOS

Early the next morning, Samuel Stoltzfus is released from the hospital. Everyone surrounding him is still glassy-eyed from sleep deprivation and achy from having sat in one position for too long. Samuel, on the other hand, slept through each of the night nurse's checkups. He whistles as he runs a comb over his hair and tugs his suspender straps up over his shirt.

"You think you could make me some *pon haus mit abbel budder* when we get home, *Fraa*?" Samuel asks, then sneers at the purple Jell-O cubes still on his tray. "After this *hutsch*, I'm right hungry."

Norman Troyer looks over at Samuel in shock. The way Helen stands with her body slanted against the wall makes it obvious that she really needs to be lying down. Her hair, which has thinned at the temples from being pulled into a bun for so many years, is oily and strubbly, her face creased from having slept with it pressed against the pullout chair. But Samuel doesn't notice this. He has not paid attention to his wife's appearance in thirty-some years; why should he pay attention now?

"*Jah*, Samuel," Helen says, giving her husband a smile

that only emphasizes the bags beneath her eyes. "I'll make you some *pon haus* when we get home."

Samuel nods in satisfaction. Tobias comes into the room with Gerald Martin.

"You all ready?" Tobias asks. Looking at the expressions on everyone's faces, he already knows the answer.

Because of Samuel's heart attack, the plans regarding the Stoltzfuses' move have changed. Helen cannot pack up the *haus* and also take care of her husband, and Tobias and Leah cannot leave their other children in his sisters' care long enough for Samuel to recover and make the arduous journey from Pennsylvania to Tennessee. Listening to this deliberation over the past three days, Rachel has known what the easiest solution would be.

But that does not mean it is an easy choice.

During the time when Rachel needed her parents the most, she was abandoned by them. But now that they need *her*, she feels compelled to help—and she knows she will feel guilty if she does not choose to remain behind while everyone else goes home. Rachel knows there is another answer to this quandary: she could travel back to Tennessee and take care of Tobias and Leah's other children, but after Tobias's behavior the night after Samuel's heart attack, she knows he would never allow Gerald Martin to drive her down to Tennessee unchaperoned.

For that matter, he probably would not want her watching over his children, even for such a short time.

So, after much inner turmoil and one phone call to Ida Mae, Rachel chooses to stay and help her *mudder* pack. She's hoping that if they both work, they can finish within the week. This would get Rachel back to Tennessee in time to tend to her reflexology patients and schedule a doctor's appointment for Eli, whose cold has left but whose inflamed lymph node has not.

Watching Gerald Martin's van drive away with her sister, brother-in-law, and nephew inside, Rachel recalls another morning—a humid spring morning the very opposite of this—when Leah left for Tennessee. Rachel had no idea when Leah climbed into the van and waved from behind the window that she was only doing so because she knew her *mamm* and sister could not see the tears streaming from her eyes. Seeing those tears would have lessened the sense of betrayal Rachel felt, but it would not have cured it. Only a week in advance, she'd been told that the next Monday her twin would be moving to the Copper Creek Community in Tennessee. When Rachel had asked why—perhaps thinking her sister had obtained a teaching position at the *schul*—she learned that a mere two weeks after that, Leah would wed a thirty-year-old widower with four children. This widower had been their *nochber* on Hilltop Road, but neither Rachel nor—if she were honest—Leah could remember Tobias King except for the fleeting image of a dark-haired man who wore a leather apron over his pants and pounded hot metal in a wooden lean-to attached to the barn.

Rachel suspected that Leah hadn't told her because Leah feared her sister would talk her out of the only decision she had ever made without Rachel's consent. Still, Rachel would have appreciated being let in on the news sooner than she was. Perhaps, given more time, Rachel could have resigned from her position at the Muddy Pond *schul* and moved down to Tennessee as well. She would never have lived with Tobias and Leah, but she could have lived close enough that she and Leah might see each other more than twice a year.

But without time, that could not happen. None of that could happen. So Leah moved to Tennessee, and two weeks later, the wedding took place as planned. Two months after that, when Leah revealed that she was with child and asked her sister to move down, Rachel felt like everything was working out as it should have all along. She resigned from her teaching position, paid a driver to take her to Tennessee, and moved into Leah and Tobias's white farmhouse—into the very room next to where Leah and her newlywed husband slept.

If only Rachel had known what devastation that move would bring, she never would have made it. Not even for the love of her sister, for what happened after that move risked it all.

## Rachel

A week after his return from the hospital, my *dawdy* wearies of his ailment and rises from his bed like a phoenix from the ashes. By this point, the entire contents of the house have been disassembled, swaddled in bubble wrap, and nestled in the banana boxes my *mamm* had the foresight to collect from Weis Market when my sister wrote saying that she and *Dawdy* should move down. Despite this preparation, there is still plenty to do before Gerald returns to pick us up tomorrow. My *dawdy* has been sedentary for so long, however, he cannot imagine another day lying around as my *mamm* and I carry boxes past him.

"Want to go to Root's?" he asks.

I look over my cup, then set it back on the counter. Sleeping beneath my *dawdy*'s roof for the first time in a year and a half has galvanized the pain his emotional absence has always caused. Because of this, nothing in me wants to spend quality time with this man who has never had quality time to spend before. Nothing in me wants to talk with this man who has said no more than two dozen words in the eight days I've been here, all of which were uttered in the same clipped tone he uses when dealing with difficult horses. But then I recall my middle-of-the-night conversation with Leah. I know if we are ever to change the dynamics of our relationship with our father, we must not duplicate the same rejection we have always felt. Instead, we will have to embrace him with all of his mistakes and hope that with the example of our steadfast love, our *dawdy* will be able to love us the way he should have from the beginning.

"Let me check with *Mamm* first. See if she can watch Eli."

*Dawdy* slaps his thighs and gets to his feet. "I'll go hook up the buggy."

When I tell my *mamm* that we are traveling to Root's Market, she seems as surprised as I. "It'll be *goot* to get that *rutschy mann* out of the *haus*. He gets underfoot when he's bored."

"Eli's still asleep." I point over my shoulder. "Do you mind?"

My *mamm* shakes her head. Her *kapp* strings sway from where they have come untied. "You watch *Dawdy* and I'll watch your *suh*. I say you have a harder babysitting job than I."

I smile, turn to leave.

"And, Rachel?"

*"Jah?"*

"Don't let your *vadder* eat everything in sight."

Balancing on that narrow seat, watching the immaculate farms of Lancaster County slip past, I am reminded of all the times Leah and I made this journey from Mount Joy to Manheim with our father. She and I would sit together rather than on either side of *Dawdy*, and the whole time, we would whisper and giggle until he quieted us with an eyebrow raised over a stern blue eye. But if I was riding alone with *Dawdy*—perhaps on our way to help a *nochber* with his horse gelding or to bring one back that we could break and train—I would sit in the buggy with my hands in my lap, wordlessly staring out the window as I am doing now.

When we were working side by side in the barn, *Dawdy* and I were both so busy feeding the horses or exercising them in the *scheierhof*, there was no need for talk. Yet in that dark, cramped space smelling of leather, oil, and horse liniment, the weight of the silence rested on my chest until I opened my mouth to keep from gasping aloud. I do not know why my father and I had such an awkward relationship—perhaps because we never had a relationship at all. In truth, I felt more comfortable around Judah's father than I did my own, and Amos King rarely said anything besides, "And how are you, Rachel?" But that simple question and having him wait—bent over and looking into my eyes—until I had stammered my answer meant the world to me. Sometimes, I imagined that my *mamm* had married Amos rather than our *dawdy*, allowing Judah to be our brother who could play with Leah and me without the daily interruption of supper and chores.

"You see the Mummaus have sold?" My *dawdy* reaches across me to point to the buggy's tiny window. "They moved to Florida," he huffs. "Of all places."

Peering through the window made from rainproof plastic,

I see a minivan parked in the driveway and a yellow toddler swing hanging from the branches of the pin oak we'd eaten beneath when it was the Mummaus' turn to host Muddy Pond's bimonthly fellowship meal. A satellite dish juts from the roof like an alien appendage; the Mummaus never even had a telephone in their barn. How Mary Louise Mummau would shudder to see her flower beds (always her pride and joy even over winter) crawling with crabgrass and the yard strewn with sticks as thick as her forearms, which were muscled from years of kneading sourdough by hand.

"Do you think our *haus* will look the same before long?" I ask.

*Dawdy* shrugs. "*Jah*, but all our *nochberen* are moving. *Bauern* can't pay the taxes on their property, even if they inherited the land."

The knot in my stomach begins to loosen. These words are the most my *dawdy* and I have exchanged since he began demanding to know—and I refusing to tell—who Eli's father is. Although this is not the deep, meaningful conversation I hope the two of us might one day have, I know it is a start. And perhaps my *dawdy*'s near-death experience has challenged his life in more ways than I have dared to dream.

Every Tuesday for as long as I can remember, Root's Market—a centipede of connecting warehouses interspersed with small wooden buildings—has transformed from a graveyard atmosphere into a festival. The summer months are the busiest. The tables running through the center of the cement-floored warehouses are covered with green tarps and heaped with cantaloupes as big as bowling balls. There are striped watermelons that could have been prizewinners at some Southern state fair but are just considered normal to Lancaster County *bauern*, who attribute their harvest bounty to a steady supply of manure tea (horse manure mixed with water and poured over each plant). There are always peaches fuzzed as lightly as newborn skin, cherries and grapes that shine like jewels beneath their clear plastic mesh, ears of corn still tucked in their husks, celery stalks freshly sliced from the fields, and heads of lettuce that flare out in layers like a woman's old-fashioned petticoat.

But even now, when the fields have long been turned under until the threat of frost has left, crowds come from miles around for the baked goods the Amish and Mennonites sell and the handcrafted items they make, such as butter churns, pie safes, and tin stars that can be purchased in the surrounding outbuildings. Walking up and down these aisles with my father at my side, I can almost imagine that I am just a child again, spending a quarter of the afternoon peering in at the quarter-sized chocolates lined up behind the confectioner's glass counter. The candies are still here, but they do not beckon to me as they once did—perhaps due to my increased height, which no longer has my gaze flush with the second row: those dark-chocolate disks with white sprinkles glistening on top like the snowdrops for which they are named. To my left is the Greek family's booth selling flaked pastries called baklava, filled with honey and walnuts. They also sell gyros, grape leaves stuffed with rice and pine nuts, and salads heavy with feta, grape tomatoes, black olives, and a tart dressing infused with peppercorns and olive oil. My father smacks his lips and maneuvers over to this Greek booth. Before I can utter a word of protest, a hot pita filled with a shaved mixture of lamb and beef is in his hand.

I watch him scarf this down while resting his hip against the booth selling dried *abbel schnitz*, pineapple rings, apricots, dates, and a variety of chocolate and nuts that can be made into a trail mix according to customers' preferences.

"Now, *Mamm* told me you can't go eating everything in sight," I warn.

My *dawdy* uses the paper the pita came in to wipe the yogurt sauce from his fingers. "This is my last time at Root's for who knows how long," he says. "I'm just getting started."

I groan, but reminding him of his heart attack will only encourage his eating further.

Under the guise of wanting to say good-bye to his "*goot* friends," my *dawdy* stops by the sub shop for a six-inch meatball and the fish shop for a deep-fried fillet lathered with ketchup and slid between two slices of Bunny Bread. He attempts to buy an *abbel* dumpling, but the woman who owns the booth bought a pony from him for her *gross-dochder* and gives the dumpling to him for free. He purchases hand-cranked peach ice cream in a paper cup, eats this, then pats his stomach and declares he is full.

*Dawdy* has gone to throw his cup away when a Mennonite woman who looks familiar takes me by the elbow. "I haven't seen you since you moved to Tennessee!" she cries. "How are you and the *bobbel*?"

The only remedy for these situations is to act like you know the person claiming to know you. "We're doing well," I say. "And how are you?"

But it is obvious, as she takes a step closer and places a hand on my arm, that this woman is not interested in giving information as much as receiving it. "And your *schweschder* . . . ?" Her eyes dart across the aisle as if searching for eavesdroppers. "I heard she's had some trouble."

Thinking of Leah's stint in the hospital, I smile and say, "She did, but now she's doing better."

"Is she?" A disbelieving frown slices a V between the woman's brows. "I take it she married the *kind*'s *vadder*, then?"

Only now do I realize that she thinks I'm Leah. I glance at the crowd parting around our bodies, blocking the flow of movement like two stones protruding from a riverbed. Nobody is paying attention to our conversation, but I wonder how many of the Plain people in this building—and the ones surrounding it—know about Rachel Stoltzfus's fall from grace and her subsequent tumble into shame.

"No," I say, not even allowing myself to blink as I stare into this woman's inquisitive eyes. "She *didn't* marry the father. She actually left the church and is now doing reflexology for an English woman."

"Oh, my!" the woman cries, splaying a hand across her chest. "That doesn't sound much better at all!"

"But it is," I say. "It is one of the best things that could've happened to her." I realize the words are true even as they leave my mouth. I wouldn't be trying to heal the relationship with my father and to find healing within myself if I were still sheltered beneath the church, which once provided me with so much false security that I didn't know how deeply I was scarred.

Smiling at the woman's astonishment, I turn and stride toward the booth where my *dawdy* stands, waiting for a cup of steaming mulled cider.

# 11

## AMOS

Rachel intended to follow Norman Troyer's advice about taking Eli to a *doktor*, but back in Tennessee, Eli seemed better, if not fully well. Plus, Ida Mae needed her help preparing the store for Christmas in the Brier—the town's annual tradition where every shop owner keeps his doors open long after closing and attempts to lure new customers in with the same kind of complimentary powdered cider, store-bought pound cake, and chewy popcorn balls offered by the shop owners before them.

The Apple Plate Restaurant (famous for its signed photograph of Dolly Parton, who visited back in '75) and Ida

Mae's Amish Country Store are the only shops in the whole lineup that do not serve this predictable fare. The proprietor of the Apple Plate, Vidalia Swanson, serves apple pie à la mode and carameled apple cider as a way of expanding her business's reach along with her customers' waistlines. Ida Mae is not the cook that Vidalia proclaims herself to be. Still, she takes just as much pride in the complimentary food she serves her customers during Christmas in the Brier. The past month alone, Ida Mae's been forced to lie numerous times, claiming she was sold out of hummingbird cake when she had twenty iced loaves rolled in Saran and stashed in the freezer. Her *Grossmammi* Meltzer's famous wassail recipe (with the splash of sherry everyone enjoys but no one talks about) Ida Mae's also hoarded for this very occasion. The farmer's, smoked cheddar, and Muenster cheeses are just waiting to be sliced and fanned out on a silver platter alongside Lebanon bologna and Ritz crackers.

Rachel spends the day preceding that evening's festivities hunkered over the countertop, festooning the miniature furniture for the dollhouses with tiny velvet ribbons trimmed in gold and setting everything up in a dollhouse that's high enough that little curious hands cannot reach. The window display must be yanked to the full height of its yuletide glory, which is difficult, considering the Amish do not believe in Christmas trees and would have an issue with the red, green, and silver tinsel draping the three-foot synthetic pine and the multicolored lights that blink at random throughout the day. This eyesore gives Rachel a headache, further irritated by Ida Mae's strict policy that a cinnamon bun candle must remain lit at all times, so customers who come in will become hungry for her baked goods (which do not taste as good as that candle smells) and also buy a candle.

It is a call too close for Ida Mae's comfort, but everything on her to-do list is completed an hour before Mayor Townsend (dressed as a skinny Santa Claus) cruises down Main Street in his yellow convertible and announces through a megaphone that Christmas in the Brier has begun. The parking lots of the shops filled an hour ago, forcing the overflow traffic to park on the frosted grass hemming in the high school grounds. After Mayor Townsend's decree, the drivers exit their vehicles and flock like a chattering group of magpies into the shops.

Ida Mae's Amish Country Store is one of the first to reach maximum capacity. Rachel comes out of the back room carrying trays laden with hummingbird cake and cheese, and then passes out cups of wassail. As she does, she is caught off guard by the customers' rude stares and ruder comments. She knew from her days running a produce stand in Manheim that her Plain appearance would draw attention, but she had no idea people would think she and Eli were just *Englischers* dressed in Amish costume.

"Him yours?" one woman says, pointing over at Eli, who is sitting on Ida Mae's lap taking everything in with round blue eyes. Rachel nods. The woman puts a hand on Rachel's arm and leans in like she's about to be privy to a secret. "Tell me," she whispers, "where'd you find such a cute getup?"

Rachel bristles. Eli's "getup"—black trousers with snaps to access his diaper, black suspenders with button fastenings, and a long-sleeved teal shirt—is one she put countless hours into making.

"I sewed it myself," she says.

"Did you?" The woman plucks at Rachel's sleeve. "Lemme guess, you made yours, too?"

Rachel nods again, then walks back through the curtain separating the store from the darkened reflexology office, which has been closed since her trip to Pennsylvania and will reopen after the holidays.

"I had to escape too," a man says.

Rachel jumps and flicks on the lights.

Russell Speck rolls the unlit cigarette from one side of his mouth to the other. "I always had to," he says. "Escape, that is. Guess being on the road so long makes it hard to be around all them people."

Rachel sits down on the stack of containers.

"You look tired. Did you get you something to eat?" he asks.

Shaking her head, Rachel smooths the material of her dress over her knees. "I don't want more cheese and Lebanon bologna. And the hummingbird cake's too sweet."

"Here." Russell holds out a paper bag darkened with grease. "Have yourself some curly fries."

Rachel hesitates, looks over.

Unfolding his bulky frame up from beneath the desk, Russell walks over to the fridge. He plunks a bottle of ketchup on the container beneath Rachel. The ketchup under the lid has congealed into a sticky maroon shell. Rachel peels it off, squirts some of the ketchup on the bag, and dabs the ketchup with a fry.

Russell says, "Pretty good, huh?"

Her mouth still full, Rachel nods.

Sitting back down, he adds, "Didja ever have curly fries before?"

All her frustrations with her customers boiling up at one moment, she swallows with difficulty and says, "What do you *Englischers* think, we Mennonites live under a rock?"

Russell throws his head back and laughs until crow's-feet stamp lines around his eyes. "Shoot-fire, you've been around my wife too long!"

"Ida Mae? But isn't she your *ex*-wife?"

Russell's smile disappears. He looks down and raps his thick knuckles on the desk made from more synthetic material than wood. "I figure you gotta have two people not wanting to be married anymore to make it official. But yeah, Ida Mae's my ex."

Rachel is silent a moment. She eats a curly fry dusted in salt and swallows. "Why'd y'all divorce if you didn't want to?"

"'Cause *she* did." Russell juts his chin toward the curtain to let Rachel know who *she* is.

"You two just stopped getting along?"

"Goodness, girl." Taking off his cap, Russell scratches his bushy red hair. "You sure you're not a defense lawyer in your spare time or something?"

Rachel shrugs. "I've just been wondering about you two. Wondering why you still come around, when Ida Mae treats you the way she does."

"Guess 'cause I feel like I deserve it."

Rachel says nothing, just looks down at the dwindling pile of fries.

"Just between you and me, though—" Russell leans over so that Rachel can smell the fried food heavy on his breath—"I'm hoping one of these days, Ida Mae and me can get back together."

Rachel smiles. "So *that's* why you keep coming around."

"Yes'm. Just gotta get her to forgive me."

Standing, Rachel picks up the soggy paper bag and sets the rest of the fries in front of Russell. She moves toward the curtain separating the office from the store. But then she stops. Turning, Rachel looks in Russell's direction without meeting his eyes. "I'm only saying this because of what I've been through. . . . I don't think you need to get Ida Mae to forgive you as much as you need to get Ida Mae to forgive herself."

In the store, Rachel continues serving customers who continue to stare. What would they think, she wonders, if they could see the scarlet stain hidden beneath her Plain clothes? The Plain clothes that evoke in *Englischer* minds a naiveté and innocence, when it is they themselves—believing the gentle people infallible—who are naive.

"Rachel!" Ida Mae yells. "You're spilling!"

Rachel looks down. *Grossmammi* Meltzer's wassail has overflowed the Dixie cup and splashed onto her cape dress. But Rachel just smiles, watching the red beads roll off the slick cotton without leaving a stain. Perhaps there is hope that her own scarlet stain can be washed from her soul as well.

At ten o'clock, when the *Open* sign flips to *Closed*, the cinnamony dregs of wassail are all that remain in the bottom of the Crock-Pot. A few cheese crumbs and slick spots where circles of bologna have rested are all that's left on the silver platter. But only ten of the twenty hummingbird cakes have been touched.

Staring morosely at these cakes that have forced Ida Mae to sacrifice her conscience, she says, "I can't freeze them again. They been setting out so long, I can't sell them full price. I don't know what I'm gonna do."

"Sell 'em half price," Russell says, holding Eli, who is a little blip on the radar screen of his chest.

Ida Mae is too tired to come back with her typical sassy remark. "You think it'd work? We've only got two days 'til Christmas. I don't even know if the cakes'll last that long."

Russell says, "If they don't, let me buy them off you. I could eat them with my Christmas dinner."

"And what's *that* gonna be?" Ida Mae rolls her eyes. "A bucket of KFC and a six-pack like last year?"

Rachel clears her throat. "Actually, I invited Russell to eat here with us. I'm going to cook." She turns to the man, who is as shocked by this news as his ex-wife. "You'll be here at six o'clock? And you're going to bring boiled custard, right?"

Russell keeps nodding because he is imitating Rachel. Ida Mae is staring holes through Rachel's skull, but Rachel decides she'll just have to deal with her later.

"Hey. What's wrong with him?" Russell jerks his chin down at Eli. "Why's he making that funny sound?"

Taking her son and placing her ear against his shuddering rib cage, Rachel can hear a watery rattle coming from deep inside his chest.

"That's not the croup, is it?" she asks Ida Mae.

Ida Mae steps closer and listens. "I don't know, Rachel-girl, but I never known a young'un to be so sickly. Wintertime or not."

"I've been meaning to make a doctor's appointment. I'll do it first thing tomorrow."

"You can't. No place is open tomorrow. And I wouldn't wait 'til Monday." Ida Mae's eyes are filled with concern. "No, Rachel-girl. This's gone on long enough. Insurance or no insurance, I think we should take him in tonight."

Dr. Riordian, a silver-haired Irishman with the swaggering aura of a retired horse jockey, is used to harried young mothers bringing their children to the emergency room at two and three in the morning when a good night's rest would set their small immune systems right again. Because of this, he is unconcerned when Rachel places Eli on the table and tells the doctor to please take a look at him. Of course, the situation is unusual from the beginning since the mother is dressed like she just stepped off the *Mayflower* and speaks with an accent to boot.

Clutching the paper wrapping the examination table, she says, "Before you do anything, I want you to know that I don't have insurance. I was in an Old Order Mennonite community, and we always shared medical expenses through the church. But now I don't go to that church. I don't live in that community."

The more words that leave her mouth, the more flustered the mother becomes until it is everything Dr. Riordian can do not to reach out and calm her. "It's okay," Dr. Riordian says instead. "We'll figure everything out as we go, but you should know that we never turn away someone needing medical assistance."

Rachel smiles for the first time since Russell was holding Eli and asking what was wrong. Watching that smile, Dr. Riordian is taken aback by how young she is, when her eyes appear so old. Dr. Riordian shakes his head, gets Rachel to lay Eli on the table, takes the stethoscope from around his neck, and plugs the rubbery ends into his ears. He places the disk on Eli's chest and listens. Moves the disk farther down and listens again. Taking the stethoscope out of his ears, the doctor begins to run freckled fingers over the sides of Eli's neck.

"He has a bump," Rachel says, as if embarrassed by the bump, when what she is really embarrassed about is the fact that she hasn't brought it to a doctor's attention before now. "It's over here." She trails a finger over Eli's clavicle and dips it down into the hollow between skin and bone.

Dr. Riordian places his finger where hers was and traces the same area.

"How long since you noticed this?" he asks, his voice as void of emotion as his features.

"Two weeks," she whispers, looking down. "I found it when I was visiting family."

"That's good," the doctor says.

"Good?" Rachel lifts her head. "Why is it good?"

Dr. Riordian knows he cannot say anything to give Rachel either alarm or reassurance. "It's good that you found it so soon," he says. "I don't know what this is. But I promise you that Mandy Vaughan is the person who can find out."

## Rachel

I cannot sleep, so I pass the time listening to the hourly trains and wondering where each car is destined to be dropped. I like to imagine that, rather than hauling coal as many trains these days do, this is a passenger line that whisks people to places that have been untouched by fear, disease, or death. Even just thinking this causes tears to well in my eyes, the tears I have been forcing back since tonight's visit to the emergency room, where I realized my son might be sicker than I thought. Climbing down the bunk ladder, I stare at Eli asleep in his bed. The strange part is that although he is sweating, he is not tossing or turning as much as I have been and his breathing is unencumbered by the watery rattle we heard before. Dr. Riordian did give Eli a steroid shot, which he said would make it easier for him to breathe, but I cannot stop hoping that my son's mysterious ailment has somehow cured itself. If Norman Troyer hadn't crossed my path when we were in Pennsylvania, I know I would not be taking Eli to the pediatric hematologist, Mandy Vaughan, regardless of how highly Dr. Riordian recommends her. All my life, I've been taught that natural remedies are the only true cure. But now, after I know that even a renowned holistic *doktor* believes in the power of modern-day medicine, I find my whole point of view has become skewed right at the time I need clear vision the most.

I nestle the afghan around Eli's body, then reach out and

take his hand, which curls around my fingers although he is asleep. When the unthinkable happened and I became with child, I stopped allowing myself to yearn for the companionship of a mate. I knew that Plain men would not yoke themselves with a woman whom the community perceived as damaged goods, even if one in the community had helped inflict the damage. Although I mourned the union I had always dreamed of but would now never have, I got through it by telling myself that I would have the resilience to bear whatever hardships came my way, even if I had to bear them alone.

All of this made sense at the time. But tonight, staring at Eli—who is oblivious to the cares of this world such as insurance and blood tests—I feel the vulnerability of our situation more than ever before. If Judah King were still here and his offer of marriage still stood, I would be sorely tempted to accept.

But would it be out of convenience—simply to make hardships like this one easier to bear—rather than out of love? Or maybe hardships scrape away life's dross, allowing us to clearly see in hindsight the person who was always meant for us . . . until he grew weary of being taken for granted and was gone.

I don't go with Ida Mae to her Pentecostal church the next morning because two inches of snow and sleet fell during the night, and the gray sky seems frozen solid with cold—conditions I shouldn't take a sickly child out in. I want to let Eli sleep as long as he needs to, but as the hours pass in silence, I find myself entering our bedroom and putting a hand to his chest to make sure I can feel its steady rise and fall. Bored at ten o'clock, I put on my warmest dress and tights and make my bed, wipe down the kitchen counters, and sweep the floor. I go into the bathroom to clean because it looks about as necessary as getting an ox out of a ditch on the Sabbath. After scouring the tub, I work on the sink and rinse the flotsam of hair and toothpaste down the drain. I glance up into the mirror to see if it's been spattered with toothpaste as well, and that's when I notice my haggard reflection.

Taking out my bobby pins, I uncoil my waist-length hair. The strands are lank and darkened from a winter of barely seeing the sun. Years ago, when I started noticing the boys starting to notice me, I would spritz my hair with lemon juice and hydrogen peroxide and lie out on the back porch with my hair swirled across the hot boards. For hours, I would let the UV rays penetrate deep into my scalp, sometimes burning the skin of my center part a vermilion that peeled and made it look like I had dandruff—which more than canceled out any pretty highlights the sun might've bleached. My parents never knew about this vanity of mine because I always waited until they had gone into town to do it. But my sister sure did. Although Leah never uttered one word of censure, the pinch of her lips relayed her disapproval. When I asked her about it, Leah said she disapproved of my secrecy more than the act itself.

Now, spooling my hair around my fist, I curl my hand under to see how my hair would look at shoulder length. The mere thought of it gives me a foretaste of freedom that is inexplicably sweet. I envision my ears pierced with the silver baubles I have always admired, shining through short, frosted locks framing an *Englischer* woman's made-up face. I bite my lips and scrub my cheeks, giving them the rosy glow they haven't had in more than a year. Carried away by my girlhood dreams that are now within reach, I rifle through the cupboard above the toilet, searching for forgotten makeup or perfume to try.

I don't find anything except a tube of cherry-flavored ChapStick and an aging bottle of Love's Baby Soft. Swiping my lips with the tube, I spray some of the perfume and wonder whether Ida Mae has any jewelry I can borrow. I never see her wearing any, but I imagine all *Englischer* women have a stash somewhere. Feeling abnormally bold, I walk into Ida Mae's bedroom and look at the wooden jewelry box sitting on top of her bureau. I check the top section for a pair of clip-on earrings, so I can see what I'd look like with pierced ears, but there are just a few strands of cheap beads that have pieces cracked or shattered. Tugging open the shallow drawer beneath the top section of the jewelry box, I am disappointed to find no jewelry—only a pair of glasses with the thick lenses so shattered, they cannot be of use. That piques my curiosity, because Ida Mae doesn't even need glasses for reading.

Finally, in the back of the little drawer, I discover a large, thick piece of paper, tightly rolled up with a thin gold wedding band around it. I pause and peer out into the living room. My search has moved beyond an innocent hunt for jewelry, and I wonder if I should stop. But my hands seem to have a mind of their own. I carefully slide the wedding band off the paper. My fingers shake as I unroll it, not because I am scared of what the paper might reveal but because I am scared that I am going to be caught. I furtively scan the document: a gold-embossed wedding certificate declaring that holy matrimony took place between Russell Maynard Speck and Ida Mae Troyer on September 15, 1992, at the Cumberland County courthouse. There is a woman's name, Erin Speck, as one witness; Norman Troyer is the other.

My eyes flit back up to that last spidery signature and read over the names again. Ida Mae *Troyer*? Norman *Troyer*? I know the odds are that this is not the same Norman Troyer as the holistic *doktor* in Lancaster. That last name is as common among the Amish and Mennonites as Smith is throughout the rest of the nation. But as I roll the marriage license up and slide the wedding band over it, I have to wonder: Are Ida Mae and Norman somehow related? And if they are, how? And how can I ask Ida Mae about him, since the only way I could have found this out was by rooting through her private things?

Before I can damage my character even further, I hear Eli begin to stir in his bed. Glancing back at the jewelry box and inside the bathroom, I reassure myself that everything is in its place and walk over to the blue room to comfort my son.

The morning of Eli's appointment with the pediatric hematologist, I am unusually silent. I know that if I begin to speak, I will have to tell Ida Mae about the second lump that I discovered when I was changing Eli's diaper last night. It was larger and firmer than the lump on his neck, and I had so quickly felt alongside Eli's other leg with my cold, panicked hands that he startled and began to cry. But even before I found that second lump, my maternal instincts were telling me that my son's sickness is from more than a wintertime cold, that Eli's slight body is being inhabited by an illness threatening to overtake it. Throughout childhood, my *mamm* said that I was far too independent, that I made decisions based on feelings rather than on sound judgment. That was true the night Eli was conceived, and though I try to fight my tendency to be rash, sometimes that is true still. But now it is not *my* life hanging in the balance according to the decisions I make, but my son's. What if the doctor needs to run some kind of test on Eli that I refuse because of my holistic beliefs? What if my attempt to protect him only thwarts his ability to get better? What if I make the wrong decision, and it is too late to turn back and find the right one?

Ida Mae pulls up in front of the clinic and slips her truck into park. Last night, we agreed that I would go into the appointment by myself and then call her when it was over. But now, knowing that I am to face this all alone, I begin shaking so badly I cannot unhook the fastenings of Eli's car seat.

Stretching across the seat, Ida Mae puts her sandpapered hand over mine. "Rachel-girl," she says, her voice softer than I have ever heard it, "you go on in. I'll call Russell and tell him to open the store; then I'll come in to be with ya."

I stare at my son's legs flailing in the car seat, then nod and blink hard to keep tears from falling onto my cheeks.

In the waiting room, the receptionist with jet-black hair cropped like a boy's and sparkly pink lipstick passes me a clipboard layered with papers that I must fill out. Sitting down, I realize that a majority of the information the papers ask for I cannot provide. Eli has no primary care physician; he has not had any of the immunizations listed. I do not have a telephone number; I do not even have Ida Mae's address memorized. I obviously cannot write Eli's father's information down. In doing so, I would be wreaking havoc in more directions than I can name. As my anxiety increases, so do the jolting feelings inside my body. I look up from the papers at the jacketed children sitting on their mothers' laps or playing with colorful plastic toys on the floor. I then notice that about half of these mothers are observing Eli and me as though we are some strange specimens trapped in a jar.

The vibrations of fear reverberating throughout my body morph into anger. I slam the clipboard in my lap. "Don't you know it's considered rude to stare?"

The women who were watching us drop their eyes to their children or to their clipboards like my own. The ones who weren't looking glance up, searching around the room for a face to match to the sound of the voice. When their flittering eyes alight on me in my conservative cape dress and black lace-up shoes, their mouths gape open like they have forgotten how to breathe. Embarrassed by my flash of temper, I draw Eli close and act like I am filling out information when I don't know how to begin.

"Eli?" a nurse says. "Is there an Eli Stoltz—" she looks down at her clipboard—"Stoltzfoos here?"

"Yes. We're here." I stand and look out the window toward the parking lot, where Ida Mae's leaning against the brick wall, talking on her phone. When she sees me, she mutters something and snaps the phone shut.

"You'll come in with me?" I ask once she enters the clinic.

But Ida Mae is already moving past me toward the nurse. "What?" she says, looking over her shoulder. "You think I'm gonna let my young'uns go through this rigmarole alone?"

# 12

## Rachel

Dr. Mandy Vaughan smiles when she comes into the antiseptic room and sees our unusual trio waiting there: Ida Mae, with her flanneled arms crossed, watching the doctor's every move through distrustful brown eyes; Eli, happily gnawing on a wooden block carved with the letter *D*; and me, wearing a cape dress whose somber hue contrasts with the bloom of fear in my cheeks.

Taking the stool opposite us, Dr. Vaughan crosses her legs and moistens her lips. She smiles again.

Eli's cooing and the ticking of the black-and-white clock are the only sounds in the room.

"Miss Stoltzfus . . ."

I nod to reassure Dr. Vaughan that I am listening, but it takes effort to register my own name.

"Miss Stoltzfus, your son's blood work came back showing that his white counts are abnormally high." She stops and clears her throat.

My eyes will her to continue, as my mouth is too stunned to work. Finally, she swallows hard and looks back at us. "Because of this and because of a small mass that showed up on the chest X-ray, Dr. Riordian and I have agreed that he should be tested further. Tomorrow, I would like to schedule an FNA—that is, a fine-needle aspiration biopsy—for the lumps in Eli's neck and groin and a CAT scan for this Friday."

"A cat scan?" Ida Mae's question is distorted by the ringing in my ears. "What on earth's that?"

"*C-A-T* stands for computerized axial tomography. Simply put, it's where patients' veins are injected with a radioactive dye, and then they are sent through a tube that takes X-rays that will reveal anything foreign in the body."

Resting my chin on Eli's head, I rotate my jaw from side to side, trying to relieve the horrible ache from having to hold back my scream. Eli's alphabet block drops to the examining table. Like an automaton, I reach down and pass it back. "What—what kind of foreign thing?" I stammer.

Dr. Vaughan meets my eyes. For a moment, I can peer beneath her bedside manner to the sorrow emanating from the difficult words she has been preparing herself to speak.

"I'm going to be honest with you, Miss Stoltzfus." She breaks eye contact and looks at her hands. "I am scheduling this CAT scan so close to the fine-needle biopsy because I want . . . I want to rule out any possibilities of cancer."

Breath empties from my lungs. My arms constrict around Eli as if they possess the power to keep the menace away, even a menace threatening to destroy my child from the inside out. "Cancer?" The word is muted into a whimper.

Still, Dr. Vaughan can read the toxic form of it in my mouth. "Yes, Miss Stoltzfus. But don't get me wrong; I am not saying that cancer is what Eli has. It's just that with his symptoms—" the doctor rattles them off like a grocery list, although, when added up, they lead to a diagnosis bringing with it the possibility of death—"high white counts, difficulty breathing, night sweats, fevers, weight loss, and swollen glands . . . Well, with symptoms like that, I want to rule out the worst. I've always believed the sooner we know what we are dealing with, the better we can deal with it. No matter *what* it is."

I bow my head over Eli and silently bathe his downy blond hair with tears. My frantic heartbeat thuds against the upper portion of his chest where the mass must be. *Oh, Lord, please,* I beg. *Forgive me. Don't pour your wrath out on my child because of what your wayward child's done.*

My son looks up as my sobbing chest palpitates against his own. Wiping my eyes with my fist, I breathe deep and attempt to smile at him. He smiles back, his blue eyes trusting that I possess the ability to keep him out of harm's way. My no-longer-restrained sobs ricochet throughout the room. Over them, I hear Ida Mae get up from the chair. The paper sheet crinkles as she sits on the examination table beside me. She wraps an arm around my quaking shoulders, buoying me up when I feel like I am drowning beneath the weight of two benign syllables that crash together to reveal a malignant word.

"I'm sorry, Miss Stoltzfus," Dr. Vaughan says, "that I even have to mention that word in regard to your son." When I do not reply in the pause, she adds, "I'll see you tomorrow, then. Tomorrow at ten."

Ida Mae, her voice thick with tears, asks, "What about insurance? I don't know much 'bout medical things, but I know that when you start mentioning biopsies and scans, we're talking big money. This girl don't got insurance. She don't even have a car."

"I'm afraid I can't help you there." My eyes remain clenched, but I can tell that Dr. Vaughan has slipped into her role of the detached doctor again. "But if more testing is required, you will be assigned a social worker who will help you figure out your financial situation. Until then, go down to the billing department on the first floor. They might be able to answer your questions."

The door clicks as Dr. Vaughan exits. Every muscle in my body spasms; my teeth chatter inside my throbbing skull. Passing Eli to Ida Mae, I turn and bury my face in the paper covering the examination table. I pull the thin pillow up to my mouth and release the scream that has been building inside my chest since Dr. Vaughan stepped into the room wearing her white lab coat and her nervous smile.

For a long time, Ida Mae does not start the truck. She and I just sit, staring through the dirty windshield up at the multitiered hospital aglitter with mica. Eli babbles in the car seat between us, oblivious to the troubled maze of our thoughts. Ida Mae says, "A biopsy . . . I'm telling ya, that don't mean a thing. I had one a few years back 'cause I had this lump in my breast, but here there was nothing to it. It just meant I was drinking too much coffee."

Unforeseen terror stops up my throat. I wonder if I'll be able to speak or fully breathe until the biopsy results are in my hands, until I know that all of this is actually nothing.

Ida Mae turns on the engine, and the radio flares to life, its jaunty tune grating against our shattered nerves. She snaps it off. "Where should I take ya? Home?" Ida Mae waits for my answer, then adds, "If ever you needed a mom and a sister, I say it's now."

"No." My frustration is evident even in a fragment. "I told you. I can't go back. Some people, they . . . they might try to stop me from getting Eli tested."

"You mean his dad, huh?"

I look at Ida Mae sharply, but she is staring straight ahead. Her bitten fingernails gouge the steering wheel as she drives out of the parking lot. "But mostly my *mamm*," I say. "She doesn't believe in modern-day medicine."

"Your mom's one thing," Ida Mae says. "But don't you think Eli's dad has to sign some kinda permission form before the tests can even be started?"

My stomach roils at the thought of that man's signature being required to save my son's life. "So far Eli's father's only been involved the night he was conceived," I say, the words bitter granules on my tongue. "I'm not about to take the chance that, just because Eli might be sick, he would feel guilty and want to become involved now."

"Welp," Ida Mae says, merging into traffic, "if you're not gonna tell Eli's dad or your momma, you still might want to tell your twin."

*"Please."* I rest my temple against the window. Leftover tears smear the glass, although my hot eyes are dry. "I really don't want to talk about this. Just take me home."

"My home?"

I sigh. "What other home do I have?"

## AMOS

On their way to the hospital the next morning, Ida Mae drives past a barbershop advertising a haircut and shave for ten dollars. "Actually—" Rachel turns and looks out the rear window—"I want to get my hair cut first."

"Your hair cut?" Ida Mae repeats. "Like a trim?"

"No. Like a transformation. I want this—" Rachel indicates the beautiful hair coiled on the back of her head—"this whole thing gone."

"But you've never had it cut."

"I know. That's why I want to."

"Today?"

Flipping down the visor, Rachel uses the mirror to locate her bobby pins. "Yes. Today." The pins begin filling Rachel's lap, and her hair unravels like yarn. "I need to be in control of something—*anything*—and this is the only thing I can think of."

Ida Mae bumps her truck over the yellow cement barriers slowing down traffic in front of the barbershop. "This is where guys get their hair cut. Not girls. You know that, right?"

"What's that matter?" Rachel says. "Hair's hair. It's not like they can mess it up."

Rachel is already smiling as she walks toward the glass door with its spinning candy-striped pole outside, and Ida Mae doesn't have the heart to dissuade her.

But twenty minutes later, a mere hour before Eli's surgery, Ida Mae wishes she had said something. Rachel is now leaning against the passenger's side of the truck with a twenty-three-inch ponytail coiled in her lap. She doesn't say anything, as she didn't say anything when the man started hacking away at her virgin hair as if he were cutting wheat in a field.

"It'll grow," Ida Mae says, reaching over and touching the blunt strands of Rachel's shoulder-length hair. "It'll grow back in no time."

Shrugging, Rachel continues to stare out the window.

Ida Mae glances over. "You all right?"

"I'm *fine*."

The air is an orchestra of silence before Ida Mae makes the turn into the hospital. Rachel, staring at the cement building, drags fingernails through her shorn hair like she is trying to scrape the remnants from her scalp. "I am not about to cry over my hair when my four-month-old son might have cancer."

"But it's okay to grieve, too," Ida Mae says. "Sometimes it's easier to grieve over something not related to your pain than it is over the pain itself."

"And what do you know about pain?" Rachel snaps. "All you've ever done was *cause* pain by sending away the man who loves you."

Ida Mae parks in front of the clinic and shuts off the engine. "Rachel-girl," she says, her hand still wrapped around the keys, "I hope you never know my kinda pain. It's the kinda pain that sneaks up on you and knocks you flat before you can even breathe. It's the kinda pain that is the first thing on your mind when you get up, and the last thing on your mind before you start to dreaming. It's everywhere and it's everything, yet it's nothing, too, 'cause nobody wants to hear it. Nobody has time for somebody's grieving twenty years after that grieving's supposed to be through."

She looks over at Rachel. Tears pour down the face of the girl whose age is the same as the age of Ida Mae's grief, tears that have been festering deep inside the cracks of Rachel's wounded soul until their poison could be drained.

"I'm sorry," Rachel whispers, wiping her forearm across her jaw. "I didn't mean what I said about Russell. About you—you sending him away."

"And it's all right if you did," Ida Mae says. "But I don't think you were talking about Russell right then. I think you said that 'cause you're feeling guilty for sending Judah away. The man who loves *you*."

## Rachel

My body thrums with adrenaline. After one week of gut-wrenching anxiety following Eli's tests, we're once again in Dr. Vaughan's office. She points over to a table splashed with rays pouring down from a skylight. I do not want to sit there; I want to run. I want to run from the hospital and from the stark reality of what the pediatric hematologist has to say. As if sensing this, Dr. Vaughan presses fingertips to the steel bar of my spine and guides me into a chair. Taking the seat across from my own, she crosses her legs and moistens her lips. Her professional reserve is the same as it was at our first meeting, yet I can discern a troubled shadow now lurking behind Mandy Vaughan's guarded eyes.

"Miss Stoltzfus . . . Rachel . . ." She squares her shoulders beneath the white lab coat. "Eli's results have come back."

Dropping my gaze, I trail my index finger over the gold threading the table's faux marble surface, buying time until I can gather courage for what I'm about to learn. "And . . . ?"

"And it looks to be what we feared. Cancerous cells were found in both of the needle biopsies taken from Eli's neck and groin, and the CAT lit up a solid mass within Eli's chest about the size of a ping-pong ball, which explains his difficulty breathing."

Dr. Vaughan reaches across the table to touch the top of my hand. But I am so shocked by this information, I cannot feel; I can't even cry. The vibrations that started in my chest the morning of Eli's first doctor's appointment, then radiated throughout my body, have finally stopped. That sensation has been replaced by an odd numbness, like I am being baptized in a frozen pond and still haven't been brought back to the surface. I wonder how long it will take for reality to come splintering in through this frozen tundra of my thoughts. How long until keening grief takes hold, even as the little one I am grieving hardly shows signs of this life-threatening disease.

"Rachel?" Dr. Vaughan says. "Do you understand what I'm saying? Do you have someone I should call?"

"It's because of what I've done, isn't it?" I ask, still staring at the table, whose pattern blurs from the tears filling my eyes. "My sin's being carried down to the next generation. Just like in the Bible."

Dr. Mandy Vaughan clutches my roughened fingers with her manicured ones. She is no longer an *Englischer doktor*, and I am no longer the distraught mother of her patient. Instead, we are two women sharing a burden before the full weight of it can be felt.

"We don't know why things happen to innocent children such as Eli," she whispers, "but they do. I've seen it time and time again. It helps no one to blame yourself for your son's sickness, to become lackadaisical because you feel like nothing about this can be changed, that this is predestined because of something in your past. What you need to do, Rachel, is prepare yourself for a battle, make yourself strong. Eli's going to need you now more than ever."

I nod to convey my understanding. Inside, however, I can feel a fire wall of self-preservation erecting itself around my heart. I do not only blame myself. I also blame the man who continues to live beneath a facade of self-righteousness, even though his soul is marred with the same scarlet stain as mine, as malignant as our son's cancer.

"Now, Rachel-girl," Ida Mae says, "don't wanna hear no fussing from you. I'm taking you home."

"But I don't have anything packed. Eli's diapers—"

Ida Mae points to the floorboard of her truck. I look down, and my mouth goes dry. That bag is the one I took when Verna King forced me to leave Leah and Tobias's home, the one Judah packed when he came to Blackbrier to ask for my hand in marriage. That single bag drags as many feelings to the surface as the cataclysmic information I have just gleaned.

"I'm not ready to go back," I say.

Reaching over Eli's car seat, Ida Mae pats my shoulder. "I know that. But I also know that when push comes to shove, family should band together and put differences behind them."

"You don't know my family," I whisper.

"And, honey," Ida Mae says, "you sure don't know mine."

I'm hoping my thoughts will return to the numbing void they fell into after meeting with Dr. Vaughan, but the longer I remain in the narrow twin bed shoved under the eaves of my parents' *dawdi haus*, the more my mind spins out the worst possible scenarios. Keeping the top quilt around me, I slip out of bed and kneel in front of Eli's pallet on the floor. I watch him slumber like the babe he is and find myself grateful that his young age doesn't allow him to be exposed to the debilitating fear of the mature.

Kissing Eli's cheek, which causes his mouth to start a sucking motion although he cannot be hungry, I lace up my shoes and tiptoe across the living room and open the front door. The night sky is heavy with the promise of snow, the stars and clouds shielded by the grayish fog preceding a winter storm. I glance over at the white farmhouse and see a light shining through the kitchen window, casting a pattern of blocks on the old snow and trampled grasses in the side yard. Leah became so distraught when I told her and my parents the news, I feared letting her walk the short distance back to her house. Now I imagine she is having the same difficulty sleeping as I.

The grass, sheathed in a veneer of ice, cracks beneath my feet as I shuffle toward the house while dragging the cloak of my quilt behind me. Climbing the porch steps, I expel a breath that becomes a puff of smoke in the cold. I don't knock on the door, as I do not want to alert anyone of my presence except for my sister sitting in that dimly lit kitchen. Using a piece of quilt as a pad for my hand to turn the icy doorknob, I enter the house and call out, "Leah?"

The heavy tread across the floor in the next room tells me the person still up is not Leah. Tobias fills the kitchen doorway with his large hands fisted at his sides. I flinch, stepping backward as he moves toward me, but he only walks faster. Seizing my elbow, he drags me toward the door. I scramble to retain my footing, and the quilt becomes tangled beneath my shoes. It unravels from my body and drops to the floor.

Tobias opens the door and tosses me out. I think he is going to close the door and lock it, but after a second, he returns and throws the quilt at me. Stepping onto the porch and shutting the door behind him, he plods down the steps. I wrap the quilt around my nightgown and follow. The two of us hunker beneath the stripped branches of a sycamore tree, and though it is the most frightful night we've had all winter, Tobias seems oblivious to its cold. He just stands there, staring at me, his eyes so dark they are impenetrable.

Tobias looks down, as do I. The grass and leftover ice have shattered beneath our combined weight. "Leah said he's bad," he rasps. "That true?"

"Yes. The cancer's spread to more than just one lymph node."

"What are you going to do?"

"Chemotherapy. Treatments start next week."

The wind peels up a loosened piece of tin and smacks it against the roof of the barn.

"Do you need money?" he asks. "A driver?"

For the past year my brother-in-law has never offered me anything but rebuke. Now, when I just need someone who understands the full depth of my sorrow, I am certain that Bishop Tobias King is simply trying to manipulate me into silence.

"No. I don't need your money *or* your driver." I hurl the words at Tobias like shards of ice. "Who would you get to drive me—the fallen woman of Copper Creek—anyway? Surely not Gerald Martin. Didn't you already pay him not to?"

Tobias clenches the tops of my arms and jerks me toward him. Peering down into my face, he brings his own closer. "You can't keep this up, Rachel." The anger in his voice is inconsistent with the sadness in his eyes. "Your bitterness will only destroy you."

"I'm not bitter, Tobias. I am angry. I am angry that you live in your white farmhouse with your family the same as you've always done. While I—who have done nothing you haven't—*I* have been cast out of the community and left to fend for myself and my fatherless child."

"I never knew any of this would happen," Tobias says. "I never dreamed—"

I shrug off his grasp and lower myself deeper inside the quilt. "We never do. It's not until consequences are made visible that we understand what we've done."

"I hope you know I would do anything for you and Eli . . . if I could."

Looking up at Bishop Tobias King, I see a man tortured by the same mistakes as I, yet with nothing to show for these mistakes except what he hides from the world. For the first time, I understand that my plight might be the easier cross to bear. "If you could, Tobias," I say. "*If* you could. But you won't. That was obvious a year ago when I told you what happened, and you turned from me."

"I had no choice!"

"And *I* did?"

"I offered you money, but you wouldn't take it."

"*No!* I wouldn't take your money. I couldn't. Not if I was going to keep my self-respect."

Folding his arms, Tobias stares out across his land that has increased in acreage since his father's death. I turn and look at it too: at the rolling hillsides iced with white, the way one field is distinguished from another only by the rustic fence posts dolloped with snow.

"What's going to happen?" he whispers. "I don't mean you and me. I mean to all of us." He unlaces an arm and casts out a hand to take in these fields. "All of *this*. What's going to happen if the truth comes out?"

"You will survive," I say, and though I try, there is no compassion in my voice. "It will be hard. At first you will feel like you are dying, but then one day follows into the next, a week becomes a month, and you realize that life goes on . . . although it is not the same life you knew before."

Tobias shakes his head. "I won't do it; I won't tell. There's too much at risk. My family, the community—"

"Your reputation, your pride."

His face hardens along with his voice. "That's enough, Rachel. You have said your piece."

"So we're back to that now, are we?" I force myself not to be cowed by his domineering tone. "You're once again the bishop, and I am the fallen woman of Copper Creek?"

"No. I may not have always been the bishop, but you have never been anything but a fallen woman. Like Eve giving the apple to Adam, *you* alone are the reason I fell."

The quilt slips from my shoulders at the same time my right hand whips out and smacks Tobias's face. Exposed to the elements for so long, my fingers have gone numb, but now they tingle and sting from the impact of skin striking skin. Tobias does not rub his bearded jaw or even wince. Angling his head, he just looks at me. In his black gaze, I can see a steely resolve that chills my bones more than the oncoming storm.

## AMOS

The afternoon Tobias came into my office and took the chair across from my desk—the desk that has been carried down through the King *familye* since we came to the New World to escape the persecution of the Old—I could see by his troubled face that something was weighing heavily on his mind. I knew Tobias had come there to discuss it, and I was honored that he trusted my discretion enough to confide in me. But I was so eager to speak with my first-born for the first time in weeks, I wanted to catch up on trivial things: the new residents being born, the ones who had died, the families who were just arriving in Copper Creek, and the ones who were leaving in hopes of acquiring more land. After we had discussed these changes, Tobias cleared his throat and stared at his hands in his lap, as if too ashamed to meet my eyes.

I couldn't understand it, because I could not imagine what my eldest had to be ashamed about. Once again, I didn't want Tobias to speak, to ruin such a delightful visit with talk that would surely upset me, since I carried each of my children's burdens like they were my own. But when I stood to check whether Verna had any egg custard pie in the *kich*, Tobias held up his hand and said, "*Dawdy*, please. Sit down. You must hear what I have come to say."

The moment those words left my son's mouth, I was taken. It happened so fast, I could not say good-bye. I couldn't get my papers in order like I had always hoped. I couldn't hug my wife or kiss my children. I couldn't push my *grosskinner* one at a time, one more time, on the tire swing attached to the sycamore. I was simply whisked from one world and placed in the next, a world unlike any I have ever known. I do love it here—with all the tears wiped from our eyes, how could I not?—but for weeks after I watched my temporal body being lowered into its earthly grave, I wondered why I died without any warning. I had thought that the Lord and I had such a sweet communion that he would tell me, like Moses, when it was time.

I have come to realize, however, that when I passed away, my affairs were more in order than I knew. My wife and I were enjoying the best years of our marriage. My children were all grown, and most of them had birthed children of their own, who all filled me with more joy than I thought was possible. I loved the Copper Creek Community, and I loved leading the humble flock of our church in seeking the ways of God.

I thank the Lord for taking me when he did, even though I did not understand his ways, which are higher than mine. Now, I can gaze down upon the grief my firstborn has caused, and I can forgive him because my vantage point here is much better than it was on earth, when I foolishly evaded Tobias's confession. You see, after I died and the paper in the *Ausbund* declared Tobias bishop, pride in his newfound title would not allow my son to confess to a deacon what he and Rachel had done. Inadvertent though it was, I condoned Tobias's sin by allowing him to remain in darkness. The only ability I long for is to help Tobias and Rachel. If I could somehow communicate to him that repentance is much more important than pride, and to her that forgiveness will break chains while anger will only keep her in bondage, I am certain they could get through this pain without causing themselves or others permanent scars. But without applying the balm of repentance and forgiveness, if Leah finds out, or—I cannot bear to think it—my precious wife, I don't know how their heartbreak will ever heal.

Even though the Lord does wipe the tears from our eyes, that does not mean this cloud of witnesses is exempt from feeling empathy for those hurting below. If I could shed tears over the direness of Rachel and Tobias's situation, I would. But I cannot. I cannot cry over it, and I cannot mend that which I have not torn. Instead, I turn my thoughts to Judah, my youngest, who has never brought anything to my life but joy.

Judah has traveled far from home, all the way to Cody, Wyoming. At this moment, he is sitting on a stool, wiping beer froth from his lip with the back of his hand.

I do not believe it is the biased opinion of a *vadder* when I say that something sets Judah apart from the rest of the men parking their sorrows at the bar. I see how the women watch him from their positions around the pool table, which holds a game they have no interest to play, as their aim is far more strategic. Cringing, I watch as one young woman with brown hair tangled down to a slender waist bends over the pool table and gives Judah a smile that somehow seems exposed. But my son is oblivious. He just keeps nursing his beer and cracking peanuts that he picks out of the shells but does not eat. I do not need this heavenly perspective to know what has hardened my son's heart and snuffed the light from his eyes. If I hadn't been so terrified of our Lancaster County bishop, I might have gone to a bar myself that first time Verna turned me down for open-buggy courting. But my son doesn't have any bishops around to fear, and I know he would not fear them even if he did. His feeling of rejection has consumed him to the point where he cannot feel anything else.

When you are twenty years old and the only woman you have ever loved has spurned not only you but also your love, it seems like life just isn't worth living. This is why Judah is seated in the Watering Trough with a fake ID purchased from a rodeo clown burning in his back pocket. This is why, when that young woman with the tangled brown hair comes sidling over and touches Judah's back, he looks at her and smiles. This, and a loneliness unlike any he has ever known, is why he invites her to sit beside him and purchases another mug of beer.

As the late-night crowd gathers, the room grows darker. The woman leans over, her perfumed hair blanketing Judah's right arm, and pulls his other arm so that his barstool spins and he has no choice but to walk with her onto the dance floor. My son has never danced in his life. This would be obvious except for the fact that this woman knows her moves. Twining her arms around his neck, she steps so close, her belt buckle grinds against his. She sways her body to the music. Judah does the same. I watch how he peers over this woman's head and out through the bar's smoke-stained window. I hope that just like Joseph with Potiphar's wife, he will flee temptation and make his escape.

Trailing her nails along Judah's neck, the woman leans up and whispers. At first his face blanches, and then red sweeps the sides of his cheeks. He nods. The woman laces her fingers through his and leads him from the dance floor. The last image I allow myself is of Judah helping the woman into her jacket and walking with her out the door.

Thankful that even in my present state, I am privileged to intercede for my loved ones, I implore Judah's heavenly Father to intervene in his life in a way I am no longer able to. I notice, not for the first time since I've found myself here, that my prayers pierce the heavens with a power

I had always imagined when I knelt and beseeched the throne from earth. I can only hope they will make a difference before foolishness destroys my younger son, just as it is threatening to destroy his brother.

# 13

## Rachel

Although I am sure Leah's meal is delicious, each bite rolls around in my mouth like sand. This morning, when Leah invited me and our parents to supper, I knew I could not decline without revealing that something was wrong beyond my son's illness. But I also knew I would be unable to act as if everything were fine when it is not. For this reason, I do not know how Tobias can just sit at the head of the table, which demonstrates his place as the head of the King home, and smile and laugh as if he hasn't a care in this world. He even attempts to draw me into a conversation regarding the expansion of Copper Creek. The hypocrisy of his acting cordial toward me in public—when he knows full well what has taken place between us in private—fills me with such loathing, I cannot unclench my jaw long enough to reply.

"Creamed *welschkann*, Rachel?" my *mamm* asks.

I shake my head, but she passes the bowl to me anyway. Perhaps she senses that if she can keep my mouth filled, I will not be able to open it. Taking an obligatory scoop, I pass the bowl over to my father, who dumps half the contents onto his plate and reaches for another heel of salt-rising *brot*.

"This is nice," Leah says, looking at her husband from the opposite end of the table. I cannot help but note how her eyes shine, which causes tears to well up in my own. "We haven't all sat around the same table since our wedding. Have we, Tobias?"

He shakes his head and smiles, swallows his small mouthful of food. For a country-raised Mennonite, he has impeccable manners, which only emphasizes my belief that you can look the part of the honored bishop but still be a barbarian inside.

"Rachel?" my *mamm* says. "Would you help me a moment?"

Pushing my chair back and passing Eli to my eldest niece, Miriam, I follow my *mamm* into Leah's kitchen. Even as a young child, I could always tell when my *mamm* was about to lose her temper from the way she would bunch the muscles of her shoulders around her neck or walk across the floor with the rigidity of a windup doll. Now she is doing both. Jabbing a finger back toward the mudroom, my *mamm* continues walking and I follow, feeling like I am five years old again and about to get my behind swatted with a spoon.

Earth and must combined with lye and freeze-dried clothes fill my nostrils. My *mamm* slants her body against the wooden shelf labeled, in my sister's calligraphy-worthy hand, with each of the children's names along with hers and Tobias's. On wash day, each cubbyhole is filled with folded laundry that the four older children then take up to their rooms and put away in their respective drawers, which are also labeled: *socks* and *underwear*, *pants* for the boys, *dresses* for the girls.

"She's some housekeeper," I remark, still staring at the shelves.

My *mamm* ignores this, grabs my upper arm. "What do you think you're doing?" she hisses. "I know you're upset, but you have *got* to stop this *ferhoodled* behavior!"

"What are you talking about?" I groan. "What did I do *now*?"

"You just keep sitting there, not saying a word to anyone. Leah's prepared this *nachtesse* especially for you, and I won't let you ruin it!"

"My son's just been diagnosed with cancer, *Mamm*. Forgive me if I'm not feeling cheerful."

"That's still no excuse! And the way you keep looking

at Tobias . . ." She digs her fingernails into the flesh of my arm. "I taught you better than that."

I do not defend my behavior toward my brother-in-law, knowing my silence will both condemn our past actions and explain my present anger.

"*Ach*, *Gott* forgive you," my *mamm* breathes as the puzzle of my child's paternity slides into place. "I don't know how it happened, but you . . ." She stops and grapples both my cheeks in one hand, forcing me to face her, to meet her probing eyes. I am filled with indignation at being treated like such a child when I have a child of my own, but I know even if I were forty-five and my mother eighty, she would treat me just the same. "You had *better* keep the secret regarding Eli's *vadder* to yourself." My *mamm* shoves my head away, and it knocks against the side of the shelf.

"I am not the only one who's sinned," I say, rubbing my cheekbone.

"But *you* are the only one responsible for *your* sin, and I won't have Leah dragged into this. She has just gotten her strength back. I will not allow you to take it from her!"

I wield my tongue to fillet her with a reply, but when I open my mouth to speak, my voice cracks. In that briefest pause, I find that all fight is taken from me. I turn to face the shelves so my mother cannot see my tears. Looking at those names my sister carefully wrote for each member of her family, however, only causes me to weep even more. "I am just tired, *Mamm*," I say. "I am tired of living with my mistakes and knowing I will die by them. I am tired of being treated like a child when I am a woman, have become more of a woman in the past four months than I have in three years, and I am tired of being punished alone for a sin that I did not commit alone."

I face my *mamm*. Even in the shadows, I can see the glint of her cobalt eyes. I think its source is anger, but then she swipes her palms across her cheeks, and I know she is crying too.

"My *meedel* . . ." *Mamm* reaches out and cups my wet cheeks, bruised by the force of her fingers. "You do not have to live with your mistakes if you're willing to admit them and turn from them. Even this can be forgiven by our *Gott*. But you will never be able to turn if you remain focused on Tobias's sin."

Pans clatter in the *becken*. *Mamm* drops her hands from my face as we turn and see the kerosene bulb sprouting to life, filling the kitchen with an illumination brighter than electricity. Leah, her voice so sweetly unselfconscious it is almost like a child's, begins to sing. *"Gott ist die Liebe, läßt mich erlösen; Gott ist die Liebe, er liebt auch mich."* She scrapes plates and dumps the residue in a slop bucket for the *sei*.

"What's going to happen?" My *mamm* sighs. "You can't hide it from her forever."

Swallowing, I say, "No, I probably won't be able to hide it from her forever, but I am at least going to try."

## AMOS

Leah remains in the kitchen long after the kerosene light has been extinguished, the dishes washed and put away, the children kissed and piled beneath enough quilts to weigh them down into peaceful dreams. But still she stays, her dry hands clasping the *becken*, staring through the window out into the snow-covered darkness. In this second, her careering thoughts stopping long enough that she can grasp the tail end of one, Leah pauses to stare at her own reflection, illuminated by the oil lamp's glow. She takes in her shadowed eyes, pointed face, dark-blonde hair scraped into a *kapp*, and wonders why someone who looks identical to her is the one her husband wants.

Tonight is the first in several months that Leah allows her suspicions to rouse themselves from the depths of her subconscious's slumber and raise their ugly head. She never questioned asking her sister to come live with her and Tobias because she knew Rachel would never do anything to cause her or her family harm. But with a courtship as short as theirs, Leah's husband was still a stranger when she married him, and this is where the danger lurked. Or at least this is how Leah explains it.

In the beginning, there were little things—things so minute Leah did not bother to contemplate them longer than it took to discard the incidents from her mind. Her husband did not like to be alone with Rachel. He did not like to sit near Rachel. If Rachel would enter a room, he would leave it. If she would ask him a question, he would not look up at her as he answered.

Leah didn't know her husband well enough to even know his personality, so she told herself that he was shy. But Tobias was *not* shy. He knew everyone in the surrounding communities and everyone knew him. If Gerald Martin picked them up in his spray-painted van and took them into town for supplies, Tobias would even strike up a conversation with the owner of the outlet shoe store, a heavyset *Englischer* with a gold neck chain and capped teeth. And if Tobias was discussing a smithing job with one of his customers, he would often become so caught up in a conversation about anything but smithing that Leah would have to send one of the children over to pull their *vadder* respectfully away for supper.

Her husband's awkwardness around her sister was something she could dismiss until the afternoon Leah risked the *doktor*'s strict bed-rest orders because she heard Rachel's cry echoing up from the kitchen, followed by the sound of breaking glass. It took Leah ten minutes to make the excruciatingly slow journey from the bed, to the floor, to the hallway, and then down the twenty precarious steps. Her nightgown was plastered to her sweaty skin by the time she stepped off the last stair and into the airless dining room. For almost a minute, Leah stood with one hand clinging to her chest and the other to the doorframe. But as soon as she caught her breath and peered into the kitchen, her breath was lost again.

At first, Leah could not comprehend what she was seeing. She had made her way down the stairs, not because she believed something clandestine was taking place, but because she believed her sister's cry to mean that she had injured herself. And even after Leah saw her husband and sister kneeling in that puddle of pickled beet juice as red as *blut*, her initial reaction was relief that Tobias had also heard Rachel's cry and hurried to her aid.

But then Leah saw her husband's face, saw a tenderness there he never expressed except upon their own marriage bed, the bed to which Leah was now confined. Leah saw how Rachel could not look at Tobias as he took an untarnished corner of his rag and dabbed the wine-colored stain smearing her cheek, but instead closed her eyes. Leah saw how Rachel's skin burned just as brightly as that stain, and she knew the only time her own skin burned like that was when her husband was watching her with that same tender expression.

Leah felt her insides collapse. In her mind's eye, she could see each organ as a wooden block; the last piece of the game had been pulled out, and the tower started tumbling down. She was tempted just to fall backward onto the hardwood floor and see what such a fall would cause. Leah did not want to harm the baby swimming and kicking inside her womb; she just wanted the pain in her heart to ease. Leah believed the only way she could stop this pain was by inflicting a different kind of pain upon herself. Instead, she forced breath into the steel trap of her lungs.

Prying her fingers from the doorframe, she brought her hands down by her sides, where they clenched and wrung her sweaty gown.

Leah again looked into the sweltering kitchen, where two strips of flypaper hung from the ceiling like sticky yellow streamers, and watched Tobias place his hand flat against her sister's cheek. She watched how Rachel tilted her head toward that touch. Murmuring something, Tobias got to his feet and let Rachel remain kneeling in that dark-red pool sparkling with glass shards.

Leah's husband strode out of the kitchen so quickly, she had no time to hide. All she could do was flatten her expectant body against the wall dividing the dining room from the kitchen like a child playing kick the can. Her breathing shortened to the point that it came out in ragged bursts. Leah thought for sure that Tobias would overhear her as he moved past. But he heard nothing; he *saw* nothing. And it wasn't until Tobias left the dining room and Leah heard the front door slam that she realized her husband had been so focused on her sister, he hadn't noticed his own wife standing in the next room.

Leah now picks the oil lamp up from the counter and brings it closer to the window. Leaning over the *becken* until the ceramic edge digs into her diaphragm, she twists the lamp's brass knob so that the extended wick flares and again studies her reflection—again thinking how much that reflection, that face, is so like her sister's. Heaving the oil lamp back until the flame glimmers high above her head, Leah prepares to smash it through the glass to destroy the image she sees along with the identical one that haunts her. But as always, common sense overrules her rash thoughts. Blowing out the lamp and setting it back on the counter, Leah drapes the *hunlomma* over the spigot to dry, turns and leaves the kitchen, and begins to climb the stairs.

The oddest thing about tonight—looking down the length of table laden with food she had prepared to honor her sister and watching how her husband and sister danced around each other in a taut configuration only they knew—was that the intuitional knowledge of their affair did not devastate Leah. It shook her, yes; it caused her to question everything she loved and everyone who claimed to love her. But since that afternoon Leah came downstairs and saw Tobias and Rachel kneeling in that *blut*-red spill, it was like Leah's life had been lived on borrowed time, and her internal clock had struck its final hour. Everything from here on was new, for she finally knew everything. Leah knew that Eli was Tobias's child, and that he was probably conceived under this very roof, in the very home she had opened to her twin. She remembers how she fought to keep Rachel here, sheltered from the community's harsh elements, even though her sister was pregnant with an illegitimate child. Oh, how Tobias must've laughed at her as she pleaded! How he must've felt that he had pulled the wool over Leah's eyes as he agreed to let Rachel, his lover, stay!

*Rachel . . . oh, Rachel.*

With each step Leah climbs, she can feel tears climbing

up her throat. But she swallows, forces them to remain deep within the wellspring of her soul, for if she begins to cry now, she fears she might never stop. It is heartrending to know that she was not enough to satisfy her husband, that he sought someone who looked identical to her but had more snap and fire, more zest for life that he thought would translate into a better experience on the carnal bed.

What is even more devastating than this, though, is her sister's betrayal. All their conjoined lives, they have been each other's best friend, soul mate, confidante. Leah was so satisfied with her and Rachel's effortless companionship, she had no desire for anything more. It wasn't until her *mudder* came up to their bedroom with the dark-paneled walls and curtains hanging limp in the windows and showed her the envelope titled with Tobias King's return address that Leah realized life was soon going to change. Either she left their yellow house on Hilltop Road or Rachel did, but either way, they would be separated.

Walking past the children's rooms where the girls and boys (except for Jonathan) are sleeping two to a bed, Leah stops outside the room that Rachel and Eli had occupied. She pushes open the door and steps inside, inhaling the cool air that has been trapped since mid-November along with the scent of the lavender sachets Rachel placed in each of her dresser drawers to adorn with perfume her otherwise Plain clothes.

Standing in the very room where she believes her husband and sister betrayed her, Leah should be filled with fury, with sorrow. She should want to tip over the dresser, yank out the drawers, and strew the floor with the lavender sachets before stomping the tiny blossoms to a bluish powder.

But she doesn't. Leah is still angry with her husband—as angry as she was when she watched him tonight, trying to lead her sister into a conversation she would take no part of—yet she cannot be angry with Rachel. She is hurt by her; she is so wounded, she is not sure her wounds will ever heal enough to enable her to trust her sister again. But she still loves Rachel, will *always* love Rachel, and she will not allow her sister's betrayal to destroy their bond, which was developed even before birth.

Leah eases back into the hallway and closes the door. Before entering Rachel's room, she'd stumbled upstairs as if her mind were clotted with sedative, but now she strides down the hall and softly pushes open her bedroom door.

Her husband is still awake. Leah can sense this by his breathing and by the stiff way his body is curled beneath the sheets. But Tobias doesn't turn toward her or even acknowledge that she has entered their room. Not a word is exchanged as Leah wrenches the cape dress over her head and tugs the bobby pins and *kapp* from her hair. She kicks her shoes into the corner and peels the second skin of her black tights off her legs. For the first time since Tobias began his nightly ritual of detachment because she could not forgive him for Rachel's leaving, Leah allows herself to care. Pulse throbbing, she slips beneath the quilt and barely moves, barely breathes, as she edges across the cold sheets until her body can feel her husband's body's warmth. Leah's fingertips trace her husband's shoulder with a tenderness that she does not feel, but which she hopes the familiarity of their union will be able to resurrect. Tobias turns. Tears stream from Leah's eyes and dampen her hair, and she prays that as she makes this last attempt to awaken her husband's love, he will not be longing for her sister.

## *Rachel*

As I enter the schoolhouse on Sunday morning, I can feel my cheeks and ears tingle with embarrassment. The community will not stop staring at me and the child in my arms; their faces twist with such open repugnance, it contradicts the passivity doctrine all Mennonites are to exemplify. I hold Eli tighter and keep walking down that never-ending aisle separating the women from the men. I come to the first bench seat I used to occupy with my sister, who preferred to sit up front out of support for her father-in-law, the bishop. Now it is out of support for her husband, who was granted Amos King's role by a tiny slip of paper. Sitting down and settling Eli in my lap, I am looking straight ahead with my jaws clenched when the double doors of the schoolhouse bang shut, causing an aftershock that shakes the glass in the four windows on either side of the building.

Bishop Tobias King is the one who has done this, the one who stalks up to the front and maneuvers behind the crude podium his father built to hold the *Ausbund* and perhaps a glass of water, not for decoration like the *Englischers*. Gripping the podium, Tobias looks at the members of his flock in turn.

By the wintry light slanting in through the school's oblong windows, the skin of my brother-in-law's face looks stretched until his cheekbones jut out like sabers and his nose like a beak. I have to wonder if the sin he is hiding on the inside is beginning to wear him down on the outside. I know some might think we are equally guilty of keeping our shared sin a secret. But I tell myself that Tobias's secrecy is worse than mine: he is trying to salvage his pride; I am trying to protect Leah, my sister whom I so dearly love.

Clearing his throat, Tobias looks down at the podium as if studying the text it holds. However, I can see from my position so near to his that nothing is there except for his closed German Bible, the same Bible he read from at his father's funeral two months ago. Tobias glances up and motions to old Elmer Schlabach, who sways to his feet and takes a pitch pipe from his pants pocket.

After he hits a few discordant notes, one makes it out free and clear. Elmer begins to lead the congregation—his voice as unsteady as his stance—in 131, *"O Gott, Vater, wir loben dich und deine Güte preisen."*

I am glad that I am seated up front so no one but Tobias can see that, instead of singing, I have closed my eyes to focus on the effortless melding of the community's voices. Each person, from the time he or she could talk, has been memorizing these hymns that have been passed down since the sixteenth century, even before our ancestors fled persecution in Switzerland and Germany and arrived on the patch of land given to us by the English real estate entrepreneur William Penn. From the voices of the people lifting anthems in praise of our heavenly Savior's kindness, you would never guess that these are the same people who have rejected me here on earth.

If I am to seek forgiveness, though, I must first forgive. I must stop nourishing the bitterness that has taken root within my heart, and I must stop believing that the majority of the community harbors evil within theirs. Back when Amos King was bishop, Copper Creek was known for its warmth and hospitality to outsiders, yet even he could not protect me from the women's wagging tongues as my pregnant belly started to expand. I never heard my name mentioned—or any man's in conjunction with mine—but as soon as the bakery door, the cannery door, the leatherworks door, the sorghum mill door would swish shut behind me, the women would bolt upright from the counters they'd been hunkered over and begin mumbling something so mundane, I knew they'd really been gossiping about me.

The hymn now completed, everyone stops singing so abruptly, you cannot hear one unsynchronized breath. Elmer Schlabach will usually lead in two or three more hymns before Tobias gives an opening sermon. This is followed by the community kneeling in silent prayer, a Scripture reading, and the main sermon. Tobias holds up his hand to show that he is ready to begin. My stomach drops. I know that today is going to be different.

Nodding at Elmer, Tobias waits for him to take his seat before he begins. "I know it is my duty as bishop to bring a sermon that can challenge you until the next Lord's day. But today, I find that the Lord has not given me anything in which to lead. Just this small portion of text I hope you will carry as a warning, not just throughout this next week, but into the coming months and years ahead."

Then, looking out over the congregation to everyone except me, he opens the Bible to Ezekiel 16 and begins to read the allegory about unfaithful Jerusalem: "'You would not even mention your sister Sodom in the day of your pride, before your wickedness was uncovered. Even so, you are now scorned by the daughters of Edom and all her neighbors and the daughters of the Philistines—all those around you who despise you. You will bear the consequences of your lewdness and your detestable practices, declares the Lord.'" Closing the Bible, which causes dust to rise up and dance in the sunlight, Tobias stuffs it under his arm and strides out of the schoolhouse, smashing both doors open just as forcefully as he had closed them.

I am sure it is obvious to anyone who listened that these verses were chosen for me, the adulteress of Copper Creek. Mortified by this singling out, I stand and gather my son close before striding down the aisle the new bishop just walked. Despite my exit being scrutinized just as much as my entrance, this time I do not blush. I do not need my sister's arm to lean on. My steps do not falter as I leave. If the community thinks I do this because I am offended, let them; if they think I do this because my pride is hurt, let them. I am not going to squander my life trying to keep the boundaries of it under Old Order Mennonite lines. I am going to live my life as a woman who has fallen far enough to know that legalism is not the same thing as righteousness.

When I exit the schoolhouse, snowflakes left over from last night's storm flutter down from the sky like tidbits of lace and cling to Tobias's black buggy and horse. A flock of red-winged blackbirds peck at the grass impaling the white landscape. Tobias mutters something beneath his breath; his rage sends the birds spiraling into the air, painting the gray clouds with every flap of their crimson-accented wings. The double doors of the schoolhouse are still flung wide, so I make no noise when I come out through them.

Because of this, Tobias has no idea that I am standing here observing him, and as I do, I see that his foot is poised on the buggy's step as if he's trying to decide whether he should mount or descend. I watch the expressions shifting across Tobias's features—anger, remorse, sadness, frustration—like each is part of a puppet's face being manipulated by a much larger hand. Trying to turn from my mistakes as *Mamm* suggested, I let my heart go out to this tormented man, not as someone who once shared my bed, but as someone who is so consumed with saving his reputation, he is in the process of losing his soul.

I bind my woolen shawl tighter around my shoulders and sweep up a piece of hair that has slipped from my *kapp*. Eli nestles closer to my bosom. The snow falls upon his face and melts upon his skin as if touching a fiery skillet. Stepping down the icy school steps, I touch my hand to his cheek and can feel the heightened temperature there. My son is running a fever. Not a high one, but high enough that his blue eyes—which I thought were just bright—now appear glassy, and his cheeks are red with something other than this fearsome cold.

"Tobias," I call, walking over to him.

His head snaps up, his dark eyes narrowing when they alight on my outstretched hand. "What're you doing?" he barks.

Putting the hand I had extended back around Eli, I say, "I just want to tell you I know why you read those verses, and I want you to know that it is all right."

"It's not my duty to make sure that you're all right."

"No," I murmur. "I would say it's never been."

Tobias silences his inner argument and climbs up into the buggy, sits on the bench seat with his hands wrapping the reins. Even from where I stand, I can see how his fingers are shaking. "You need to go," he says. "You don't need to be seen talking here with me."

Behind me, I can hear the clomp of shoes on the

schoolhouse steps, the distant chatter in Pennsylvania Dutch as the people make their slow way toward the double doors. I say, quietly so that no one else might overhear, "The truth of the matter is, Tobias, you don't want to be seen talking here with *me*."

But he's turned deaf. I shake my head and turn to greet the person who is walking toward me. My sister. Her steps are measured as her blue eyes flit between me and her husband with a questioning look I have never seen in them before.

Dread punches the breath from my lungs. Smiling to mask it, I walk over and take her arm. "Didn't our sons do good during the service?" I ask. But Leah says nothing, just watches Eli reach for his cousin and entwine their pudgy, drool-covered hands. Although they are very different in coloring, Jonathan and Eli's facial features are becoming more and more similar the older my son grows. It is a bittersweet pleasure to watch how, even in infancy, the two cousins interact as if no distance has ever come between them.

Nothing like the distance I feel emanating from Leah now.

The entire congregation has filed out of the schoolhouse's doors and is shuffling through the snow toward the individual buggies that look so identical, *Englischers* are mystified that we can tell them apart.

Tobias leans out of the buggy and calls brusquely to his wife. "Come now, Leah."

Nodding at him, she turns back and looks at Eli and

Jonathan through unseeing eyes. "Don't you think it's odd," she says, separating our children's conjoined hands, "how our sons could almost pass as brothers?"

Feigning a migraine, after the church service I ask my *dawdy* to take me back to the *dawdi haus*, and then I watch through my parents' front window as the caravan of horses and buggies begins the three-mile journey to Abner and Sadie Glick's, whose turn it is to host the bimonthly fellowship meal. Not wanting Eli to sense my distress, I play with him on the pallet before lying down beside him. I stare at my child for a long time after he has fallen asleep—marveling at his dimpled hands clutching the silken edge of his blankie and praying that despite the sterilizing effects of radiation and chemotherapy, those hands will one day hold a child of his own. Willing tears from my eyes, I ease off the pallet and tiptoe into the kitchen. I take a seat at the table and look out the window to the sun glittering off the thawing patches of snow and the bare black branches of the sycamore sheathed in ice that drips like tinsel. Seeing the tree that Tobias and I stood under two nights ago calls to mind another tree that once sheltered me—not from the frigid wind, but from the summer's heat.

One month passed between the time Tobias touched my face while we knelt on Leah's stained kitchen floor and the afternoon of the Masts' barn raising. The women were seated beneath a maple tree whose orange-leafed branches fanned out over the yard, providing enough shade to keep both us and the leftover food from expiring beneath the Indian-summer sun. I tried to work on a quilt block but had never learned this typical Mennonite trade since, throughout childhood, I had always used the excuse that my fingers were not as deft as my sister's. Setting the tangled thread in my lap, I peered out over the sun-parched field, watching the men climb up and down ladders with nails clamped between their teeth and hammers hooked over their pants pockets. Sweat trickled down many of their faces and necks, darkening the backs of their blue, white, yellow, and brown collared shirts. The few men who were not soaked through were so ruddy from exertion, I feared they might collapse, which is more than just a hindrance when you are putting tin on a fifty-foot roof.

Servitude did not come naturally to me, but it did to my sister. I knew what Leah would do if she could have been there. After refilling the bucket from the well, I went over to the fencerow and broke off a bundle of the meadow tea Katie Mast had uprooted from her Pennsylvania yard and replanted when they moved down to Copper Creek. This I tore into sprigs and dropped into the bucket. I let the water steep in the shade until the mint had blanched from the leaves, flavoring the liquid like tea. I carried this bucket and a wooden ladle across the field. The women stopped chattering among themselves as I drew closer to the men, but at that time—and as Leah's sister—they did not question my motivations. At the time, neither did I.

Tobias was the first to come down the ladder. I had seen him on the roof peak, shading his eyes as he watched me make my way across the shimmering field. His smile widened as he drew closer, a white slice in a tan face heavy with beard. I felt my cheeks turn red from more than just the sun.

Pointing to the bucket, Tobias said, "You did this for me?"

"Not just for you," I countered. "For *all* the *menner*."

Tobias grinned, reached for the ladle, and dipped it into the well bucket, which I held with both hands. He took a long swig and dumped the rest of his ladleful over his head. The meadow leaves clung to the dark waves of Tobias's hair; two water droplets glistened off his earlobes like jewelry.

Wiping his face on his shirtsleeve, he looked over his shoulder, where the other men—his brother, Judah, among them—were climbing down the ladders and making their way toward us. Tobias thanked me and turned away. But then he stopped. "Rachel," he said, his back to me, his light shirt darkened with sweat and the water dripping off his hair, "I am glad you're here. Before you, I . . . I never knew this land could be so dry."

I kept watching Tobias walk away, even after Judah came to pick up the ladle and place his lips where his brother's had been. He began to say something, but I could not pull my eyes away from Tobias long enough to pay attention.

Perhaps my ears were as closed to Judah as my heart because he was not the one who shared a relationship with my sister. And perhaps—in the inmost parts of me, where that child craving her *dawdy*'s attention still lurked—I did not want Leah to enjoy another tender relationship with someone whose tenderness I could never know.

Now, lowering my forehead to the table, I keep my sobs silent so as not to awaken my son. My sister never had the relationship with our *dawdy* that I had imagined and therefore envied. If anything, her relationship with him was even more distant than mine was. I have destroyed two relationships in an attempt to feel the intimacy of one: Leah's relationship with her husband, and my relationship with her husband's brother, Judah King. I have closed my heart to him so often, I fear I will never have the chance to show him that I would put the world on hold just to hear him speak my name again.

# 14

## ⁂ AMOS ⁂

Russell Speck notes Rachel's swollen eyes and the slope-shouldered way she follows him from her parents' house to his truck, but he believes it must be because of Eli's illness, and his heart goes out to her. Eli's illness, though never in the back of Rachel's mind, right now is not at the forefront of her problems.

Leah is.

Before starting the truck, Russell says, "You need to go somewhere first? Say good-bye or something?"

Rachel faces the window and shakes her head.

"Alrighty, then," he says. "Just checking."

They are halfway to Blackbrier before Rachel asks, "Is Ida Mae okay?"

Russell says, "She is," but Rachel notices that he keeps his eyes a little too focused on the road.

"Right as rain?"

Turning to look at her, Russell says, "Huh?"

"When I called her cell phone, you answered because Ida Mae wasn't feeling well, and you said that today she'd be right as rain."

Russell's grin relieves her. "I don't know if I'd go that far, but she's doing pretty good. Sometimes it just takes Ida Mae a little while to get her handle on things again."

"You mean since what happened to her husband?"

Flexing his meaty fingers, Russell rewraps them around the steering wheel. "In one day, I took everything from that woman, and I've spent every day since trying to patch her life back together . . . to make it whole again."

"You can't take that on yourself," Rachel says. "Nobody should live under that kind of burden."

Russell shakes his head. "Nope. I don't suppose nobody should, but sometimes it's hard to remember that God's removed our transgressions as far as the east is from the west, when we keep standing smack-dab in the middle."

Resting her head against the truck seat, Rachel lets his words sink in. Perhaps, just perhaps, she should stop feeling condemnation for her sins, when the instant she turned from them and asked God to forgive her, he did.

Only now, Rachel wonders if her sister can be that forgiving.

When Russell drops her off at Ida Mae's, Rachel finds that the blue room she and Eli share has been changed to a salt-water green so pale, it would be hard to discern it had any color at all if not for the calming presence the new paint exudes. Curtains as fine as dandelion seed hang over the small window and are pulled to the side with green ribbon, allowing light to flood in where the heavy, Western-themed material once blocked it. The bunk beds have been traded for the wrought-iron twin that was covered with quilts in the store. An eyelet-lace coverlet and pillows replace the blue and red comforters. A white crib with yellow covers and bumpers is against the wall where the toy chest used to be. A changing table is also there, covered with the same material as the crib.

"You don't like it?" Ida Mae asks, mistaking Rachel's silence.

Rachel pulls Eli against her chest, which heaves with the magnitude of love she feels for this woman who was a stranger a few months ago but now feels more like family than her own flesh and blood. "Oh, no. It's the kindest thing anyone's ever done for me." She smiles at Ida Mae through her tears and kisses Eli's forehead. "Anyone's ever done for us."

Ida Mae waves her hand in a self-deprecating gesture, yet it is easy to see the pride on her face. "Oh, it was time for a change."

"But how'd you do this all by yourself?"

"Easy," Ida Mae says. "I didn't do it by myself. I had some help."

"From whom?"

Rachel is surprised to see a blush creep up Ida Mae's neck and settle in her cheeks. "I had help, is all," she says, then turns and grabs Rachel's bag by the front door and lugs it into the pale-green room. "Now enough with your yammering. Let's get you and Eli settled. We've got us a big day tomorrow."

Ida Mae Speck is not prepared for the fact that Eli's new doctor comes strutting into the hospital room—where he's kept them waiting for over an hour—wearing a Rolex watch and shoes that stick out from beneath his dress pants like a pair of lacquered boats.

*Know how he afforded them,* Ida Mae thinks, folding her arms and raising one eyebrow.

Unaware of this scrutiny, pediatric oncologist Taizeen Sengupta pushes Gucci glasses higher up on his nose and runs through the steps required to prep Eli for surgery later that day. Rachel calmly nods when told about the removal of two of her child's lymph nodes. She nods when Dr. Sengupta mentions the bone marrow aspiration that will surely be just as painful as it sounds. But after discussing the installation of a port in Eli's chest—so the nurses can pump chemotherapy into him without having to search for a vein that is still so small that the continual pressure of a needle inside it could cause it to collapse—Rachel begins to question her decision to bring her child to a place that would slice open his chest, then sew something back inside it as if Eli's body were as unfeeling as a doll's.

"You're sure all this is necessary?" she asks.

Over his glasses, Dr. Sengupta cuts Rachel with one laser-sharp look. His face softens as he sees her terrified expression. "Your son," he says, "has childhood non-Hodgkin's lymphoma. Which is the third-most-common childhood malignancy and is very curable, yes. But the subtype is anaplastic large-cell lymphoma. ALCL, as it is widely known, composes only 10 percent of non-Hodgkin's lymphomas, and although patients in the low stage like Eli often achieve 100 percent event-free survival within two months of intensive combination chemotherapy, many of these patients with ALCL are subject to future relapse."

If you could see inside Rachel's mind, it would look like a Rubik's Cube: the tiny colored squares frantically struggling to rotate and find a match that is uniform, that makes sense. But Dr. Sengupta has been in the medical profession for so long, he cannot understand that the "layman's terms" he gives his patients' families aren't layman's terms at all.

Ida Mae's mind, on the other hand, isn't even scrambling to keep up with the doctor's. Instead, she puts her hands on her hips and says, "I'm 'bout fed up with all you educated people trying to make us feel like hayseeds. You need to start talking some sense, or you'd better stop talking."

Dr. Sengupta gives Ida Mae the same look of reproof that he gave Rachel. Instead of seeing a pale slip of a woman, however, he sees an overweight battle-ax with fire shooting from her eyes. "Okay," he says to Rachel, inwardly wondering how these two very different people ever became acquainted, "I'll put it to you like this: if you do not allow us to give your son all these intensive combination chemotherapy treatments, his chances of relapse are going to rise and his chances of survival are going to drop."

"Finally," Ida Mae says, looking at the doctor while patting the now-sobbing Rachel on the back, "you're speaking our language."

The doctor leaves. Ida Mae continues circling her hand across the girl's bent spine. "Rachel, look at Eli," she says.

But Rachel doesn't look up, only grips the railings of the hospital bed and sobs harder.

"Rachel-girl," Ida Mae says, "look at your son."

Heedless of the tears streaming down her face, this time Rachel does look up.

"See how he sleeps?" Ida Mae asks. "He's not in pain. I know it may be hard for you to believe that, but it's true. They got him all cozy and sedated for surgery, so that he don't know which way's up."

Rachel begins to speak. Ida Mae holds her hand up, then goes into the bathroom and returns with toilet paper. Rachel mops her face and blows her nose before continuing. "When Eli does wake up, he'll start feeling the nausea, the pain, and he's too little to understand why . . . and he doesn't understand why I am doing this to him. I just can't live with that." She licks tears from her lips. "Not for two whole months."

"Not even if it saves his life?" Ida Mae asks. "Not even if it means that little child lying there can grow up into a man?" Ida Mae spreads her hands to take in the machines, the bed, the bare walls, the constructed skyline beyond. "Eli won't remember none of this, Rachel. All this will just be something you talk about at his graduation, at his wedding, when you hold your first *grosskind* in your arms."

Rachel is silent and then says, "I don't want to do this anymore, Ida Mae. Raising Eli alone. I thought I could. . . . I thought we'd be fine, but it's too hard." She turns and presses her face in Ida Mae's lap, a twenty-year-old mother desperately needing to be someone's child. "It's just too hard."

Ida Mae doesn't bother reassuring Rachel that she isn't alone. She knows the companionship Rachel craves is from someone other than a middle-aged woman rubbing a hand across her back and passing her a bundle of toilet paper to wipe her nose. No, what Rachel Stoltzfus desires is the companionship of a man. A good man. Running her fingers through Rachel's hair, Ida Mae knows who this man is.

The man she now must find.

## Rachel

On Wednesday, my *mamm* shows up at the hospital before breakfast has even been served. I am so relieved to see her that I forget about our altercation at Tobias and Leah's, get up from my chair beside Eli's bed, and fall into her arms.

Pushing me back by the shoulders, she looks into my eyes. "Now I invited somebody along," she says. "I hope you're not offended."

"Offended? Why would I be offended?" I step around her to look toward the door. "Did you bring Leah?"

"No," *Mamm* says. "I didn't bring your sister. Tobias won't let her come."

"Who, then?"

Before she can answer, a man with a long white beard and silver braces on his arms shuffles awkwardly through the door. He smiles; then his gray eyes alight on the person sleeping in the chair on the other side of Eli's bed. "Ida?" Norman Troyer says, his smile turning into a caricature of disbelief. "Ida Troyer? That you?"

Ida Mae blinks against the fluorescent lighting and swallows so deep, her parched throat clicks. "Who?" she sputters. "Who said that?"

The Lancaster County *doktor* doesn't move from his position by the door, whether from weariness or wariness I cannot tell. "Ida," he calls instead, only louder this time. "Ida, this is your *bruder*-in-law, Norman. Norman Troyer. From Pennsylvania."

Ida Mae rouses like a bear who's been asleep all winter and doesn't appreciate the first glimpse of spring sun. Her wiry hair is whipped all over her head, her face creased from where it was pressed against the chair, her eyes—after a night of nurses filing in and out to monitor Eli's elevated temperature—pasted partially shut. Ida Mae peers across the bed and up at Norman. "What on earth!" she cries. "Don't you look like something the cat drug in."

Rather than giving her the sarcastic retort that Russell would, Norman just shrugs. "I drove straight through the night."

"You're driving now?" Ida Mae says. "But you're still dressed as Plain as a pilgrim."

My *mamm* pulls out a chair for Norman. Sinking gratefully into it, he rests the weight of his upper body on his braces. "I left the Amish years ago, Ida. I'm New Order Mennonite now."

"Looks like we're both shunned, then," she says. "Must not be too handy for your voodoo business."

Norman says, "Actually, now that I can travel and make house calls, my holistic practice has only grown."

Ida Mae rolls her eyes. "Am I just another one of your house calls? You drove the whole way down here to see if I'd changed my ways?"

"Ida," my *mamm* says, a note of warning in her voice, "*I* am the one who invited Norman down here. I knew he could help Eli if he'd just take a *goot* look at him."

Finding my voice, I decide it's time to insert myself into

this surreal conversation. "And why didn't you run this by me first?"

My *mamm*'s eyebrows lift at my disrespectful tone, but after three days of no sleep and little nourishment, I am far beyond standard protocol.

"Because I knew you wouldn't let him come," she says.

"But am I not Eli's mother?" I say. "Doesn't that still make it *my* choice?"

Squaring her shoulders, my *mamm* raises her chin. "You can live and die by your choices, Rachel Stoltzfus, but I am *not* about to let my *grosskind* live and die by them too!"

Ida Mae leaps up from the chair—her hair and clothing still wildly disheveled—and marches around Eli's bed. "Rachel's an amazing mother," she says through gritted teeth while glaring at my *mamm*. "But you don't know that 'cause you just come in here whenever it suits you and throw your little powwow *doktor*ing weight around!"

I am about to step in when Norman Troyer stands up and hobbles over, angling his broken body so that it forms a barrier between the two women, forcing them to drop their defensive stances.

I knew the first time Ida Mae and my mother met at the Amish Country Store that their possessiveness over me would eventually lead to a confrontation. But I never imagined that this confrontation would lead to blows. Now, looking at the way their chests heave and eyes blaze, I am no longer so sure.

Ida Mae keeps threatening to put me on a four-thousand-calorie diet composed of hamburgers and milk shakes if I don't stop losing weight. Although I can see the wings of my hips and the ridges of my ribs whenever I take a bath, I cannot sit beside my son's hospital bed and eat hot meals when I know that his mouth is so sore from chemo that the liquids fed through his port are the only nutrients keeping him alive. This is my sixth week on a raw-food regimen and Eli's third week off in his one-week-on, one-week-off round of combination chemo.

At first, Ida Mae thought my new "fandangled" way of eating was because of pressure from my *mamm*. Once she realized it is, rather, my feeble attempt at controlling something when my entire world is spinning out of orbit, Ida Mae decided to offer support by eating organic whole foods too. I was skeptical, since her fried-food habit is just as bad as her ex-husband's, but this morning when I made a spirulina-and-carrot-juice smoothie, Ida Mae held her hand out for a cup of it as well. She did plug her nose and grimace like she was being forced to partake of hemlock, but she drank that smoothie down to the brownish dregs, and then stumbled off to the bathroom to gargle with Listerine.

"How you holding up?" I ask her as a customer leaves.

Groaning, Ida Mae drops her forehead to the countertop. "I need coffee. Chocolate . . . butter." She looks up at me from beneath a spiky fringe of bangs. "Who came up with this whole organic thing anyway? I bet it's a conspiracy from the government. They're not putting pesticides on our food anymore 'cause they're trying to poison us with bugs."

Rolling my eyes, I say, "You're so full of it."

"Nuh-uh," Ida Mae says. "Not anymore. That green stuff I drank this morning cleaned me out."

"Ida Mae. Really. I would've been better off not knowing that."

After one more customer and two hours of solid complaining, Ida Mae blows out the cinnamon bun candle and flips the store sign to *Closed.* I put the fruit pies and fried pies in the refrigerator. Arm in arm, we head back to her cottage with the electric candles glowing in the curtained windows and the white picket fence whose entrance is guarded by a passel of green-eyed cats and one obese dog. Smoke from the neighbors' fire uncurls lazily from their chimney and catches in the branches overhanging our roof. Leaning back, I look up at the stars and imbibe the wood smoke's earthy perfume. I am suddenly overwhelmed by the emotions that I can't put into words, and I squeeze Ida Mae's arm.

"I know," she whispers, "it's mighty good to be home."

My *mamm* and Norman are ready to leave as soon as we come in the door. Every other afternoon, the two of them make the hour's journey from Copper Creek to Blackbrier in Norman's old Buick Skylark. As Norman peers into Eli's eyes to check on something only he knows how to see, and then prepares some herbal concoction to heal what the chemotherapy has hurt, my *mamm* will be in Ida Mae's tiny kitchen, soaking vegetables and fruits in alkali water, chopping and dicing so we have enough food until she comes again. I haven't minded their company, and though it may seem callous to say it, having a two-hour break now and then from being Eli's mother restores my senses and gives me strength to face the week of chemo ahead.

"Won't you stay for *nachtesse*?" I ask. "We're having . . ." I look over at my mother and grin. "What are we having?"

"Boiled red cabbage, sweet *grummbeere*, and a spinach salad with Greek yogurt and walnuts."

Ida Mae unzips her Carhartt jacket and slings it over the back of the chair. "Sounds delicious," she quips.

I am awakened by a strange sound around midnight. Fearing that Eli has become sick again, I toss the covers and walk over to his crib. I turn him on his back and rest my hand on his forehead. His skin is cool and dry, and his chest not labored with what seems to be a daily effort to breathe. His lips are open, though. Even in the darkness, I can perceive the small sores that ring them, which have made it difficult for him to nurse and heartbreaking for me, who cannot give him the nourishment his ailing body needs.

But this is the first day in weeks I have not cried; I cannot break that record now. Taking Ida Mae's robe off the peg, I wrap it around myself without tying the belt and walk into the kitchen. That's when I hear it: that strange sound again, like a mouse has gotten trapped in the cupboards. Grabbing a rolling pin from the crock beside the stove, I reach over and flick on the lights. Ida Mae is sitting cross-legged on the tile floor, crouching possessively over a whole fudge pie (or what was once a whole fudge pie) from Hostetler's Bakery. Her mouth is dark with chocolate; her eyes gleam with a recklessness I've seen in my *dawdy*'s horses before a storm.

"Don'chew 'udge me," Ida Mae garbles. Swallowing, she smears her mouth on her pajama sleeve. "I been living on nothing but pinecones and berries for days and days. . . . And I've *had* it. I ain't *never* eating that organic junk again."

I don't say anything, since I'm afraid I will laugh and awaken Eli. Instead, I pull out a drawer in the cupboard and reach for a spoon. Lowering myself beside Ida Mae with her old paisley robe pooling around me, I fold my legs to the side and hold my spoon over the pie. She clamps the lid back on the box and pulls it against her chest.

"Aren't you going to share?" I whisper.

Ida Mae whispers back, "Only if you go pour us two glasses of milk. I'm 'bout dying of thirst." Her face pales. She reaches out and touches my knee. "I'm sorry, Rachel," she says. "That—that came out wrong."

"You're fine," I whisper, getting to my feet and opening the refrigerator door. "*We're* fine. Right now, I just want to eat my pie and drink my milk like Eli's cancer never happened."

After pouring the two glasses of milk, I sit back down. Ida Mae takes one glass from me and taps it against the other. "I'll drink to that," she says.

# 15

## AMOS

Even though Judah has been living in Cody, Wyoming, for three and a half months, the single-wide overlooking the Shoshone River is bare except for an old mattress clumped with pillows and blankets, a coffeemaker, and a miniature fridge. Judah is hunkered over the kitchen sink with the cordless phone clamped between his neck and shoulder. All my son wears is a pair of low-rise jeans that look like they need washed as badly as his bathroom towel. His hair is so long, it laps at his neck in sandy waves, and his broad shoulders are blotched with freckles left over from the summer afternoons he and the *nochber* boys spent swimming in the cow pond after they'd finished morning chores. He is more muscular than I remember, but I haven't seen my son without his shirt since he was ten.

The one-bedroom trailer suddenly seems to shrink with Judah's violent intake of breath, and I know that Ida Mae must have revealed to him the news. "Is Eli okay?" he asks, gripping the sink like a crutch. "Is Rachel?"

There is a moment of silence as Ida Mae replies.

My son spins to face the spartan bedroom and drags a hand over his face. "Is there anything I can do? . . . *Really?* You don't think she'd mind?"

Ida Mae must put her whole heart into convincing him, because when she is finished, Judah says, "All right. I'll start as soon as I can."

## *Rachel*

Nighttime is the hardest. Parents throughout this city are zipping healthy children into footie pajamas and tucking them into bed, and I spend the hours like an insomniac, clutching my son's hand and begging the Lord not to take him from me. There have been many nights like this. For some reason, though, tonight is one of the worst. Perhaps it is the urgency surrounding Eli's elevated temperature, causing the nurses to cycle in and out more often to check his vitals, after which they say nothing, as if sensing I do not want my fears confirmed.

I have tried reminding myself that the moment I repented and asked for the Lord's forgiveness, he wiped away the scarlet stain of my sin. But when I look down at Eli, whose face is wet with tears even in sleep, I feel like surely this tribulation is punishment for what Tobias and I did. That if I had married Judah King and we had conceived a child inside the parameters of God's sovereign plan, the child would be healthy and whole and not tasting the bitter wine that his parents' wanton actions have pressed.

"Lord, please . . ." I rest my forehead on Eli's thigh, swaddled with soft cotton sheets that remind me of a funeral shroud. "I know I have already asked your forgiveness for my adultery, but I need to know that you really forgive. That you are not punishing my child for the sins I have committed. That my sins are truly separated from me as far as the east is from the west. That you do not withhold from your child any good thing, and so you are going to bring redemption to *my* child, to this situation that seems so impossible to redeem."

The night-shift nurses do not often knock, not wishing to disturb our sleep. So I am still praying—still letting tears drip on my son's body—when the door opens and Donna comes into the room. "Can I get you anything, Rachel?" she asks. "Sprite, water?"

It doesn't matter if it's ten at night or two in the morning, Donna never whispers. But tonight this does not irritate me. I am just grateful to rest in her grandmotherly presence when Eli's cancer makes me feel so ill-equipped to be his *mamm*.

"Thank you . . . no," I reply. "I'm fine."

Donna turns from the computer's blue glare and glances over her bifocals at me. I wince, knowing she has heard the tears in my voice. Slipping a thin plastic sheath over a digital thermometer, she leans over the bed and carefully inserts the elongated tip into Eli's ear.

"My son was here too," she says. The thermometer beeps. Donna turns and types in the information. "Well, not here . . . but over there at 11 North." She points toward the window, as if the adjacent hospital can be seen at night. "Robert had aplastic anemia. You know, where your body stops making platelets to clot up your blood?" I nod, but I hadn't known. "He was given a bone-marrow transplant by an anonymous donor, then—five years later—a clean bill of health."

Donna slips the thermometer into her pocket and fingers an earring glinting in the frosted tips of her hair. "I don't often tell patients, because sometimes even happy endings don't help when you can barely wrap your mind around your own story, but I thought that you might need to hear it tonight."

Wiping my eyes on the corner of the sheet, I sit up. "What's he doing now?"

Donna rolls her eyes. "Nothing . . . and everything. After the transplant, Robert went back to college on a scholarship with the marching band. He graduated five years ago, and now he's married with two little ones. The youngest is a girl about Eli's age, named Leah."

My heart catches in my throat; somehow I murmur around it, "Leah?"

Donna nods. "A precious creature with huge dark eyes and a temper like her daddy." The soles of her sneakers squeak as she walks past Eli's bed to where I am seated on the edge of the chair. In the darkness, I watch her reach up again into her hair. "Hold out your hand."

I do, and Donna places in its center one tiny gold earring shaped like a drum. "There was a time when I didn't think Robert would ever play again. But he did. And soon, all that racket made me wish he would stop." She laughs and curls her warm hands around mine, closing my fingers around the gift. "Just know that whatever happens, you're not alone. He sees everything. Everything you're going through, as if your lives were cradled right there in his palm."

After Donna leaves, I place the earring on the sheet, the gold plating brilliant even in the dim light. I take Eli's hand. But this time, I do not hold on to it like I alone can keep him here. Instead, I hold it with the assurance that despite the tribulations we must face, we are also being held.

## AMOS

By the time Judah hits Kansas, his eyes are so heavy despite the caffeine jittering through his veins, he parks at a truck stop crowded with snoring semis. But no sooner has he lowered the driver's seat and rested his head on the pillow of his jacket than his mind floods with images of Rachel and himself throughout childhood: poring over contraband *Englischer* books in the dairy barn, teaching her how to read and write just so he had an excuse to spend time with her, playing kick the can with the other *nochberen* and tweaking Rachel's pigtails so she would chase him—only him—so he could let her catch up and then collapse with her onto the grass and laugh until both their sides were stitched with knots.

He recalls other memories—memories too recent for time to have subdued their sting. After Rachel moved from Muddy Pond to Copper Creek, Judah thought the camaraderie they'd shared in Pennsylvania would continue in Tennessee. But though she ate beside him during fellowship Sunday and once stopped in at the smithy to visit after buying King Syrup at Kauffman's General Store, the camaraderie between them wasn't the same at all.

Judah consoled himself with the fact that adult propriety would not let them demonstrate the same affection their youth had allowed. He also understood that Rachel's independent nature—one of her personality traits he loved most—would initially balk against letting him court her, just because it was what the entire community had predicted before she had moved down.

Plus, Rachel was busy taking care of her sister and his brother's family. Surely once Leah's baby was born, he and

Rachel might have a chance to rekindle their old friendship and perhaps, over time, awaken something more. Until then, he would give her the space to realize that marriage to him would not take anything from her. He just wanted to build a life with his best childhood friend and grow old together with her.

Then word spread throughout the community like wildfire: at nineteen years of age and without the legitimacy of a husband's last name, his best childhood friend, Rachel Stoltzfus, was herself with child.

Judah recalls how, after Tobias broke the news to him, he marched out to the barn, grabbed a pitchfork and a wheelbarrow, and furiously began mucking out the heifers' stalls—only stopping in between loads to wipe the burning mixture of sweat and tears from his eyes. Judah usually found that the mind-numbing tasks of farm life took away the worry surrounding life's questions that never received answers. But once the stall was scraped clean and the new straw bales spread, Judah's beleaguering thoughts returned.

Slanting the pitchfork against the wall, he collapsed next to the milk storage tank just like Rachel and he used to do when they were young and innocent. He must have sat there for hours on the dirty cement floor of his brother's barn, digging fingers into his skull in an attempt to rip out the visuals of her with a man who wasn't him, who would *never* be him; then—once his anger was spent—crying over the girl who'd become a woman he didn't even know but whose heart had somehow already claimed his.

Judah cannot take any more memories. Snapping his seat into the upright position, he cranks the engine of the blue Ford, guns it up the ramp and back onto the interstate. He turns the local rock station as loud as his radio will go, more to block out his thoughts than because he enjoys the words.

He knocks back Red Bulls and then tosses the crushed cans to the floorboard; he digs through an open bag of pizza-flavored Combos he keeps in his lap. Grating lyrics screech to a stop and then drive full-throttle into the next song; radio stations fade in and out; DJs' velvety voices disappear into the void of airwaves, only to be replaced by another slew whose voices are just as gravelly as the others were silken. All the while, Judah wishes something would occupy his mind besides Rachel. Besides Eli. Besides himself and his own mistakes.

Just as the sun rises over I-24, turning the four lanes of asphalt from gray to gold, Judah crosses the Tennessee state line. He pulls over at another truck stop on the outskirts of Nashville and pays for a shower whose availability is called out over the intercom like an order of fast food.

He is standing at the sink in a fresh set of clothes, shaving off his three-day beard with a two-dollar razor and soap from the dispenser, when he pauses and stares into his eyes. They are bloodshot from lack of sleep and an overabundance of caffeine, but there is something different about them that is due to more than just exhaustion. He then realizes that his eyes—albeit the same honeyed brown—are as hard as fossilized amber. Though my son avoided the more overt temptations, he knows a lot of his innocence has been lost in the short time he's been away. Judah's only hope is that Rachel will not see this, for he fears she might blame herself, when Judah knows he has only himself to blame.

Bundling up his dirty clothes in the stiff towel that is even dirtier than they are, Judah walks out into the truck stop's store and purchases from a rotating glass case a crystal figurine of a horse that is small enough to fit inside a thimble. For Eli, he gets a bouncy ball that lights up when thrown and is too large to be swallowed by a six-month-old throat. These gifts are a paltry attempt at consolation, he knows, but the idea of walking into that hospital room empty-handed and hollow-eyed fills Judah with so much dread that he would never have the courage to go in.

Thirty minutes later, Judah enters the south garage of the Vanderbilt Children's Hospital. The ceiling is so low it makes him feel claustrophobic as he circles his vehicle around and around the numerous levels trying to find a space.

He marches up the sidewalk with his heartbeat roaring in his chest as loudly as the thoughts inside his head, wondering if Rachel will even want to see him or let him see Eli. Walking through the double set of automatic doors into the hospital, Judah is amazed by its festive appearance when the people who come here do not have much to be festive about. There is a wide, curving staircase with a star-and-ribbon banister, and just past the elevators, an elaborate train set encased in protective glass that winds past minuscule homes, snowy lakes, and evergreen forests whenever a patient presses a red button.

Judah walks into the waiting elevator and presses the button for the myelosuppression floor as Ida Mae instructed. In the elevator with him is a hospital volunteer with a Rubbermaid cart heaped with toys and a young Spanish couple whose son looks completely healthy but is wearing a white hospital wristband. Stepping off the elevator when it reaches the sixth floor, Judah walks over to the intercom box and is buzzed in once he can reveal to the nurse the room number and name of the person he is visiting.

Slipping his truck-stop gifts into the pocket of his coat, Judah rubs his hands with the mandatory disinfectant and strides down the ocean-themed hall toward Eli's room. His breath grows shallow and his legs weak the closer he comes to that door. Taking the gifts out of his pocket, Judah holds on to them with everything he has, hoping that such small tokens can be enough to let him back in.

## *Rachel*

I am furious when someone raps on the door. This is the first time Eli has slept without whimpering in two days. Springing from the chair, I cover the hospital room in four steps and fling the door wide. I begin to say, "No visi—" but cannot finish the word.

"Judah?" I ask, although it can be no one but him. His hair is longer, his face harder, the skin pulled across his cheekbones coarse and burned as if he has been someplace that, even in winter, sees the sun. Because of these changes, or because of the guarded expression in his eyes, he looks more like a man than the boy who walked off Ida Mae's porch into the rain three months ago.

Even though I opened the door ready to send whoever had come to visit right back home again, my emotions are so unstable that I now cross the hospital room's threshold and bury my face against Judah's chest. All I can hear is his thundering heart keeping time with the beeping machines behind us, and then he eases both arms around me. I begin to weep as he does, for I don't know how long it has been since I have been held and not the one doing the holding. Turning his torso, Judah slips something into his pocket and closes the hospital door with one hand. Judah moves this hand up between our bodies and uses the rough pad of his thumb to skim the tears from my cheeks. It is a simple gesture, a sweet gesture, yet the same one his brother did the night I realized the full magnitude of what the two of us had done.

This memory brings me to my senses. I step away from Judah and watch as his face falls; then his arms fall in slow motion back down to his sides.

"You cut your hair," he says.

I turn my head so that his outstretched hand doesn't touch my severed locks. I lace my arms to hide their shaking. "And I see that you *haven't* cut yours."

Judah grins, and I think nothing in him has changed, that he is still that same mischievous boy I knew from before. But that shadow in his eyes soon returns, and he glances over at the hospital bed where my tiny child is struggling to recuperate even as more chemo is being pumped into his system.

"How is he?" Judah asks.

I move over to the bed and fold Eli's blankie down so that it doesn't come in contact with the plastic tubes snaking from his port.

"It's hard to say." I am relieved to drop my upbeat performance for the people who barely know us, who just ask about Eli so they'll have the details of another sad story to tell. "We're almost through treatments. But every time we come back here, it feels like Eli's closer to dying."

"That's how chemo works, isn't it? The doctors kill off the good cells with the bad, then let the good ones rebuild themselves again?"

I shrug. "Most of the time I don't know what's going on. I just have to trust that these complete strangers know what they're doing when they take my son's life in their hands."

"I'm so sorry, Rachel."

I have heard those rote words so often, I usually don't hear them anymore. But this time I do.

I can tell by the pained expression on Judah's face as he looks at my son that if he had the power to scoop Eli up from that hospital bed and make him well again, he would; if he had the power to take me in his arms and heal my heart again, he would.

I sit in the chair again. In my shattered state, I do not trust myself to keep from going over and leaning against Judah in an attempt to absorb the strength his presence exudes. I do not know what has happened to me or to him in the time since he's been gone, but looking at Judah now—leaning against the door of the bathroom with his hands sunk in the pockets of his faded jeans and his wavy blond hair brushing the hood of his hunter-green jacket—is like looking at a stranger. Besides the color of his eyes and the crooked angle of his smile, I can see no semblance of the boy I knew in childhood, the boy for some reason I never thought could turn into a man until he was gone.

"Where did you go?" I ask. "I mean, after here?"

Judah strolls over to the window and splits the blinds so he can look down on the happenings of Music City. Taking his other hand from the pocket of his jeans, he folds his arms and turns back toward me. "Wyoming," he says. "Cody, Wyoming. I was a farrier for the rodeo."

"But how'd you get out there? How did you get that job?"

"I hitchhiked. And had some money saved. So when I got to Wyoming, I got my driver's license, then bought a truck and drove over to the rodeo and told them I knew a thing or two about horses."

Maybe it's the way he won't look in my eyes, or the way his sentences are so halted it is as if he's making them up one fragment at a time. But something about his story doesn't ring true. Or maybe there is something about his story that he is not telling me. With a sinking feeling in my stomach, I realize what it is.

"You've met someone?" I ask. "From Wyoming?"

"Nobody's from Wyoming," Judah says. His gaze remains fixed on the few stubborn wisps clinging to Eli's scalp that I haven't had the heart to cut. "At least not in the rodeo."

My cheeks grow hot; I realize he has evaded my question. It is all I can do to keep still, not to pace and fidget like Judah is doing in front of the window. I am grateful that he didn't look me in the eye as he said this, won't even look my way now. If he could see my face, he would know the envy that is inside my heart.

I hate myself for these fickle emotions. I am acting like a normal young woman with boy problems even though I am sitting next to a hospital bed occupied by my diseased son. I hate myself because this envy is rooted in selfishness, letting me know that I have not changed much at all. My dear childhood friend deserves to find someone who will cherish him for the man he is, not a woman who couldn't stop self-destructing long enough to realize what a treasure she had before it was too late to claim it.

I am opening and closing my mouth, attempting to dispel the tension between us but not finding the right words, when Ida Mae taps the door, then comes in. "How's our little man?" she asks, bending down in front of the miniature fridge to replenish the juice boxes and carrot sticks I ate yesterday.

"He had a solid BM this morning, and they're taking him down for a PET at noon," I explain. Ida Mae nods. She and I often communicate in medical acronyms that would never make sense to anyone listening from the outside world.

"Your mom and Norman been by yet?" she asks, then closes the fridge and turns. "Oh, hey there, Judah. Aren't you a sight for sore eyes."

My own eyes flit between them. Ida Mae doesn't seem the least bit shocked to see Judah standing here after months away, and I never did find out how he'd known of Eli's sickness and which hospital room he was in. The moment I start to ask these questions, Ida Mae tosses a juice box at me. "Now, you two are too young to be inside on such a pretty day. Why don't y'all go take a walk around town?"

"Aren't they calling for sleet?" I waggle the plastic straw into the juice box and take a sip. "I saw it on the news."

Ida Mae waves her hand. "Those doom-and-gloom weather reporters don't know what they're talking about."

Judah turns toward me and shrugs. Getting up from the hospital chair, I place the juice box in the fridge, kiss Eli's forehead, and retrieve my coat and scarf from the closet. Judah holds the door open, and I pass under his arm into the hall. We ride down the elevator in charged silence, our unspoken words electrifying the air. When the automatic doors of the hospital open, ushering us out into the street, I gulp the biting wind and let my lungs fill until they feel like they will splinter.

"I haven't left the hospital since Dr. Sengupta put Eli on a supplemental IV," I explain, working my fingers into my red mittens and coiling the matching scarf around my hair, the first red items I have ever been allowed to own. "Even this freezing cold feels wonderful."

Judah touches my arm, looks down both sides of the street. "Where you wanna go?"

"Anywhere."

Nodding, he takes one of my mittened hands and tucks it in the bend of his arm. We walk without speaking up Children's Way and cross Twenty-First Avenue onto Vanderbilt's deserted campus, receiving inquisitive looks from the few students brave enough to face the harsh elements. I guess it must appear unusual for a Plain-dressed woman to have her hand wrapped around the arm of a man who is garbed like an *Englischer*, but in the light of Eli's illness there are certain things that do not matter to me anymore. Keeping up with appearances is one of them.

We've traveled less than a block when sleet begins to spritz from the muted sky, the icy granules bouncing across the sidewalk like translucent pearls.

"Seems those weather reporters *do* know what they're talking about," I quip.

Judah says nothing. If not for the steady pressure of his

hand over the one I still have tucked in the crook of his arm, I would think he has forgotten I am even here. I study him from the corner of my eye as we retrace our steps, but the hood of Judah's jacket is pulled up. I cannot see his face except for his reddened nose and the frosted sweep of his lashes.

"Do you want to go up there?" He points to a wrought-iron pedestrian bridge burnished with gold that links the university's historic section to Peabody College. It seems an odd choice of shelter as the structure has no solid covering that I can see, but Judah is acting so strangely, I agree without question.

I climb the slick steps in front of him. I can feel his palm against the small of my back as he attempts to keep me from falling. We reach the top; Judah strides over to face the four streams of traffic passing slowly beneath the bridge. Despite being midmorning, almost all the vehicles have their headlights on and their windshield wipers whipping back and forth, brushing sleet into double arches that condense at the sides before spattering the blacktop that is turning gray beneath the thickening sheen of ice.

I stare at Judah's back—at the way his bare hands clutch the iron railing and the sleet that glitters on his green hood.

Coming to stand beside him, I am silent before asking, "You okay?"

The driving wind and sleet make it hard for me to discern my own words, but somehow Judah hears them. He releases his grip on the rail as if his strength is responsible for holding the bridge together, yet he has no choice but to let it go. Sweeping back his hood, Judah looks over at me. For the first time, I see the tears that are melting trails down the frozen skin of his face.

He drags his coat sleeve across his eyes and shakes his head. "I never should've left," he says. "If I had stayed—"

"If you had stayed, nothing would have changed."

The sentence has barely left my mouth when the hurt flickering in Judah's eyes tells me that he has misinterpreted my meaning and I have misinterpreted his. I thought he was crying because he felt responsible for Eli's cancer. Now I realize his tears are because he believes if he had remained, I might have relied on his strength over these past three months and that reliance—given time—might have turned into love.

What he doesn't realize is that the moment he walked out of my life was the moment I knew I already loved him. Have always loved him.

Judah is grappling the railing again with his broad shoulders hunched to ward off the cold or the impact of my words; I cannot tell which. Stretching out my mittened hand, I place it over his. "Nothing might've changed had you stayed, Judah, but I know that I am glad you have returned."

He changes direction so abruptly that I step back. As he trails his hand over one side of my red scarf, the thawed sleet beads across his fingers. He places these cold, damp fingers to my cheek, but his touch feels more like a burn. Sliding his other hand down the base of my spine, he presses my body against him, as if I am a piece of fine china whose unseen fractures might crack. "There's no one else, Rachel," he whispers, patching my temple with a kiss whose tenderness forces me to close my eyes. "There's never been anyone but you."

As the wind unspools my scarf and the sleet lashes our unprotected skin, Judah leans down and touches his frozen lips to mine.

Though I am painfully aware that nothing and no one can take precedence over my battle to reclaim my son's health, I cannot stop myself from twining my fingers into Judah's wet hair and leaning into his kiss, into this moment stolen on a bridge where two people are suspended in a world fraught with ice and fire.

# 16

## Rachel

Ida Mae and I are drinking the tea I heated in the microwave of the family lounge when there is a quiet knock on the door. I call out a welcome, and Norman Troyer comes limping in. Looking between the two of us, he takes off his black hat and feeds the brim around and around in one square hand. "I wanted to check on Eli," he says, still staring at the hat. "See if there was anything you might need before I left."

"You're heading back to PA?" I ask.

He nods. "*Jah*, I put Leah and Tobias out long enough."

"I'm sure they didn't mind. We all loved having you here."

Ida Mae snorts. When I look over with wide eyes, she just smiles and takes a sip of tea.

"Do you care if I take one more look at him?" the holistic *doktor* asks, motioning to my son.

"No, please." I move to give Norman more room. "I'd feel better if you did."

Ida Mae knocks the tea back although the temperature must scald her tongue. Setting her mug on the food tray table, she gathers her belongings and stuffs them into the Salvation Army backpack she uses like a purse. "You think they'll release Eli in the morning?" she asks.

I shrug. Dr. Taizeen Sengupta can change his mind about Eli's being released or being forced to stay as quickly as the wind can shift its course. I keep telling myself that the doctor is keeping my son in the hospital for his own good. Sometimes, I even believe it.

"Welp," Ida Mae says, "give me a call when you need picked up. If I'm running the store, I'll send Russell to fetch ya."

"He's back in town?" I ask.

Ida Mae nods, keeping her eyes away from Norman Troyer. Her ex-husband has been away for a month and a half, the same amount of time that Norman, her first husband's *bruder*, has been in Tennessee. I don't know why Russell Speck has made an effort to avoid such a docile man, but I'm sure it is the same reason Ida Mae has avoided talking about Norman whenever I've found the chance to ask why he's no longer a part of her life.

Norman Troyer keeps staring at the door long after Ida Mae has said good-bye to us and left. He then turns and shuffles toward the hospital bed. Taking a flashlight from his pants pocket, Norman rests his weight on the railings and guides the beam down into Eli's eyes. My son is asleep, but the instant his eyelids begin to flutter, Norman shields the flashlight's brightness with his hand and peers around it. Norman only looks at his eyes for a few seconds before clicking off the light and returning it to his pocket. Immediately, the pain medication filtering through Eli's port causes his eyes to shutter into sleep again. I wipe tears as my son's slack mouth opens and drool dangles from his sore-crusted lips.

Drying my eyes, I ask, "How is he?"

Norman doesn't respond. I cannot tell if it is because he is afraid to, or if he does not know how to tell me what he sees.

I push the chair that Ida Mae had occupied closer to the bed. Norman rocks back into it with a sigh. "You should get another scan done," he says. "I don't like how yellow his eyes are."

"They did a PET today. They'll probably have the results tomorrow."

Norman bobs his head and lays his braces over one knee like canes. "That's good," he says. "Let me know what they find out. If I need to come down again, I will."

These past two months spent watching Eli battle cancer have sapped my confidence in both conventional and holistic medicine. Because of this, I do not really care if

Norman Troyer makes that long journey from Pennsylvania to Tennessee regardless of Eli's scan results, but considering that Norman is an old family friend, I cannot reveal how my faith has waned regarding his abilities.

"I'll let you know," I say. "Or I can send a message through my *mamm*."

"That'd be fine. She calls to order herbs anyway."

"Why don't you ever call Ida Mae?" I have so many questions, I cannot help asking the one that has plagued my mind since I discovered Norman Troyer's signature on the bottom of Ida Mae and Russell's marriage certificate. "Your *bruder* might be dead, but she's still your *schweschder*-in-law, right?"

Norman stares at my son before replying. "*Jah*, Ida married my younger brother, Henry. But after Henry died and Ida was shunned, I was still in the church and—"

"And," I interrupt, "you couldn't talk with her and keep from being shunned yourself?"

"No, it wasn't that. Ida hurt us not by leaving the church like she did, but by marrying the man who killed her family."

*The man who killed her family.* I remember Russell's hands clasping the steering wheel as he said, *"In one day, I took everything from that woman, and I've spent every day since trying to patch her life back together . . . to make it whole again."* I murmur now, hoping my words are true, "Surely it was an accident."

Norman nods. "We never should've been out that day.

It was getting too dark, but we were on a deserted road, and I thought the triangle reflectors were bright enough to keep us safe."

"It was a horse-and-buggy accident?"

Looking over, Norman tilts his head. "What kind of accident did you think it was?"

"I—I wasn't sure." I am too embarrassed to admit I thought it might have been an armed robbery attempt before Russell found the Lord.

"Russell was driving truck for Dutch Valley at the time." Norman lowers his arm braces to the floor and rests his upper-body weight on them. "He was going too fast for the narrow road, but—like I said—it was too dark and we shouldn't've been out. I had both my nephews with me . . . and my *bruder* Henry's *familye* was up visiting from Ohio, and we were in a hurry to get home because my *mudder* was cooking a special *esse* in their honor. But then we came around that corner and saw headlights. Headlights that made the inside of that buggy look like day. The semi was coming so fast, we had no time to get off the road and Russell had no time to brake. If we had been in a car, I could've swerved. We might've been fine."

I murmur, tears filling my eyes, "But you weren't in a car."

Norman wipes the sorrow that pools in his own eyes, even after all these years that are supposed to lessen grief. "The impact splintered the buggy into matchsticks. Killed the horse instantly. Along—" Norman chokes, clears his throat, and tries again—"along with my *bruder* and my younger nephew. My legs were so badly mangled in the collision that I couldn't move. I would've died in that buggy if Russell hadn't helped us. I told him to get my nephew first. The one who was still alive . . . Daniel. I *begged* Russell; I *screamed* at him, but he saw the blood covering Daniel's face from having broken off his teeth in the wreck, and Russell thought he was too injured to save. So he helped me out of the buggy first."

Norman shakes his head, as if trying to dislodge the painful memories. I want to reach out to him, to somehow ease his suffering, but I know that remaining quiet and still is the kindest thing I can do.

"Russell carried me over to the side of the road and carefully laid me on the grass. Something must've sparked in his truck that ignited the gas spilling from it, because by the time he turned around to get Daniel, the buggy had burst into flames. I wailed there along the side of the road. I wailed so hard, veins ruptured in my eyes. Since my legs didn't work, I tried dragging myself over to the buggy with my arms. I remember how the fire was so hot, even the blacktop seemed to melt beneath my hands.

"It seemed like a long time, but it was probably only seconds that I didn't know where Russell was. I thought he'd been killed in the fire, but then he came walking out of the carnage with this wall of flames behind him. He was carrying Daniel in his arms, and even from that distance across the road, I could see how his blond hair was singed to the scalp and the clothing branded onto his skin."

Norman is crying harder now. I get up and rip some toilet paper off the roll in the bathroom. Coming back, I pass it to Norman just like Ida Mae passed it to me, knowing from experience how the simplest gestures provide the greatest relief.

Norman wipes his face and blows his nose. I sit with my back straight and hands folded as the details of this horrific recounting play on the silver screen of my mind.

He clears his throat. I open my eyes to see that Norman is ready to continue. I sense then that this is not just a story he is telling me; more than that, it is a story he has long needed to tell. "Ida would've kept Daniel on life support forever, but he was so badly burned, if he ever *did* come out of that coma, he would never have lived a normal life." Norman sighs, lifting the shackles of his braces. "A life even harder to live than mine.

"The Amish church, as you know, shares medical expenses. Even after Russell's trucking company paid their part through insurance, there were plenty of bills rolling in long after the accident. And once the church heard that Daniel was probably never coming out of his coma, they decided they didn't want to pay the medical expenses of someone who was only alive because of machines. Ida fought them. She fought the Amish church like it was a matter of life and death. In her eyes, that's exactly what it was."

Norman swallows, wets pink lips surrounded by white beard. "Russell was really scarred after the accident. Not physically, but emotionally. He started drinking, lost his job—which he didn't even want anymore—but once he sobered, he moved from Tennessee to Pennsylvania to fight alongside Ida. I guess it was his own kind of penance. The church did not agree with fighting at all, but especially against them. Ida was asked to repent for rising up, but she was so angry that this only made her fight harder. She and Russell tried pooling what little money they had and hiring a lawyer, but the only lawyer they could afford was an inexperienced one who doubted a case could be won against a group of people who would never fight back. The wheels of the *meiding* were put into motion then. Ida Mae knew it, but she didn't care. She'd already lost those she loved most, so she left the church before she could be shunned."

"So her *kind*, Daniel, was taken off life support?" I whisper the words, as if that will negate their meaning.

"That's just it," Norman says, seeming surprised by the unfolding story, although I am sure he has rehashed the nightmare countless times. "Ida is the one who took Daniel off life support, *not* the Amish. Eventually it had to happen, but it was as if once she'd lost everything—fought everybody—she was at peace to do what needed to be done."

I remember how angry I was after Tobias blackmailed me into leaving Copper Creek, an anger that caused me to reject to the same extent I had been rejected. I am thankful that I did not have to lose everyone I loved before I was willing to make peace with my past.

One of the night nurses, Leslie, knocks on the door and

opens it without waiting for my reply. She must sense that Norman and I are in the middle of a deep conversation, because she doesn't pause to start one with us. Walking over to the computer monitor, Leslie rolls out the keyboard beneath it and types in the information required before she can give Eli his treatment. She slips on a pair of latex gloves she has pulled from the cardboard box next to the bed, extracts from her scrubs pocket a capped syringe, then reaches into her other pocket for a glass bottle shaped like a baby food jar.

Taking off the cap, Leslie stabs the syringe's needle into the top of the jar filled with clear medicine, then expertly pulls the plunger back until she has the specified amount. With a fingernail that glows lime green even through her latex gloves, she points the syringe to the ceiling and taps the barrel to make sure no air bubbles are trapped inside. Leslie leans over the bed and inserts the filled syringe into the color-coded lines trailing like serpents from Eli's port. She does this same routine three more times—reaching into one pocket for a capped syringe, reaching into another pocket for a jar of medicine—and each time I wince, although I am told that Eli cannot feel the poisonous medication slithering through his veins.

Leslie discards the syringes and bottles of medicine in the metal hazardous-material bin with the red trash bag and rolls off her gloves from the backs of her hands to her fingers so that the gloves are inside out. Throwing these away as well, she smiles and offers a little wave, which Norman and I return. The door clicks shut. Norman and I face each other, oddly shy in the light of such blinding revelations.

"A month later," Norman continues, "Ida and Russell married at the courthouse. I went down to Tennessee for the wedding because *blut* was so bad between Ida and the Amish that no one else would be her witness. That was such an awful day. Attending that wedding brought back memories from my *bruder* and Ida's own wedding eight years before. Even now, I don't know why Ida and Russell got married. I think the two of them were just so bound up in their mutual agony surrounding the accident that they confused it with love, and they feared that losing each other would just bring the pain of their loss back.

"I was still so angry at Russell for not leaving me in that buggy and saving Daniel that as soon as the wedding ceremony was over and the marriage license signed, I went outside and told my driver to take me back to Pennsylvania. Some time later, I heard through one of my patients that Ida and Russell got divorced before their third anniversary. For nineteen years, I didn't see Russell or Ida again. And our lives probably never would've intersected again if your *mudder* hadn't called two months ago and invited me down to look at Eli. That's when I walked into this hospital room and found Ida Troyer—forgive me, Ida Mae Speck—sleeping next to your son's bed."

I remember the mask of disbelief Norman wore while watching Ida Mae sleep, and how angry she had been when he woke her up—an anger she used to defend me to my *mamm*. "That must've been quite the shock," I say.

"It was. But I'm sure it was a shock for Ida Mae, too. Waking up and seeing me here would've been like seeing my dead *bruder* all over again."

"Your brother, Henry—did he wear glasses?" I ask, recalling the crushed pair I'd found in the back of Ida Mae's jewelry box.

Norman nods. "We looked so much alike, that was the only way some people could tell us apart."

"Did they survive the accident? The glasses, I mean?"

"They were shattered," Norman says, "but, *jah*, they survived. When Henry was thrown from the buggy, the glasses were thrown too. A fireman found them when he was sorting through the wreck." Norman smiles sadly; when he speaks, tears coat his voice. "I guess you could say everything that survived the accident was shattered in one way or another. Henry's glasses, my legs, Russell's heart. . . . Before that night, I am told that Russell Speck was a very happy man."

Eli emits a pain-filled sound that should never come from someone too young to speak. I go over to the corner sink and run a *hunlomma* under warm water. Wringing it out, I wipe my son's swollen face, then refold it and drape it across his forehead. Even without having heard the results of Eli's PET scan, I doubt Dr. Sengupta is going to release him tomorrow.

Norman says, "I should go." I am suddenly too tired to protest.

It is considered inappropriate for Plain men and women

to embrace or even to shake hands. But before Norman Troyer leaves, he gives me a hug and even rests his large hand on my head like a benediction.

"Remember," he says before closing the door, "I'll come back if you need me."

It seems impossible that I have any tears left after these emotionally taxing months. But listening to Norman shuffle down the hall, I find that tears stream down my cheeks as if they have never stopped.

How very different my life would have been if Norman Troyer had been my *dawdy* rather than Samuel Stoltzfus, who hasn't been to check on his *grosskind* in the weeks we've been in Vanderbilt, while Norman's been here every day since he arrived. I have forgiven my *dawdy* for his detachment, which prompted me to seek an intimacy I should have never known, and I know I cannot blame him for my mistakes. Still, I believe that if Norman Troyer had been my father, my unholy union with Tobias wouldn't have been one of them.

## AMOS

Although Tobias has convinced himself that if not for Rachel's powers of seduction, he would not have been seduced, as he now peers out the window at crows forming curlicues across the frosted sky, he admits that the night he entered Rachel's room as if by accident was no accident at all. The lust for his wife's twin had grown at such a slow rate that—like a steady spreading of cancer that's not detected until it chokes out a vital organ—Tobias didn't know it was happening at all. Of course, he was aware of Rachel, had been aware of Rachel from the time he was twenty-two and she was ten. He sneers at his stupidity, recalling how he would forge a horseshoe in the fire and watch Rachel run up and down the hill beside his parents' Lancaster County home, chasing Judah. Her braided pigtails (a lighter blonde than they are now) would flutter out behind her and her laughter tinkle with this sound trapped inside it, like brass bells in a stone church. Tobias was not captivated by her then, and even though he was aware that she was a pretty girl soon to grow into a beautiful woman, he was not even attracted to her. He just knew that Rachel Stoltzfus was as different from her identical twin, Leah, as two roses that happened to grow from the same vine: one choosing to spread its blossoms in the sun, while the other remained ensconced in the shade.

My eldest son does not dig deep enough into his psyche to uncover the darkness that lurks there—that festers as it continues to grow without the antiseptic of light—but Tobias envied Judah from the moment he was born, and envied him even more when he realized that I was going to protect Judah from his abuse and the abuse Tobias encouraged in his siblings. At twenty-one years old, when Tobias should have been a man above such childish behavior, this envy he harbored for nine-year-old Judah extended over to the young girl Tobias knew his young brother idolized. As Judah's tales bordered on garrulous, Tobias listened; he listened to how Judah would insert Rachel's name into a dinner table conversation or watched his elaborate gestures describing the simple things the two of them had done: making mud pies along the cow pond, playing kick the can with Leah and Eugene, drinking *millich* from jelly jars out in the dairy barn. Tobias would nod and smile, take a bite of dried *kiehfleesch* or a sip of sassafras tea, acting the part of the indulgent older *bruder*, even as he was counting the days until he could take away from Judah the one thing he wanted most.

After two years passed, however, Tobias realized his quest to get back at Judah was going to take too much time. He did not want to wait five more years until Rachel was old enough to court and then another year to marry. Tobias resigned himself to a long-distance courtship with Esther Miller from a community in Bird-in-Hand, Pennsylvania. She was a dark-haired, dark-eyed girl with a clear complexion and a singing voice almost as musical as young Rachel's laugh. Yet Tobias did not love her. He did not know if this was because, for years, he had placed in his mind that one day he would take Judah's bride away before the two of them could even contemplate being wed, or if those summers he spent watching Rachel run and laugh up and down the hillsides had welded in his heart as irrevocably as he had welded the horseshoes with the forging hammer that the woman he would one day marry would have the same wavy blonde hair and stormy blue eyes as twelve-year-old Rachel.

Once Esther died shortly after Sarah's birth, Tobias's old pact to make Rachel his bride was what caused him to avoid her at his and Leah's wedding ceremony. He was beyond grateful to marry Leah, a soft-spoken *mudder* to nurture his *kinner* during the day and a soft body to warm his bed at night. But whenever he looked at Rachel sitting there in a cape dress the same hue as her eyes, it was all he could do to turn away and look at the blushing woman who—after listening to three hours' worth of sermons and exchanging a few words—would become his second wife.

Throughout that humid spring day in the schoolhouse, then at Verna's and my place for the wedding *esse*, he couldn't help comparing the two sisters, which was easy to do as they were often side by side. Their features were the same—a snub nose, a thin but shapely mouth, eyebrows a shade darker than their hair, and those blue, blue eyes—but there was something about Rachel's personality that turned these regular features into something ethereal. It was the way she would tilt her head in conversation like she was gripping every word; the way her cheeks could so easily burn with passion or become extinguished and pale; the way her eyes tilted up at the corners, giving the appearance that she was smiling even when she frowned; the way she moved across the room like her feet, although encased in the same clunky shoes as the rest of the female community, never touched the floor.

All these things Tobias saw, making a point not to look Rachel's way. It was as if the harder he tried to fight his attraction to her, the stronger that attraction grew. By the end of his and Leah's wedding day, his obsession had become so consuming that Tobias feared he would not be able to perform his conjugal duties that night, and later—as he held his trembling bride on their marriage bed, kissing Leah's temple and closing his eyes—he willed these images of Rachel back to the pit from whence they came. But they would not leave. And so that first night, the only way Tobias could get through the act that made him and Leah truly husband and wife was by envisioning that he was not caressing his bride but the woman who looked identical to her, the woman he had wanted for almost ten years.

In the early months of his and Leah's marriage, this carnal illusion never waned. When Rachel came to live beneath their roof, Tobias let himself imagine that she was coming down not to care for her bedridden sister, but because she cared for him. Before fantasy eroded his reality, Tobias knew this was not true. But the more time that passed and the more interactions he and Rachel had, the more he began to believe that she wanted him too. Soon afterward, Rachel dropped that jar of beet juice in the kitchen. Tobias desired her so much as he was wiping the scarlet stain from her red face that he had to get up and leave, stalking out through the living room without minding his shoes and smacking his way out the front door. My son spent the rest of that afternoon in the blacksmithing shed, heating wrought iron over the fire until it bent like taffy, then forging it into a shape he was never going to use, for the moment it hardened, he melted it down and forged it into shape again. This monotony lasted for hours. Sweat coursed down his forehead and stung his eyes. His clothing clung to his back and his ribs heaved with the intensity of labor. But he did not stop. Tobias *could* not stop. He was determined that he would not go home until he had pounded out the demons that tormented his mind.

When darkness swept its cloak over the community, the demons were still there and the refining fire burning out. Tobias walked home—blistered hands hanging like anvils at his sides—and all he could see for twenty miles were the stars arching over Copper Creek Mountain, like a bridge constructed in the heavens, and the oil lamps burning behind netted screens on the farmhouse porches. When Tobias came to the V in the lane, he began walking up toward the huge dwelling, its white clapboard a beacon in the night, contradicting the unease he felt when he was inside it. He saw a lamp lit in an upstairs window, and his pulse thumped. Had Leah been able to wait up for him? Had the nursing *bobbel* for once not sapped her strength?

As Tobias got closer to the house, he realized the light shining in the window was not coming from his and Leah's room. It was coming from Rachel's. With a heavy heart and an empty stomach, Tobias let himself in, mounted the staircase, and let his blistered hand slide up the banister, relishing the pain caused by the abrasion of raw skin on unsanded wood. He paused at the landing. His breathing grew ragged; his blistered palms became slick with sweat not brought forth by the temperature increase upstairs. Tobias could imagine Rachel sitting behind that closed door in a cotton nightgown like her sister wore, with her blonde hair hanging long and loose. He imagined that she had worried about him throughout the afternoon and evening, that her face had burned with the remembrance of their kneeling together in that stifling kitchen. All of this caused my son to stride toward her door. He even stretched out one hand to turn the knob. But the moment his raw skin touched the cool metal, Tobias jerked his hand back like it'd come in contact with a branding iron.

He could not do this to Leah, could not enter her sister's room when their own room was right next door. Leah was still his wife regardless of his years-long fantasy that Rachel was his bride. Releasing a shaky breath, Tobias took three more steps and turned the doorknob to his and his wife's room. The bedroom was dark and hot and smelled of diaper cream. Despite the heat, the covers were cinched around Leah's body as if she didn't want them or her disturbed. Their child, Jonathan, was asleep in his cradle at the foot of the bed. Peering in at him, Tobias shed his sweaty garments, draped them over the cedar chest where Leah stored her wedding dress and Jonathan's outgrown things, and slid beneath the sheets. Tobias reached out a hand and placed it on Leah's shoulder.

But she did not stir or make a sound.

Tobias was filled with such longing to reconnect with his wife and drive out the thoughts of her sister that he contemplated making love to Leah even if she was not awake. But he knew that was wrong. So my son flung off the covers, turned on his back, and stared at the moonlight polishing the dull ceiling silver until his exhaustion overcame his fear that he would not have enough strength to fight the feelings he harbored for Leah's twin.

# 17

## Rachel

Pushing open the heavy door, I step into the wind buffeting the concrete park attached to the hematology and oncology unit. To my right is a twenty-foot castle, icicled with turrets and porticoes, which the children have long since abandoned for the warmth of inside. To my left is a dragon whose mosaic scales shimmer in the late-afternoon sun. Planters filled with dry potting soil and crumpled leaves left over from summer punctuate the maroon playground mats along with three bench swings made from metal and wood.

At first, I think the kidney-shaped park is deserted, but

then my nose is pricked with smoke. I look in the corner to see the young father who sometimes comes out here to sneak cigarettes and cry. Scrubbing a hand across his dampened face in embarrassment, he nods at me, tosses his cigarette butt on the sidewalk, and stalks back inside.

He has a four-year-old daughter with leukemia.

I walk over to the secluded area where that young father stood—his smoke hanging thick on the air, his cigarette embers still glowing orange on the gray cement—and stare down at the city.

Nobody out there knows what is happening in here; nobody out there knows our stories or our struggles. Not the bohemian college students who squander time loitering in coffee shops and call it studying; not the suited workers who log in their forty hours a week one begrudging day at a time; not the homeless people who trudge up and down the sidewalks, packed down with everything they own like lackluster gypsies.

I do not blame these people for their oblivion. I did not know much about cancer and its rippling effects throughout daily life until my own life was assaulted with it. Now that I do, I would like to sink into oblivion as if it were a tepid bath and let the water close over my head, blocking all distraction and sound.

But I cannot sink into oblivion. Although I haven't recuperated from the last battle, I must prepare myself for the next, a battle that is going to make the last two months look like mere training ground. You see, Dr. Taizeen

Sengupta found cancer lurking inside Eli's bones when he performed the invasive bone marrow aspiration that left my son bruised and sobbing for days. In less than two months, the cancer's not only been unresponsive to the chemotherapy treatments, but the malignant cells have seemed to feed off the poison, flaring up in new places that never showed up in any of Eli's PET or CAT scans before. Because of this uncanny aggression, in such a short time Eli's non-Hodgkin's lymphoma has skipped from Stage II to Stage IV, those two innocuous numbers dropping Eli's chances of survival by 40 percent.

Yesterday, after spending the majority of the day conferring with pediatric oncologists across the nation, Dr. Sengupta took the elevator up to Eli's room. He rested his back against the corner sink, took off his designer spectacles, and anxiously twirled them by one ear stem as he explained the next step he would like to take. It was a radical step, Dr. Sengupta said, but one he believed was necessary to oppose the radical form of my son's disease. Dr. Sengupta wants to wipe out what little immune system Eli has left with intensive combination chemotherapy formulated to be more aggressive toward cancer cells than the last round. After this—after Eli's white cells are completely destroyed, leaving him so vulnerable to infection that a bouquet of flowers sent to the room could send my son to critical care—Dr. Sengupta would like to perform a bone marrow transplant.

Dr. Sengupta was kind enough not to gloss over the cold, hard fact that a bone marrow transplant is a risky procedure even for someone ten times the size of my son. In one hundred days, the patient's body has to either accept or reject the new bone marrow that has been placed inside it using a small bag filled with the yellowish fluid that drips down through an IV or a Hickman line like the one burrowed inside Eli's chest. Accepting this alien bone marrow would mean that the strands of Eli's six-and-a-half-month-old DNA have been totally revamped; if he were to cut himself, he would bleed the DNA of someone else's blood. But rejection means graft-versus-host disease (or GVHD, as the acronym-loving medical field refers to it), which is when the patient has not grafted the new bone marrow into his or her body, causing the body not to recognize these alien cells and to go into combat mode against itself. This new disease can affect the skin and the interior of the bowel, and if not treated, GVHD has the power to kill a patient faster than cancer ever can.

I have not told my *mamm* or Ida Mae what Dr. Sengupta said. They both know the chemotherapy did not do as intended and that the bone marrow aspiration Dr. Sengupta performed revealed more cancer. But they do not know about the possibility of a bone marrow transplant. I have not told anyone about this possibility because I am not sure what I am going to do. Dr. Sengupta might suggest a bone marrow transplant, but it is still just that—a suggestion, if an imperative one. In the end, the decision to bring my son through hell and hopefully back is up to me. I wish it weren't. Over half of Eli's life has been riddled with pain; am I now going to extend that pain over the next three months while Dr. Sengupta performs a procedure that sounds like something from a science fiction novel?

For twenty-two hours, I have been calculating the pros and cons of this quandary, trying to come up with a solution yet finding none. Although Dr. Sengupta has wisely given me my space, I can feel the tension radiating from the nurses as they cycle in and out to do their rounds. Many of the younger ones—like Leslie with her red hair and glow-in-the-dark nails—have not assumed that professional aura placing between themselves and us an invisible barrier that cannot be breached. I can see how their eyes sometimes mist as they look down at my son, whose angelic face is ravaged by the side effects of the chemotherapy more than the disease. Over the past two months, these nurses have been the first ones to see me awake and the last ones to see me crying myself to sleep at night. They have been the ones I run to when Eli's machines start beeping and I don't know why. The ones who chat with me in the darkness as they punch in the information the computer requires—the whole time acting like they haven't come in and seen me huddled in the pull-out bed, praying and sobbing while holding my son's fragile hand in both of mine. Almost all of these nurses I know by both first and last name. I know how many children they have and what grades they are in school, which subjects and sports they favor. At times, I feel like I know more about the nurses' lives beyond this hospital than they do about mine, but I think it is easier for them to share these empty details than to ask about our families and our lives, knowing that we are in the middle of being torn apart by this malignancy called cancer that someday could also affect them.

Last night, after Russell and Judah reassured me that they would remain with Eli, Ida Mae drove me to her tiny tin-roofed cottage between the highway and the train tracks. I was so weak as I climbed down from her truck that she had to run over and wrap her arm around my back to keep me from falling. In the house, she lowered me into a rocking chair and turned on the gas logs. I stared at the contorting flames, listening to Ida Mae drawing a bath for me. I could smell the lavender she poured into the water, and when I got up and staggered through her bedroom into the bathroom, I saw that the water was saturated with so much oil, the top glistened with an iridescent sheen.

Ida Mae forced me to sit on the closed toilet lid as she lit candles on the shelf, casting shadows on the walls that—in my sleepless delirium—looked like the face of a crying child. Motioning for me to stand, Ida Mae carefully slid out the straight pins that bound my cape dress together and pulled my legs free from the constricting black tights. As she continued to assist me in shedding the layers of my Plain garments, I recalled that Sunday morning I'd spent trying out her cherry-flavored lip balm and spraying myself with ancient perfume, envisioning that I was pierced and painted and parading the latest fashions like any other *Englischer* woman without troubles to her name. That dream seems so removed from me now; the only one I yearn for is that my son can make it out of that children's hospital alive.

Rolling up her sleeves, Ida Mae licked beads of sweat off her upper lip and slipped two arms beneath mine. My legs felt like Norman Troyer's must, as if every movement they made was for the first time. Water and lavender oil sloshed over the sides of the claw-foot tub and saturated the shag rug as my body sank weightlessly into the bath. In the week since Dr. Sengupta told me about the transplant, I hadn't bothered to bathe beyond what I could do in the hospital room's sink. In such a short time, the muscle lacing my flesh appeared to have sloughed off my bones. Ida Mae took the purple loofah from the shelf above the tub and squeezed some of Eli's No More Tears bath soap on it. Passing it to me, Ida Mae supported my upper body as I ran the sponge over my lower. Droplets of moisture struck the top of my head. I looked up and saw tears falling down Ida Mae's face even as her features were cast into a mold of fierce determination not to cry.

"You'll get through it, Rachel-girl," she whispered, taking the loofah and running it gently across my back. "But you gotta let us carry some of your burden. Your shoulders are too little to carry this all by yourself."

Just the thought of trying to speak required energy that I did not have to spare. Ida Mae seemed to understand. She bathed the rest of my body in silence, then squirted shampoo into her hands and massaged it through my hair until I fell asleep with my body nestled in the lavender water and my head resting against the sloped back of the tub.

Ida Mae, at almost sixty years old, must have carried me from that bathtub over to her bed. I do not know how she did it. Even though she is strong and I have lost weight, a body encumbered by sleep is somehow far heavier than when it is awake. But she must have, for this morning when I opened my eyes, the first thing I saw was not my son's atrophied face or the tubes snaking from his port, but the early spring sun spiraling in through Ida Mae's curtained bedroom window.

I yawned and stretched, peeling back the covers to find myself garbed in one of Ida Mae's huge tattered nightgowns. Snuggling deep down inside it like a scared child reassured by the familiar, I pulled the blankets back over my head and slept so hard, I dreamed of magical passenger trains that whisk people to places untouched by fear, disease, or death.

## AMOS

The past three months Leah hadn't gotten her monthly, she dared not hope that she had conceived again. But then—in the midst of nursing her other child—she recognized the brief flutter in her lower abdomen that was the slightest stirring of life, a butterfly unfurling inside her womb. Jonathan's violent birth had scarred her insides so much, the *doktors* didn't think she could conceive another child. They'd also cautioned her and Tobias that it would be wise not to do so, even if a miracle took place and they somehow could. The wall of Leah's uterus was so thin and pocked with holes, one stout kick from a fetus's limb could puncture through it; the *doktors* told her that she would probably have to be on bed rest not just for the last five months as she'd been with Jonathan, but for the pregnancy's entire duration.

In spite of these worries, I've noticed that Leah has told no one she is expecting—that, according to her estimations, she is already three and a half months along—for the pleasure of it is almost sweeter unshared. Each morning she awakes, rather than becoming torn between the pain she feels for her nephew and sister's plight and the pain her own husband and sister have caused, Leah instead thinks about this child—this miracle child—who is already finding his or her way inside her heart and swaddling a balm of peace around her mind. Taking a nine-by-thirteen pan of baked oatmeal laced with apple *schnitz* out of the oven, Leah places a hot pad on the table and slides the pan, wrapped in an old tea towel, onto it. Beside this, Miriam sets a crock of *millich* from the Guernsey and stirs it with a long wooden spoon to keep the cream from separating. A mason jar of *abbel budder* is opened along with a jar of crunchy peanut *budder* made from last year's crop. The four older children take their usual seats on the benches flanking the long pine table, their faces scrubbed after early morning chores, and clean hands folded in their laps although their feet tap the floorboards with an impatient staccato.

Leah waits five more minutes for Tobias to return from the barn. When he doesn't—the first time he has been late for breakfast in two years—she bows her head for the silent blessing, then motions for the children to begin dipping up their bowls. Even Miriam, who is too old to be excited about such a treat, smiles as she swirls *abbel* and peanut *budder* in her baked oatmeal, then pours on top of the steaming square *millich* that puddles around it as thick as whipping cream. My daughter-in-law knows she must act nonchalant for the children's sake, but inside she is wondering where Tobias could be. Before dawn, he awoke and went outside to milk and feed the animals, a chore that takes, at most, two hours.

After the dishes have been cleared and washed and Miriam has finished feeding Jonathan his own serving of oatmeal softened into a pasty mush, Leah asks Miriam to watch the children and heads outside to find her husband. She checks the barn first, but it is only occupied by the Guernsey, Mabel, whom Tobias keeps around for the extra cream so their family can have fresh *budder*, and a gray cat eating table scraps. Exiting the horse stalls, Leah walks past the sixty-foot Harvestore silo with rust streaking down the navy metal like dried *blut*. The air holds only vestiges of winter's chill as the weather catches up with spring, but Leah shivers once, twice, as her mind searches over the many places her husband might be.

Since that night Leah attempted to use her body to awaken her husband's love, the two of them have not really talked or touched. Still, she can see how her husband has aged in just a few months. Leah hears the words Tobias mumbles in his sleep when he stops tossing and turning long enough to tumble into restless dreams. Sometimes my son continues the conversation my abrupt death stopped. Sometimes he talks to Leah, the tone of his slumbering voice far more gentle than when he is awake. Sometimes he even talks to Rachel, but any word he utters is always barbed with anger.

Leah is on her way to Schlabach's Leatherworks when she changes her mind and walks to the schoolhouse instead. She does not know what leads her there other than the fact that her husband, in his distress, might return to the place where I had preached for years. The place where Leah and Tobias were married, the place where Tobias's peace used to be both sought and found. But besides a rabbit with a twitching nose and cotton-ball tail, there are no signs of life in or around the one-room building. Leah is about to resume her walk to the smithy when she hears a muffled sob coming from behind the schoolhouse. Thinking it is a child, Leah lifts her dress to her knees and dashes around the building toward the community graveyard. And although the sobbing does sound like it is coming from a child—from a broken child—it is not a child who is crying but a full-grown man.

Closing the wooden gate so its creaking does not disturb the mourner, Leah softly calls, "Tobias?"

But the person sprawled over my grave is not my elder son. No, ever since the first fingers of light prodded awake the nighttime sky and helped it change into dawn, Judah has been out here talking and crying to me, his earthly father, and railing against his heavenly Father for the pain being dealt out to the child and the woman he desperately loves. My youngest does not know why he felt so compelled to come back to a square, unmarked stone stuck above my sunken grave. He just knows that after Rachel told him about Eli's need for a bone marrow transplant—its substantial risks and exorbitant costs—he wanted the comfort of his father's touch, the comfort of his father's words. But that is something I can no longer offer him, and the grave where my earthly body rests is the closest he can come to being close to me again.

"Judah?" Leah takes small steps toward him. "You all right?"

My son sits up and wipes his face with the back of his hand, smearing the red earth that has turned to mud from his tears. Shaking his head, his breath twists in the frigid morning air. "The chemo didn't work." Judah looks to the side, at the other simple gravestones wedged in the soil like rows of teeth. "The doctors are going to have to do something else."

"Do they think that . . . that he'll still make it?" Leah isn't even aware she is crying until the wind hits her tears' salty warmth and turns them to twin streams of cold.

"They're talking about a bone marrow transplant," Judah says. "But first, they have to find a donor."

"A donor? For bone marrow?" Leah tramples the sodden ground and kneels before her brother-in-law, not even caring about the dirt that is grinding away the flowered pattern of her dress. "Can anyone be a donor?" she whispers. Her mind cannot traverse the conundrum of the medical field, but somehow her spirit knows that everything that has taken place until now—all the heartache, the tears, the emotional pain bringing with it an onslaught of physical repercussions—has happened for a reason.

Trying to recall what Rachel tearfully revealed to him last night, Judah says, "No, not anyone. It has to be someone whose bone marrow is an exact match for Eli's."

Leah swallows and shifts her right knee that has found a pebble lodged in the earth. "Like a parent?"

Judah shakes his head, and his sister-in-law finds momentary relief. Perhaps that premonition she had felt had been nothing; perhaps this new turn of medical events will not bring everything into the light that is safer kept in darkness. Even secrets kept from a husband by his wife. For Leah—sweet, naive Leah whom Tobias would never suspect of deception—has secrets of her own.

"No. A parent wouldn't be a close-enough match," Judah says. "The best donors are usually siblings."

"Siblings," Leah breathes, the fear of her words trailing on the wind like smoke.

Judah's eyes are so swollen that he cannot see the panic flaring up in hers. "But since Eli doesn't have any siblings, he's been put on a waiting list to try to find a match. Now we just have to hope one is found before it's too late."

"You don't mean that . . . Eli could die?"

"Rachel didn't say as much last night, but she wouldn't be this bad if Eli had hope beyond a transplant."

"How long since she's known?"

"Rachel?"

Leah nods.

"A few weeks." Judah sighs. "She kept it from us for as long as she could."

"Why would she do that?"

"I guess she didn't see any point in telling anyone, since Eli has no siblings. And Rachel's had to carry so much on her own, she didn't think one more burden would make any difference."

Leah can hear the accusation threading my son's innocent words: that she hasn't been to the hospital since Rachel and Eli have been in there; that she hasn't helped support her sister's burden even after Rachel moved down from Pennsylvania to help support the weight of hers. But Judah does not know the whole story; he does not know the secrets that were created beneath Leah and Tobias's roof. Leah springs to her feet. She marches toward the gate with old leaves clinging to her dirtied dress and determination hardening her spine.

"Where are you going?"

But Leah does not stop. Opening the graveyard gate, she lets it slap shut behind her. "I've got to get back to the barn. To make a call."

"Wait!" Judah cries. "Use my cell phone."

Leah freezes before she turns back to face him. She accepts the small flip phone that Judah is holding out. "Do you have Norman Troyer's number?"

Nodding, Judah steps so close she can smell his lemon aftershave as he helps her scroll through the programmed names to the one she wants.

Leah takes a deep breath as she looks at Norman's office number. "I'm going to need some privacy," she says.

Five minutes later, after Leah has confirmed her mounting medical suspicions with the only medical professional she knows besides her *mamm*, she steps from beneath the pine tree overshadowing Abram Beiler's grave and squints up at the bleached disk of sun. The juxtaposition of light and darkness has never felt like such a presentiment to Leah before; that soon—perhaps within weeks, perhaps within days—the truth is going to be illuminated for the entire Copper Creek Community to see.

"Judah," Leah calls, and then pinches her lips to stop their quivering.

My son stands from the resting place of his brother's first wife, Esther, and brushes from his hands the vinelike tendrils that had been crawling up around her gravestone's simple base, threatening to erase the proof of her short existence until he plucked them all away.

"Can you take me to the hospital, Judah?" Leah asks before her resolve has a chance to fail. "Can you take me to see my sister?"

## *Rachel*

Three weeks have passed since Dr. Sengupta placed my seven-month-old son, Eli Michael Stoltzfus, on the bone marrow donor list. Yet nothing has changed. Even the oncology nurses seem subdued by this endless purgatory of waiting. Red-haired Leslie no longer prattles about her boyfriend, who picks her up on his tandem bicycle with a wire basket in the front. Even Donna files in and out of Eli's hospital room, smiling her dimpled smile but not meeting my troubled eyes. It is as if they fear my sorrow is catching, but I know they just do not know what to say.

I don't know what to say either. I don't know what words of comfort to give my *mamm*, Ida Mae, or Judah because I fear that whatever I tell them will only be false hope and lies. All I do know is that every day when I wake up on that pullout bed and watch the sun rise over Nashville, I pray that Dr. Sengupta will come up and tell us that a bone marrow donor match has been found. But then the hours drag by.

I flip through one of the hardback classics Judah brought, which I am too tired to read, or I look at the TV, although my eyes cannot focus long enough to watch. And as the city lights flicker on to dispel the gathering darkness, I know that we are one day further from hope of finding a donor and one day closer to the death of my son.

My eyes are scanning the litany of *Faith, Hope, Love . . . Faith, Hope, Love* stamping the chapel walls in cursive script when my head sinks down onto my chest, and I find that I am softly snoring without my mind being fully disengaged in sleep. Stirring myself, I drape my body across the upholstered seats. The chapel was deserted when I entered, and I haven't heard anyone enter since. Perhaps I can take a short nap and then return to Eli's room before the milk shake I purchased for Ida Mae is completely melted.

I have no idea how long I have slept when someone shakes my shoulder. Bolting upright, I wipe a hand across my mouth and look up into the smiling face of my twin.

"Hated to wake you," Leah says. "You looked peaceful."

The fog of slumber clears from my mind, and I find myself again amazed at the nonchalance with which my sister approaches our reunion. I have not seen Leah since that snowy day outside the schoolhouse when I felt such distance between us. But now, here she stands in her flowered cape dress and black bonnet, smiling down at me as if she doesn't know the turmoil I have endured over the past three and a half months. The turmoil, if it had been up to her, I would have endured alone.

"Where have you been?"

"What do you mean?" Leah asks. "I just got here."

"No. Where *have* you been." I point to the stained-glass window depicting a multiethnic array of children smiling and laughing because their young lives have recently been freed from disease. I point out the words *Faith, Hope, Love* parading around the room, reminders of all the things the patients and their parents have in short supply. "Where *were* you when my son was throwing up in his crib? Where *were* you when his tube slipped from his port and blood gushed down his chest? Where *were* you when he had such a high fever, I wasn't sure he'd live through the night?"

Exhaustion removes my filter, and the condemnation of my words pours out of me, toxic as gall. Tears pour down my face, but they are only a visual extension of the anger erupting inside. Mopping my face with my sleeve, I suddenly panic and turn toward the double doors of the chapel that are standing wide. But no one is viewing this quarrel between two oddly dressed women who are identical twins.

Leah follows my gaze and then looks back at me. Giving me the same measured glance as that Sunday she came out of the schoolhouse to find me talking to her husband, she walks over to the doors, kicks the stoppers away with her black lace-up shoes, and lets them swing closed. She grabs a box of Kleenex, tugs out two tissues, and dabs the skin beneath each eye. Balling the tissues up in her fist, she strides toward me with her narrow shoulders squared.

"I did not come here today to confront you," she says

in Pennsylvania Dutch, her body and voice shaking. "But then you come at me like this. You tell *me* that I have betrayed *you*, when you, dear sister, are the one who has betrayed both me and yourself. You, who I fought for when no one else in our family, no one else in the community, would. You, who I let remain in my home when no one else, knowing the full depth of the situation, the full depth of your betrayal, would. But I didn't *know* the situation; I didn't know that you had betrayed me. I was too blind to see the adultery taking place beneath my own roof. The adultery taking place in the room right next to my husband's and mine."

My thoughts crash over one another like waves racing toward shore. But my heart does not race so much as it ceases to beat. If my sister had walked across the chapel and slapped me across the face, I could not be more surprised; her words and the tone in which she conveys them are a slap in the face in themselves. And though every word is painful to hear, I find an odd relief in having my culpability exposed by the person my selfishness has destroyed.

"Even when you first moved in with Tobias and me," Leah continues, "I had to repress this feeling that you were the other woman, his other wife. I thought it was just because of how we were in childhood, me always vying for *dawdy*'s attention while you had it effortlessly, and that it had scarred me to the point I carried it over into adulthood. I told myself that I was being foolish, even immature. That I could trust my husband. And even if I couldn't, I could at least trust *you* . . . my sister, my twin."

Leah's voice cracks, the only disclosure of pain she gives. Staring at the lacquered floor running down the chapel's center aisle, she says, "Even after that day I saw you and Tobias kneeling together in the kitchen, I never thought you would betray me. To this day, I *still* cannot believe it, but somehow I know it's true. I know it by the anger you and Tobias have for each other—an anger that was spawned through the debasement of immoral love. I know it by how frustrated Tobias is whenever you come around. This frustration that he takes out on his children, on me, was created because of what the two of you have done. And yet . . ." My sister's head comes up. Anger settles in her cheeks. If someone from the community saw us, they would think we have never looked more alike than we do now. "And yet, Rachel—my sister, my twin—I cannot help but love you. Despite everything you have done, despite how you have betrayed me and betrayed my family, I do not want to cause you the same level of pain that you have inflicted. I do not want your son to suffer even more because of the sins of his father. Because of the sins of his mother."

My voice is both confused and contrite as I ask, "What do you mean?"

"I mean, why I came here today: not to confront you about your betrayal with my husband, but to give you the most precious possession I have ever had."

I am so perplexed, I can't ask any more questions because I do not know where they would begin.

"Eli's bone marrow transplant," Leah says. "I think I have his match."

Shaking my head, I say, "But he doesn't have any siblings. The doctor put him on a waiting list for a donor—"

"Rachel," she interrupts, "you're wrong. Eli *does* have a sibling."

"What are you talking about?"

"Genetically," my twin says, like this should be common sense, although I have never been more mystified, "genetically, Eli *does* have a sibling." Leah puts a hand on my arm, a smile returning to her face even as her cheeks are still bright with anger. "Rachel, he has my son."

# 18

## AMOS

Leah has not mounted the first porch step when Tobias digs a hand into her forearm. "Where have you been?" he snarls.

Her curved spine straightening, Leah scrapes his hand away like it is leeching blood from her flesh. "I was at the hospital."

"I already told you—" Tobias scrutinizes her features to gauge if she is lying—"you can't go see your sister."

"I wasn't going to see my sister." Leah marches up the steps, turns, and looks down at her husband, who is no longer in position to tower over her. "I went to see our nephew."

Slamming his truck door, Judah strides across the yard and spits from between his teeth, "Or, not your nephew so much as your *son*."

Tobias knocks Judah's accusing finger away from his chest, dismissing both his younger brother and his younger brother's viewpoints as he has always done. Judah's temper that has been simmering since Rachel's confession reaches its boiling point. Rearing back, he shoves his brother with both hands; the impact sends Tobias sprawling on the division line between gravel and grass. But my firstborn does not remain down for long. Scrambling to his feet, he crouches low and drives his head into Judah's stomach, ramming the breath from his lungs. Judah staggers backward but remains standing. In the middle of the driveway in front of the white farmhouse, my eldest and youngest begin circling each other—their fingers outstretched and nostrils flaring—resembling a dark and a light alpha wolf from the same pack.

"Leah and I know everything," Judah gasps. "Rachel told us. . . . She told us that *you* fathered Eli."

Tobias cuts his eyes up to the porch. Seeing Leah's face, her wan features highlighted only by her blonde hair and tear-filled eyes, his black gaze narrows into slits. "Why would you believe that harlot?" he growls. "I bet Rachel can't even remember every man she's slept with."

Judah lunges. Binding both arms around Tobias's torso, he drives the arrogant bishop to the ground. In Tobias's thirty-two years and Judah's twenty, neither has been allowed to fight. Now, it seems the energy they have suppressed throughout childhood comes surging through their adult veins, causing them to grunt and curse as they wrestle more than swing fists. But the tumbling of their flesh across stones lances blood from their faces and scores cuts and bruises into their skin.

"You knew I loved her," Judah cries through broken lips, his wrath transforming into pain. "You knew I loved Rachel for years and you—you slept with her!"

Flipping his body on top of his younger brother's, Tobias grabs Judah's head with both hands and smashes it back against the gravel, the golden curls spilling over gray stones. "I did *nothing* to Rachel that she didn't want," Tobias hisses, the spittle of his words carrying further than he knows. "She wanted it all. She *encouraged* me." Judah turns his head from the stink of his brother's sweat and lies, but Tobias grapples Judah's cheeks, forcing him to listen to these words Tobias knows have the power to wound his brother more than any physical blow. "Rachel *never* loved you."

Tobias actually does not know if Rachel ever loved Judah or not. In this frenzied moment, he just wants his younger brother to learn the lesson that Tobias has yearned to teach him for years. That Judah—the overindulged child the Lord granted to Verna and me in our old age—cannot have everything he has ever wanted without sacrificing anything in return. Judah cannot have Rachel, the woman he dreamed would be his bride, for Tobias has already taken her, and in that one fleshly act, he has already taken her from Judah.

"She *never* loved you," Tobias repeats, not able to resist pouring salt into the wound he has just inflicted. "She never has, never will."

"Stop it!" Leah releases the porch post and stumbles down the steps as if awakening from a dream. "Just stop it!" she wails. "*Both* of you!"

She is almost to them when—without closing her eyes or breaking her fall—her knees give way and her body crumples onto the gravel. Clambering to his feet, Tobias runs over and scoops his wife against his chest. Leah's reed-thin legs dangling over his arms, Tobias rushes up the porch steps and bangs the front door closed with a hind kick of his boot.

Judah remains lying in the bloodied gravel outside his elder brother's farmhouse with tears leaking from his honey-colored eyes and sliding into the roots of his hair. He is grieving the loss of the woman he loves. But more than this, he is grieving the loss of the life with her that he will now never have.

## *Rachel*

The day Dr. Sengupta went through the innumerable risks Eli faced if a transplant match was ever found, he also explained that there would be no real risks for the bone marrow donor himself. The donor could not be very active for a few weeks, but in comparison to Eli's being confined to a hospital room for one hundred days and not being allowed to be carried into the hall without a mask first placed over his face to protect him from airborne infection, the side effects for a donor were really quite mild. When Dr. Sengupta told me this, I had pictured the donor as a thirty-five-year-old man with shaggy hair and an athletic build, a person who would bounce back from the surgery not feeling like something had been taken from him but that he had given something away. A gift, the incomparable gift of life.

But now that Jonathan might be going through the procedure involving a hollow needle inserted into the wings at the base of the spine to extract bone marrow, I am filled with dread. What if something goes wrong? What if Jonathan gets an infection? What if the transplant does not work and he lives with survivor's guilt, even if he cannot remember the infant cousin who died? With this perspective, a bone marrow transplant no longer seems like the best choice out of a selection of impossible ones. Yet, as I sobbed these questions through the sieve of Leah's skirt, she stroked my hair and reminded me that we were beyond the spectrum of best and worst choices, that we were at a crossroads where we must do whatever it takes to sustain life—even if it means risking the life of someone we love as much as the life we are hoping to save.

Leah and I must have remained in the chapel for over an hour; the milk shake Ida Mae had requested showed no semblance of its former state once I gathered it to leave. Still, no one entered the chapel in all that time. Twice, I heard one of the double doors open, then close, the people—displaying empathy only known when you have been in such a distraught place yourself—understanding that my sister and I needed the sanctuary of the chapel's walls a little more than they did.

When Leah and I returned to Eli's room, Judah and Ida Mae looked up from the foil wrappers holding their hot dogs and tater tots. "What happened with y'all?" Ida Mae took a slurp from the milk shake she must have asked Judah to get, since I never returned with her order. "You two get in a fight or something?"

Judah's eyes darted between my tear-streaked face and my sister's uncomfortable one. Wiping his mouth with a napkin, he cleared his throat.

"Cat got y'all's tongues?" Ida Mae prodded.

Leah chose to lead. "We think we might have a bone marrow match for Eli."

"Yeah?" Ida Mae popped a tater tot into her mouth. She garbled, not bothering to swallow, "Who?"

My sister's smile was a combination of triumph and nerves. "Jonathan," she said. "My son."

*"Jonathan!"* Ida Mae squawked. "That won't work. He might be a cousin, but he ain't no brother."

Breathing hard, I glanced at Judah. The whole time he visited Eli and me in this hospital—bringing my favorite foods and books and the card game Dutch Blitz that he and I, and sometimes even Ida Mae, would play in the family lounge if Eli was sleeping—Judah never once hinted about that day we kissed in the sleeting rain. I knew Judah remained silent because he wanted to let me focus on my son's health. Though I appreciate his consideration, Eli was not the reason I could not allow myself to speak. I loved Judah. I believe I always had, but my heart had been so encrusted beneath past scars, it could not reciprocate a healthy love when the opportunity came. But now that my heart had healed enough to realize that Judah always had a place inside it, Judah was about to learn the truth—causing me to believe that our love would never again be spoken of. This time, however, Judah would remain silent not out of consideration, but because he would no longer want a life with a woman whose past was as desecrated as mine.

I took another deep breath, and Leah slipped an arm around my waist. The reassurance of her support when I least deserved it was what gave me the courage to say, "Actually—" I paused and shifted my eyes away from Judah's—"Jonathan *is* Eli's brother. At least genetically. And genetically is all that matters as far as bone marrow transplants are concerned."

"I don't get it," Ida Mae said. "I don't get it at all."

My eyes drifted over to Judah's, but his were closed. A mottled flush had crept up his neck and soaked into his hairline. Standing, he pivoted and faced the window. Ida Mae might not have grasped the situation, but Judah King somehow did. I had to wonder if Judah knew without understanding every medical detail because a part of him had always known that Tobias was Eli's father.

"Ida Mae," I said because I could not bear to make Leah have to say it, "Tobias King, Leah's husband . . . he—he's Eli's father."

Ida Mae looked at me, then at Leah, then from Leah back to me. This ping-pong reaction reminded me of the times my sister and I had been at Root's Market or at the New Holland horse sale and people—both *Englischers* and Plain—stared between the two of us before asking if we were twins. This time, though, I knew that Ida Mae was looking for more than an uncanny resemblance. She was searching between the two of us to see what difference there could be in our character to make one twin and not the other fall so far.

"You saying that you—" Ida Mae took the straw from her mouth and pointed it at me—"you had a baby with your twin sister's husband?"

I nodded. Although Judah was still looking out the window, I knew my silent response was confirmation enough.

Spinning around so the get-well cards and balloons trailing along the window fluttered with his movement, Judah looked at Leah. "You ready? Everybody's probably wondering where you're at."

My sister took her arm from around my waist. Devoid of her support, I felt my body would collapse in on itself like a Chinese fan. I wanted to cling to Leah, to entwine myself around her slender frame that had grown in such strength. But I couldn't. She had to return to her home, to her husband, and this was when I realized something so obvious, only in my deliriously hopeful state could it have slipped my mind.

"Tobias." My grip on Leah's upper arms communicated the desperation I felt. "We forgot about Tobias. We can't use Jonathan for a bone marrow donor if we don't get his permission too."

My sister pried my fingers off her arms. "Don't worry, Rachel," she said. "Let me take care of him. You just take care of yourself . . . and Eli."

Leah stepped away from me and over to my son's bed. The pain medication the nurses had given him to counter the burning from the radiation to the growth inside his chest caused Eli to be so drowsy, he wasn't even aware that anyone else was in the room. My sister reached out and placed her palm to his forehead. I knew from all the times I had done the same action that she would be surprised by his skin's dry texture that was so hot to the touch.

Sealing his forehead with her lips, she moved away from the bed and wrapped her arms around me. For the briefest instant, I could sense the sorrow emanating from below the surface of her determined frame. I held her even tighter and wept. "I'm so sorry."

Her stomach heaved. Again, I felt the slight bowing in Leah's womb that matched the swell left over from Eli. But the bulge in her womb, even though five months older, was strangely larger than my own. Moving a hand between our bodies, I pressed it to Leah's lower abdomen and looked up. There was such beseeching in her eyes, I held my tongue.

Judah maneuvered his body around ours. The door clicked shut. "Don't worry," Leah said, releasing me. "Everything will work out in the end."

I knew my sister spoke not only of her and me, but of Eli and Jonathan and the promise of a bone marrow transplant, of this baby growing inside her womb when that womb was not supposed to bear the weight of any more children.

Not knowing what to say when there were so many things I couldn't, I murmured, "Please, take care of yourself."

Leah touched the back of her hand to my cheek. "I will," she said. "You take care of yourself, too."

Then, calling out good-bye to Ida Mae, my twin was gone, the only trace of her a crushed leaf that had fallen from her dress and a clod of dirt that had dropped from the bottom of her lace-up shoe.

## AMOS

Leah had collapsed enough times to recognize her body's warning signals and, even better, to know exactly how to fake them. At first, the ruse was not meant to manipulate her husband in one direction or another. She just knew the only way to stop the fight between Tobias and Judah was to cause a diversion, and the physical distress Leah felt at that moment—looking down from the porch as her husband and brother-in-law wrestled over her twin—would have caused even the stoutest of hearts to grow faint. The rapid breaths, dilated pupils, frantic pulse, and pale skin: these symptoms of another collapse were quite easy for Leah to duplicate.

After she did collapse, Tobias carried her upstairs to their room and stretched her out on the bed. He eased her shoes off her feet and dragged a blanket up to her chin as though Leah were a child. Tobias looked so alarmed that she had to suppress the impulse to sit up and smile, to tell her husband that everything was fine. But there was no faking the fact that everything was *not* fine. That their marriage had been a hoax from the moment Tobias's letter arrived in her parents' mailbox outside their yellow house on Hilltop Road, and that it had only grown into more of a hoax as the years passed by.

Leah was tired. She was tired of living a lie, and she was tired of the lie's repercussions. She might have known it was wrong to respond to that letter addressed in Tobias's hand, but surely such a simple deception was not worth such a punishment of sorrow and loss. Surely it was not worth having your husband and sister conceive a child beneath your own roof, in the room right next to the room where, five months before, your own child was conceived. These thoughts revolving around her son and her sister's child were what drew Leah out of the past and back to the present. She had promised Rachel before leaving the hospital that she would take care of Tobias if Rachel would just promise to take care of herself, that she would somehow talk her husband into letting Jonathan become Eli's donor. That was when Leah realized, by continuing this ruse of illness, she could manipulate Tobias into helping save her ill nephew's life.

Three days have now passed since Leah resigned herself to self-imposed bed rest, the longest three days of her life. When she was on bed rest before, she had felt so unwell that the room for the most part had felt more like a refuge than a cage. But whenever Leah hears the children downstairs eating a meal that Miriam has prepared or the screen door slapping shut as they venture into the balmy warmth of spring, it takes all her willpower to remain in bed. She knows her ruse of sickness is working, though, which strengthens her resolve to stay. Each time Tobias comes up to check on her, she can tell by the expression haunting his dark eyes that he believes everything that has happened to her has been his fault, and he would do anything to rectify it. Anything to make her well again. Despite this, Leah has not made her request known. She has been biding her time so that whenever she does mention it, Tobias will have no need for suspicion.

There is a rap on the door so gentle, it is more a brush of knuckles on wood than a knock. Nudging the door open with his hip, Tobias brings in an oil lamp and a bowl of *hinkel rivvel supp* and places both on the cedar chest parallel to the bed. Tobias sits on the edge of the mattress, which hammocks beneath his weight, and takes his wife's hand, threading her fingers with his. "How are you feeling?" he asks, resting his other hand against her cheek.

Leah manages a fatigued smile even as her heart starts to pound. She wonders if this is the time to bring up the origin of Eli's birth and how their son could now save this illegitimate child's life, *his* illegitimate child's life. For despite the shame surrounding Eli's conception, he is still Tobias's son, is he not? Wouldn't Tobias still like to see Eli whole even if that meant revealing to Copper Creek that *he* was the child's father?

Leah licks her lips. Mistaking her nervousness for thirst, Tobias stretches over to the cedar chest and brings her a cup of water. She smiles her gratitude and takes a sip. Tobias fluffs her pillow before she settles back against it and, for a moment, Leah's resolve to ask him these questions fails her. Looking up at Tobias, she instead tries to discern this man she married who is such a shifting amalgam of darkness and light. But by the gilded wash of the oil lamp, she cannot tell where one part of him lets off and another begins.

"Tobias," Leah says.

Her husband leans down and smooths a strand of unwashed hair behind her ear. "What is it?"

"Aren't we ever going to talk about you and Rachel?"

His hand drops from her ear. Sitting up higher on the mattress, Tobias folds his arms. "What is there to talk about?"

"I think there is plenty." Leah has to make an effort to keep her voice weak.

Striding to the end of the bed, Tobias winds both hands around the carved footboard. "Like what? What's in the past should remain in the past."

"Not when it's affecting the future of your son."

Tobias's head snaps up. "Jonathan?" He points at the cradle although their child is playing downstairs. "What does *he* have to do with this?"

"Everything," Leah says. "Eli needs a bone marrow transplant, and Jonathan could be his donor."

"His donor? What do you mean, his donor?"

"Because you have fathered both Eli and Jonathan." The muscles of Tobias's face spasm, and although Leah's insides are trembling, she forges ahead. "And because my sister and I are identical twins, Eli and Jonathan could share as much DNA as siblings. Norman Troyer said there would be a 25 percent chance that—"

Tobias's arms fling wide, the span of them almost the width of their bed. "You talked to that powwow *doktor* about this?"

"Yes." Leah forces herself to stare into her husband's hostile eyes. "I talked to Norman. I had to ask him if it was even a possibility before I got Rachel's hopes up again."

Tobias stalks toward the front of the bed. "How many know?" he asks.

"Ida Mae from the Amish store. Judah, Rachel, Dr.

Sengupta, and—" Leah's body cowers beneath the covers, but she sticks out her chin—"and my *mamm*."

Tobias's beard twitches as he clenches and unclenches his jaw. His fists following this same movement, he creeps toward her. "And why did you tell your *mudder*?"

"Because . . . because she came over here when she heard that I collapsed in the yard, and I told her that Eli might be able to have his transplant after all."

The light of the oil lamp captures the dark sheen lurking in her husband's eyes, and Leah knows which side of Tobias's dual character has won out. Peering down at his wife for a suspended moment, Tobias draws his hand back—the hand that had caressed her—and brings the splayed flat of it against the side of Leah's face. Her head cracks to the side, her loosened hair floating before settling back around her shoulders. Tears fill Leah's eyes and trickle over her face, but these tears are caused more by the pain rupturing her heart than the pain inside her head. Pressing the sleeve of her nightgown against her bleeding nose, Leah glances up at her husband and is amazed by the transformation she sees. Tobias's face is pulled back in a deathlike mask of horror. The obsidian of his eyes that Leah had glimpsed right before he struck her has been replaced with such shock, the dark irises are completely ringed with white.

"I'm . . . I'm sorry." His tongue stumbles over the syllables. "I never meant to—to hit you."

Leah would like for her sister or *mamm*'s strength to

rise up in her now. But right when she needs it most, Leah finds that all the strength she has exuded since Rachel left Copper Creek has vanished from her painstaking reserve. Instead, Leah looks up at her husband, who has somehow captured her heart even as he was in the midst of giving his own away, and weeps. She weeps so hard that the pulsing sensation in her nose balloons across her skull, causing yellow starbursts to dance before her eyes. Leah knows that if Tobias were to climb into the ruse of her sickbed and hold her that she would let him, that she would weep against his broad chest and forgive him for everything, *everything* that he has ever done.

Yet Tobias does not hold her.

The image of his twenty-year-old wife curled up in their bed with blood spilling from her nostrils is too searing for him to bear. Muttering an oath, he stalks across the room and jerks open the door. Leah lies there in their defiled marriage bed, staining her pillow with blood and tears, and listens to the sound of Tobias charging down the steps as if the whole world is on fire.

# 19

## Rachel

The call comes at midnight. At first I think the tinny beeping is the monitor saying that another tube has become disconnected from Eli's port, but then Ida Mae sits up from her cot and staggers across the hospital room. Slinging her arms left and right, she slaps her hands on the food tray table until they land on the cell phone.

Ida Mae flips it open and grunts, "Yeah." The caller hasn't talked for long when Ida Mae pinwheels the arm not holding the phone. I dart over, wide awake.

"Who is it?" I ask.

"Your momma."

"What's wrong? Let me talk to her!"

Ida Mae hands over the phone.

"Everywhere," my *mamm* sobs. "We've been looking everywhere!"

"What for?" I ask. "What did you lose?"

She gasps for breath. "Not what, Rachel. *Who!* Tobias. He's disappeared!"

I am not too alarmed. If Tobias dropped off the face of the earth, I would be sad for Leah and their family, but I wouldn't exactly grieve for him. But if he is not here to sign the permission form for Jonathan to be Eli's donor, I know Dr. Sengupta will never go through with the transplant.

"When did this happen?" I ask.

"About three hours ago. He and Leah got in this awful fight, and he just left. Didn't take a horse and buggy . . . nothing."

"They got in a fight?" I don't know what surprises me more: the fact that Tobias has vanished or the fact that he and my sister—who was so passive throughout childhood, she would never even raise her voice in play—have quarreled.

My *mamm*'s sigh is so immense, I can feel the weight of it through the phone. "Rachel, he struck your sister."

"No." My body flushes with heat even as goose bumps prickle across my skin. I begin pacing the floor in front of Eli's hospital bed like a horse on a short lead, my nightgown swishing around my ankles, my bare feet making sucking sounds on the tile. Ida Mae watches all of this with concern but doesn't mouth any questions I do not have the answers to. Crushing the phone against my ear, I hiss, "Tell me he didn't."

"*Jah.* He did. Leah said they fought about the bone marrow transplant. Tobias doesn't want the community knowing he's Eli's *vadder*. After he hit Leah, he ran out of the *haus*. Leah sent their *buwe* out looking for him—they even searched the woods—but he's nowhere. Reuben came over and got *Dawdy* and me out of bed about an hour ago, but we can't do much but wait. Judah's out looking now."

"I'm going to come."

I hear my *mamm* sigh again, but this time from relief. "I hoped you would. I didn't want to ask . . . not with Eli."

"I'll have to get Russell to come here before we can leave."

"Don't be too long, Rachel," my *mamm* warns. "Leah needs you. I don't think—I don't think Tobias is well."

"I think you're right, *Mamm*." I watch the peach-colored city lights sparkle through the blinds and remember that night I saw the sun rise over Copper Creek Mountain, knowing as it did that my life would never be the same. "I don't think Tobias has been well for quite some time."

This is the first I've ridden with Ida Mae that she has not played the radio, and I am relieved. My mind is so cluttered with thoughts, I do not think it could withstand any more stimulation. Resting my head against the window, I try to keep my breathing regular as I replay an incident as shocking as Tobias striking my sister before disappearing into the woods.

Those five months after I moved down, so many questionable episodes took place between my sister's husband and me, it is now hard to determine which was the catalyst that set the events of that raw December night into motion. A night so cold, no amount of covers and shivering could get my body warm. I was padding downstairs to make tea when Tobias came into the house, holding his muddy boots in one hand. His suspenders were looped down on either side of his black pants, his white shirtsleeves rolled to his forearms and stained around the edges.

"Leah?" Tobias squinted up at me standing on the moonlit steps.

"No," I clarified. "Rachel."

"Rachel."

A shiver arched up my spine. I tried to keep my voice steady as I said, "How's the horse?"

"Not *goot*. The Epsom salts didn't work."

"Did you try packing the frog with calcium sulfate?"

Tobias shook his head.

I listened to the wind howling around the house like it was searching for a way to get in, to the glass chattering at the windowsills like teeth. "Perhaps I should take a look at her?" Tobias knew how much I had helped my *dawdy*.

He pointed over his shoulder. "It's bad out there."

"Can't be worse than Pennsylvania. Let me get my coat."

When I came downstairs, Tobias had his boots back on and was facing the door, clutching a lantern in his hand. I went to stand beside him, still in my nightgown but weighted with my coat and a satchel of holistic medications my mother had forced me to take in case Leah needed them.

"You're sure about this?" Tobias searched my face without meeting my eyes.

In response, I smacked open the door and marched into the blustery weather. Tobias followed, the lantern he carried throwing circles of light across the dead grass. The wind cut our cheeks and sliced through our jackets like a knife. Side by side, we stepped into the barn's shelter, which felt immeasurably warmer than outside. I inhaled the muddled compost of hay, fermented silage, saddle soap, and dung: the scents of my childhood.

Tobias held the lantern high. "She's in here," he said.

I motioned for him to lead, then took one step and tripped over a pitchfork. Tobias turned and caught me. Staring up at him, I watched pieces of sawdust filter down from the haymow and dust his broad shoulders and hair. I reached out and brushed a strand of hay from his right shoulder. His grip tightened on my ribs. My sister's husband leaned his head closer to mine. Even by the lantern's murky glow, I saw Tobias's pupils bleed into his dark eyes. His lips parted.

The infected horse stamped once and snorted. Tobias removed his hand from my back and strode into the stall. I took a breath and followed. The huge Clydesdale was standing in the far left corner, favoring her right foreleg with the abscess. Her head was down, her nostrils dripping, velvety lower lip hanging slack. With every wave of pain, her powerful muscles rippled beneath her smooth, fawn-colored hide. I knew her case was hopeless even before seeing how far the tentacles of infection had reached.

I tossed my coat over a loosened hay bale the horse had been too sick to eat and rolled the sleeves of my nightgown. Kneeling beside the mare, I tapped the back of her right knee. "Lift," I commanded, squeezing her feathered hock. "Good girl."

Her hoof was the size of a serving platter. The fever snaking up through the soft lamina radiated out through her skin and warmed my hand like a flame. Though drained of pus, the flesh still smelled like rotten cheese. Breathing through my mouth, I asked, "You have a hoof pick?" Tobias nodded. "Can you run it through the lamp's flame first?"

He did and passed the silver pick to me. I prodded the inflamed frog, but my first instinct had been right: the infection had spread so high up the white line connecting the hoof capsule to the bone, there was little we could do besides euthanasia. I still had to try. Growing weary of her awkward stance, the Clydesdale began to rest her massive weight on me. I crab-walked into a firmer position. "That bag over near the hay bale," I said. "I need a bottle that says calcium sulfate."

Tobias sorted through the contents and dropped the blue bottle in my lap. I unscrewed the cap and tilted the bottle until a steady stream of powder poured out into the softened frog. Batting at the cloud hanging over my head, I asked Tobias to pass me a spool of gauze. This I wound around the frog to seal in the calcium sulfate and block out any more infection. I slid the hoof into a burlap sack that Tobias held out for me, fastened this with a strip of twine, and lowered the mare's foot to the freshly mucked floor.

Hobbling to my feet, I rested a hand against my lower back and stroked the mare's muzzle. Her limpid brown eyes flicked up and met mine with such a look of intense suffering, they almost seemed human. "Oh, Tobias," I sighed. "I don't think there's anything we can do."

Tobias rose from the bucket he'd turned upside down and used like a chair. Coming to stand beside me, he slipped his arm around my lower back. This time, I did not look up at him in confusion or try to decipher his actions. I just leaned against his body, savoring its warmth and strength when I had no right to.

My brother-in-law and I were silent as we exited the horse stall and crossed the short distance between the farmhouse and barn. My pace was far more hurried, causing the wind to iron my nightgown to my legs and flap open the lapels of my coat. Plodding up the porch steps, I opened the front door without letting the screen door slam behind me. I was halfway up the staircase when Tobias came in. I did not turn or say good night, but continued mounting the steps until I'd reached the safety of my room. Leaning against the door with my heart rushing in my ears, I could still feel Tobias's eyes burning their way through the wood, burning the clothes off my back as they had the entire time I climbed the stairs.

Bathing my face and hands in the *weschbohl* of frigid water on the dresser, I unbuttoned my nightgown and dabbed at the skin of my neck and chest with a cloth. Even without the mirror we were forbidden to possess, I knew how flushed I was. I could feel a fever roaring through my body as aggressively as that infection was spreading throughout the horse. I was attracted to my sister's husband. I had known this since that hot afternoon Tobias so tenderly wiped the stain off my face as we knelt in the kitchen. But I had never admitted how much this attraction consumed me until now. I had thought that he and I could just continue living a hairbreadth away from each other while aware of our temptation, yet doing nothing about it. Recalling how the two of us had locked eyes after I stumbled in the barn—our bodies trembling although our limbs barely touched—I knew it was no longer safe to remain here, to remain sheltered beneath my sister's roof when that meant sleeping one thin wall away from her husband.

There was a gentle rap on the door.

"Yes?" I said.

The door opened as I turned from the dresser and put down the cloth. My breath caught. There Tobias stood with my sister's wedding-ring quilt draping his arms like an offering. But when his gaze fell on me—on the moonlight spangling my open nightgown and flushed skin—the quilt fluttered from his arms and pooled at his feet. Tobias reached behind him and closed my bedroom door without taking his eyes from my face. Trampling the quilt, he strode across the room; his steps were so careful on the floorboards that, although the whole house was moaning with the wind, there was not a single creak.

Tobias's breath pattered against my face. I could smell the salt on his skin. "Rachel?" Leah's husband asked.

I did nothing to shield my nakedness or to shield the naked look of longing in my eyes. "Yes," I said, not knowing what he had asked or what I was really answering. "Yes, Tobias."

And as Tobias's head bent, bringing the first touch of his cool lips against mine, the fever raged throughout my body. I knew then that whatever happened tonight, both he and I were consumed.

"Wake up." Ida Mae pushes my shoulder. "We're almost there."

My eyes snap open. Pressing my body against the passenger door, I clench my forehead as tears drip between my fingers like rain.

"Rachel-girl," she says, squeezing my knee, "they're gonna find Tobias. Judah's probably done found him, and in all the hubbub, they've just forgotten to go out to that barn and give us a call."

I wail, "But I don't *want* them to find Tobias! I wish he were dead!"

"Rachel Stoltzfus!" Ida Mae chides. "You can't go wishing people dead, honey. No matter how much you might hurt. Take it from somebody who knows. That kinda hate will eat you from the inside out and leave you just a husk of what you once was. Like a locust shell stuck on a tree."

Drawing in a shuddering breath, I wipe my face on the front of my dress. "Did you hate the Amish church for what they did to you? For making you take your child off life support?"

Ida Mae clutches the steering wheel and shifts the wad of snuff to her other cheek. "Russell Speck," she spits, blaming him for my knowledge of her past and not Norman Troyer, the man who told me. Swatting her right blinker, Ida Mae careers her truck up Copper Creek Mountain. Her brights bounce off the narrow, corkscrewing road. "Yeah," she says. "I hated everyone in Flat Plains so much, I wished they'd all keel over like flies. But then, after the smoke cleared and I was the only one standing there—the only one in my immediate family who wasn't in the grave—I realized the person I hated the most was myself. You see, I made my sons, Jacob and Daniel, go with Norman and Henry that day 'cause I wanted them out from underfoot. I packed 'em all a big picnic lunch and told them not to come back before supper. Such a wonderful day I had. I loved having every minute to myself: no cooking, no cleaning, no wiping up spills or taming strubbly hair. I took me a long nap, then went for a walk around my in-laws' land. I had no idea that that day I ate up the quiet would be the first day of the rest of my life that the quiet reminded me of everything I'd lost."

I begin to cry again as I watch tears wind down Ida Mae's face. "For a long time . . ." She pauses. "For a *very* long time, I blamed myself for my sons' deaths and for the death of my husband. And the only other person in the world who understood my pain was the man who believed he was responsible for it."

"Russell," I say.

Ida Mae nods. "I didn't marry that man 'cause I loved him—'cause I sure didn't at the time. I married that man 'cause every morning I woke up with Russell Speck in my bed was like putting flowers on my sons' graves or taking down the books they'd made that were still at their *gross-mammi's haus*, laying out to dry, when that state trooper come driving up that lane and told me about the accident."

"And the blue room? The bunk beds?" I ask, recalling how it used to look before I returned from that upsetting weekend at Copper Creek and found everything repainted green. Everything made fresh and new like a thawing spring rain after the last winter storm.

Ida Mae drags a flannel sleeve across her nose and clears her throat. "That stuff was never my sons'. After me and Russell split up 'cause looking at him stopped being a balm and started being the knife that kept peeling scabs right off my wounds, I no longer had no monument of grief to wake up to every morning. That's when I decided to make that blue room. I went to Goodwill and yard sales and decorated that room with everything I imagined my boys would have wanted if they'd been English."

I ask, "What made you give it away after all that time?"

Ida Mae slows the truck. I can hear gravel crackling beneath the tires. Leaning over, she rests her weathered hand against my cheek. "You did," she says, tears spilling from her eyes even as she takes her thumb and wipes my own away. "You and Eli did. After the doctors told us about his cancer, I realized how much I loved that little man. How much I loved *you*. I knew then I couldn't keep living with one foot in the past and another in the grave when that little man needed me, when *you* needed me. I know it sounds awful, but Eli being diagnosed with something that could take his life gave me something to live for. 'Cause for the first time in twenty years, I had something to *fight* for."

"So you repainted the room."

Ida Mae smiles. "Yep. I painted over that room and burned everything I could within Blackbrier limits. Russell Speck helped me that whole weekend. He never left my side 'cept to go home to sleep. I knew then how lucky I was to have this good-hearted man still standing by me after all these years I'd been so hateful to him. So, you see—" Ida Mae takes the left side of the lane that divides Tobias and Leah's house from Verna King's—"if I hadn't let go of the past, if I hadn't let go of all that hate and let myself love again, I'd be missing out on so many good things. Things like you and Eli and that confounded man, Russell Maynard Speck."

She flips her headlights to low, but not before I notice Judah King leaning against his truck's back bumper with his arms crossed and eyes squinted against the brightness. Ida Mae pulls her truck up behind Judah's and lurches it into park. Turning off the ignition, she stares at him before looking over and touching my face. "Promise me, Rachel-girl . . . Promise me you won't let hate for Tobias make you miss out on love. No matter what this community does or whether Leah forgives you, you gotta promise me that *you* will forgive. That you won't live your life wishing you could do it over. That your life will keep moving forward, that your life will keep going on."

"I promise," I whisper.

I climb out of the truck, and my twin rushes down the three porch steps with one hand over her battered face to stifle her sobs. Closing my eyes, I pray for the Lord's infinite mercy. Without it, I do not know how my life can keep moving forward. My life is the reason so many other lives will never be the same.

# 20

## AMOS

I do not know how long I have watched Tobias run through the woods with branches slapping his face and brambles lashing his skin. But I do know that he must stop soon. His rib cage is laboring like fireplace bellows. The small portion of his body that is not stippled with blood from its collision with briars is covered with sweat that plasters his torn shirt to his chest and gleams like silver on his skin. Right after Tobias struck his wife and went charging into the night, I approached my heavenly Father and beseeched him to let me go—once, just this once—back to Earth to speak Life into my son. I could see how Death leered down from the trees and lurked in the corners of Tobias's desperate mind. I could see how every breath my son released into the air was putrid and as dark as the wilderness Tobias dove into.

In three days, my son had come to the end of himself. He had nothing left to live for, nothing left to gain or lose, and the voices hissing in the recesses of his mind told him that he should then choose to die. Taking death into his own hands was the one last thing Tobias could do for his wife and family, as they didn't need such a volatile man wreaking havoc on their lives. It would be insufficient to say that Tobias was not thinking clearly as he charged into those Copper Creek woods. Tobias was not thinking at all. His thoughts had been left to their own sinister devices for so long, now that he wanted to rein them in and take control he found that he *had* no control. So he gave in to these thoughts that had wielded their power over him for years when he believed he was the one who, regardless of his dalliance with lust, still held dominance. He gave in to the thoughts that told him he should just end it. End the torment, end the suffering . . . end it all.

These tormenting voices are the reason—hours later and as winded as a green-broke horse—Tobias continues to run. The reason he runs until he doubles over and vomits the bile of his soul into the twisted undergrowth of the woods.

*Please, Lord,* I plead in my spirit. *Please let me go to him.*

But still, I am not released.

I grasp the gilded arm of the park bench. My son clatters down a ravine, clutching at saplings and kudzu roots to alleviate a fall. Springwater splatters his leather boots and saturates his pants up to his ankles. Tobias's nostrils flare and his mouth gapes wide as he struggles to suck in oxygen his body is too exhausted to absorb. The waning crescent flickers through the trees hardly budded with enough foliage to shield their skeletal forms. Through this filtered luminosity, I can see the ravine—no more than a darkened slash in the earth—yawning open to a cliff whittled from shale.

A grin slithers across my son's features, but I sense he is not the one causing its form. His troubled soul sees this cliff too, causing Tobias to believe his end is found. Stretching out his arms as if to embrace it, Tobias begins his reckless descent. I yearn to cry out, but no words I utter from this celestial park will ever reach his ears. Hanging my head, I close my eyes. I cannot watch my eldest son go over the precipice from which there is no hope of return. This is why I do not see so much as hear Tobias's dampened feet become ensnared, and his body begin tumbling beneath a Force far more powerful than gravity. I look up. My son flips down the ravine, his white shirt and black pants a checkerboard kaleidoscope. Smiling, I think, *Your ways are not my ways, Lord.*

With one wild somersault loosening pebbles and clods of decomposing earth, Tobias's body ceases its kinetic momentum. He is so close to the cliff edge, his left arm dangles like it is hanging over a bed. Not a finger on that hand moves, not a muscle on Tobias's body twitches, not an eyelash flutters against his cheek.

My fatherly heart aches watching my son, yet I trust that our heavenly Father—who loves him even more than I—has allowed Tobias's fall from such a great physical and metaphorical height. Peace floods my mind and renews my spirit. My eyes clench shut as the heavenly realm begins rushing up at me until I can hear the thunder of a thousand galaxies zipping past my ears. My eyes open. I can see years streaking by—time reduced to the tail end of a fiery comet—along with the explosion of supernovae in that unexplainable void called space. Closing my eyes again, I bow my head as I begin my journey through the opalescent haze of the Milky Way to a foreign planet I called home a mere five months before. My descent through the Earth's atmosphere appears the same as when I check in on my family from time to time, but it does not feel the same. Not at all. Although I am not back in the flesh that once housed my spirit, my soul feels weighted with the cares of the world I hadn't known I had left behind until now.

The greenish-gray shape of the Americas surges up at me, resembling a cookie cutout slid on a place mat of blue cloth. I spread my arms and fingers and let the air buffet against my body, easing me down through the layers as a feather floats on the wind. To my left is the spiny black ridge of the Smoky Mountains connected to the larger vertebrae of the Appalachian chain. My speed increases the closer to my destination I draw. The must of lichen, mossy wood, and wet-weather creek beds clotted with old vegetation fills my nostrils. It is a familiar scent: the scent of my community, the scent of home.

Swooping past feathered pine boughs and hardier deciduous trees, my body comes to rest on wet grass that cushions my limbs like a quilt. I sit up and brush twigs off my clothing—the plain black suit I was wearing when Verna and I wed—and pluck pieces of fern from my hair. *My hair!* Laughter bubbles up from the well of my chest and spills out my mouth, chiming over the mountainside with the resonance of bells. I didn't have hair for the last twenty years I was alive. Looking down, I see that my beard is the same tawny blond it was in my youth. The hands that pat at my suit are no longer knotted with arthritis and crowded with veins.

I hear a groan. My joviality ceases. My legs could carry me for ten thousand miles, but as I stand and walk over to Tobias's prone form, it takes all my willpower not to collapse. I kneel before my firstborn. The instant my fingers touch the damp cotton covering his back, a pop of light goes off like an amplified burst of static electricity. I glance down at my hands still shielding Tobias's spine and flex them. They do not ache, yet they look the same as when my precious wife crisscrossed them over my unmoving chest. My beard is now also long and white. The hair I have just rejoiced over has been removed from my head. Then I understand this second transformation that is as surprising as my first: I must appear to my son as the father he remembers so that my words can be received.

Taking my newly ancient hands, I again place them on Tobias's back. He groans and rolls over. A thread of blood unravels from the wound on his forehead.

"Tobias," I say.

As when he was young and I would rock his shoulder and tell him I needed help birthing a calf or colt in the barn, my son swims up through the dense strata of sleep, struggling to awaken.

"You need to get up, my son. We do not have long."

Tobias's eyes fling back like shutters on a vacant house. His fleeting soul returns. *"Dawdy?"* He wets his lips and closes his eyes, but I am still here when he opens them again. "*Dawdy?* You—you can't be here. You're dead." His eyes widen. "Am I . . . Does this mean I'm dead too?"

I do not know what to call our meeting between this world and the next. I just know it is a rare gift I do not want to squander.

"No, Son. You're not dead," I say. "You're dreaming. You hit your head running in the woods."

The pain of Tobias's memory returns. Tears seep from the corners of his eyes. "I hit her," he wails. "I hit my own wife."

"I know, Tobias. I know."

"I was just so angry. I love Leah; I do. But I didn't want anybody finding out about—"

"You and Rachel." It is not a question, but a statement.

My son's face blanches above the contrast of his beard. He looks down as his tears resume their fall. "I'm sorry, *Dawdy*."

"I am no longer here, Tobias. You do not need to be apologizing to me."

"You mean I need to apologize to Leah."

"Yes." I nod. "And also to Rachel."

Tobias looks up with that old flash in his eyes. "Why should I apologize to *her*? Rachel's the reason this all happened!"

"Really? Weren't *you* the one who entered her room that night?"

"Yes, but *she's* the one who invited me in."

"When you knocked on her door to give Rachel that quilt, you knew what you were thinking."

"But those were just thoughts, *Dawdy*. They would've never been actions if Rachel hadn't turned around with her—" Tobias shakes his head in disgust, unable to remove the images trapped within the strongbox of his mind.

"Even then, Tobias, you still had a choice."

His forehead ripples with so much frustration, the congealing cut on the upper left splits. "A choice?" he rails. "Would *you* have turned around if you'd been in my place?"

"The turning should've happened long before that night. But yes, with the Lord's help, I believe I could have."

Tobias snorts and wipes his bleeding forehead with his arm. "Then you're a far better man than me."

"I wasn't always," I murmur, recalling how jealous I'd been watching Samuel Stoltzfus down in the New Holland show ring with *Englischer* girls prancing their gaudy feathers before him like birds of paradise. If one of them had pursued me to the same extent, I wouldn't have tossed their phone numbers to the sawdusted floor like Samuel had. I would have taken advantage of those numbers. Lord forgive me, I would have taken advantage of the women who had written them down.

Tobias's ragged breathing is disrupted by the throaty hoot of an owl.

"How did you change?" he asks.

"I didn't change; I *was* changed. I realized I hated the man I'd become. But I knew I didn't have the power to change myself, so I asked the Lord to change me."

"That simple, huh?"

"It *could* be that simple if you'd just lay down your pride. If you would ask the Lord's forgiveness and forgiveness from those you've wronged."

"I can't tell them what I've done, *Dawdy*. I can't let Jonathan be Eli's donor. If the community finds out, I'll—I'll lose *everything*. My *familye* will disown me. I'll have to step down as bishop—"

"I won't tell you you won't lose everything, Tobias," I say. "Because you might. But what are a few years of temporal loss when you have gained your eternal soul?"

The moment these words leave my mouth, I can feel something inside of me break loose as if I am fragments pieced together by the seamstress of time. Resting my hand on my son's shoulder, I say, "Tobias. I have to go."

"Don't leave, *Dawdy*!" He twines his arms around my waist even as my body splinters apart. "I can't face this all alone!"

I hold my firstborn child as tightly as I can. "You're never alone, Tobias. Even if I have to leave, there's One who never will."

My temporary body dissolves back to dust, and my spirit begins to ascend. *"Ich liebe dich,"* I call down to my son.

With his arms outstretched and tear-streaked face upturned to the heavens, Tobias's wail echoes across the mountain ridges like a feral cry: *"Forgive me!"*

I don't know if Tobias is asking for my forgiveness or for the forgiveness of Someone far greater than I. Either way, I believe that after this night my eldest son, Bishop Tobias King, will never look at this life, or the next life, in the same way.

# 21

## Rachel

The residents of Copper Creek heard my twelve-year-old nephew, Reuben, ring the schoolhouse bell at three o'clock in the morning, alerting everyone to our emergency before we wanted that emergency made known. Carrying so many lanterns that they dispelled the darkness more effectively than a row of streetlamps, the community followed Reuben up the lane and have been keeping vigil in front of Tobias and Leah's farmhouse. The men gather in a tight, conspiratorial circle in the front yard—their heads with the uniform black hats lowered as they discuss the possibility of foul play. On the porch, the women hunker beneath shared quilts and shawls—their faces puffy with interrupted sleep, their eyelids slitted with the suspicious expression they've worn since they went upstairs to check on my bedridden sister and saw the left side of her face that grew darker with the coming of the dawn.

The porch steps protest as I descend them. The community shifts to watch me bear the ineffectual offering of hot drink on a cold morning. During the Masts' barn raising, I assumed this position as hostess because I knew it was what Leah would want. Now I use this act of servitude to counter the times all the community saw in me was pride.

Keeping my hand on the lid, I refill the cups I brought out three hours ago. Elvina Hostetler barely acknowledges me, but Rebecca Risser murmurs, *"Danke,"* and reaches out to touch my hand. The men say nothing, which is expected. At least they do not turn their backs.

My chest tightens as I look at the eastern rim of the yard. Judah leans against a fence post, waiting for the ashen sky to transform to ocher, when the community will begin its search. For hours, he continued combing the fields and the outbuildings of the neighboring farms. He returned to the farmhouse only to see whether Tobias had been found before leaving it again in a desperate quest to find his brother. But I wonder if this quest has also been to avoid me.

A prayer rises from my mouth, the words steaming like the carafe warming my hands. I cross the yard and take Judah's cup from the fence post. Whipping cream dots the untouched surface.

"You want more?" I ask.

He shakes his head. "I'm too sick to drink."

"Judah. I'm sorry."

"It's not your fault."

Wind stings tears from my eyes. "But I am partly to blame."

"Don't you know I blame myself?" His voice breaks. He looks up at the clouded bowl of sky. "I could have protected you better. Told Tobias I suspected—"

"Judah, please," I interrupt, setting the carafe on top of the post. I reach out and take his hand. "Forgive me. I know I've hurt you."

"Forgive you?" Judah turns. His eyes glow against the backdrop of the rapidly changing light. "How could I *not* forgive you? I've loved you my entire life, Rachel." He lets go of my hand and clasps my elbows, drawing my body toward his. "I can't stop now. . . . I've tried."

The community erupts into chatter. We break apart and see Tobias limp from the woods as first light treads gold dust across the fields. I gasp at his gruesome appearance; Judah does the same.

Blood has crusted into a maroon birthmark that melts into Tobias's beard. His pants and shirt are torn. A suspender trails behind him like rope. Looking at him, one would think my brother-in-law has been in a battle. But I can think of no battle other than the one that, for months now, Tobias has been fighting with himself.

Puncturing the fog with his exclamation, Judah begins

to run. No one gathered in the yard or on the porch says a word as the eldest and youngest King offspring draw closer to each other. Tobias's wary stance conveys that he does not know whether his brother is coming to attack or embrace him. I am grateful my sister must remain in her sickbed and cannot watch this unpredictable exchange. Sweat moistens my hairline despite the morning chill.

But there is no need for my fear, no need for my suspended breath. Two steps before reaching Tobias, Judah pauses and looks up at his elder brother. I cannot hear the words exchanged; I do not know if any are even said. Still, I can tell by the tears on Tobias's face that the brothers are communicating more clearly than they ever have before.

Minutes pass. The sun punctures through the clouds to the frosted earth, making it impossible to see either brother without first shielding our eyes. Judah slides his arm around Tobias, and they begin the slow journey across the field.

Watching the brothers—who do not look like brothers at all—I cannot believe I ever thought Tobias was more of a man. For years, I dismissed Judah's love as boyhood infatuation and brushed off his advances as if his heart had the same depth of feeling as a fly's.

Oh, how I wish I could take back those years of indifference! Oh, how I wish Judah and I were once again having that conversation on Ida Mae's porch, watching the sheet of rain unfurl off the green tin roof because it was safer than looking in each other's eyes.

But I promised Ida Mae that I would not live my life wishing I had a chance to live it over. And so now, standing here against the fence post as a new day breaks, I vow that I will begin loving Judah as if the two of us are making up for lost time.

Wiping tears, I smile as the two brothers pass me and enter the yard. Tobias has just mounted the first porch step when he shakes his head and extricates himself from Judah. Moving back into the yard, the bishop of Copper Creek stands before his community as if before the judgment throne: broad shoulders bent, head hanging low, hands folded as he prepares to face his reckoning.

Swallowing deep, Tobias looks up at the faces of some of his congregants: Apologetic Lemuel and haughty Elvina Hostetler from the bakery. Newlyweds Leon and Katie Mast with their silver-framed glasses, timid brown eyes, and slender builds. Alvin and Rebecca Risser, appearing bereft without their brood of flaxen-haired children, who are probably stretching and yawning themselves awake in their beds. Elmer and Mable Schlabach, the ones who moved down with that first group led by the deceased bishop, Amos King. My *dawdy* and *mamm* are also here, along with Tobias's own *mudder*, Verna, whose dark eyes are shadowed with worry.

More of the community is represented than this, but Tobias does not take the time to look at them. Instead, he clears his throat and says, "I am standing before both God and man today . . ." He wipes his shirtsleeve across his face, smearing the cotton with more dirt and blood. "I am standing here because I need to ask you—my community, my family—for forgiveness. I need to ask my wife for forgiveness. And her sister. But most of all, I need to ask God. The past two years of my life have been a lie. Even before I married my wife, Leah, I fell in love with her sister. Rather than asking the deacons to help me, to keep me accountable, I chose to keep my pride by concealing my sin."

For the second time in my life—the first being at Amos King's burial service, which was overseen by the same man who is speaking now—my face burns with the heat of a hundred stares. No one murmurs their shock, for, regardless of Tobias's confessions, his position as bishop still commands their respect. But I can see their eyes dart around the yard until they land on the woman on its outskirts, who must have used every ounce of her feminine wiles to lure such a righteous man into temptation. The sweat that had gathered along my hairline pools at the waist of my cape dress. I dig my nails into the post. A sliver breaks loose and spears the soft pink quick of my nail. But I am thankful for the sting. It is almost a pleasant sensation compared to the discomfort of so many eyes resting on me.

Tobias scans the faces of the crowd gathered outside his home. When he follows the direction of their gazes, he says, "Now, Rachel's not the one you should blame. Last night, after I fell in the woods—" Tobias fingers the wound on his forehead—"I dreamed that my *vadder* came to me. He helped me learn that *I* am the one responsible for my actions. No one else is to blame. I never should have slept with my wife's sister, but I did not sleep with her because she seduced me. I slept with my wife's sister because of the way I allowed my lust for her to consume my conscience until my conscience couldn't check my desires. And now—as I stand here before you all, my community, my witnesses—I would like to ask Rachel's forgiveness for not being the man I should have been. For not being a better brother-in-law, a better husband to her sister, a better servant of God."

I am so astonished by Tobias's words, I find none with which to reply. But it is as if he doesn't expect me to say that I forgive him or ask him for his forgiveness. And only at this moment do I believe that whatever vision Tobias had of Amos must have performed a miracle of biblical proportions.

His eyes bright and dry, his voice ardent as he delivers what he must know is his final address, Tobias continues, "Because of my sin, Eli was conceived. But that does not mean he should be punished for my wrongs. As most of you know, Eli is lying in a hospital bed in Nashville, waiting for a bone marrow transplant that could save his life. Since Leah and Rachel are twins, my son Jonathan has the possibility to be Eli's match. Until last night, I had no intention to allow Jonathan to be Eli's donor. Not because I was afraid of what would happen to Jonathan, but because I was afraid of what would happen to *me* once you all knew the truth. Then last night, in my dream, my *vadder* told me that I would never find freedom if I did not ask forgiveness from the Lord, from my wife, from Rachel—and from all of you."

Tobias's shoulders are still curled forward, but I notice with every secret brought into light, his spine is straightening and his swarthy countenance is growing clear.

"So now you know the truth," he says. "Now you all know the man I was for the past two years. But I hope that by my revealing these things to you, you also know the man I hope one day to become."

After such a plethora of shocking news, not even the sternest of tongues can be suppressed. The entire Copper Creek Community murmurs among themselves, and Tobias and I stare at one another in silence. For the first time since I have known him, I can look into those dark eyes without feeling attraction, censure, or shame. I do not know how so few words have the power to wipe away so many wrongs. But there is such buoyancy in my spirit—there is such hope in my heart—that I know those few words of true repentance were the panacea Tobias and I needed to move on.

"I forgive you," I murmur; then—because it is not enough for the promise he has given to both me and our son—I say, "Forgive me."

A smile stretches across Tobias's weary face. He nods and looks at his feet. Then his head jerks up, and there is only one name on his lips. *"Leah."*

Cutting through the wake of the community who have

begun filtering down the porch steps, Tobias flings open the front door, almost colliding with his daughter Miriam, who was about to open it from the other side.

Tobias takes her by the shoulders. "What's wrong?"

*"Mammi!"* Miriam wails. "She's bleeding!"

My knees buckle and my vision blackens. Tobias looks over at me with terror in his eyes. Judah flips open his cell phone.

"Call Ida Mae!" I cry. "She's at the hospital!"

"There's no time," Tobias calls from the porch. "Call 911. Come now, Rachel, your sister needs you."

I peel my fingers from the fence post and walk across the yard. As I move through the stunned community and step into Leah and Tobias's farmhouse, I am afraid. Tobias and I might have found forgiveness for the immoral act we committed, but that does not mean our family will be exempt from paying its price.

## AMOS

Rachel and Helen sit side by side on the couch with their fingers clenched in their laps and ankles snapped together. With every agonizing tick of the *uhr*, it is obvious that regardless of their best efforts, nothing more can be done. Yet as soon as Tobias—holding Jonathan in one arm and wiping tears from his face with the other—and the four older children file out of his and Leah's room and descend the stairs, Rachel and Helen do *not* stop.

As if her efforts alone will keep Leah with them, Helen packs the area between her daughter's legs with fresh towels, trying to stave off the bleeding until the ambulance arrives. They are soaked through within minutes. Rachel no longer takes time to wipe tears away. She is trying to save her twin sister, but all the shepherd's purse and raspberry leaf that Rachel applies will not squelch the blood that keeps pouring from Leah to such an extent it is no small wonder she and the baby are both still alive.

Leah suffers through their frantic ministrations for two more minutes. "Stop," she says. "Please . . . okay? Just stop. I'm fine. I'm going to be fine."

Holding on to the bedpost, Rachel turns to the side and lets a sob rip through her body without her mouth emitting a sound.

"*Mammi.*" Leah smiles from her fake sickbed that, within a few short hours, has become unbearably real. "I love you, but I need to speak with Rachel now."

Helen's alarmed eyes ricochet between her daughters. With a resigned sigh, she presses a kiss to Leah's cheek and leaves the room.

Waiting for the door to shut, Leah pats the spot next to her where Tobias always sleeps. Rachel does not move.

"It's all right," Leah says. "Just come. Be with me . . . for a little while."

Rachel takes her shoes off and stretches out on top of

the quilts. Leah leans her head against Rachel's shoulder and entwines their arms. Regardless of her resolve, Rachel's body quakes. Leah turns on her side. "Oh, Rachel," she says, "my dying's not your fault. It is just a part of life. And sometimes life does not go according to plan." Leah turns her twin's face toward hers. "Will you promise me something?"

Rachel dries her eyes on the quilt. "Anything."

"If I die today—" Leah silences her sister's protests by placing a finger to her lips. "If I die today or tomorrow or twenty years from now, I want you to look inside the purple martin birdhouse beneath the sycamore tree." A blush steals over Leah's pale face. She looks down. "The letters will explain everything," she says, "but make sure you read the top letter first. The yellowed one from Tobias. His letter will explain the most."

"I'm not going to read Tobias's love letters to you," Rachel says. "I've taken enough from your marriage as it is."

"Rachel." Leah places a hand on her sister's tense body. "The letter was not to me. The letter from Tobias was addressed to you."

"To me?"

"Yes. *You* were the one he wanted, not me . . . never me." Tears flood Leah's eyes. She closes their lids down hard, willing them back. "Two years ago, a letter came in the mail addressed from Tobias to you. *Mamm* had heard of his wife's death, and she believed she knew what the letter entailed."

"She read it?" Rachel asks.

Leah's words fall faster. "Yes, she read it, and then she gave it to me. She told *me* to respond to Tobias and tell him that you had received the letter but you weren't interested in becoming his wife. He hadn't seen any of us in so long, *Mamm* said he wouldn't know the difference."

"But why did you do it?" Rachel says. "Why did you leave?"

Leah sighs. "You had all these boys wanting to court you when I didn't have one. *Mamm* told me that you would marry soon and leave, and I would be left behind on Hilltop Road if I didn't respond to Tobias's letter and choose to leave first."

"Tobias didn't think it strange that you wanted to take my place like that?"

"He was too desperate. He had a baby and three other children to tend. He needed a wife and a *mudder*, and I was willing to become one. So . . ." Leah smiles, but the brilliance fades before reaching her eyes. "Although I knew I was just a substitute for the person Tobias really wanted, I married him. I married and moved away from you because I had convinced myself that you were moving away from me."

"Oh, Leah."

Leah clasps her sister's hand. "Don't you *get* it?" she says. "I told you because I don't *want* you to keep feeling sorry for me. I don't *want* you to keep blaming yourself for everything when all of this is not your fault."

"But most of it is."

Leah smiles ruefully. "Perhaps most, but not all."

Down the lane, they can hear the ambulance siren. Leah's face grows white. Rachel rubs her sister's hands, but no matter how hard she massages, the warmth will not return.

Leah stares out the window. Her voice is clipped as she turns and says, "Rachel. Look at me."

Rachel does and can see that her sister's eyes are glassy.

"When I visited you and Eli at Vanderbilt, I first asked Ida Mae who your doctor was, then went and told Dr. Sengupta that I was expecting. I told him that the baby I carried would probably have the same genes as Eli, since our children have the same father and we're identical twins. I knew there was a possibility Tobias wouldn't let Jonathan donate bone marrow, but I thought he couldn't stop me from donating the cord blood from the new baby."

"But how did you—"

"How did I know? *Mamm* didn't just teach *you* the medical basics, Rachel. Plus, I called Norman Troyer and ran some questions by him."

"So you—you . . . ?"

Leah smiles. "Yes, I filled out the paperwork that will allow my unborn child's cord blood to be used for Eli's bone marrow transplant."

The sobs that Rachel had suppressed rush up from the fount of her soul.

Putting an arm around her sister's shoulders, Leah strokes the dark-blonde hair. "There're some other things

Tobias will have to fill out," she says over the sound of her sister crying and the ambulance howling up the lane. "Dr. Sengupta was going to see if I could donate the cord blood without my husband's permission. But now—now, I don't think Tobias would protest even that."

"What if . . . ?"

"What if the baby and I die?"

Rachel nods, sobs racking her body.

"I don't know," Leah says. "I don't know if the stem cells would be developed enough for the doctors to harvest them."

The farmhouse door thwacks open; the brisk stomps of the EMTs' boots ascend the stairs. Leah's lips clench shut. The twins cling to each other as they did throughout childhood and adolescence. The steps draw closer. Even then, no words of love are uttered. Each sister knows that the bond they have shared since the womb has been frayed, but never broken. And regardless of what this life or the next life brings, that bond of love will continue still.

# 22

## Rachel

The wooden gate creaks as I push it open. Orange and red leaves, stripped from the trees during last night's storm, tumble across the graveyard and splay like painted hands across the five rows of simple, dark stones. Eli drops my hand and totters across the uneven ground. His thin curls flutter in the breeze; his steroid-swollen cheeks are flushed bright with cold. Turning back to face me and grin, my son's overconfidence in his newfound walking abilities does not match his bearings. He collapses onto the cushion of his diaper and, startled, almost cries until finding a pinecone nestled amid the leaves, which he proceeds to beat happily on the ground.

Reassured that Eli is not going to bring the pinecone to his mouth, I walk over and kneel before the newest stone placed beside the grave of Tobias's first wife, Esther King. The vines have curled back over both bases, despite my many attempts to clear them all away. Tears flood my eyes as they have every time I've come to the Copper Creek graveyard over the past five months.

Most people would not understand the depth of my grief. They would not understand how I could have harbored such love in my heart for my two-pound niece, whose short lifetime was spent inside an incubator and whom I never even held. But without that two-pound child—without Leah and Tobias's daughter, Serenity Joy King—I would not have my son. Through Serenity's cord blood, harvested after her premature birth, Eli was given a second chance at life. A chance that could have never come through Jonathan, who turned out not to be a match for Eli.

Digging into my coat pocket, I take out the thimble-sized crystal horse Judah gave me on the day of Eli's transplant. I place it in front of Serenity Joy's grave and clear the weeds from her stone and Esther's. Scooping my son into my arms, I press his warm body against me. He pushes against my chest and looks up into my face.

*"Ich liebe dich,"* I murmur. *"Ich liebe dich."*

Carrying Eli, I stroll out through the graveyard gate, past the schoolhouse, and up the long gravel lane. The line of stores comes into sight with their shake-shingled roofs and painted window boxes brimming with purple and white pansies. A few cars, minivans, and buggies are parked at each pristine location, proving that though the scandal surrounding the former bishop of Copper Creek swept the whole way up to the communities in Canada, it has not hurt business the way the store owners feared.

The glass door to Hostetler's Bakery swings wide. Elvina stalks down the handicap ramp with the rubber entrance mat in her hands. She lifts it over her head and whacks it over the handrail. Dust and coin-sized leaves flutter through the air. The brown apron of her cape dress lifts with the breeze, revealing thick calves sheathed in black tights. I raise my hand in greeting. Letting the mat flop over the rail, Elvina folds her arms and stares. Not moving, not saying a word. Eli sees her too. Delighted to meet a potential friend, he smacks a kiss into his left palm and then his right. He wags his christened hands and gives her the grin that won over so many nurses on the myelosuppression floor.

Elvina's lips begin to twitch—proving that not even a miser can withstand my son's unstudied charms. She lifts her hardworking hand and waves at Eli. And then she nods at me. I smile as tears blur her stout figure.

Any customer watching this exchange between a young *Englischer* and an Old Order Mennonite woman would not think it unusual. But this simple interaction with the unofficial gatekeeper of Copper Creek shows that though I will never reenter the community, I am no longer outside its fold.

With grace in my step, I continue walking. Eli babbles in my ear, but I do not hear his nonsensical words. My mind drifts to the seven-month journey our family has been on. A journey whose destination I sometimes could not see, and therefore did not think I had the strength to reach.

The deacons contacted the head bishops in Pennsylvania the same day Tobias confessed his affair in Tennessee, the same day his wife almost died and his daughter was born. It did not matter that Leah was hospitalized or that Serenity was in NICU; that next week Tobias was summoned to stand before the bishops' judgment seat. It must have been a rude awakening for Tobias to see that he was on the bottom rung of the hierarchy in Lancaster County, even though he had reached its pinnacle in Copper Creek. He repented before the bishops, as he had repented before us. But it made no difference in the outcome. I am sure he never expected it would.

Tobias resigned from his position the day he returned home. Rumor was, the deacon who made the call to Pennsylvania was the same deacon who opened the pages of the *Ausbund* to find the paper declaring him the new bishop. Only this time, the mantle was one he had long expected to wear.

Tobias was not bitter. He even dismissed the allegations that his forced resignation had been selfishly devised. This made me realize that he had truly changed. A part of this change took place the day he emptied his burdens through confession. But losing Serenity Joy was the pain-filled metamorphosis that cemented his faith. At that point, he could have turned his back on God. He had risked everything to cleanse his soul, and in recompense, he lost everything. Amazing as it was, Tobias did not waver in his pursuit of righteousness. I knew then that Tobias was not predestined to be bishop of Copper Creek, yet he was meant to lead others in seeking the ways of God—just as his father, Amos King, had done.

Leah and I did not talk often after Tobias stepped down. Eli was confined to the myelosuppression floor, and she was confined to the NICU with Serenity Joy. Occasionally we would meet in the hospital's cafeteria to drink watery coffee and eat thick oatmeal cream pies the remarried Ida Mae Speck smuggled in from Hostetler's. For a short time, we were two young *meed* seated at our *mamm*'s scarred kitchen table. Then silence would loom between our adult selves like a dam built by my betrayal—unspoken turbulence blocking the tranquil flow of our conversation.

In this, I have paid a hundredfold for one night of thoughtless passion. The only comfort remains in the thought that perhaps, with time, our new intimacy will be cherished all the more for our having lost the old.

On the knoll, the tall white farmhouse with the ten rooms and ten plain windows comes into view. Coils of steel-gray smoke twist from the chimney. Leah and Miriam are at the *kochoffe* inside, preparing the last *esse* that will be shared among the Kings and the Stoltzfuses before Tobias and Leah's family moves to Canada. The community has not asked the Kings to leave, but neither have they asked them to stay. It will be hard for my sister to leave behind everyone she loves, but the dynamics of our relationship being what they are, Tobias and Leah know they must start afresh rather than remain in a place dank with what should have never been.

Resettling my son's comforting bulk on my hip, I stride down the lane toward the farmhouse, relishing the feel of jeans and the wind running its fingers through my short hair. In the breeze, my earrings tinkle like chimes. Eli reaches up and touches one.

"Don't pull," I warn, kissing his fingers.

With a whine, the farmhouse door opens. I look up. Tobias King is standing on the top porch step. Even before Serenity's death, silver had threaded his black hair and beard. Although he has not regained the weight he lost over the past twelve months, peace usually reigns in his eyes, where they were once evidence of his inward war.

But today, despite my brother-in-law's eyes still being filled with the peace that passes all understanding, they are also filled with sadness. For a moment, those dark eyes lock with mine. That one silent glance communicates what a lifetime of contrite words could not. Tobias then shifts his gaze down to this beautiful, innocent child cradled in my arms—the child he and I created—and I know the sorrow he feels is not over the past, but because of the future. For throughout Tobias's life, he will remain only a distant uncle to this child, when he should be so much more.

The front door opens. I look past Tobias to his younger brother, Judah, whose face splits with a smile mirrored by my own. Wiping his calloused hands on a dish towel, Judah tosses it over his shoulder and plods down the porch steps. His soft, honeyed eyes igniting with joy, he extends his arms toward me—toward his *familye*—and I step into them, ever so grateful that Judah King has awaited my return.

# A NOTE FROM THE AUTHOR

I was born on a hot August day in the heart of Amish country. My family moved to Tennessee when I was only three years old, but my childhood was filled with stories of Pennsylvania Dutch ancestors hiding TVs from bishops and concealing permed hair beneath *kapps*. However, this unique heritage did not interest me. Instead, I pouted as my mother divided my waist-length hair into plaits and then forced me to change from purple overalls into a jean skirt and sneakers in preparation for a visit to our Plain friends—knowing, even at the tender age of six, that this combination was a fashion faux pas. Playing hide-and-seek or kick the can with my Old Order Mennonite peers, however, I soon became grateful for that skirt, which helped me transition from Southern *Englischer* to intimate friend.

Years passed. I knew my Mennonite playmates had traded braided pigtails for *kapped* buns, yet on a visit to the community, I rebelled against my mother's instructions and arrived with unbound hair. During supper, which was eaten beneath a popping kerosene bulb, the hostess came and stood behind my portion of the bench. She slid out my blue satin ribbon and plaited my hair as I stared into my bowl of *grummbeere supp* accented with homemade *brot.*

The winter of my seventeenth year, I returned to the community to visit a once-raucous playmate whose ill health had transformed her into a soft-spoken friend. The whites of her deep-brown eyes had yellowed from liver complications. Her family and my own gathered around her bed, which was heaped with spinning-star quilts, and sang hymns whose Pennsylvania Dutch words I did not know, but whose meaning struck my heart with such clarity, tears slid down my cheeks.

One week later, I stood beside her grave, wearing a thick black headband to hide my newly pierced ears with the fake diamond studs that stabbed the tender skin of my neck, giving me a migraine further magnified by jaw-clenching grief. I remember how the somber community huddled around her family as if their physical presence could shield them, not only from the slashing wind and sleet, but from the reality that the body of their *dochder* and *schweschder* was about to be placed into the cold, hard ground.

I left for college that summer, almost eighteen years to the day after I had been born in Lancaster County, Pennsylvania, the first person in my immediate family to attempt a higher education. As I unpacked my flared Lucky jeans and beaded sweaters into wobbling dorm drawers, I thought I was leaving my Mennonite heritage along with a certain broad-shouldered, hazel-eyed man whose father had attended my father's Mennonite high school.

Three years, one death, and two lifetimes' worth of tribulations later, I realized that I had not lost the precious attributes surrounding my Plain heritage so much as I had needed to go away in order to find myself.

In the cool autumn of 2008, I married my broad-shouldered, hazel-eyed Dutchman, thus making my last name as difficult to spell as my first. I kept wearing my Lucky jeans and layering my wrists with jewelry, but I was also drawn to a simple life, reminiscent of the one I had once tried to flee. My husband and I purchased a forty-acre valley nestled at the base of softly rolling Tennessee mountains.

Upon moving into the *haus* my husband built with determination and his own two hands, I began to write a fictionalized version of a story that had once been told to me—a story regarding the power of desire and the reverberating cost if that desire is left unchecked, a story that, shockingly enough, took place in an idyllic Old Order Mennonite community.

In Nashville, I was introduced to a genial, white-haired man who was as excited to hear my Dutchy last name as I had been to hear his. He had attended the same Mennonite high school as my father (and my husband's father) and, as a literary agent, he was interested to read the portion of the story that I had completed.

He read the first twenty-five thousand words while flying home from a book festival in Brazil and wanted to read more. I continued to write as my expectant belly continued to grow. Two months after the birth of our daughter, Tyndale House accepted the manuscript; they were as excited to promote my modern retelling of *The Scarlet Letter* as I had been to write it.

And so, wearing Lucky jeans (the same pair, actually), chandelier earrings, and un*kapped* hair, I continue writing stories about the Pennsylvania Dutch heritage that once brought me acute embarrassment but has now become a creative outlet with no closing doors.

Thank you for joining me on this journey.

# About the Author

***Jolina Petersheim*** holds degrees in English and communication arts from the University of the Cumberlands. Though *The Outcast* is her first novel, her writing has been featured in venues as varied as radio programs, nonfiction books, and numerous online and print publications. Her blog is syndicated with the *Tennessean*'s "On Nashville" blog roll, as well as being featured on other creative-writing sites. Jolina and her husband share the same unique Amish and Mennonite heritage that originated in Lancaster County, Pennsylvania, but now live in the mountains of Tennessee with their young daughter. Follow Jolina and her blog at www.jolinapetersheim.com.

# DISCUSSION QUESTIONS

1. Why does Rachel agree to leave Copper Creek? Do you agree or disagree with her reasons? How do her feelings of guilt play into her decision? Have you ever been tempted to avoid an issue or a loved one because of something you've done? How did you resolve it—or is it something you still need to address?

2. Although Leah and Rachel are identical twins, their personalities are starkly different. How do their personalities change as the story progresses? In what ways do they remain the same?

3. Have you known any identical twins? Did the author's portrayal ring true? Why or why not?

4. Imagine that Judah King was the one who withdrew the sheet of paper from the *Ausbund*, declaring him the next bishop of Copper Creek. How might he have addressed Rachel's sin, given the way he loved her?

5. Do you believe that our deceased loved ones in heaven view the pain we go through on earth? Did you find Amos's viewpoint believable? Why or why not?

6. If you were in Tobias King's place, would you have chosen to forsake your child or your pride? The choice may seem easy in theory, but if it involved confessing a shameful sin, would it be? What factors might influence your decision?

7. If you were in Judah's place, could you have forgiven Rachel and still built a life with her? If you were in Leah's place, could you have forgiven your sister's betrayal? Have you ever been faced with a heart-rending situation like this? If so, how did you handle it?

8. What are some of the biblical allusions in *The Outcast*? What did they add to the story?

9. Holistic and conventional medicine are compared and contrasted throughout *The Outcast*. In the end, do you feel one was more effective than the other? If so, why? Why is there a tension between the two approaches? Have you or your family encountered this tension?

10. Ida Mae and Rachel were both rejected by the communities that once sheltered them. Compare their individual responses. It's natural to want to turn around and reject others in the same way we've been rejected. How have you responded in the face of rejection?

11. In the end, Leah and Tobias decide to leave Copper Creek because of the painful memories it holds. What's the difference between forgiving and forgetting? Why is it sometimes difficult—maybe impossible—to forget a wrong, even when we've worked hard to forgive? Does true forgiveness have to include forgetting? Why or why not?

12. Was it startling to learn that the Plain communities struggle with the same sins as the English? Why do you think these communities tend to be viewed in a utopian light?